Tethered Souls

MIRANDA GRANT

I0721890

TETHERED SOULS

MIRANDA GRANT

BY MIRANDA GRANT

WAR OF THE MYTH
Elemental Claim
Think of Me Demon
Tricked Into It
Rage for Her

FAIRYTALES OF THE MYTH
Burn Baby Burn
The Little Morgen
Bjerner and the Beast

DEATHLY BELOVED
To Have and to Lose
Death Do Us Part
For Better or For Worse
To Love and To Perish

BOOK OF SHADOWS
Madness Behind the Mask
Cursed to be Mine
Tethered Souls

TETHERED SOULS

This is a work of fiction. All characters are products of my imagination and should not be seen as having any more credibility than fake news does. Any resemblance to organizations, locales, or persons living, dead, or stuck in purgatory is entirely coincidental.

Copyright © 2023 by Miranda Grant
ISBN: 978-1-914 464-02-7

authormirandagrant@gmail.com
mirandagrant.com
Facebook: Author Miranda Grant

All rights reserved. No part of this book may be used or reproduced in any manner whatsoever without written permission by the author, except in the case of brief quotations embodied in critical articles and reviews.

Edited and published by Writing Evolution.
Cover design and interior artwork by Writing Evolution.

To Micha:

I fucking hate you.
I also love you, you bitch.

TRIGGER AND CONTENT WARNINGS

(These are also spoilers)

Look, after *Madness Behind the Mask*, nothing seems that bad anymore. I mean, this has some descriptive torture and gore in it, but I think that's about it?

However, if anyone reads this and thinks, oh no, there are absolutely some triggers for non-messed-up people, can you please email me so I can add them to the below link?

Thanks!

https://mirandagrant.com/tethered-souls

PROLOGUE

HIM

He's fighting for his life, but I'm just working out my frustrations. Twisting out of the way of his knife, I pivot sideways. My right arm snaps into his nose. He stumbles back, and I follow, kicking his kneecap. He sinks to the ground on a scream. The blade lowers, and I'm on him in a second, through the gap in his defense. Grabbing both sides of his head, I jerk it down as I lift my knee straight up into his nose.

Crack!

The broken bones of his face fly into his brain. Blood sprays down my leg. The knife clatters to the padded floor of the gym. Releasing his head, I shove my foot into his chest, kicking him onto his back.

The air shifts behind me, and the next prisoner runs at me.

My nostrils flaring, I breathe in his scent. I shouldn't be able to pinpoint where he is by that alone, but my senses have always been *more*. Another reason I'm a freak.

Jumping as I spin, I kick him in the side of the head. He staggers sideways, his eyes crossing, the light fading. Then he is dropping, the bones near his temple having severed the underlying artery when they shattered.

He's practically dead, but I keep going. A foot to his chest. Another to his face. His body hits the ground, but my frustrations don't die with him.

"You're nothing but an abomination."

"You don't deserve to be Boss."

A third man rushes me.

I'm a witch without magic. Nothing but a thing to be put down. My father left when I failed to enter my ascension – that moment where a child of the supernatural world comes into their powers around puberty.

My opponent ducks low to wrap his arms around my waist, hoping to lift me despite my two hundred and fifty-odd pounds of muscle. I bring my hands together and slam them into the back of his head before he can even try. The bones at the base of his skull fracture beneath my blow. His arms go slack, but he isn't dead. Just unconscious.

My father was a progeny, his range of telekinesis was unheard of in a witch. He was picked for that reason alone to breed with Mother, so their children would be powerful, untouchable.

Yet, here I am with no innate powers, no healing magic. I can't even work any learned spells or summon a demon or even use a fucking pre-spelled wand – three things a mere *human* can do.

"You're a failure to the Shadow name."

I shove my opponent off me, but I'm not fast enough to avoid the new knife at my back. I'm not *good* enough. Pain flares across my ribs as I twist and the blade cuts a five inch line from near my spine to my side.

"Don't!" I snap as my brother, Khalid, shifts ever so slightly.

He's my bodyguard, the reaper of this Family, and he's standing off to the side of our gym, waiting to intervene as necessary. But it isn't fucking necessary.

Only allowing the prisoners to come at me one at a time isn't *fucking necessary.*

I need more. A higher risk. But Khalid, won't let me take it. I'm too *valuable.* And he's too full of responsibility and guilt over one mistake he made thirteen months ago. So I make do with what I have. Frustrations but no complaints. I crack his ribs, rupture his veins. Bruises and more freely flowing blood form beneath his clammy skin. I pull back, dodging the wild swings of his knife, then dart in again. My feet hustle left and right, keeping me moving. The man swings, and I follow. My back burns. Blood seeps down it, but I don't stop.

"You're an abomination."

Yeah, I am.

So fucking what.

"You don't deserve to be Boss."

No, I don't.

But neither did any of those who ruled this Family before me. We were all born into this role. No one earned it. No one had to *fight* for it. A few killed off their older siblings so they could gain the title of heir, but their claim was still only respected because of their bloodline.

The same blood that runs through my veins.

"You're a failure to the Shadow name."

Perhaps.

My knuckles *crack* into the man's ribs. He stumbles to the side, gasping through swollen lips.

The ones on my other hand follow.

I breathe out quickly but not harshly, controlling it, not letting it control me.

Perhaps I am a failure.

Perhaps my ancestors are rolling over in their graves on the Plane of Monsters, also known as the Shadow Domain – a name we took to name our own Family.

But who fucking cares?

My fist rocks into his flesh.

They are dead –

I duck and come back up again, an uppercut rattling the last of the man's resolve.

– and I am alive.

I throw all my power behind the punch. My knuckles slam up into his chin. His head snaps back in a telling *crack*. Blood rushes down his face from his previously broken nose, that rich copper smell filling my stomach. But he doesn't jerk, doesn't gurgle. Doesn't scream either. He just sways, unconscious. I dart forward and grab his head with both hands. A sudden *snap* has him dropping to the floor. Now he no longer breathes.

I look down at him as he crumbles to the ground.

Blood runs down my knuckles. My back.

My nostrils flare as the sting of the air caresses my cuts.

I *am* an abomination.

But I am also the Boss of the Shadow Domain. Anyone who doesn't like that can fucking try their hand at killing me. They might even succeed at becoming another scar on my back, but they *will* become another body in the ground.

But that isn't the issue, is it?

That's not why I'm down here in the middle of the night. The floor of our family gym littered with bodies.

Turning on my heels, I head for the wood bench against the pale-gray wall that Khalid stands beside. I grab the hand towel he offers me. I want to tell him to get more prisoners, but that is – *was* all we had. Most don't live long enough to be captured. Khalid is too efficient in his responsibilities. These were only brought in alive because I demanded it.

Low rats wanted for questioning.

"You see your girl?" I ask as I wipe the sweat from my face. My brother raises a healing wand to tend to my back, the warmth of the magic seeping into my skin.

"No."

"You should." Being away from her is eating at him like *this thing* is eating at me, and at least one of us should find some sanctuary.

But his jaw only tightens as he steps around me to put the wand back into the cabinet beside the bench. "Not until I kill whoever it is who's trying to kill you."

Scar number thirteen. Received as many months ago. The sly fucker hit me from behind, nearly killing me with a knife to my chest. If I hadn't turned in time, he would've pierced my heart. Khalid was off stalking his girl, watching her instead of me, and his guilt over that is crippling. Especially since Mother had to use her magic to save me. Any power she uses will drain her life – a last parting gift from Father, who died cursing her, sacrificing himself to strengthen the spell about a year ago.

Ever since that night, Khalid hasn't been to see his girl. A foolish endeavor considering we don't have a lead to go on; I woke up remembering nothing about the attack or how I managed to make it back to one of our warehouses before collapsing in the door.

I start to tell him someone's always trying to kill me and that isn't an excuse, but just then my neck prickles, the fine hairs warning me of someone's approach, and I pivot to face the door.

It clicks open, and Mother steps inside, looking every inch the high-class woman despite the early hour. The sun isn't even up, and already she is dressed to the nines – her hair and make-up styled to perfection, diamonds glistening around her neck, gold bands around her wrists, a rich red dress flaring out at her hips. The only thing she doesn't wear are earrings, but with her long black hair hanging free, they would be lost anyway.

"I used to find your father here whenever he couldn't sleep," she says, her eyes going around the room, looking at memories long gone.

Khalid tenses beside me, but he doesn't leave like he normally does whenever Father is mentioned – in the rare moments he is. He left us when I was twelve, came back three years later, only to take one look at me and leave again. But I remember how he used to be. The warm smiles. The tight hugs. The laughter, the teasing, the pure love he had for us.

All until I didn't hit my ascension.

Then came the fighting.

The screaming.

The drinking.

The lashing out at me and Mother.

She loved him. Still does. I can see it in the yearning of her eyes right now. But then her green gaze shifts between all the corpses at my feet, and her face saddens. "You must be working through a lot."

The muscles of my back clench tight as I'm forced to confront the reason I'm up in the middle of the godsdamn night. I swipe the towel across my face again, then toss it on the bench.

The Death Hunt, the werewolves led by Antonio Garcia, have started massacring the vampires making up the Blood Fangs. After two millennia of our three Families being on equal footing power wise, the wolves have finally found something to tip the scales. Aleric Zadar, the vampire Boss, has tried to keep the attacks hidden, but his numbers are dwindling fast. It won't be long before Antonio turns on us.

The thirty-eight-year-old treaty between the Families of St. Augustine, the one mother forced them all into before I was born, is about to be broken. We're about to head into an all-out war.

We need more soldiers.

And there's only one way to make more witches.

My jaw tightens.

"I need an heir." Just forming those words makes me want to hit something. If I father one and they inherit my inability to wield magic, they will be killed.

And so will I.

As much as I can accept that I am an abomination, my genes cannot be. The Boss of the Shadow Domain *must* be able to pass down the shadow magic that gives us our name, allowing us to shift into shadows and travel the Plane of Monsters.

"It's about time you gave me some grandkids," she says with a smile I don't return. Sighing, my mother closes the gap between us, her humor gone. "Your children *will* inherit the shadow magic, Varius."

"You have no way of knowing that." Even if her sixth sense is stronger than most, she isn't a foreseer. Turning, I grab the two black rings I left on the bench and slip them on over my middle fingers. They're magic tools that give me increased strength, putting me on par with a vampire.

I turn back to face her, but she doesn't say anything. Then, "I'll start the search."

I glance at Khalid, and he holds my gaze, his lips tight. Neither of us voice the fact that as reaper, he will be the one tasked with killing me and whatever abomination I father.

"Would you like me to give you a list of candidates?" my mother asks as I head for the door, Khalid behind me.

"No," I say. "Just sort it."

I don't want to know anything about her. I don't want to fall in love with a woman who might have to watch her kids die because of me. I don't want to die knowing she'll get passed on to Leno, the second oldest, and everything about me will be erased so he can "be" the firstborn.

A thing like that might finally succeed in doing what all the assassins and the slurs directed at me have not.

It might utterly destroy me.

ONE

HER

"I can't believe he fucking married Lou off!" Snarling, I kick the door shut as my best friend and I enter the empty apartment, a man slung over my shoulders, a duffel bag full of supplies on Dayne's. Throwing my magic across the room in a spray of purple embers only I can see, I visualize them wrapping around my father and burning him alive. It does little to curb my anger.

I stomp over to the bedroom on the right. The man on my shoulder groans, but the magical drug I gave him keeps him out. Placing him on his feet in front of the window, its blinds closed, I wait for Dayne.

"How are you surprised?" my best friend asks as he puts his bag on the floor, then takes over holding our patsy up from behind, his hands on both sides of his head, his fingers spread wide. "She's utterly useless as an assassin."

I glare at him before I drop to the floor and rummage through the bag. I pull out the case with the handgun, then the gun itself, my gloves keeping my prints off it. I place it in the man's hand and line it up with the window. "She just turned sixteen," I grumble. Which makes her new fiance a verified creep. Then again, even if Lou was pushing thirty, that wouldn't change my opinion of him because my little sister is marrying Varius fucking Shadow.

The stories surrounding him twist my stomach, and I'm a fucking Black. My Family are the ones boogiemen call when someone has wronged them. The assassins who kill without question or hesitation regardless of the target.

Peeking through the blinds, I peer out at the park across the street. I aim the man's arm at the playground full of children, getting the angle of the projection right so when the police checks for gunshot residue later, it will match the line of fire. We don't always bring along someone to frame for our kills, but the police won't ignore multiple deaths at a public park, especially not on this side of town where heavy wallets have weight. Best to give them a case-closed suspect to keep them digging too deeply.

With my other hand, I draw a sigil in the air, pulling on one of the tattooed runes beneath my shirt. Using innate power doesn't require focus, but anything else is a constant fight to use. Magic is dangerous and needs a firm hand to sharpen it into usable energy. My runic tattoo buzzing with power, I force the air around his body into a bubble to stop the sound and the bullet from escaping.

"He still out?" I ask without looking up, concentrating on my magic.

"Yes."

"Then fire."

Drawing on his own innate magic, he sends an electric spasm through our patsy's brain. His finger twitches. The gun fires, throwing residue on his hand and clothes.

Three more shots ring out in utter silence.

The man groans. His eyes flutter, and I remove the gun

from his hand. Placing it back in the bag, I pull out a vial of red liquid. Dayne tilts the man's head back, and I pour a few drops of the potion down his throat. His eyes shut.

Pocketing the vial, I help Dayne lower him to the ground. "If I showed up with a body tonight, would you help me hide it?" I ask. He's helped me hide many bodies at many hours of the night, and I have done the same in my pajamas without question. But this is Varius Shadow I'm not so subtly not talking about, and although he doesn't have any magic, he does have power.

Vast power – his empire enormous and his reach even bigger than that.

Plus, he has that bodyguard he takes with him for all his meetings. Now *that* guy has magic, terrifying magic that can kill from anywhere in the world. Khalid is literally the reason I first started shaving my head twelve years ago. Leaving hair at a crime scene is amateurish in our line of work. Leaving DNA for Khalid to collect and use in his soul dolls, magical creations that make your body and soul his bitch, is stab-yourself-in-the-face stupid.

Dayne raises a brow as we stand. "Starting familicide early, huh? Perhaps you should marry Khalid, really cement this deal between your two families, you know?"

I look at him dryly. Khalid is a reaper – the one tasked with killing members of his Family who turn traitor, and there have been a *lot* of them over the years. Varius' lack of power is an ember to a fire that will never go out. All it'll take is one little blow, and another uprising will rage across the Shadow Family. A Family my little sister is marrying into.

"Seriously, though, Lou can't marry him. He'll break her."

"She's not fragile, Micha. She can handle herself."

"Um, hello? Have you met her? She's utterly useless." If she picks up a sword, she is definitely the one getting cut. If she tries to shoot a gun, that bullet is going into her fucking foot. Whatever Varius or his family wants to do to her is going to happen. Worry eating at me, my eyebrows draw together. "Seriously, Dayne. I need your help."

Sighing he asks, "How are you planning on bringing this 'body' to me?"

I chew my lip for a bit, then glance to the left, knowing he's not going to like this. He never likes my plans. "Dead," I say slowly.

"Micha," he says dryly. "We've been over this. That's not a fucking plan."

"But planning's just a waste of time! *Nothing* ever goes to plan." Seeing he's about to start the same argument we always have, I jump in first. "Just yesterday, you *planned* to kill that SCU agent who shall not be named for *reasons.*" Reasons being her partner is godlike, so can probably listen in whenever her name is spoken or some other bullshit thing like that. "You wanted us to sneak into her house and kill her while she slept. And what happened?

"Oh yeah," I say, not waiting for him to answer. "You didn't realize her dog was a fucking *hellhound* on loan from Hades –"

"That's a bit of an exaggeration."

"And she is mated to a fucking *archangel!*"

Luckily, said archangel wasn't in her house when we broke in. Otherwise, we'd both be very much dead, our souls never to reincarnate. Probably. Not a lot is known about what happens when you get offed by an archangel because it so rarely happens. And not because they aren't super badass and incapable of killing people. Oh no. But because all their time is spent *policing the gods.*

Which we are most certainly not.

We're witches. Aka: *mortal.*

"No, she isn't." Dayne rolls his eyes, having said this a thousand times since yesterday. "Archangels were created before souls were split. They don't have lifemates."

I cross my arms. "Well, penguins didn't have their souls split by the gods just for kicks, and they still have mates."

He rolls his eyes. "It's not the same thing."

"I bet it is to him. He's probably gonna strike us down at any moment once he traces our soul signatures."

"That's not a thing."

"I doubt he's going to have much mercy for two assassins who tried to off his girl in her sleep."

"One, he probably isn't even an archangel. It's not like we have a database to run his face through, and two, we didn't exactly *do* anything, so..."

"Aha! That was my point," I say triumphantly, having totally not forgotten why we were having this argument again in the first place. "Your *plan* didn't work. You can only have so many contingencies, I always say."

"You never say that."

"The best way to hit someone is to go in fast and adapt accordingly."

"Like you did in New York?"

I wince, my side burning from the phantom pain of an eknor rage demon's claws. That wasn't my best 'plans are for wussies' moment, I'll give him that.

"And going back to last night," he continues, "if we'd gone in fast with the 'plan' to adapt accordingly, we'd both be dead. It was only because my plan had been to find out more about her first that we discovered she *might* have the eye of a guy who *could be* an archangel."

That might be a lot of 'mights' and 'could bes' but you just didn't chance it with an archangel.

I snort. "Yeah, okay. Of course you'd see it that way." It didn't help matters that it was also the truth.

But gods, I hate planning. It's so boring. I like to just jump up and stab things in the face. Which is why Dayne and I work so well together. He plans. I kill. The money pours in from all the jobs we do.

"Fine," I sigh, dragging the word out in my annoyance. "Tell me the plan."

It is his turn to snort. "You can't make a plan to kill Varius fucking Shadow. He's *Varius* fucking Shado–" He laughs as he dodges my ball of purple fire. He's unable to see it, but he knows me well enough.

"You're an ass," I say as I snuff out the flames before they catch something on fire.

He grins, completely unabashed. "But you bring me his body, and I'll help you hide it."

"Thanks." Joking aside, I'm seriously considering it.

Because I'm not letting my little sister, who doesn't even want to join the Family business (instead, wanting to go to college to get an art degree – which screams I am not ready for the real *human* world, let alone one full of dangerous witches, werewolves, and vampires and all the boogiemen you can think of) get married to that monster.

The timer on my phone buzzes, signaling it's three in the afternoon – the time our target arrives with his nanny. The hunt is now on, and my mind focuses sharply. As much as I love my sister, Dayne is my partner, and getting distracted now could get him killed.

Peeking through the plastic blinds, I scan the heads of all the kids in the playground. Their parents might think they can protect them from all the little boo-boos they might get, making sure they're not climbing on something too sketchy or running off with strangers, but the truth is, there are some dangers no amount of planning and careful watching will ever stop.

Like it didn't with Bambi. My eyes fall to the tattoo I have on my left hand – the geometric stag with a code that says 'Bambi' down one side and the date I hurt that little girl down the other. The day I was forced to sell my soul so I wouldn't stain the family name with my *morals*.

I pull my eyes from my black tattoo, from my constant

reminder of who I really am and scan the adults across the street. Despite having negotiated exclusivity in our contract, I don't trust a selfish bitch like our client to actually honor her word.

And fuck, is half of me hoping she doesn't.

Because then I'll get to kill her – a consequence that's clearly outlined in our Ts and Cs. Don't fuck with us doing our job, and we won't fuck with you.

We deal with a lot of assholes in our line of work, but there's something about this particular client that rubs me the wrong way. She's a stepmom entrusted with the care of her dead husband's child. A monster with diamond-beaded cheeks already prepared for six-year-old Ron's funeral.

"Target spotted climbing up the slide," Dayne says.

My gaze lands on a small head of brown hair sticking out of a red hat. Bundled up against the cold of February, he's wearing a thick coat and gloves. His cheeks are round with baby fat, but his hazel eyes are far from innocent. He knows pain and misery, and anger burns inside me for the injustice I am about to aid.

Picking up the handgun, I place it between two blinds of the window.

"Old man on the bench at two o'clock. Cane beside him," Dayne says, and I glance in that direction. I find the man quickly. He has yesterday's newspaper open on his lap. His legs are crossed.

"Confirmed," I say.

"Woman by the tree at eleven. White hat, blonde hair."

My eyes track to the left. She's standing, her shoulders hunched, her head down. Long sleeves and trousers. A man walks by her, and she flinches. "Confirmed."

"Preteen male at twelve. Black wife beater."

I tense even as my gaze picks him out in the crowd. It might be the beginning of February, but today's the first day the sun has been out in a while, and the park is busier than normal. The boy is young. Ten maybe. Or eleven.

"Dayne," I say. We agreed to kill three others. Our client paid the quarter million fee, the first half made six months ago, when her husband was first diagnosed with stage four pancreatic cancer. One hundred thousand for the kid. Fifty for each one thereafter as they aren't specific targets, just extras to hide the real crime. But in cases like these, we are always particular in our choices.

No 'good people.'

And no kids.

The old man is hiding an erection between his crossed legs and newspaper. Maybe it's a coincidence. Maybe he has priapism, but his eyes are on the kids instead of down in embarrassment.

The woman is being heavily abused, her bruises hidden behind long sleeves and a curtain of hair over her face. But she is out here with her child, free from *him*, and she isn't running. She's going to go back. Take her child back to *that*.

"Look at him," Dayne says softly, and my gaze sharpens on the kid.

There aren't any bruises on him. His head is up, and he's standing with his mates, a metal water bottle in his hand. He passes it to a friend, and she takes a swig before pulling a face and coughing. He laughs, but my eyes are on the arm he uses to grab the bottle back. A gang tattoo covers half his forearm. And his knuckles are red and raw.

I think back on the man the woman flinched from. He's the same build and has the same hair color and cut as her son.

"He's beating her," I say.

"Most likely."

Dayne never confirms any of the deductions we make. To him, they're merely deductions, never confirmations. To me...they're simply enough for me to live with the choices I make.

"She's a mercy killing," I say. A mother being beaten by her own son. She loves him too much to stop him. But even if he dies, she'll most likely drink herself to death. Either due to the judgment of others for having failed as a mom. Or her own voice judging her too. A civvy might argue that she could break the cycle of pain, that she could beat the statistics, that there is such a thing as hope. That she could come out stronger...

But everyone in this park has the *potential* to change. A future that could be worth saving.

Target Preteen approaches his mom, and she instantly fumbles inside her purse and pulls out another bottle. He sneers at her as he takes it. A psychopath who gets off on seeing her fear. Otherwise, he would have just left her at home. Ditched her to be cool with his friends. Instead, he trained her well.

Exhaling, I say, "Confirmed."

"Target now on the swings." Dayne opens the slats, then slides the window up.

Keeping the gun inside the apartment, I line up the shot, watching as our target swings back and forth. His eyes are closed. There's a smile on his face.

I wait for him to fall back to the lowest point.

And then I fire into his skull.

TWO

HER

The park erupts into chaos as I swing my gun to Target Preteen. The bullet rips through his lung. The next one goes into his mother as she rushes to his side. I turn my weapon to the old man as he runs away, his cane forgotten. The shot goes in his back. He falls on a scream. As he starts to crawl, I fire again. He no longer moves.

Turning to Dayne as the panic outside rages, I find him sitting our patsy up against the wall. The man groans, his eyes fluttering again. Squatting in front of him as Dayne zips up our bag, I place the gun in the man's hand, then raise it to his temple. His eyes are glossed over, but they latch on to me. Like so many people, I'm the last thing he sees. Bits of brain spray out the other side of his skull. A public shooting, followed by a death by suicide – painting him as just another statistic.

Removing my hand from his, I watch as he sags over. Then I turn to Dayne as I rise. "Do you think if I put out a hit on Varius, Father will take it?"

He laughs as we head for the exit.

"What?" I ask grumpily. "I don't get why assassins are looked down on if we put up our own hits. I mean, we get paid for killing people. The time we spend killing our own people is time we could get paid better for killing someone else's people. It's just good business sense."

He shakes his head as we enter the hall. The door clicks firmly behind us, locking shut. "That's not what's funny. It's the fact that you think there is a number *your dad* would be willing to accept to try to kill Varius for, and I am *really* stressing the try."

"Well, if he dies, it'll be a win either way," I mumble as I cover us in a magical shield that hides us from human eyes. The hall is empty, everyone minding their own business, as you do when you hear gunshots next door, but there are cameras near the elevator and stairs.

"Not going to happen. Marrying Lou off to the Shadows will bring in more revenue than what you have in your bank account, especially since you spend so much of it on porn."

"Okay, one, romance novels aren't porn. That's erotica. And two, I've not had any dick in –" I hold up my fingers to count all the time I've been alive. Yanking open the door to the stairwell, I say, "Twenty-seven years. I need to get off somehow."

He snorts. "I'd tell you you could try not scaring all the men who are into you, but there're no men who are in to you."

I look at him dryly. "Thanks for the reminder, bestie."

He grins. "You'll have more fun with yourself anyway. Most men are really shit at it."

"Speaking from personal experience?"

"From the men I fuck. Not me, obviously."

"Uh huh."

As we step outside, my humor fades. A little girl with her

teddy bear has been left screaming inside the slide. There's no one in sight, and the rage I feel for whoever abandoned her makes my blood boil.

But I can't kill everyone.

I can't protect everyone either.

The world is simply too fucking cruel.

So I ignore her, knowing that the threat is over, that she's safe despite her fear, and instead, I make my way over to our target.

Dayne places the duffel bag down on the ground beside the boy's body, then unzips it. I grab the healing wand out of its outside compartment as he lifts out the last item in the bag we've yet to use: the corpse of a six-year-old child who died in a school shooting three days ago. Our client will push for no autopsy, wanting to put this behind her as quickly as possible, and Dayne's magic has kept his body fresh.

He has the same fragile build as our target. The same hair. A similar gunshot wound to the head, though not quite exact. I shot our target through his right lobe and missed his brainstem, giving him a chance to survive. But the corpse in Dayne's arms... No healing magic could've saved him. Nor any of the seven others who died in his school because some asshole parent let their son get access to their assault rifles.

Placing the wand at our target's temple, I reduce the swelling in his brain and close the wound. The bullet will be removed later by an actual healer as a wand isn't powerful enough to replace surgery.

After stabilizing him, we swap their clothes, then bundle him into the duffel bag. We carry him between us, away from the park just as the sirens sound.

"You good with sorting this?" I ask Dayne as we make it to our cars. He knows what I'm asking. Stay with the kid. Make sure he's okay. Get him a new family, a new identity. Transfer half our payment into a bank account for him to access when he's eighteen.

"Yeah," Dayne says as he takes the bag completely, then slides it onto the backseat of his Ford Transit. "You go and save your sis."

My lips tight, I nod at him. "Thanks. I owe you one," I say as I open the door of my own car.

"You owe me six, but who's counting?"

A small smile fluttering at my mouth, I shove my key into the ignition and take off. As I race towards home, all the horror stories I've heard about Varius, though, bang in my skull, and that smile's soon gone. My foot grows heavier on the gas.

Whatever it takes, I won't let my little sister marry that monster.

THREE

HER

My adrenaline pumping hard, I enter the pompous two-story mansion I grew up in, its decoration screaming shady politician rather than infamous assassin. Father likes to host parties here, likes to pretend he's Bruce Wayne because who would ever accuse Bruce of killing a bus full of children just so it isn't obvious Robin was the target? Granted, all those extra kids cost, but being greedy is the least of his sins.

"Stefaan!" I yell as I make my way to the grand double stairs – crisp white marble with deep-red mahogany rails. His study is on the second floor, and he's most likely in it.

At the top of the stairs, I march across the white carpet, my finger twitching at my side as I imagine lining a gun up with Varius' head and firing. All it will take is one twitch...

And, you know, getting close enough to take the shot without being killed by Khalid...

Ignoring the unsupportive voice in my head, I shove the

door open to my father's study. He sits behind his desk, his dark-blue eyes on his laptop as he types something. He acts as if he didn't hear the banging of the front door or my earlier shout for him. He doesn't even look up or respond to me in any way as I march over to his desk, slam my hands on this side of it, and snarl, "You can't sell her!"

Not a single reaction.

"Did you hear me?"

Of course he heard me. I'm full on yelling. Our neighbors probably heard, and we have forty-nine acres of well-tended lawns to ourselves.

He's just ignoring me until I can talk more "reasonably."

The urge to reach forward and slam his laptop shut has my fingers pressing hard into his desk. But I'm angry, not suicidal, so I calmly step back and take a deep breath.

"She's only sixteen, Stefaan. She can't get married. That's not even –" He looked up when I started, then dropped his head again when my voice rose on "married." Clenching my jaw, I struggle to control my volume. "Legal," I finish, very much the respectable fucking daughter.

I dig my nails into my thighs as I wait for Stefaan to bless me with his attention. My jaw clenched, I tell myself one of these days, I'm going to dance on his grave and piss on his tombstone. Then set it on fire.

He finally looks back up at me, but he doesn't take his hands off his laptop. Clearly, he is aware of just how pissed I am and just how likely it is I'm going to lose my temper again. Ironically, that just pisses me off even more, but it also gives me fuel to better control myself. Anything to spit in my father's face.

"Then you'll be pleased to hear," he says, his voice the epitome of calm, "that she isn't getting married."

That doesn't make any sense. And then it *does*, and my eyes widen. The son of a bitch.

"You said you wouldn't sell me if I became an assassin," I growl. Nothing in my life is my own, never has been, but that was one thing, one fucking thing I had control of. "You gave me your fucking word."

"Next time, get a blood oath." A magically binding vow.

Fire flickers around my fingers. Rage boils beneath my skin. I want so badly to lunge across the desk and burn my palm into his face, but I know I'll never reach him.

"I'm not marrying him. His whole family is stuck in the caveman era."

"You are," he says sharply, "and you *will* be the wife he wants."

I grind my teeth, knowing that I can protest as much as I want, but if I refuse, I'll be hunted down by my own Family, which is why he made me believe it was Lou being the one sold. I would've fucking risked it and run.

But now I've lost my head start.

I'll be dead by morning if I tried.

"Perhaps you'll finally learn how to be a woman of class," Father sneers.

"A woman of *class*? Fuck that and fuck you and fuck all the caveman neanderthals who have to resort to arranged marriages to get a bride because they're too fucking stupid and ugly to manage it themselves." I snort. "I bet Varius can't even rely on his dick to get a wife because it's so fucking sma–"

"Micha, that's enough!" he roars, slamming his hands on his desk as he rises.

"No, let her speak." The newcomer's words are soft but sharp in their lethality and confident in their ability to be not just heard but *obeyed*. A shiver runs down my spine as I spin on my heels, praying it isn't Varius who's behind me.

Fuck.

And hot damn, the boy is not ugly. It's embarrassing how quickly my protests die in the face of his chiseled jaw and crooked nose – broken at least once. Dark hair. Dark eyes that have absolutely nailed the smolder. Thick arms dressed in a black suit. If he rolls up his sleeves while looking into my eyes, I'm pretty certain I'll just instantly become Micha Shadow.

"I want to hear what she was going to say about my cock."

A flush hits my cheeks. The urge to look down has my eyes burning, but I know if I do that, I'm going to lose the ability to talk. I can laugh in the face of death, but put me in front of a hot-ass jerk with a dirty mouth, and my tongue trips over my feet.

Though dear gods, he might not even have to do any talking to get me to shut up given the heat of his stare. I can feel it tracking across my breasts, down my stomach, as if his fingers were lightly grazing my skin. My pussy clenches when his eyes linger on it.

"Turn around," he says.

"No." I'm not some damn mare that needs assessing.

His eyes rise to mine. He doesn't say another word, just watches me. Waits for me to listen.

My pulse quickens.

My resolve weakens…

I turn abruptly to address Father, deciding he is the safer option, but two words from Varius stop me in my tracks.

"Good girl."

My brain melts.

My pussy kegels.

I clench my fists to stop myself from spinning towards him as my back prickles, my skin suddenly too sensitive, too aware of his presence. He isn't even close to me, but I can feel him everywhere. Feel his eyes running down my body and lingering on my ass.

"Your father says you're a virgin."

I'm facing him again in an instant, my rage overriding

my arousal. "That is none of your fucking business."

"Micha," Father snaps, but I ignore him, knowing that for once he isn't the most important man in the room.

"Everything about you is now my business," Varius says simply.

My eyes narrow. "It's the twenty-first century, you ne–"

"You are welcome to check her," Father says. Shock slaps the rest of the words out of me, and before I can find them again to protest, Varius inclines his head, and Father and his brother, Khalid, who I've only just noticed, exit the office.

He takes a step towards me, and I take one back before I force my legs to lock in place. He keeps walking forward though. A slow, purposeful stride that is starting to cause my heart to jump all over the place.

Swallowing hard, I say, "Tell me you've never seen a vagina without telling me you've never seen a vagina." Only an idiot thinks they have a seal of virginity you can just look at.

But now he's right in front of me, the gap entirely closed between us, and my sarcastic courage is starting to run for the hills. My pulse pounds in my throat as he crowds me against my father's desk.

He grabs my hip with one hand, and the warmth of his skin burns me beneath my clothes. I try to think of another thing to say to put him in his place, but his other hand is snapping open the button of my black cargo pants, and my mind is melting beneath his hot stare.

He pulls down the zipper tooth by tooth.

When it reaches the bottom, he lifts his hand to the top of my underwear, then slides his tips inside. The brush of his fingers across my curls causes me to jump. My ass hits the edge of the wooden desk.

He caresses me, slowly rubbing down between my lips, then back up again. His eyes never leaving mine, he brushes a finger across my clit. I jerk, my hips lifting away from the desk, my mouth parting as a soft breath escapes. I've never been touched like this, and my nerves are far too sensitive.

"That's not where the hymen is," I blurt, needing to say something before I just become a mess in his hands.

"No?" Varius murmurs, rubbing me mercilessly, sending shockwave after shockwave through my pussy. "Must be my caveman upbringing."

My eyes widen. My cheeks burn.

His fingers glide smoothly south.

Then come up again, stroking me between my lips.

I start to squirm against the desk. His nostrils flare as I stare at him, my eyes half-hooded, my legs shaking. His two fingers dip low again, this time coming to a rest right at the opening of my pussy.

My breath catches.

His fans hot against my cheeks.

Holding my gaze, Varius pushes a finger inside me, going slowly, taking his time as he stretches me. I have only ever masturbated by stimulating the outside of my pussy, never put anything inside me. It's too overwhelming, and I grab his hand in a pathetic attempt to stop him from going in any further.

"Have you ever come with a man?" he asks, his eyes darkening as he pushes his finger in deeper.

I'm struggling to form words, so I just shake my head, too turned on to give him any lip right now.

"Good." He draws his finger out, and for a second I think he's finished with me, but then he pushes two fingers all the way in, stretching me completely. Dear gods, if I feel this full already, how is he ever going to get his cock inside me?

My lips part on a silent pant.

"I'm not after a wife," he says.

I raise my eyes to his, confusion furrowing my brows.

"I just need heirs."

My back stiffens. I try to push him off me, but he curls

his fingers, and a bolt of desire rips through me. My nails dig into his wrist as I arch on a small cry. My entire body trembles. My pussy clenches around him, begging him to do whatever he just did again.

"You'll be ready for me whenever I want you." He presses his palm against my clit and rubs soft circles across it.

I want to protest the barbarity of his request, but every time I start to form words on my tongue, he does something that makes me forget them all over again.

"Occasionally, you'll host a party. You will dress the part, and you will act the part of my wife, but there will never be love between us."

His fingers curl, and my hips buck as I chase that high he's dangling in front of me. I ride his hand shamelessly, not a protest in my mind about him never loving me. I could never love a monster like him either, but I can sure as hel come on his fingers. They curl. They thrust. They take me to the edge of ecstasy. But he doesn't let me over it, changing his rhythm every time I'm about to come.

A soft whimper escapes me as I try to rock my hips in the way I need to, but I have only ever come from outside pressure, and I don't know what I'm doing.

"Any questions?" he asks.

"Please," I say as I lift my hips. "I need…"

His breath quickens, but Varius doesn't say a word. He doesn't give me that last bit of pleasure either. He just keeps alternating between what he's doing, dragging me to the edge every time, only to then back away.

A whimper tumbles out of my lips. "*Varius*," I rasp. The pleasure is starting to turn into pain, into desperation, into an addict's need as their eyes latch onto their special brand of poison, and this might very easily become mine.

"I can't…" I cry, my breaths hard and fast between soft noises I can't control. "I can't… I need… Varius, *please.*"

He pulls his fingers free of my underwear, and I'm left on

that damn edge. My limbs shaking. My breath heaving. My pussy spasming with so much *need*.

"*No,*" I protest as he steps away from me.

"I'll let your father know I'm satisfied."

"Well, I'm not!" I sputter. I was so fucking close.

Still *am* so fucking close.

Whimpering, I shove my own hand down my panties, but he's on me in a second, his fingers hard around my wrist as he ducks his head down to mine. I meet his gaze head-on. My fingers stroke back and forth between my lips as I glare at him. I want them to go lower, to slip inside me, but he's stronger than I am and manages to hold me still.

"Why not?" I damn near whine.

"Because the first time you come is going to be on my cock."

My mouth runs dry.

He leans in until his lips graze my ear. "Now be a good girl and pull your fingers out."

My pulse pounding in my pussy, I remove my hand. He raises it all the way to his lips, then licks the tips of my two fingers before sucking them deep into his mouth.

My nostrils flare, and my thighs clench with unbearable need.

His eyes hot, he pops my fingers out of his mouth, then pushes his back inside me. I arch on a cry, but the pleasure is gone too quickly. Pulling free, he sucks on his fingers. A rumble echoes from his chest. My lips part on a whimper.

"Go pack a bag while I finalize things with your father," he says, his voice tight. "We have a long drive, and I don't want to wait much longer to fuck you."

Hoping off the desk, I practically run for the door, for once in my life not bristling at being given a command.

"And, Micha?" he says, stopping me in my tracks. "Put on a dress and take off your underwear."

FOUR

HIM

Micha leaves the office, and I head for the dark wooden cupboard beside Stefaan's desk. Opening its door, I pull out a thirty-five-year-old Karuizawa and two tumblers as Khalid and her father enter. A more polite Boss would have waited for Stefaan to offer; a ruder one would've rummaged around to see if there's anything better, but I simply don't give a damn for social politics. I just want to drink the required toast and be gone.

Placing the tumblers down on the desk, I turn back to the cupboard to search for the bottle opener, but Stefaan is already there, holding one out to me. He must have jogged across the room to get there in time. That or he kept one on him.

I take it from him with a nod of thanks, then break the wax seal and unscrew the lid. He says something about the quality of the bottle, but it's just worthless spiel in my ears.

The whisky can't trump the taste on my fingers, and his

company can't compete with me sinking into the pussy of my fiancee – my soon-to-be-wife, but we won't marry until I can get her pregnant. Shadows don't divorce. So if she can't conceive soon, the engagement will be called off, and I'll have to find another.

My lips flat, I pour us both a shot, then pass him one as I pick up the other for myself. I'd offer my brother one too, but I know he won't take it. Khalid stands by the door, his eyes on Stefaan, his senses trained on everything in this room and beyond its closed door. His magic seeks any threats; his festering guilt keeps him ready. The person who attacked me thirteen months ago is still out there. We have no leads, and although I doubt it was a Black who was hired, we don't know for sure it wasn't.

Looking over at Stefaan as he holds his glass out to me, I lift mine in a toast. "To future ties."

"To grandchildren," he counters. He isn't a family man. Doesn't care about his own children, let alone any of theirs. But Micha's heirs will give his Family power like he's never known. He might be the head of an assassination gang, but they don't hold territory. They don't hold sway between Families, can't give the green light for other gangs to move onto unclaimed streets like I've just done – the trade I made for his daughter.

I nod, and we drink. I don't savor it. Just tip it back and then I'm gone.

My ears twitch as I enter the hall. My nostrils flare as I suck in air...and the scents my brother can't. The small trace of Micha, her specific gleam of sweat mixed with the last lingers of raspberry and cream – a body wash perhaps that has nearly worn off. And the smell of her arousal...

I inhale deeply as I follow her trail down the staircase, pleased she isn't still in her room, isn't taking her time when I want her in the car waiting. My cock jerks against the cotton of my pants; her scent's getting stronger with every step I take.

She can't be wearing any underwear with how freely it marks the air, not hidden under the layers of fabric she had on earlier. My fingers twitch as I imagine them back inside her, curling, making her scream, making me hard as I watch her come undone.

I nearly took her in her father's office. Nearly stepped between her thighs and buried my cock inside her after tasting her on her own fingers. But I can't fuck her here – when there are too many variables for Khalid to handle on his own. We might've entered into a relationship with the Blacks, but just because they're allies doesn't mean they're not enemies. And I want her to be the only thing I have to concentrate on rather than having an ear trained for anyone approaching outside, for anyone trying to attack while we are divided.

Khalid might be my bodyguard, but he's still my little brother.

When I step outside, my eyes go to her immediately. She is sitting in the passenger seat, wearing a spaghetti strap black dress, and my cock hardens at the idea of rewarding her for her obedience. But then I spot the phone in her hand as she texts someone, giving them her attention rather than me.

My gaze narrows as my feet eat the distance between us. I open the driver's door, and she jumps, tucking her phone down the outside of her thigh, the one further away from me, hiding it. My jaw ticks, but I don't say anything. I don't want a wife, someone to care about or be jealous over. I just need a womb capable of bearing a child who can survive the requirements of my Family. Who isn't born an *abomination*.

Settling behind the wheel as Khalid circles the car to sit behind her, I turn on the ignition. She jerks when my hand lands on her bare leg, right above the knee. I want to go higher, to trail the black fabric of her dress up until I can push my fingers back into her naked pussy, but I don't.

I want to tease her first. To get her worked up. To get all her attention on me, on every little brush of my fingers, on every squeeze of my palm. We have an eight hour car ride back to St. Augustine, Florida, and I want to enjoy every minute of it smelling her arousal.

Pulling out of the drive, I slide my hand further up her thigh. She jumps, a quick breath in, her muscles tense, and I can practically hear her thoughts concerning my brother. About how he's in the car, sitting right behind her, able to tell what it is I'm doing.

But I know he doesn't give a damn. Khalid ran into some woman on the street nearly two years ago, and he's damn obsessed. I don't know her name, and I haven't met her, but I see the effect she has on him. Nothing else can compare to the brilliant star she is in his mind, twinkling in the dark that is his world. He's even celibate now. Hasn't looked at another girl since. Hel, the guy hasn't even jacked off to porn. In the few times I've caught him masturbating, his eyes have been closed. No doubt imagining her. *His girl.*

A pang of envy hits me hard, a yearning for the chance to be that close to someone, but my mind quickly cuts in with all the reminders about why that can never happen.

How many times have once-trusted capos attempted to kill me? Family uncles and cousins – men I grew up with, broke bread with, who gave me their vow of loyalty only to turn traitor. And Micha is a hitman for hire. A Black. She'd kill her own family if the pay was good enough.

But even if she was a civvy and I wasn't a target…our child could be murdered because of *my* genes. How can there be anything real between us when I'm keeping that from her?

Shoving those feelings down, I run my fingers back and forth across her lower inner thigh. Soft hair tickles me, and my cock jumps at the knowledge that I'm touching her in a place no one else gets to see. I trail my tips towards her knee, searching for that line she can't be bothered shaving past and find it right above her kneecap.

I feather my hand back up her thigh, my cock jumping at the first brush of hair against my fingertips. This is mine and no one else's.

My cock hardening, I push my hand higher. She squeezes her thighs together, trapping me, and I glance over at her as we head down the mountain pass.

She looks at me, her cheeks flushed red, her lips parted, her eyes glazed in utter need and tinged with a slight panic born from inexperience. From innocence.

My cock jerks against my pants, growing painful.

Holding her gaze, daring her to keep denying me, I push my hand up higher.

Her lips part wider as a soft noise escapes. But she doesn't deny me. Doesn't stop me from taking what is now mine.

"Good girl. Now spread your legs for me."

Her mouth drops open all the way. Horrified heat floods her saucer-sized eyes. Her legs snap together. Her gaze flicks to the mirror, to Khalid sitting well within hearing range before coming back to me.

Her lips move wordlessly when all I want is to hear her scream.

"Do not make me ask again."

Her muscles trembling under my hand, she slowly parts her thighs.

"Good girl," I murmur.

A blush floods her cheeks, overflowing directly into my cock, filling it, thickening it. Seeing her desire is feeding mine, and – I glance at the clock.

We still have seven hours and fifty-odd minutes to go.

Fuck.

Turning my attention back to the road, I slow down for

our turn, heading for interstate twenty-five. After we merge onto it, I move my hand down her thigh again, my fingers teasing every inch of her skin.

I want her bouncing on my cock with her tits in my face. She doesn't have a large set – A's, if that. I could fit her whole boob in my mouth. Suck on it as she squirms and blushes and pants.

My fingers trail across her thigh, stroking back and forth as she leans her head back in her seat. Her legs part even more, and my cock jumps, wet with need, precum pooling against the cotton pressed against its head.

I shift my hips, searching for a bit of relief but failing.

Fuck.

I glance back at the clock.

Seven hours and forty-five minutes...

My fingers sensitive to every shift of her body, to every hair on her leg, I keep exploring, keep teasing, keep inhaling her arousal as the car eats up the miles. She's slick with need, waiting to be filled, her scent growing so strong, it's making all my blood rush south. I can imagine her wrapped around my cock, sinking down on me before rising again. The picture strengthens with every breath of her I breathe in. It fills my lungs, my head, my throbbing cock until I'm damn near going to come in my pants.

It's been years since I've touched another – my first and only interest just wanted to get close to me. She didn't try to kill me herself. She just opened the door for her surprise boyfriend to do so. Neither of them walked out of that room, but the worst part of it was, I didn't even get my cock wet.

But in another godsdamn seven hours, I'm going to for the first time. And I'm going to take my time, explore every inch of Micha's body. Fill every hole. I'm not leaving the fucking room until she's lying in a mess of my cum, unable to move, unable to breathe, and I know what every part of her tastes like, both before and after I mark her as mine.

Shit.

I hate this fucking clock.

Seven godsdamn hours.

My fingers trail back and forth, rising higher with every return north. She spreads her legs wider, a silent plea as she clenches her hands. My cock jerks, throbbing on the verge of release, but I beat my orgasm back. The first time I come is going to be inside her.

But I can touch her now. I can slip my fingers inside her pussy and fill this car with the smell of her arousal. It's already eating away at my control, at my ability to keep my eyes on the road. I want to bathe in it. I want it smothered all over my cock and fingers and face until I can't smell anything else with my heightened senses.

So I don't stop. Don't trail back down to her knee. I go up and up, and her gaze flies to me as she finally realizes what I'm about to do. She grabs my wrist, but there's no power in her grip, her limbs weak and trembling.

Turning my head, holding her gaze, I stroke a finger through her pussy lips. A soft noise escapes her, breathy and low, and her other hand flies to her mouth as her eyes go to the rearview mirror again. To my fucking brother.

He's staring out of the window, keeping his focus off us, his eyes peeled for anyone who might be trailing us. We're nearing Death Hunt territory, and although we're currently at peace with the gang of werewolves, a war *is* coming. It's only a matter of when. Khalid and I are alone, the rest of our brothers back in Florida. It would be a good time to strike – for them or any of my other enemies.

But even if Khalid wasn't distracted, Micha is just going to have to get comfortable with his presence as he rarely leaves my fucking side.

So I stroke her, sliding my fingers up and down her wet lips, spreading her arousal even more as I learn every part of her. She hasn't shaved, hasn't had a need to, and my cock is begging me to pull over and sink into the pussy that is now mine. To claim it in the oldest of ways.

My eyes dart to the clock on the dashboard.

Six hours, forty-eight minutes.

Fuck.

Letting go of the wheel –because to hel if I'm going to let go of her– I quickly undo the button of my pants and pull down my zip. I don't free myself, just give myself a bit of room so it isn't so godsdamn painful.

A sharp inhale sounds from the passenger seat, and I grip the wheel hard, my knuckles white, so I don't reach over and pull her onto my lap as I'm driving. Nor do I grab her hand and direct her to touch me as I'm touching her. If she does that, there's no chance I'll manage not to come all in my pants.

Six hours, forty-two minutes.

My jaw clenches. I exhale slowly, finding that control I am known for.

I focus on the feel of her lips hugging my fingers and the smell of her pussy invading every part of my nose. I trail my tips up, searching for her clit. She jerks when I find it, and my cock grows painful again despite the extra space. My hand tightens on the wheel, but I force it to relax before my knuckles turn white again.

Control…

I am in control…

For the next six and a half fucking hours.

I trail my fingers down, cupping her completely with my palm. She squirms beneath me, soaking me, soaking the car seat as she bites her lip and tries so very hard not to moan.

I accelerate to overtake a car in front of us. I don't slow down after I pass it. My foot flat to the ground, I wish I had the power to phase; teleporting us into my room would be a fucking good skill to have right about now.

Rubbing my palm across the outside of her pussy, I apply

pressure. She shifts in her seat. Her breathing quickens. At the sight of her arms trembling, her fists clenched tight, I stop the path of my fingers and just cup her. Hold her. Wait for her to come back down.

She rocks her hips, but I pull my hand back the same amount of distance, keeping that pressure featherlight, not giving her what she wants, what she *needs*.

She places her hand on top of mine while she looks at me, and dear gods, she's beautiful. Her cheeks flushed. Her eyes desperate and half-hooded. Her lips parted on breathy pants. I want to give her what she wants. I want to let her demand anything of me, want to give her the pleasure she craves, that I crave to see her take.

But I want our first time to be together.

However foolish that is.

She isn't my girl; she's just a womb that will potentially lead to my death if our child inherits my disease.

So I should just let her come.

I should step back and force that distance between us.

But if all I can ever have from her is sex, if that's all I can ever give, I want that, at least, to be *good.*

So I just hold her pussy in my hand, my palm applying a slight pressure to her clit, my fingers between her lips but not in.

The miles pass.

The wheels of the car turn beneath the rumble of the engine.

My body buzzes every minute of the journey, my hand so fucking sensitive, if she trails her fingers across it, I'll come. But she hasn't moved, hasn't tried to demand again. She just waits like a good girl, and I want so badly to reward her.

Reward us.

I glance at the clock.

Six more fucking hours.

But at least she's come down again. At least I can start touching her once more. I curl my fingers up and down the lips of her pussy, and she jerks with a soft sigh, her head falling back, her legs spreading.

My cock hardens as I push a finger inside her, just the tip, only to still instantly, her pussy gripping me, trembling against me, holding my orgasm in the palm of her hand.

I can't move. Can't curl or thrust my finger inside her. Can't pull it out to bring to my mouth and suck on it. If I do any of those things, I'm going to come. I just need a few minutes to step back away from that cliff edge...

She whimpers and lifts her hips.

Fuck.

"Micha –"

"*Please*," she whispers, so soft and desperate, I can no longer deny her.

Swerving into the right lane, cutting off a car who feels the need to honk, I enter the hard shoulder. Woods spread out along the road, leading into the Blue Mountains. Khalid starts to lean forward, no doubt to tell me we're in the Death Hunt's territory and aren't allowed to stop without permission, but I just say, "Deal with it."

His lips in a thin line, he gets out of the car and pulls out his phone to call Antonio, their Boss. We might be going to war with them soon, but at the moment, they're leaving our Family alone, focusing on wiping out the Blood Fangs, the vampires we share our home city with.

As my brother deals with what needs to be dealt with, Micha looks at me, her eyes hungry. I unclip my seatbelt, keeping my other hand between her thighs. She trembles beneath my touch, and the rapid pulse of her heart seems to vibrate inside my own veins, connecting us.

I push my finger deeper, watching her face as she moans, as she damn near comes apart from just that. Then I pull out and reach across her to open the door, the chill of the day cutting through the heat inside.

I unclip her seatbelt. "Run."

"What?"

I look at her, the hunger in my veins bleeding into my eyes. "Run. And when I catch you, I'm going to fuck you until you can't breathe."

Her eyes widening, she sucks in a breath. But she doesn't move. So I grab her chin and murmur, "Run, little monster."

She's not some little deer or mouse or some other animal incapable of fighting back. No...no, my girl has claws, and I'm looking forward to having them scratching down my back.

She sucks in a breath.

Time solidifies, covered in molasses to hold this moment still. To slow it down so I can see every flutter of arousal on her lashes, every blossoming patch of red on her cheeks, every beat of her desire as it pumps at the vein in her neck.

I'm filled with pure need, my teeth aching, desperate to feel the softness of her skin beneath my lips. I start to drag her onto my lap, but she turns on a jolt and fumbles with the already open door, then stumbles out of the car.

She looks over her shoulder at me, her eyes half-hooded in arousal and uncertainty. I allow my gaze to linger on her face as I lift my wet fingers to my mouth. I suck them in, tasting her, and electricity crackles between us. The musky tang of her arousal hits my nostrils, causing them to flare.

"Run," I growl.

She jerks back, then turns. And like a deer who has just caught wind of a wolf, she bolts straight for the woods.

The primal instinct to chase floods through my system, and my fingers curl around my door handle. But I wait for her to get a bit further away, to nearly disappear between the trees before I step out and fix my pants.

Breathing deep, I catch her scent along with the burn of the cold air. My ears twitch as I hear a soft *thump* that slowly grows louder as I hone in on it, separating it from all the other noises. Her heartbeat fills me, consumes me, and my cock throbs in rhythm to it.

I glance at Khalid, and he gives me a nod while slipping his phone into his pocket. We've been given the green light for a stop. Though even if it was red, I'm not getting back in that car until Micha comes all over my cock.

My pace casual, I reach the treeline. My heart pounding in the tight thickness of my cock, I walk through the woods, control in every step. But then the snap of a twig acts like the starting gun, and I'm full-on sprinting through the trees, following her trail, my pulse spiking with every stretch of my legs.

Branches lash across my skin as I move without grace, but each burn of a cut strengthens my arousal until it hurts to move, my cock strangled by the confinement of my pants. Twigs crunch underfoot, as well as up ahead. She's moving quickly, running at full speed. My nostrils flare. My lungs burn.

Picking up my pace, I vault over a fallen log. My senses strain as I listen for anyone else's approach, the paranoia I was forced to embrace forever keeping me company. We are in the middle of the woods, having stopped abruptly. The chances of anyone else being out here at the same time are minimal.

But they're not zero.

But the only person I can smell is her. The only person I can hear is the little monster running ahead, her footsteps loud in my ears, her arousal leaving an easy trail in the air. I breathe her in, my lungs burning with the need to taste her fully, not just lick her off my fingers, a teasing taste that leaves me with an even stronger desire rather than relief.

I'm closing the distance between us. The snapping twigs and crunching dirt half-frozen under her feet are growing louder. Her scent is growing stronger. And I can almost feel the beat of her heart pounding in my own veins, consuming me, pulling me through the woods like a beacon leading home.

I catch a glimpse of her, a flash of movement. A shaved head ducking around a tree. She doesn't know which way to go, isn't thinking about the best path forward. She's just moving, her adrenaline rushing through her body and out of her pores, filling the air along with her arousal. I want her beneath me and screaming.

I want her on top of me and whimpering.

I want her until she's too exhausted to move.

Too finished even to moan.

Fuck.

I need her now.

Pulling on the abilities I keep hidden – the extra keen senses, the burst of power, the increased speed – gifts from the gods in exchange for my lack of magic perhaps, I barrel into her. She twists right before I reach her, her own senses honed. She looks so fucking beautiful with the heat in her hooded eyes, the flush of her cheeks, the parted lips with both surprise and desire.

I wrap an arm around her as we fall. My other shoots out behind her to hit first, transferring the energy to me rather than through her. My body presses into her, crowding her into the twig-littered floor. I push my thigh between her legs, and she arches against it. Her fingers run through my short hair and grip hard.

"For being a good girl by wearing a dress and no panties, you get my fingers inside you." Threading an arm between us, I slide my hand beneath her skirt and push my fingers in as deep as they'll go. She arches on a whimper.

"For running like a good girl, they get to move." I pull them out slowly, then push them back in hard. She cries out, her legs falling apart as she trembles beneath me.

"Every time you're good, I'll reward you." I curl them,

making her scream. "Every time you're not..." I pull out of her, and her eyes snap open, looking at me in utter betrayal. I groan at the sight of her desire, but that doesn't stop me from removing my hand all the way and up to my lips. "I'll reward myself." I pop my fingers into my mouth.

Her nostrils flare as she watches me. I stare down at her. Her taste is all over my tongue. My muscles strain tight as my fingers dig into the cold earth beside us. "You're not to come with my head between your legs," I say.

She gasps as I shuffle down. Sitting up, she starts, "I've not shaved –"

"I am aware." And it's making my cock hard, knowing she has no one else, doesn't even think about the possibility of another. No crush she's hung up on. No hope that she might run into them. No one else but *me*.

I need her beneath my tongue already, but I take my time dragging the fabric of her dress up her skin, feathering it across all the fine hairs on her thighs. She sucks in a breath as I lower my head to her stomach and press a kiss to her abs.

She squirms, crunching twigs as I trail my mouth lower. The warmth of her inner fire runs through her veins and caresses my lips. Her fingers tighten in my hair, urgent and demanding but I take my time, learning every inch of her skin, every magical tattoo she has on her stomach, the buzz of power beneath the ink making my lips tingle. I pause over a terribly drawn smiley face on her left hip. It looks to have a cock for a nose, and it clearly wasn't done for the purpose of making a spell easier to use. Nor was it done professionally. Perhaps a friend did it...

A growl builds in my chest as I think about a *boy* friend being that close to her, touching what's mine, becoming too fucking familiar with her skin, even if it's just the side of her hip, above her pants line.

The ink is faded, done a long time ago. When she was a

teen, and he was horny? Did he have an erection while he touched her? While he placed his fucking hands on her body? Did he go back home and jack off to what is *mine*?

Snarling, I lean forward and bite that damn tattoo. It's not a gentle nip. Not a love bite. It's feral and possessive and causes her to jerk on a sharp inhale. I swipe my tongue across it, soothing away a bit of the pain, and suck hard. She groans, her hands pressing me to her, but there's a tightness to her grip, a wariness like she's ready to pull me off at a moment's notice.

I don't like that. I don't like that at fucking all. "Spread your legs wide and keep your hands above your head."

She hesitates, and my eyes narrow as I raise my head to look at her. Then she's lifting her arms, bending them at the elbow like a good little girl. The tightness in my chest eases a little, and I move away from the tattoo I've covered with my bite mark and hickey.

I place another kiss on her stomach, right above her belly button. Settling between her thighs, I run my hands up and down them. She shivers. A moan escapes her parted lips, and I frown, trying to figure out how I can taste her and see her face at the same time. I want to watch her come undone. I want to learn what she likes. The way her cheeks darken, the way her eyes grow heated. I want to memorize every note she hits, the highs and lows, the gasps and whimpers that tell me she's close.

My cock grows wet with precum, pulsing hard on the verge of release. Dipping my head, I look at her pussy. Its lips are hidden beneath black curly hair, keeping what's mine secret and safe from the eyes of others. It's like a wrapped gift, all ready for me to open, and I trail my hands up her thighs as I look at her. My fingers skim through the arousal soaking her, and I breathe in deep as she whimpers and spreads her legs even wider.

I stop, my hands stilling as my shoulders tremble from

the force of my control. My orgasm sits tightly wound in my balls, begging for release. Ready to go without even being touched.

I brush my thumbs across the top of her inner thighs, and she sucks in a breath, rocking her hips up, begging me to continue.

But I can't. Not yet.

I want to come inside her, not in my damn pants.

So I take my time to beat my orgasm back, to step off that ledge before I plummet over. I trace my fingers up and down her legs, obsessing over every hair, over every part of her that even she doesn't give attention to. But I will.

Stretching out between her legs, I lower my head to her pussy. My hands finally touch her *there*, and she moans as she moves. Ever so softly, I run my fingers across her pussy lips, pulling them back so I can look inside.

She whimpers, and I suck in a sharp breath. So much precum leaks out of my godsdamn cock, I'm certain it's stained through my pants.

"So pretty and pink," I murmur. I've never had a favorite color before, but I fucking do now. "So nice and wet."

She whimpers and lifts her hips just a little as my breath blows across her sensitive skin.

"Do you want me to fuck you, little monster?"

Another whimper.

But that wasn't an answer, and I want to hear her say it.

"I asked you a question." My words are tight, my eyes latched onto her arousal as it drips between her lips. I lick my own, so fucking desperate to taste her.

"Yes," she breathes, her pussy quivering.

"Yes, what?"

She whimpers again. Then pushes out, "I want you to fuck me."

"Are you going to come with my tongue in your pussy?"

She moans. A clear fucking yes. "No."

"If you do," I warn, "that's it. We're done. We'll get back in the car and not stop until we get home."

She blows out a frustrated breath, and I lift my eyes to see her half glaring at me.

And fuck, I want to take my time down here, want to trace my tongue over every part of her pussy, lapping up her arousal and spreading it all over my chin. But I can't. She won't last and neither will I.

So I quickly duck my head and lick her – a long, steady pass of my tongue through her pussy lips. She cries out. Her hips buck. My balls tighten. Precum leaks down my length under the pleasure of her scream. Her taste fills my mouth, my lungs, my *control* until it's damn near breaking.

Stepping back, I take off my shoes, then my pants and boxers. Too desperate to take the time to remove my shirt, I drop to my hands and knees at her feet. Crawling up her body, I grab my cock and line it up with her pussy as she lifts her hips. With a groan, I sink into her.

Just the tip before she stops me.

Her eyes wide, she shakes her head as one hand goes between us, pushing against my stomach.

"It'll fit," I say.

She shakes her head again.

I clench my jaw as I hover over her, my arms straining as they hold my weight. I can just push her hand aside and take what's mine, but there's a silent plea in her eyes that I can't ignore.

It's her first time too, and something hurts.

Ducking my head, I breathe in sharply, then grab her hips and roll her on top of me, careful to keep in just the tip. She gasps as she spreads her legs on either side of me. Her palms land on my chest. Then they're pushing my black shirt up and over my head. My fingers dig back into her, pulling her down just a bit more before she winces.

Releasing her, I sit up to peel off her dress. She looks at

me, her lips parted, her eyes on my mouth. The urge to lean in and kiss her, to taste her lips with her pussy on mine sends a jolt through me. But that's a line I won't cross – that level of intimacy, that pretense that there'll ever be anything more than just this. I'm already lying to her via omission. I won't add to those sins.

So I turn my focus south to where she's teasing the tip of my cock. She's squeezing me so hard, so pleasurable that I don't know if I'll be able to hold back before she even makes it all the way down.

Grabbing her hands, making sure she can't use them to weave any spell while I'm beneath her, I pin her palms to my chest as I lie down. "Set your pace," I say, my words strained as I struggle to hold my orgasm back. But fuck, her pussy looks delicious sitting over my cock. My balls are damn near blue, and I squeeze her fingers as I fight for my own control.

She lifts up a bit, coming off me, and a growl rumbles from deep in my chest. Her eyes on mine, she wiggles her hips, repositioning herself before she settles back down on top of me. My heels dig into the soft earth as I sink in that first inch. Her lips part on harsh exhales as she slips down past my head, then stops. I suck in a breath at the feel of her squeezing me. At the heat of her body enclosing mine. At the wetness of her arousal sliding down my cock before her pussy does.

Fuck.

I groan.

I'm too godsdamn close.

Dragging my eyes off her pussy, I try to concentrate on something else to cool myself down. But my gaze snags on her breasts, and all I can think about is pulling her down so I can suck on them. I jerk my eyes up...but the sight of her looking down at where we meet, her cheeks flushed, her lips parted, her eyes half-hooded in unfiltered need absolutely destroys me.

My balls draw tight, then explode cum up my cock and deep into her. I groan as I pulse inside her, my tip becoming so fucking sensitive, it hurts. My hips buck on their own, and she cries out as her nails dig into my chest. She tries to rise, to get off me, but I grab her hip with one hand to keep her still.

My cock is still emptying itself inside her. With every jet of my cum, the pleasure intensifies until I'm left wondering why in Hel's name I never did this sooner. Fuck, does she feel better than my hand.

Fucking hel.

My orgasm finally fading, I release her hip to grab her hand again. "Don't stop," I rasp as I look at her. "Keep going until you're all the way down on my cock. I want to watch you come. I want you to feel me hardening inside you and know that you can take." I lift my hips, sinking into her just a little bit more. "*It. All.*"

Her breath catching, she holds my gaze as she slides down another inch.

"Good girl," I growl, my jaw clenched as the sensitivity of my cock borders on pain. "Good fucking girl."

FIVE

HER

My nails digging into Varius' chest, I clench my jaw. I want to take him. I want him to fill me so fucking bad, but dear gods, I can't move down another inch. Sweat beads on my skin. My muscles shake. Breathing out heavily through my nose, I hover over him, not moving.

"That's it," he murmurs as he squeezes my hands to his chest. "Take your time. Do you know how sexy you look sitting on my cock like this?" His words are hoarse and raw as he looks at where he's entering me, and heat blossoms across my cheeks. I duck my head, and my breath catches at the sight of us.

He's too fucking big.

I'm not even halfway down him.

A low whimper escapes me as I lift off him.

But his groan stops me. The way he tosses his head back and arches his body. His fingers are almost crushing mine, and the pleasure on his face is hot and wicked.

Biting my lip, I sink back down.

He hisses in a breath.

His eyes snap to mine.

My heart slamming wildly in my rib cage, I start to rock on top of him, up and down, up and down, just small inches of movement.

But now he's breathing heavily.

And so am I.

And fuck, he's going in a bit deeper.

My pussy quivers around him, pleasure mixing with the slight discomfort until it overrides all pain. I take my time, getting used to him, and he doesn't rush me in the slightest. He just coaxes me, calls me a good girl, lets me set the pace until eventually, I'm halfway down him.

Then a bit further.

I stop, panting hard. He's filling every inch of me, his cum dribbling down my legs. The only thing I can focus on is his cock, ruthlessly demanding my attention. I squeeze my eyes shut on a shudder.

"Eyes on me," Varius growls, and there's a rawness to his words that has my gaze back on him. A satisfied smile curls his lips.

I rock up and down, and he groans. His fingers tighten on my hands. His cock starts to thicken inside me, pressing against my walls, causing panic to flood my system. He's already stretching me too much, and he's not even all the way hard.

"I can't..." My muscles lock, freezing me stiff.

"You *can*," he growls. "You can take all of me. Just relax like a good girl."

I shake my head. No amount of "good girl" is going to make me wet enough to defy the laws of physics.

He simply *doesn't fit.*

"Think about your mom," I blurt, then wince, horrified at what I just said. But I need his dick to go back down. It's too much. It's stretching me too tight. "Or your dad. Fuck, think about your mom with your dad."

"Micha," he growls, grabbing my hips as he pushes me off him. My pussy cries hallelujah even as shame heats my cheeks. That was my first time, and the only way I could've made it worse was if I broke his penis.

And oh my gods, there's a part of me that's tempted to cut it in half. Or fourths. Then maybe it'd fucking fit.

But as I kneel beside him, having a mini crisis, he sits up and pivots so he's behind me. His movements are too fast, too smooth, and the next thing I know, I'm facedown on the cool forest floor, on my knees with my ass in the air, and he's stretching out above me. His cock rubs between my ass cheeks, and I suck in a breath at how hard it feels.

My legs trembling, I try to speak despite the dryness of my mouth, but he wraps a hand around it.

"Just relax, Micha," he growls in my ear, then pushes the tip of his cock into my –

My eyes widen. "Wrong hole!" I shout against his palm.

His teeth find my ear and nip as his other hand bands around the back of my neck, holding me still. "Every hole of yours is mine. Your body is mine, and if I want to fuck you balls deep, you're going to shut up and take it."

He pushes in, and I grit my teeth, the stretching of my ass feeling so different to how my pussy did. This is rougher, less pleasurable, more sharper in pain, and I instinctively relax as my training kicks in.

Blacks don't break under torture.

We empty our minds, focus on a place that isn't *here*. We move out of the tight confinements of our body, setting our thoughts free. To someplace better. I can't even feel the pain anymore, my body numb. My mind floating away –

"*Fuck,*" he groans, his fingers digging into my hips and snapping my mind back to this moment.

I tense automatically, expecting the burn of my ass, and

he grunts, then groans as he collapses on top of me.

"Don't move," he growls, his heart beating wildly against my back.

I still, not wanting to increase the pain, but then I realize my ass doesn't hurt. It feels *good,* and my body buzzes with a need to move. Biting my lip, I rock my hips slightly back, trying to discern how deep he is. If he can go further.

"Fuck, Micha," he says, his words harsh and raw, and I realize that despite being on my knees, I can make him beg. That knowledge makes me heady, makes my heart beat loud in my ears as a budding confidence fills me.

I wiggle back again.

He groans, and his teeth dig into my left shoulder. "Stay. Still," he growls.

"Or what?" I ask, a half-smirk curling my lips as I push deeper onto him.

His hand bands around me to touch my pussy, and a finger pushes between my lips. Desire floods me as it flits across my clit before sliding back down. "Or I'm going to tie you up next time so you can't move."

I pause, a delicious thrill shooting through me as I weigh the future with the now. The thought of being bound by anyone should terrify me given my upbringing, but with him it sounds like a promise of pleasure. And I want it.

I want it so fucking bad.

He brought me to the edge hours ago in Father's study, but I have yet to actually fall over it. My thighs are soaked, and his cum adds to the sticky mess all over my legs. His cock pulses inside of me, so thick and filling and hard, and I am *desperate* to come.

So I wiggle back, impaling myself deeper onto his cock, and his weight presses down on me even more, the strength leaving his limbs and flowing into me. Heady desire fills me, making me bold, and I start to rock back and forth on him. He hisses in a breath that turns into ragged pants to match mine. He groans as I slide up and down his cock. His hand drops from my pussy, but the noises he's making in my ear, the deep grunts of pleasure that border on whimpers and pleas are just as erotic as his touch.

I pant heavily as I rub my entire body against him as I fuck him slowly. The hairs on his chest tickle my back, and the friction of our skin leaves me breathless. The heat builds in my pussy, strengthened by the pleasure in my ass and the harsh groans in my ear, the breath he fans across my neck.

"Fuck," he growls as he presses his lips to my shoulder. "Ride me like you are, Micha. Ride me until I'm coming in your ass."

I suck in a harsh breath as I quicken my speed on his cock. My ass slides up and down him with ease now and no burn. Just pleasure. A foreign feeling that I can't explain or compare to the filling of my pussy, the curling of his fingers, or the lick of his tongue. I'm just consumed by it. This need to come. This sensation of him inside me.

My thighs shaking, I whimper as I chase the thrill of ecstasy.

"That's it, baby. You're going to make me come. Make me fill your ass like I did your pussy."

My lips part as I pant, his breath on my neck, his words in my ear making me tremble.

"Fuck, do you know how good you feel riding the tip of my cock, baby?"

A whimper escapes me as I push back on him faster, going deeper, harder until I'm certain he'll split me in two. But he feels so damn good inside me. His growls in my ear sound so wicked. So hot. So deliciously fine.

Pushing onto my hands, I struggle to lift his weight. He aides me, lifting himself as he grunts and groans and hisses in sharp breaths of uncontrollable pleasure. I am on my knees for him, but he's right here beside me, on his knees for *me.*

And fuck, is that hot.

His unfiltered desire. His want for me to fuck him raw and fast. To make him shatter on an orgasm so strong, it'll have us both collapsing onto the forest floor unable to move, unable to breathe.

"Fuck, baby."

"Just like that."

"You feel so fucking good."

He groans, and this time when he digs his teeth into my shoulder, I can't help but scream. The pleasure rips through me, erupting like a volcano, shaking me like an earthquake that could cause tsunamis halfway around the world.

It is all consuming, all powerful, and my toes curl as I arch my back on a breathless scream. His name builds on my lips, in my lungs, in every part of me that matters in this moment. My pussy and ass spasm, and as I come on a wave of intense ecstasy that leaves me half-mad, I scream –

"Dayne!"

SIX

HER

My eyes widening, I try to scramble away, but Varius grabs my hips and slams in deep. I cry out, a flash of pain erupting through my ass.

He wraps a hand around my throat and yanks me up, arching my back and forcing my head to the side. My gaze latches onto his, then starts to flick away, back to my best friend, who is now standing in the middle of the woods with us, alongside Khalid. *Why is he here? How is he here? Wh–*

Pain flares through my throat as Varius' grip tightens. My eyes fling back to his. His fingers loosen, allowing me to breathe. "Da–" I start, but my air vanishes once more under the vice of his hand as he rams into me.

He doesn't say a word, but I hear his order. *Eyes on me.* Attention on *me.*

I whimper, my pussy spasming from my release as his cock fills me so fucking deep. He dips his head as a growl rumbles from his throat. Then his teeth are on my shoulder, biting me. I moan as delicious pain meets wicked pleasure. A blush creeps across my cheeks as I'm all too aware of our audience, but I can't stop the noises from escaping, can't stop my ass from rocking back into him as I chase the last tremors of my orgasm.

Nibbling his lips across my shoulder, he bites the base of my throat. I jerk beneath him as a groan rumbles from his chest and through me. I can feel my pulse between his teeth, feel his cock pulsing inside of me. Feel the heat of his cum in my ass.

He trails his lips higher, this time to suck on my neck, and I know he's leaving a hickey, marking his territory for all to see. My eyes snap open. My pussy spasms. For all my talk about how his family is a bunch of neanderthals, dear gods, that *does something to me.*

Releasing my neck, he pushes down on my back. My cheek hits the forest floor, my arms too weak to hold myself up. My body still trembling, I fall apart completely. Earthy smells fill my nose as my heart pounds loudly between my ears.

Fucking hel, I might need to rethink if I am, in fact, a feminist.

Or if women should just keep to the bedroom...

Or the woods...

Gods, I wonder if I can ask him to wear a mask next time. Or if he'll refuse so I know it's *him* chasing me.

Shuddering, I draw in a ragged breath.

Varius pulls out of me, and a rush of warmth flows down my left thigh. My ass in the air, I'm vaguely aware of the head of his cock rubbing up my leg, scooping up his cum and pushing it back in.

I shudder.

My ass spasms around his tip.

And then I freeze.

Suddenly remembering Dayne and Khalid are standing

right there.

Oh gods!

I jerk my head up or try to, but his hand is still firmly on my back.

"How did you find us?" Varius demands, and the blood rushes from my face as my tattoo on my left hip tingles.

Panic flooding me, I shout, "He's gay!" I try to wiggle away from Varius, but his hand might as well be a damn boulder.

"Are you saying he used gaydar?" he asks deadpanned.

"I'm *saying* you have nothing to be jealous of because he's *gay*," I stress, my heart pounding in my throat. The urge to attack him with my fire makes my fingers burn. Because there's no fucking way he's going to like that I'm practically microchipped by another man.

"If I was jealous, I would cut off his erection and feed it to him," he says, a monotone statement of pure fact. "But as you can see, he still has it."

"I can't *see* anything because you're pinning my head to the ground!" Panic rising, knowing damn well Dayne can't take Khalid, I try to think of something else to say. "And all this stress isn't good for making babies!" I wince, but the words are already in the air. The pressure on my back eases, and I don't care if I said something so utterly stupid. It got me free. And now I'm up and on my feet, standing in front of Dayne, trying to figure out how the hel I'm going to keep these two neanderthals from hurting him.

We could take Varius given his lack of magic, but Dayne and I still can't take Khalid. And Khalid doesn't even have a blade to my friend's throat. He is just using one to carve into an apple and eating slices off it, and that shouldn't be scarier than seeing his twelve-inch hunting knife against my best friend's neck, but dear gods, it is. Khalid doesn't even look on edge. He looks relaxed. And hungry. And fucking confident that he can move faster than either of us.

Strike harder. More deadlier. Chills run down my spine.

"How did you find us?" Varius repeats.

"I texted him," I blurt as I turn to face him. The strike is going to come from Khalid, but the order isn't. I need to get Varius to stop beating his chest like a gorilla just because I called someone else's name... I clear my throat.

"You gave him our exact coordinates?" He doesn't say it like he doesn't believe me, but only an idiot would. I have no idea where we even are.

"There's an app on my phone," I try next, and it's not a lie. An app can also be deleted; the only way to stop Dayne from being able to find me is by killing him.

Varius' eyes finally dip to mine. "Lie to me again, Micha," he says softly, "and I won't let you come for the next week."

I snort. "That's not going to scare –" My words die at the promise in his eyes. I shift on my feet, trying to convince myself that I have not become addicted to his dick in only a few hours.

Dayne is my ride or die. I'd venture into Hel's Niflhel or Hades' Underworld to get him back. I sure as hel would stand up to my libido. I made it twenty-seven years without dick. I can deal with another week.

"Micha," Dayne says in a secret language we made up. "It's dangerous to lie to someone as paranoid as him."

By the narrowing of Varius' dark eyes, talking like this is dangerous. He could kill Dayne right here, right now, and no one would care but me. And even that wouldn't matter because Father sold me. Sold my *womb*. Varius could cut off my arms and legs or knock me into a coma or just bind me to a bed for the rest of my life. He doesn't want a wife. He wants a body to breed.

He owns me. Every part of me.

I have never felt so powerless.

So angry.

"You shouldn't have come," I hiss at Dayne, continuing

our secret conversation.

"You stopped texting me abruptly and then your heart started going a million beats a second. I thought you were being tortured for doing something stupid to save Lou. Forgive me for not realizing you were getting your insides rearranged by a fucking monster cock."

A blush burns across my cheeks as my eyes dip to said cock, still at half-mast. My eyes widen. There is no fucking way that whole thing went in.

Suddenly aware of my body, I hug my waist in a poor attempt to feel like I'm covering myself. The most skin I've ever shown was by wearing a tank top and a pair of shorts. Now I'm butt naked in the woods with three men around me. *And there's cum dripping down my legs.*

My cheeks flush hot, but my embarrassment is instantly killed by Khalid.

"Say another word I don't understand," he says between apple slices, "and I'll cut out your tongue."

I swallow hard as it takes everything inside me not to turn to face the monster at my back. I might be terrified of him, but I know he won't move without a command.

Holding Varius' gaze, I try to think about what lie I can tell him that will protect Dayne.

But there isn't one.

"Varius, please," I say, not above begging to save my friend. "Just let him go."

"If he has a way to find you, he has a way to find me."

And that's not something he can leave out in the wild. Even if he trusted him, he wouldn't trust him not to crack under torture. Varius has many enemies, and none of them would hesitate to kill one man to get to him. This isn't the gorilla chest beating competition I thought it was. This is just the life of a Boss who has been hunted all his life.

"Then take him with us," I say desperately.

"Micha!" Dayne starts, but Varius cuts in.

"Put him in the car."

I start to spin towards Dayne, to tell him everything will be okay, but a hand on the back of my neck spins me back around. Movement behind me whispers in the wind. And then it's gone, the world silent save for the birds, and I know we're alone. My pulse spiking, I watch Varius like he is a snake about to strike.

"You answer my question, and he lives," he says simply, his fingers tight on my skin.

Some things are worse than death though. Like life as a prisoner. Dayne was held in a cage and beaten his entire childhood. He won't go back to that life. If he thinks that's his entire future, he'll commit suicide. It won't be deliberate, but his attempts to escape will get more and more desperate.

"Give me a blood oath that you won't hurt Dayne Stevie Killeen-McCarthy physically or mentally."

His eyes narrow slightly on mine. "Tell me how he found you, Micha."

"Blood oath first."

"This isn't a bargaining –"

"Please."

"I'll give you my word."

"That's not good enough." Not for Dayne.

"That's all you'll get. My trust is not given on command."

"Is it ever?" I snap, my frustration bleeding into my tone.

He doesn't say anything, and I clench my jaw, trying to keep control of my temper. Letting it go in a place basically made of kindling would be foolish. "We're assassins," I say finally.

He waits for me to elaborate, and each word is pulled from me with a pair of pliers.

"As a safety precaution, we've tattooed a location spell on each other. If we concentrate, we can sense the other's heart rate."

His eyes dip to my hip, to the terrible smiley face tattoo

Dayne gave me over a decade ago. "That can't stay on you."

"It's a safety precaution for work –"

"You're not an assassin anymore, Micha." His eyes lift, drilling into mine. "All you are is my fiancee. Break the spell."

My back grows rigid at his command. My middle finger twitches as my eyes narrow into slits. "No."

His lips tighten. Grabbing my hand, he places it over my tattoo. "Remove it, or Dayne dies before you make it back to the car." He presses my fingers deeper into my hip, holding my gaze without an ounce of remorse or care.

I am so fucking tempted to burn him to ashes where he stands, but there is a gleam in his eye, a challenge, a desire for me to try that catches me off guard. He has no magic. I am a seasoned assassin.

And yet, looking into eyes that bleed of death, a red tinge in his brown, I shiver.

There is something not right with Varius.

Something dark and monstrous right beneath the surface.

Lifting my chin, I glare at him. Removing the tattoo is going to hurt like hel, more so than a simple burning of flesh. Breaking magic releases dark energy; it'll feel like rubbing salt into the wound. Then acid. And then another round of salt – if I manage to live that long; the magic will want to kill me. It'll fry all my nerve connections there, my innate healing unable to fix it. The damage and scarring will be permanent.

But it'll save Dayne's life.

"Fine," I say, lifting my chin. "Let go of me."

He stares at me, a flash of something lurking deep in his eyes. Too deep for me to see clearly. And then his hand falls away, and he steps back, giving me space.

Sucking in a breath, I call on my innate magic and let my fire burn in the tips of my fingers. Pain explodes down my side as the smell of searing flesh, of bacon sizzling away on a pan fills my nostrils. My teeth clench hard. Beads of sweat collect all over my face. My legs sway, but I don't let up.

Pushing my fire between the magical ink, I attack the spell Dayne left beneath my skin. It flares up against me, drawing power from my other tattoos. When he first drew it on me, it was only his power holding it to me. But then I added my own tattoos over the years, as witches do, giving ourselves cheat codes and shortcuts for the common spells we use. And every year, Dayne and I retrace each other's location spell, binding it to our other magic, strengthening it.

So it can't be severed.

So we can never lose contact.

Screaming, I build a fireball in my palm and shove it through every layer of skin over my hip.

The bond between us breaks.

Shatters.

Magic explodes between my fingers, and the blast tosses me back. My flesh feels like it's been burned away to bone, and I land on my ass before collapsing back. My hand falls from my side as I curl into a ball on the forest floor. My legs kick as I spasm uncontrollably, pain flaring through every inch of me, a boiling fire in my veins.

Squeezing my eyes shut, I focus on the path the magic is taking, trying to cut it off before it reaches my heart. But my body is jerking in sheer agony, and my mind is a mess of uncontrollable jittering. Just silent screams for the pain to end. I can't concentrate, can't stop the dark energy from raging through my body.

You can! Remember your fucking training.

Clenching my teeth hard, I bite back the pain. Then I trace the path of burning fire in my veins, rush ahead of it, and throw up a magical dam. I stop it right as it reaches my chest, and I gasp as scorch marks blacken my lungs.

The spell slams against my shield over and over until it

peters out, but not before it's left me on my final legs, my last juices, and vomiting from the pain, I pass out.

I open my eyes to find Varius squatting down in front of me. He's still naked, so I can't have been out that long. But fuck, do I feel like I've been tortured for days.

"If you're faking the spell's removal," he says simply, "I will skin off every tattoo you have."

I force my eyes to focus on him. Double vision makes it hard, but I'm stubborn and pissed off. At him. At myself for ever thinking that just because he took the time to wait until his dick didn't hurt that he wouldn't hurt me.

A fool. An utter fucking fool I was.

But I won't be again.

"With charm like that," I grit out, my body still shaking, "I can't believe you had to revert to an arranged marriage to get a girl."

"I don't need a girl," he says dismissively as he stands. "I just need a womb."

SEVEN

HER

And I just need to stab a knife into your fucking heart.

But that isn't ever going to happen despite how much I wish it. Khalid has Dayne, and he's probably ripping out a chunk of his hair right now to keep as collateral. Killing Varius and running for my life with my bestie will never be an option when the reaper can kill from any distance as long as he has your DNA.

So I just grit my teeth as I stand. Pain lances through me, straight down my leg like I've just shoved it through a wood chipper, and I collapse back to the ground. My fingers dig into the earth as I shudder. Varius doesn't turn to me at all as he gets dressed, and I glare at his back, wishing I could shove a knife into it.

Sever his spine. Puncture a lung. Happy thoughts.

My teeth clenched tight, my body slick with sweat, I try again. On the fourth try, I manage to actually stay standing.

By that point, Varius is fully dressed and on his phone. But his eyes are on me, tracking me as I stumble around the woods, looking for my dress.

"Who?" he asks whoever's on the other end.

Then, "Where?"

And, "When?'

"What?" I say loudly and sarcastically, but he doesn't react in any way. Muttering curses with his name, I pull on the dress I stole from Lou's room. Then I curse the fact I did something nice for him by having left my underwear while blatantly ignoring the small voice in my head that says it was also nice for me.

Fuck him.

Fuck the voice.

Fuck the whole fucking world other than Dayne and Lou.

And especially fuck my father for selling me in the first place.

Anger burns my eyes as I think about all the sins and black marks I've committed in the belief that I'd be saved from a life like this.

That I would be *free*.

Gods, I was so stupid.

Wincing, I bend down to dig a twig out of my tennis shoes. Even if Lou's shoes weren't too big for me, I wouldn't have stolen a pair. I'm not putting on death traps I can't fight in.

Varius hangs up his phone just as I fish the twig out and flick it away. He stops in front of me, looking down. "Are you good to walk?"

"Like you give a damn," I snap.

"Stress could be bad for the baby."

I laugh. "You're an idiot. You can't conceive that quickly. Your sperm is probably lost anyway, just as dumb as their father."

"Then let's hope they take after their mother."

And gods, I hate him even more. He was being sarcastic, throwing my earlier words back at me, and I fucking missed it. It went right over my head until he practically spelled it out for me. Ugh.

Exhaling harshly, I struggle to my feet. He grabs my arm to steady me as I sway. I want to pull away, but godsdamn it, I don't have the strength. Not if I want to stay standing.

"I'm fine," I growl. Totally believable. My face is most definitely flushed, and I feel like I'm going to puke from the pain still rolling around my chest.

He pulls something black out of his pocket. "Then put these on," he says, handing me...

My jaw drops. "I'm not wearing your boxers."

"You're not talking to another man naked."

"I'm wearing a dress, and it's *your* fault I'm not wearing anything underneath it."

He doesn't say anything, but I can hear his ultimatum. Put them on or don't talk to Dayne. Glaring at him, I bite back the words, *Go fuck yourself.* Snapping the boxers out of his hand, I lift one foot to put them on.

But I sway, nausea hitting me hard on the curtails of pain, and he grabs me with his other hand. Steadying me. Holding me up in a mock embrace.

I stare at him as the moment extends, growing too fast, too quick for either of us to contain it. Until it grows into something it shouldn't be. Something heavy and hot and wicked.

His gaze darkening, he slides his hands down my arms, leaving goosebumps in his wake. His eyes dip to my lips, and I suddenly realize he hasn't kissed me yet. He fucked me like a lover, but he never kissed me.

My cheeks hot, I glance away.

He doesn't move for a moment. Then he's tugging the boxers from my weak grip and dropping low to put them on me. With his underwear around my ankles, he looks up. My breath catches. He's on his knees. His eyes are hot.

He might say he just wants a womb, but there's no doubt that in this moment, he wants *me.*

Rising slowly, he slides his boxers up my legs, his eyes growing hotter with every inch they cover. My skin is too sensitive, the brush of the fabric making me shiver, and I'm forced to grab hold of his shoulder to keep my balance. His eyes dip to my pussy, and I'm suddenly aware of just how close his mouth is.

Gods, I want to just climb onto his shoulders and ride his face.

But I don't.

Because he's a jerk.

And the pain in my side is a brilliant reminder of that. Like a hit pop song telling me not to go back to my asshole of an ex because I dumped him for a reason.

Grabbing the hem of his boxers, I yank them up. The moment breaks, shatters, is gone, and I hiss in a breath as the burn on my side flares in agony. The elastic sits right over it, and walking with it constantly rubbing against me is going to be a bitch. But there's nothing to be done. They're too big to sit any lower; they need to be under the tight part of my dress or else they'll slide right off.

I start to turn to walk back to the car, but I'm suddenly in the air, cradled against a chest that's hard and hot and *close.*

Too close.

"Put me down," I snap.

"I'm not waiting the hour it'll take you to hobble back to the car."

"And here I thought you were being a gentleman."

"A *gentleman* wouldn't fuck your face to shut you up."

I open my mouth for some witty comeback, but all that escapes is a strangled, "And you will?"

"Yes." Short. Sharp. Honest.

My pussy spasms, and I remind myself I made it twenty-seven years without dick. I don't need it.

Then again, even if I didn't want it, I'm still going to get it. My life is no longer my own; I'm just the prize of a mafia Boss, a thing to be bred whenever he wants an heir.

"Tell me about Dayne," Varius says as he walks through the woods, taking twisted paths so I'm not whacked by all the twigs and branches blocking our way. I'm just hit by about ninety percent of them instead.

But it is, I begrudgingly admit, thoughtful. For an asshole neanderthal.

"He's gay," I finally say.

"That's his entire character, is it?"

I glance up at him, surprise widening my eyes. He said that so deadpanned, I can't tell if it was a joke, but... What else could it have been? And dammit, I like dry humor.

"Well, no. He likes burgers..." I add.

He glances down at me, and I can practically hear him calling me an idiot. But he doesn't say anything, and I look away, wondering where the hel my brain has gone because it's clearly no longer in my skull.

"I like burgers," he says flatly.

I glance at him, but he's already glanced away, his lips thin, and I am uncomfortably aware that we're doing a lot of glancing.

So I glance away.

But then I think I see him glance at me, so I glance back, only to find him most definitely not looking at me.

Feeling awkward, I shift in his arms, then hiss in a breath as my side explodes in agony.

Thank gods for that reminder. I almost lost my feminism there. Clenching my teeth, I shudder beneath the onslaught of pain.

He doesn't say anything, but his pace smooths out. He takes more care with his steps. Walks a bit further rather than ducking under a low branch.

And I hate that show of chivalry.

Because there's a part of me that understands what he did. That knows I would have demanded the same in his shoes. There are no easy choices in what we do. No good versus evil. No right versus wrong. Just blatant survival, and Varius has been stabbed in the back too many times by those he trusts.

He doesn't even know Dayne.

Doesn't know me.

But instead of outright killing the man who snuck up on us, he gave him a chance to explain.

Not many Bosses would have offered that same courtesy.

My father sure as hel wouldn't have.

But I don't want to understand Varius and his actions.

Not when I'm in this much pain.

And not when I don't know what's going to happen to Dayne.

The sound of the highway traffic grows louder, filling the silence between us, and then we're back on the side of the road. My gaze instantly searches for my friend, and a breath of relief escapes me at the sight of him, leaning back against the hood of his car, his eyes on me, his lips tight.

Varius walks towards him, still holding me, and I wonder if he's going to put me down at all. But then I'm on my feet, and his hands are on my waist, keeping me up. As soon as I'm steady, he releases me.

"You survived," Dayne says, his eyes dipping to my hip.

"Just."

Khalid's attention snaps to me, and I instantly still, my fingers itching for a knife. My magic isn't going to affect him. He's a reaper, and it's the worst kept secret that they have a way to mute others' powers.

I want to sarcastically ask him, "Worried about me?" but I'm not stupid enough to taunt Khalid. Only a fool dances with death when it knows all the steps and you don't even know the playlist.

"Show him," Varius says as he steps beside me.

It's so fucking demanding, I instinctively refuse to listen. But then Khalid nods at me, and Dayne warns, "Micha," and I begrudgingly lift up my dress with one hand while holding Varius' boxers up with the other. I am suddenly grateful I am wearing them. Dammit.

"It looks worse than it is." Before I can release my dress though, Khalid lifts his eyes to mine, and my hand freezes.

"Let me take away the pain," Dayne says, but I don't want him wasting energy on me. If Khalid's given the order to kill him, I want him to at least have a shot.

However minuscule that might be.

"I'm fine," I say.

Ignoring me as he so annoyingly does, he steps forward, muttering a healing incantation. Between the two of us, he's the better healer, having intensely studied the human body for his innate magic anyway. I have no idea where the tibia is, let alone what a healthy one looks like. I can heal skin cuts and muscle tears, fractures and sprains, but anything that requires actual rearranging? No chance.

Pressing his hand to my burn, Dayne rebuilds my nerves and reshapes my skin. He can't get rid of all the puckering; he isn't strong enough, but he eases as much pain as he can. Even the burning ache in my chest fades, washed away by a warmth that leaves me drowsy. As if I'd laid in the sun too long.

Raising his hand, he waits until I drop my dress and then pulls me into a hug. "Glad you survived."

"That's because your magic is shit. Breaking it was easy."

He snorts as he pulls away.

I glance at Khalid – or rather, where he was. He's now off with his brother, and they're talking in low tones. A buzz interrupts them, and Varius pulls out his phone. He glances at me before answering.

"What?" he says, and I wonder if he's mocking me for my earlier tease or if he really is just that rude when he answers his phone. My eyes narrow slightly, but his face gives nothing away.

"You okay?" I ask Dayne, turning my attention to him. "Khalid didn't –"

"Not a scratch. He appeared in my car just as I started to brake and then very calmly told me we were going for a walk." He lowers his voice. "I nearly shit my pants."

I grin.

"I for sure thought it was going to be an execution. But then I heard you moaning, and I thought my fate might be even worse than –"

I punch him in the arm.

He laughs. "So how does it feel to no longer be a virgin?"

"Virginity is a bullshit invention invented to control us, and the *only* reason a man would want a virgin is so they wouldn't know he was full of shit when he said he was good in bed."

"Except for Varius, clearly, given how much you were screaming." He looks at me smugly. Before I can sputter out a response, he drops his voice. "Jesus Christ in a spit roast, did you see his dick?"

"Uh, duh. It was *in* me."

"Not all the way, it wasn't."

My jaw drops. "What?" Horror fills me. "No." The word comes out as a whimper, a plea, a begging for mercy from the gods. "No. It had to be. It felt so fucking –" I stop, unable to say the words.

Dayne laughs. "Oh, you are so fucked."

Grabbing his arm, I pull him further away from Varius and his goon and lower my voice. "What am I going to do? Dear gods, Dayne. I can't take all of his dick. It'll *literally* tear me in half."

"It'll be a damn good way to die though."

"I'm serious, Dayne! There's no way it's going to fit." I nibble my lip. "How much did he put in?"

"A bit more than the head?"

"What!"

"Well, the angle wasn't great, and I was distracted by his hand on your throat..." He raises his hand to his neck and shivers. "Gods, I'd let him rail me."

"Good. You can take my place. Your ass will be fine. We just need to figure out a spell to make you look like me –"

"No."

"But –"

"You know how dangerous transformation magic is. I'm not risking my balls just so you can't get laid."

"Not just laid, Dayne. *Ripped apart from the inside out.* Like an xenomorph is popping out of me. Oh gods." Both hands press over my stomach. "I bet if he rammed into me hard enough, his dick would actually pop out of my belly."

Laughing, he grabs both my shoulders and shakes me. "Calm the fuck down, Micha."

"I don't want to die from a dickomorph," I whisper in utter horror.

Collapsing against me, he starts to howl. It takes me a moment, but then the annoyance comes. Here I am spilling my greatest fears, and my *best friend* is laughing. At me. *Hard.*

Shoving him off me, I snap, "You're an ass."

He wheezes, shaking his head. "Oh girl, you so lucked out."

My eyes narrow. "Um, hello?" I wave a hand at my side. "How is being forced to endure intense pain *lucking* out."

Lifting his head, he then straightens, the laughter gone in an instant. "Any other Boss would've killed me," he says simply.

I hate that he came to the same conclusion I did. I don't want to like the man who's practically kidnapping me. Who bought me and took my freedom.

"What's happened has happened, Micha," he says gently. "You need to make the best of it so you don't do something stupid like *try to kill Varius*." His voice rises on that last part, and I hit him in the arm.

"Shhh." My eyes dart over to the reaper. Khalid holds my stare, and I break it immediately. "Why the fuck did you do that?" I hiss.

Dayne looks at me in exasperation. "So Khalid knows to keep an eye on you and not let you do anything stupid before you do something stupid."

Crossing my arms, I glare at my so-called best friend. "I don't need a babysitter. I'm an assassin."

"Oh, yes, that mentally stable profession."

My eyes narrow on him. Then I growl and huff out a breath. "*Fine*. I'll try to give him the benefit of the doubt." I lower my voice to a whisper. "But if I rock up in the middle of the night, you'll hide me, right?"

His smile shines in his eyes. "Obviously."

Grinning, I throw my arms around his waist. I don't want to leave him, the only rock I've ever built a foundation on, but just because I don't want to do something doesn't mean I can avoid it – story of my fucking life.

Blowing out a breath, I pull back a little. "So... Aaron has just lost his partner."

Dayne's face sours as he shoves me away. "Stop trying to set me up with your brother. He's an ass."

"True, but you can marry him, kill him, and then we can be siblings."

Laughing, he ruffles my hair like my older brother never has. "We're already family, Micha."

My chest squeezes. "Yeah. Yeah, we are."

With a final hug, he turns and gets into his car. I can feel Varius' eyes on me as he walks towards me, but I don't look at him, keeping my gaze on my best friend as he starts the engine and pulls away, a small wave his last parting gift. Hoping like hel that isn't the last time I see him, I breathe out and try to stop the ache in my chest from spreading.

"Get in the car," Varius says.

My legs root in place, that instant defiance my father accidentally beat into me rearing its head. Out of the corner of my eye, I see him draw close, and electricity buzzes along my spine. Logically, I don't know him well enough to think he won't hit me, but there's a part of me that already knows he won't.

Maybe Dayne was right. Maybe he could be a lot worse...

But just as I start to turn towards the car, Varius steps in close behind me, his body heat warming me from the cold wind. "Get in the car, little monster, or get on your back and spread your legs."

My pulse jumps. My mouth dries. "Not get down on my knees?" It comes out sarcastically, a default setting as my mind struggles to do anything other than spasm out. "Please yourself if I don't listen?"

He pulls up the back of my dress, and his hand slips beneath the boxers to run down my ass. I dig my heels in so I don't press into his palm.

His fingers trail down to my pussy, and I try not to focus on the inhabitants of the cars passing us, how I can see them so clearly. How they can see me. All they need to do is turn their heads and look.

My cheeks flush, I swallow hard as he strokes between my lips. A groan builds in my chest. My pussy clenches. His breath hits my neck, causing goosebumps along my skin.

"It'll please me," he says in a deep rumble, "to lick your pussy until you're crying." His finger pushes into me, and I whimper as I shudder.

As he thrusts, I'm tempted to lie down on my back, to take that option, but I'm absolutely certain he doesn't mean in the woods. He means right here, in front of everyone, a neanderthal proving his claim, and I can't handle that.

So I stumble towards the car. He groans behind me, deep and feral, and I know he's sucking on his fingers. My pussy kegels as I go to open the door.

But I'm suddenly shoved up against the side of the car, his body pressing against my back. He doesn't say anything as he feathers his hands under my dress to the top of the boxers. I don't need them now that Dayne's gone.

He pulls them slowly, dragging the elastic over my ass. Dropping to his knees behind me, Varius slides the material down the rest of the way. Shuddering, I lift one foot and then the other.

"Good girl," he says, his breath hitting my thighs.

My pussy spasms. He's so damn close. Just another few inches and his tongue could be inside me. He only teased me with one lick earlier, and dear gods, that was one of the best feelings of my life. I want him to eat me out here and now, with the car shielding us from the many passersby, but instead he stands, dropping my dress back down, and bites the lobe of my ear. "Get in the car, Micha."

He steps back, and I fumble with the door handle. My legs weak, I collapse inside. Khalid settles in behind me, and I try not to think about how he saw me naked. My soon to be brother-in-law. My cheeks hot, I duck my head.

Varius walks around the car and gets into the driver's seat. Our seatbelts on, he pulls away.

Then his hand is on my thigh, pushing up my dress.

Parting my legs, I lean my head back in my seat. Dayne's right. I can't change the fact that he bought me. I can only change how I live with it. Fighting him will only lead to pain.

My hips lifting, I try not to get addicted as Varius fingers me all the way to St. Augustine. Six full fucking hours.

EIGHT

HIM

As I take the last turn home, Micha leans forward to peer out the window. Leaf-bare trees line either side of our long, winding drive before opening up to a meadow of flowers still in bloom despite it being early February. I park behind the other cars at the side door of the house. Khalid doesn't move to get out and nor do I. That call I got in the woods demands my attention. Removing my finger from Micha, I lick it clean, then lean across her to open the door. "Get out."

She looks at me. The car's still running. Our seatbelts are still on. "Where are you going?"

"Out."

"Nooo. I never would have guessed."

My eyes narrow. "I've allowed you a level of sarcasm–"

"You've *allowed* me?"

"–to adjust to your situation. But that ends now. You will

not speak to me unless spoken to, and when you do speak, it will be with respect."

"That's barbaric."

"That's survival. You break the rules, and I'll find another womb." And her father won't take her back. He'll kill her for the stain she'll leave on their Family.

"You'll have me executed over a simple question?"

"The rules are there for a reason. Learn them and know your place." The words are deliberately chosen to rile. I need to know she can hold her tongue. My capos are all arriving here next week, and one wrong action from her, one sign that I can't even control my fiancee, and the allies that have yet to turn traitor will begin to talk about how I am not fit to be Boss.

We cannot afford to be divided when a war is coming.

"My place?" she says flatly. "Let me guess. In your bed?"

"No. Your bedroom is downstairs."

She blinks.

"But I expect you to be in my room every night. Do not make me search for you. Now get out, Micha."

Her eyes speak of killing me, but her voice is ever so polite when she says, "Yes, *dear.*"

She gets out, grabs the bag at her feet, and slams the car door shut. I'm out before she can cross the hood of the car. I push her against it, bending her back over the metal, and she stares up at me with wide eyes that are quick to narrow into slits.

"Get off –"

She starts to push me, but I grab her hands and pin them over her head. One palm wraps around both her wrists. The other fishes around an outer pocket of my jacket, and I pull out the black balisong inside it. Diving my hand beneath her dress, I press the metal of the knife between her pussy lips.

She jerks, her legs lifting a bit off the car as she tries to scoot back, but there's nowhere for her to go.

I push the end of the balisong inside her. "You will learn to be a lady," I say. "Or you will learn to be a slave who only ever sees the inside of her bedroom."

Leaning down, I bite the side of her neck, right over the hickey I gave her in the woods. My cock hardens as she turns her head as if to stop me, and I want to let her go and order her to run. So she can get out her frustrations as she flees into the trees surrounding our home before she falls onto her back and spreads her legs so I can get out mine.

But my time is limited.

And she needs to learn her place.

Sliding the folded over handle far inside her, I catch her earlobe between my teeth. "For slamming the car door, the knife's to stay inside you until I get home."

I release her ear and look down at her. My finger runs between her pussy lips and rests on her clit. It's hard and wet beneath my pad, and I rub it slowly. She glares at me, but her lips grow slack, and a hot breath escapes her pretty little mouth. My eyes dip to her lips before flicking back up. "I'm not a forgiving man, Micha. Do not test me."

Straightening, I head back for the driver's seat. She stays leaning against the hood, but when I reverse, she jumps up and turns to face me. Her dress falls back to her knees. Her middle finger twitches at her side.

My lips flick upwards. So much fire.

Then they flatten as I turn the car around.

"Don't hurt her again," Khalid says as he appears in the front seat, coming out of the shadow he shifted into to crawl up here. My annoyance flairs even though I knew this was coming as soon as we were alone. A reaper must be neutral in all things, and Khalid is...except when it comes to things like this.

We might be brothers. He might be my bodyguard, but I am not ignorant enough to believe that he would not strike against me if he thought I was hurting my girl.

My girl...

My jaw tics as I relax the suddenly tight grip I have on the wheel. I try not to think about the fact that I told her I like burgers. Who the fuck even says that? Everyone likes burgers. Even vegans with their fake meat and cauliflower and beans. *"I like burgers,"* is something you say to a girl you want to like you when you don't know what the fuck to say.

"I like burgers."

Fucking hel.

All I need is for the sex to be good.

And it is. My dick's hard from having pushed that knife into her cum-soaked pussy. I don't need anything else from her. Not the loyalty she gives so easily to Dayne. Not the willingness to nearly kill herself to save him. Not the smile, the light tilt of her tone even as she said his name in utter surprise and horror at being caught with my dick inside her.

My fingers flex across the wheel. "It was her decision," I say. "And she isn't my girl."

"She's to be your wife."

"Chosen by Mother."

"Accepted by you." He turns to me, his face flat, his eyes hard. "To be the mother of your children."

And that is the fucking problem. The leather of the wheel feels damp beneath my skin. Skin that itches and burns and is desperate to move. To slam into a punching bag. To dodge the slash of a knife, adrenaline demanding my attention rather than this fucking silence.

"I like burgers."

Fucking hel.

My jaw clenching and unclenching, I say softly, "What if I can't save her from the pain of losing a child?"

"Then save her from everything else."

My eyes snap to him even as I keep my head forward. He stares ahead too, not looking at me, giving me privacy in the close confinement of the car. I turn my gaze back to the road as my hand squeezes and releases the wheel.

We drive in silence, that single sentence playing over and over in my mind.

He makes it sound so simple. So final.

To him, Micha is already my girl.

But to me…

"I like burgers."

And my mark is all over her body.

The car stops outside the house of one of our landscaping clients. A rich fucker who's only here a couple times a year but pays us thousands to keep his gardens tended. It's a two story, Spanish-style mansion lined with pillared terraces and an attached seven-car garage for vehicles they never drive.

Opening my door, I get out. The sound of crickets mixes with the rush of water – a walk-in waterfall out back that runs into a heated saltwater pool. Italian stone paves our way to it, leading through a shimmer of blue. Like a heat wave rippling through the air, just the slightest tinge to it that humans can't see. As soon as we step through it, our bodies heat as the magic wraps around us, searching our souls to see if it's allowed to kill us.

I tense automatically despite knowing I shouldn't, that doing so will make it worse. And as if on cue, the magic digs its claws into my chest, sharp pain that has me nearly collapsing to my knees.

The wards have been made to keep out every sup but a witch, to stop Aleric or any other born vampire from being able to phase inside. But due to my lack of magic, it always takes a few passes for a ward to accept me as a witch.

Gritting my teeth, I force my legs to lock. The feeling of knives slashing across my body intensifies, and sweat beads down my face as my limbs shake from the agony. But if I try to push through, it'll end in certain death.

Khalid stands on the other side, having passed through without a hitch, and now he turns to face me. He holds my gaze, giving me strength in his proximity, and I latch onto that, focus on it to turn the pain into something bearable.

But then the magic slams into my back, straight into my heart, and my eyes snap open as a memory hits me. The cut of a blade in a dark alley. The smell of soap before the rush of blood. Electrified agony sweeps through me, spreading out from that cut, and I cannot decide if it's from now or then. If it happened when whoever tried to kill me struck me from the back.

In an instant, the magic releases me, and I stumble out the other side, my breaths ragged, my body slick in sweat and still burning from the trial of the ward. My hands on my knees, I struggle to hold on to the smell I recognized, but it is already fading.

"You okay?" Khalid asks, and the smell vanishes, wiped from my mind completely, like the fading senses of a dream.

As I straighten, my eyes dart over to the group of people already inside the ward, waiting for us. Two of my brothers and our only uncle, but their gazes aren't on us – used to giving me privacy whenever I pass through a ward.

Still, I lower my voice, not wanting any of them to hear. "I knew them," I say, staring at Khalid.

Whoever it was who tried to kill me over a year ago got close. They didn't know I can sense a heartbeat or smell the adrenaline seeping out of their skin. They didn't mask the beat of their pulse, the musk of their body as they snuck up behind me. I noticed they were there. I *smelled* them.

And I simply *did not turn*.

Because I trusted them at my back.

Trusted them like a brother?

My eyes shift to the two behind Khalid, their backs to me

as they stand around the swim up bar, their attention on the writhing vampire strapped to it. Their voices carry, words of urgency as they try to keep Jerry, the bloodsucker, alive.

I look at Leno – my Underboss. My second in command. The brother who might take my place and my fiancee...

Then I look at Maddox – the youngest of us. A psycho who likes seeing what he can get away with. Did he leave me alive on purpose? Only want to see if he could get past Khalid for the fucking hel of it? No harm meant?

I fucking wish he did...

Because the alternative –

"If you want to talk to him, you better hurry up before he dies!" Uncle Myers shouts as he struggles with the vampire on the counter.

Khalid waits for me to elaborate, but I don't. We need to know what Antonio has been doing to the Blood Fangs. He's been grabbing them off the streets for months, never to be seen again – or at least, never to be seen by *us*. Aleric has been tracking them down himself, phasing to them as soon as they reappear on neutral ground. Meaning, if he's that desperate for us not to see anything, he's either in league with the Death Hunt...or his own Family is on the verge of collapse. Neither of those are good for us.

"Later," I say as I pass him and head for the swim up bar. Jerry, one of Aleric Zadar's higher ups, is lying on his back, naked, on the teak counter. Maddox and Uncle Myers are fighting to pin down his thrashing arms and legs. Near his left shoulder, opposite to Maddox, a large dog is standing up on his hind legs, staring intently at Jerry's face. Red coat. Large pointy ears. Gold eyes that look almost human.

One hand pressed firmly on the vampire's forehead, Leno curses as he tries to pour some sort of bubbling blue potion down Jerry's throat, but he's having a hard time. Not just because of the head jerking around, even though it is.

But because the skin is bubbled and blistered so badly,

that it's slipping off in chunks, and with every movement, a part of his lips fall back into his mouth, choking him.

"Shit," Leno growls, then changes tactics. Releasing the vampire's head, he holds his arm out towards a nearby rose bush and calls upon his magic. A stem of thorns shoots forward and grabs the glass with the potion, holding it in the air. Now with both hands free, he twists them around each other. One of the palm trees bends over, twisting under the canopy of the bar, then drops a branch into his hand. A dozen small shoots grow out of the end of it, curling like the face tentacles of Cthulhu.

Just as we get close, Leno shoves it down the vampire's mouth, and it splits open at the top, creating a funnel. A few seconds later, the pieces of lip that had fallen off and were blocking his throat come hurtling out. They splatter across my brother's black tee. Grabbing the potion from the stem of thorns, Leno pours it down the wooden funnel.

"Fuck!" Maddox curses as the vampire's arm comes off in his hand, ripping free at the shoulder, the skin no longer strong enough to keep it connected.

But his spasms are weakening, whatever Leno gave him working quickly.

The stem of thorns, his third hand at this point, dives into the open canvas bag at his feet and pulls out a glass jar of powdered yarrow, a natural styptic. He sprinkles some on the vampire's armless shoulder, then places his hand over it. Green magic flows beneath his fingers, turning the powder into a scab. It won't save him though. Whatever the wolves did to him is killing him quickly.

"How long?" I ask as I stop beside the dog, who turns to look at me, my blind brother, Leno, seeing through his eyes.

"A few minutes." Leno shakes his head. "Maybe."

"Take the funnel out."

He pulls it free slowly, but he still manages to rip bits of skin out of Jerry's mouth. One of the pus-oozing boils on his lips pops, and a rotten smell explodes out of it, churning my stomach. Piss and shit and blood leak free from him, and skin sloshes off every inch of his naked body like an ice-cream dropped on the sidewalk by a clumsy child.

"Jerry," I say, but there's not one feature I can identify him by. His nose is slipping down his left cheek. One eye is missing, pink gunk clinging to an open hole, and the other is swollen shut by sacs of pus yet to pop. But Maddox and Uncle Myers both say it's him.

As shapeshifters, they have learned to memorize every detail of a stranger's face so they can shift into them, and Jerry is far from a stranger. We've dealt with him a few times when moving through Aleric's territory.

"Tell us what happened to you."

His mouth opens wide, and it takes me a second before I realize he's screaming. Because there's no sound other than a fragile hiss of air. His vocal chords are gone, screamed raw perhaps. Or maybe the inside of his body matches the outer, organs and tendons and muscles just turning into slush.

Whichever it is, his limbs start spasming again, smacking against the bar as his convulsions increase. More skin falls off, and he becomes useless to me. I pull out a knife, but Maddox cuts in.

"Given how weak his skin is," he says as he holds up the vampire's detached arm, "can I try pulling his head off?"

I stare at him.

He stares back.

Then I step to the side and let him have at it. It makes no difference to me how he dies. Turning to Leno, I ask, "Did he say anything?"

"Not a word."

My jaw tics. It would've been nice to know he was mute before I came out here, but I don't say it. Instead, I turn to Uncle Myers. "Have you come across anything like this?"

His lips tight, he shakes his head.

"Then get me Cara Jervis." I start to move, wanting to head back home and get some sleep. I'm exhausted, not able to top up my reserves like the others can with their magic. And being out here in the middle of the night, not knowing if I can trust any of my brothers anymore... It's making me paranoid. My hairs rise every time one of them shifts even slightly.

"You can't be serious," Maddox says as he moves around the bar, and I unconsciously rock onto the balls of my feet. "Ma'll be pissed."

"Let her."

He lets out a humorless laugh and shakes his head. "Your funeral." Grabbing Jerry's head with both hands, he yanks it hard to the side.

Crack!

But it doesn't rip free.

So of course he tries again.

Crack!

"Regardless of Mom, Cara's not going to come," Leno says as he bends down to pick up his bag, and for a split second, I think about kneeing him in the face and crushing his nose into his skull before he can make the first move. My hands itching, I step back.

"She's fully on Aleric's side," he says as he rises.

"Then don't ask her."

His lips purse, but he doesn't protest the impossibility of that request. Cara is a powerhouse, and the only reason she isn't a Boss of a Family anymore is because she murdered them all for being incompetent a couple years back, her crimes hidden under the spread of Covid. But she still holds territory in the midwest. No one has been dumb enough to try to take it from her; she's *that* powerful. Mother says she was responsible for the Spanish Flu, which despite its name actually originated in the US when Cara Jervis and Terra

Harrison went to war. The only reason I know Covid wasn't her creation was because it's nowhere near as deadly as she likes her viruses to be.

Pop!

Jerry's head tears free, and Maddox stumbles back, like he wasn't expecting that to happen. His wide eyes say the same and then he laughs as he tosses the head into the air. Bits of flesh fling everywhere, and my eyes narrow on him.

His smile falling, he quickly goes to grab Jerry's head. But though his hands make contact, the skin they touch slides straight off the vampire's face, and the head drops to the ground, then rolls across the Italian stone. Snorting back laughter, he hurries after it, and I wonder how the fuck he managed to make valedictorian in high school *and* college.

Clearly, the world is full of dumb people.

"Bottle up some of the blood, then clean up." Leno, his dog Krypto, and Uncle Myers all turn to glare at Maddox, who doesn't even have the decency to look sheepish at the extra mess he's just caused. Normally, Rudy, a specialized cleaner and brother of ours, would deal with it, but he's down in Miami on another job.

Some idiots thought they could fly in under the radar, moving women and children through a massage parlor on our streets. So some cugines decided to set the place on fire with them in it. Show them what's up. Impress us enough to join our gang.

So now they're all six feet under. We don't recruit those that are so fucking stupid as to call the attention of every cop in the area. Examples are done by my capos, not some wannabes with no sense of finesse.

Moving around the counter, the hairs on my nape rising as I pass my brothers, I head for the ward. My back burns from where I was stabbed, the memory of the magic cutting deep. The thought of one of my brothers being the traitor cutting deeper.

Closing my eyes briefly, I let the grief hit me.

And then I shove it down.

Stepping through the shimmering blue wall of magic, I brace myself for the pain. It comes quickly but doesn't stay anywhere near as long, remembering me from before. No new memories come either, and soon I'm out the other side and climbing into the driver's seat of my car.

I wait for Khalid to settle in beside me, then turn around and head home. The miles pass, and it's not until we get back to the city limits of St. Augustine that I tell Khalid what I remember.

What I suspect.

That a brother is out to kill me.

For a long time, he's silent. And then…

"You're not an abomination," he says softly.

But he doesn't say the one thing I want to hear. That I'm being paranoid.

That none of them would ever do that.

NINE
HER

"Shit!" The word explodes out of me as I'm tempted to throw a fireball at the wall of this damn ensuite. My foot is perched on the closed toilet seat, my dress is off as it kept getting in the damn way, and my fingers are groping around my pussy trying to get hold of the damn *fucking* knife that has disappeared *all the way up in there.*

I knew I should've taken it out as soon as Varius turned the car around, but I hesitated in case he had eyes on me in the rearview mirror. Then his mom came out and ushered me inside, and I had a choice to make – waddle like a duck to stop the balisong from slipping out and dropping at my feet in the most embarrassing meet-his-mom ever or shove it in all the way and squeeze it tight.

I dumbly chose the latter.

And now it's stuck.

I can't get it out.

And dear gods, I'm trying not to panic.

Bending down to my phone perched on the kitchen sink, already open on a call to Dayne, I hiss, "I can't reach it!"

He's still howling in laughter, which is what he's been doing for the past five minutes, since I first called him.

"Dayne!"

His laughter doesn't stop, and purple fire crackles across my fingers. I wish I had the power to send it through the phone and right into his face.

But I don't.

Ugh.

"Will you laugh about this later and just fucking *help me,* please?"

His howls grow louder. "If you go to...the ER, don't get into...a MRI..." I can't make out the rest of his words, but I highly doubt they're useful.

Clenching my teeth, I flip my phone the finger. He can't see it, but me telling him to, "Fuck off," is just going to make him even more hysterical.

Giving up on my utterly useless best friend, I end the call and try once more to grope around my vagina.

But my arm is too fucking short. I don't have the reach to hit the happy spot, let alone manage the correct angle to grab the knife. If I was thinking at the time, I would've told him to hold up and tie a string to it, but my fucking brain took a walk, slipped on the soaking wet mess I made all over the floor, careened right into a wall, and passed the fuck out.

"Don't speak unless I give you permission. Don't ask questions. Don't be anything but a fucking sex doll," I growl beneath my breath as my fingers brush the end of the knife.

"I should've slammed the car door right into his face." Ignoring the whole, his face was in the driver's seat and safe from any door, I visualize his nose bleeding and both his eyes blackened.

"I'm going to use this knife to stab him in the face." If I

can get the damn thing out. But I can't get a fucking grip on it.

"Fuck!" I grunt as I try various angles, cursing Varius with each one that fails. I'm just starting to think that maybe I should suck it up and ask his mom for a pair of pliers when the door opens behind me.

I freeze, my eyes the only movement as they grow wide.

No.

Please no.

"I told you not to make me come get you," Varius says, his voice low and dangerous.

My spine snapping straight, I turn to face him. "You wouldn't have to *come get me* if you weren't such a fucking *neanderthal,*" I bite out.

His dark eyes narrow as he stands there wearing nothing but a pair of gray sweatpants. Remembering the respect I'm supposed to talk to him with, I add, "*Sir.*"

A small light flickers behind his eyes, a bit of humor perhaps, before they dip to my pussy, and realization crosses his stupidly handsome face. "Come here," he says, looking back up at me.

I cross my arms so I don't give in to the urge to slap him. I want to tell him to go fuck himself with a pineapple, but we are not on equal footing. I can either be a lady or a slave, and I am not dumb enough to choose the latter.

I start to paste on a fake-as-fuck smile when he asks, "Does it hurt to walk?"

I blink in surprise. "It's uncomfortable."

He walks towards me, and my nerves dance across my skin with every step he takes. The bathroom suddenly feels too small, too constricting with not enough exits. And I hate this feeling of being trapped, of being forced to cower under a bigger threat. I became an assassin so my father couldn't make me feel this way.

Yet here I am, standing against a man without magic,

feeling like I'm about to be eaten. Mauled under a moonless night where no one can hear me scream.

Because even if I manage to kill him, I will not manage to escape. If Varius is in my room, I do not doubt Khalid is close by. Perhaps just right outside the door, in the hall, waiting to see if he's needed.

Fucking Dayne making him paranoid. Some damn bestie he is.

My magic burns beneath my skin, itching to fling free as Varius continues towards me. But he doesn't strike me for my disrespectful tone. He simply bends down and scoops me into his arms. Walking out of the bathroom, he places me on the edge of the bed as I gawk at him.

"Spread your legs for me," Varius says as he drops to his knees, and my breath catches at the sight of him before me. He's had a shower, his hair still damp and smelling of soap. His mouth is just *there*. But it's the fact that he seems keen on actually helping me – unlike my asshole of a bestie, that has me doing what he asked.

Leaning back on my elbows, I try not to concentrate on the fact that I still haven't shaved. Or had a shower yet, and his old cum is still all down my legs.

I swallow down my embarrassment as he spreads my lips open with one hand. "Can you get it out?" I ask. I've never had this happen before, and I really, *really* don't want to ask his mom, who is a healer, to take her son's impromptu toy out of my vagina on the first night I met her. If I try to use magic for this myself, I'm likely to accidentally rip out my ovaries, and then there goes my one worth to this family.

My life would be over.

"Relax," Varius says as he presses two fingers between my pussy lips. His invasion is slow and methodical, but it doesn't feel like a doctor doing an exam. His touch is too electrifying. His breath is too hot as it feathers across my thighs.

My nerves drumming tighter, I blurt, "So do you do this to all your girls then? Sorry, your *wombs*. So you can take it out and act the hero? … *Sir*."

He looks up at me, a half-smirk hiding in his eyes, and I don't know what that means. If he's laughing at me or the situation or if he thinks my rambling is "cute" like my best friend does.

It's definitely not cute though. It's embarrassing. But my mouth will just not shut up in front of a hot man.

Give me a knife and I'm fine. Throw me in a cage with a werewolf on the full moon, and I'll die without ever being nervous. But put me on my back with a wicked neanderthal kneeling between my thighs? I turn into a bumbling idiot no matter how much I try to bite my tongue.

"No," Varius says as he dips his eyes back to my pussy. "First time."

I blink. "First time putting knives up someone's vagina or…" I trail off on a little laugh, my nerves clearly getting to me. Of course he isn't. That'd be silly. He's Varius fucking Shadow. Probably fucked his way through half the state.

But when he doesn't dismiss the notion, I bolt upright.

"I almost had it," he says, but I don't care about that now. Him being a virgin when we met makes him seem human. Flawed. Not so untouchable as Varius fucking Shadow – the boogieman to the boogiemen. The asshole neanderthal who only wants me for my womb.

"But you're so good at it," I blurt. "How can that have been your first time?"

He looks at me dryly. "I came in seconds. That wasn't a clue?"

"But in the office, you kept fingering me until I was about to come and then stopping! And you did it repeatedly!"

His lips flatten. "That wasn't deliberate."

"That wasn't –" I slam my hand over my mouth as a little giggle crawls up my throat. "Oh my gods, you were just shit at fingering."

"Thank you," Varius says so deadpanned, I struggle not to laugh. His dark eyes narrowing, he returns his gaze to my vagina. "Lay back down," he commands, and I flop back, still reeling from that reveal.

"I was your first?"

"That is what it means."

"You were mine, you know."

"I know."

I scrunch my nose, thinking him an idiot for trusting that 'exam' before I catch myself. I lean up on my elbows just in time to see him pull the balisong free. He flicks it open and twirls it around in a sequence of spins and tosses. My eyes linger on the knife even as he snaps it back shut. I'm happy he got it out, but my focus is on him. On the potential future here that might not be that bad.

"But not from the test," I say slowly. "Because you know they don't work; you just play into the whole neanderthal thing."

"I don't *play* into anything. You decided what I was, and I didn't care to correct you."

Sitting up fully, I scoff at him. "You *bought* me. In the *twenty-first* century. What was I supposed to think?"

"Your father sold you. Our Families are not so different."

"Our women are allowed out of the kitchen."

"You're not in one now."

"But I will be, won't I? I'll be expected to cook for you. Clean for you. Pop out babies with no dreams of my own."

"And what do you dream for, Micha?"

I open my mouth, but my chest squeezes tight, and no words escape. He looks at me, waiting, and I swallow as I struggle to think about what I dream for. I want Lou to be safe, to have her own life, to pursue her dreams of going to college for a damn art degree. I dream of saving all the kids I agree to kill from the pain of knowing someone wanted them dead. I dream of there being a world that isn't so full of death and despair. I dream of Dayne getting therapy for his childhood trauma even though I know he never will.

But none of those are dreams of *mine.*

Because I've never really had the luxury to dream.

And he knows it.

I glance away, expecting him to call out my ignorance, to tease me for being so naive, to brag that he is right. But he doesn't. He's too busy grabbing my ass and hauling me up to his lips.

I cry out as he buries his face in my pussy. His tongue strokes me, long and slow, and my hips buck as I fall onto my back, my arms giving out, my breaths ragged and harsh as I let the sensations overwhelm me. To focus on the sex rather than what this moment almost became. My legs wrap around his head as his tongue sweeps between my lips, up and down repeatedly. Arching, I dig my hand into his hair and scream.

He takes his time just like he did in the car. Learning every inch of me, changing his pace and rhythm based on my cries, how they increase whenever he does something so fucking wicked. His licks start to build into a technique, a slow learning that has me shaking with need.

But despite how good it feels. Despite how much I want to come, I don't. I can't. The sensations are too different to what I'm used to.

Whimpering beneath his onslaught, I ride his face with my hand in his hair. He grips my ass and pushes me up the bed as he crawls onto it after me, keeping his head between my legs. My eyes slam shut as I try to chase that last high, that final explosion of stars that'll knock me off my feet.

But it keeps dancing away.

And the harder I try to chase it, the faster it runs until I'm begging for it to take me, my entire body shaking like an addict out of reach of her needle.

A sharp nip on my pussy causes me to jerk up on my elbows. My gaze lowers to see his eyes burning hot. But not just with arousal...with jealousy.

The neanderthal is jealous I'm *in my own head.*

"Relax," he growls, but I hear the words he doesn't say. *You're mine. This moment is mine. Your attention damn well be mine.*

And fuck, do I find that hot.

My chest rising and falling rapidly, I hold his gaze as he lowers his head back to my pussy. He watches me as he eats me out, and my breath catches. My toes curl. My eyes grow half-hooded as the sensations of ecstasy come slamming back into me. But this time I don't chase them. I don't try to change this moment from what it is. An exploration of his tongue. A learning between two souls. A simple pleasure of licks and kisses and moans with no end goal in mind other than him tasting me.

My fingers tightening in his hair, I start to moan again. My breaths turn shallow and fast. My toes curling, I cry out as I arch back onto the bed. The sensations are building too strong, too heavily, but they still sit poised on that edge, denying me any relief. Tears fall down my cheeks as I rock my hips into him, as I squeeze my thighs around his head.

He pushes a finger inside me as he continues to lick my pussy, and my cries strengthen. Rise in pitch. My spasms increase. Then dear gods, he starts to growl, and those deep vibrations *do* something to me.

Whimpering, I fuck his face as I toss my head side to side. His hips lift and press into the mattress as he starts to chase his own release.

A momentary relapse hits me, a feeling of shame that he might be able to come but I will not. I tense, and his teeth dig into me.

"Micha," he growls as his finger fucks me faster. "I told you to relax."

I start to tell him that's not how relaxing works, but then his finger curls, and I can't remember a damn thing I was going to say.

Grabbing one of my hands, he places it on my pussy. "Show me," he says as he lifts his head just a little. "Show me how you make yourself come."

My lips parting, I start to touch myself as he watches, as his finger rocks slowly in and out of me, his concentration on my hand, not on the pumping of his own.

I moan, my limbs starting to shake as the both of us work to get me off. He keeps his thrusts slow and leisurely, the highlight of his focus on me. On my hand. On how I ride my palm and stroke my clit to make myself come.

Panting, I lift my hips, sliding further onto his finger. Harder. Deeper. *Faster.*

"That's it, little monster," he says, his voice a deep rasp that leaves me weak. "Let me see you come."

My thighs snap together as the tension builds. His eyes rise to mine, a snarl on his lips, and my legs fall back open.

"Good girl," he growls as he curls his finger and lowers his gaze back to my hand. "You keep those legs open. I want to see your pussy squeezing my finger."

Leaning forward, he licks me. Then groans as he pulls back so he can watch me. My fingers dip between my lips, riding on top of his. I push them in just a little, not able to go far with my short arms. My release is just out of reach, and I whimper in frustration. "Please," I rasp as I refocus my attention on my clit. "I need another finger inside of me."

He doesn't hesitate to oblige, and I arch back as my other hand rises to my breasts. I cup myself, my nipples hard and demanding, and he hisses in a breath as he watches me. He fucks me faster, and I cry out on another wave of frustration before I rapidly shake my head.

"Slower," I order. "It's all about...the rhythm." I moan as I grab his hand and show him the pace I like. The slow firm thrusts. The slight hesitation before he rams in that gets me squirming in anticipation.

My gasps build again as he takes over, fucking me hard but slow. My hand goes back to stroking the outside of my pussy as my other massages my breast.

He licks my inner thigh, and I arch on a small moan, my skin too sensitive, too fucking *good* with all the nerves taut and raw.

I cry out as my orgasm rips through me, making my thighs clench around his head. The spasms shake all the breath from my body, leaving me a gasping mess. I pant hard as he pulls his fingers out and grabs both my hips. Pinning my thighs to his head, he flips us, pushing me up onto my knees as he buries his tongue into my pussy.

I moan as I jerk beneath his licks, each stroke causing my muscles to twitch uncontrollably. My hips buck as I ride his face, smothering him fully, my body no longer capable of holding itself up.

He releases my hips. One hand comes up to fondle my breasts. The other wiggles under my leg, and I realize he's reaching for his cock. Turning my head, I suck in a breath. I never thought I would like watching a man masturbate, but fucking hel, the way his hips jerk up to meet his hand, the way his precum leaks down his thick head...

I want his cock inside me.

I start to wiggle back, but the sharp bite of his teeth on my thigh locks me still. Then he groans, throwing his head back as he arches off the bed, tossing me onto my hands and knees. Hot wet splodges land on my ass. He pants beneath me, and I look down at him, peeking between my thighs to see his still throbbing cock. Cum is streaked all across his abs, and I lick my lips, wondering what it tastes like. Lifting his head, he buries his face back in my pussy for a long slow kiss. Then he drops back to the mattress. His finger scoops up some of the cum on his belly.

And pushes it into me.

I whimper as his finger fills me as far as it can go.

Then it pulls out to scoop up more cum before pushing it deep inside of me. I collapse with my ass in the air and my face on the pillow, my arms no longer willing to hold me. My entire body is lax, even my eyelids as they struggle to stay open. He wipes the cum off my ass and pushes that in me too.

A warm buzz flows through me, reminding me of a cat stretching lazily in the sun. Every part of me is content, like a zen-touched soul… Like all the pieces to a puzzle…

With one last lick of my pussy, Varius flips me over onto my back. Standing, he leaves without a word. The door closes behind him with an abrupt *click*, but I'm happy he didn't linger.

Because I'm absolutely exhausted, and his mother told me earlier I have to be up at six o'clock to make him fucking breakfast.

Fuck.

My.

Life.

Though dear gods, Varius can fuck me…

TEN
HER

The hot spray of the shower washes the sleep from my eyes but barely. I need coffee. Or a knife thrown at my face. One or another; nothing like a bit of danger to get the blood pumping.

Grabbing the shower head off the railing like a zombie, I lower it to my vagina. The sudden burn of a cut causes me to jump, waking me up just a little bit more. I wince as I wash, taking care of whatever little tears Varius' cock has caused. Or perhaps it was his knife.

The next time I see Dayne, I owe him a punch to the face. "Useless fucking friend," I mutter as I finish cleaning it, then the rest of me, lathering soap across my body.

"And who the hel sticks a *knife* up a vagina? Tell me I've only ever seen porn without telling..." I trail off, my cheeks hotter than the spray hitting them. Varius is a virgin. *Was* a virgin. Just like me.

"Don't be daff," I mutter as I rinse the soap off my body,

pushing aside the budding desire to make a connection that isn't there just because we shared a moment.

Monsters can still be virgins, I tell myself. *In fact, they all start off as virgins.* Varius opening up to me means nothing. Him being kind enough to help me get the knife out means nothing. Because he put it there.

He dragged me into this situation.

Told me my only worth is in my womb.

That I can't speak unless spoken to.

So any kindness he shows –

No, any kindness I *trick myself into believing he shows* is just stupid.

I am a womb.

Nothing more; he made that clear.

Scowling, I wrench the shower off. Then sigh. Or is it more stupid of me to keep seeing him as a monster?

After all, I cannot change the fact we are engaged, that I am forced to spend the rest of my life with him. Shadows do not divorce, so would it not be wiser to let myself believe he is capable of kindness so I'm not so fucking miserable all the time?

I groan. "No. No, it's way too early to be having this kind of debate without coffee."

Stepping out of the glass cubicle, I grab the towel off the heated railing and pat myself down. Throwing on a clean pair of sweatpants and a black tank, I leave my room and head down the hall. The smell of roasting beans fills my lungs, and I inhale deeply as I step into the kitchen. Sau, Varius' mother, sits at the large wooden table, alone but with a cup of coffee in her hands.

I look around to see if there's a coffee pot half-full, but my eyes snag on the curved zebrano counter that splits the kitchen in half. The table Sau's at is in front, the cooking area behind it. Power hums from it, deep and rich, and the hairs on my nape rise.

In old times, a witch's kitchen doubled as their spellroom to make potions and brews. Now, they're more commonly located in attics or basements or spare bedrooms, but as I stare at the magic shifting under the stripes and the knots of the wooden counter, I know this kitchen has seen some shit. Perhaps even a human sacrifice given the darkness clinging to its surface. I can practically see a naked woman laying on the counter, her eyes empty as well-dressed men shove forks inside her cracked open chest. Lovely.

"Shall we get started?" Sau asks.

And it takes me a moment to realize she doesn't mean shall we join the men in cannibalism. Ripping my eyes – and imagination away from the counter, I say, "I know the shops aren't open yet, but I'm A-okay with breaking and entering to steal some perfectly made store-stolen waffles."

She looks at me in sympathy.

"Alternatively, I can make a mean bowl of cereal," I say hopefully.

"He is lactose sensitive."

Great. I now know what to put in his food. Though if he's still capable of eating waffles, maybe I should just jump straight to using poison.

Pushing such dangerous thoughts down before the joy of his demise dances in my eyes, I yawn. "I need coffee."

She rises and crosses behind the counter. I follow her to the post of fresh brew.

"The cups are here." She points to a cupboard hanging on the wall beside the counter, then waits expectantly. I open it to find it full of mugs, glasses, and plates. There's also a container of small spoons for stirring. I reach for a random cup, then stop, my eyes widening. They flick left and right, opening even further. "Holy shit. There's a row of dicks." *Photographed* dicks wrapped around custom-printed mugs.

"You can't drink out of those," she says as if I just said something about the weather. "Pick one further back."

Clearing my throat, I try really hard not to look at each cup to try to figure out whose dick is whose. Although the only brother I've met so far is Khalid, having been dropped off when the house was dark and shown straight to my room by his mom, I know there are six others. And the twins are known for *vibrating* their cocks. A lot of other men with telekinesis have tried to copy, but concentrating on magic that well while balls deep in someone? Turns out, it's *really* hard.

Hard.

Like cocks.

Fuck.

My cheeks on fire, I grab a random cup from the second row. My eyes dart to the cock mug in front of it, then quickly away, then back again. Lingering on it, I realize it's a completely different skin tone to that of this family. It's full-on Caucasian. And the one beside it is Black. Clearly, they're not the boys' dicks at all, and that kind of makes me feel more at ease. More capable of looking them in the eyes later.

I quickly close the door. With an apron now tied around her waist, Sau flits around the kitchen, pulling out mixing bowls and ingredients for the waffles. I pick up the pot of coffee and pour me a black. Gulping half of it despite the heat, I slowly start to feel alive.

"So do the boys actually drink out of them?" I ask as I try to picture serious-looking Varius with a dick mug to his lips but failing.

"When they're forced to, yes."

"Forced to?" The disbelief is clear in my tone. This is the house of the infamous Shadow brothers. Who the hel can force them to do anything?

Turning to me with a box of eggs in her hands, Sau smiles. "A woman might serve a man in this family, Micha, but do not ever think we are weak because of it. When they piss you off, and they absolutely will, get creative with their punishments."

"They don't just grab a different cup?"

"Not if they want to eat; everyone but Khalid is a shit cook."

My mouth drops open in awe. "What did they do?"

Her eyes narrow. "Maddox thought it was funny to make cups of the women in this Family a few years ago, and the others didn't protest. We are to be bred, yes, but they will do it with fucking respect."

Placing the eggs on the counter, she smiles at me. "Now come. I'll teach you how Varius likes his waffles."

ELEVEN

HIM

I slam my fist into the bag. It rocks back, and I follow it, extending my arm to pound my knuckles into its leather. The bag swings from its hanging point. My feet shift. My body twists. With each blow, I imagine the cut of a blade sliding deep into my back.

One of my brothers tried to kill me.

Keeping my head low, my arms up, I hammer my left fist into the leather. The bag swings, and I dart forward, then back. Dip. Right hook. Three rapid punches from my left. Dip, another punch, then shuffle to the side.

I dance around it like I dance around the questions in my head.

Which brother do I suspect the most?

Whose alibi can I tear apart?

And can I really give the order to treat them the same as every other traitor? An instant death at the hands of Khalid.

My breathing turns heavy as I continue to work the bag.

My lungs strain. My naked chest becomes slick with sweat. I don't stop even when my knuckles begin to bleed. When I can feel the fractures of the bone. The swelling tenderness from deliberately mistiming my swings. So the punches are not correct. So the angle of them *hurts*.

Grunting, I pound the bag harder. Break my bones more.

But I can't stop the thoughts from riding my ass just as hard.

The traitor isn't one of the twins as they would have used their telekinesis to cut me down rather than get close.

It can't be Khalid because no one would accuse a reaper of treachery; it's his job to kill anyone who will hurt this Family. He could shoot me in the face in front of all my capos and get off scot-free.

Grunting, I drive my elbow upright into the leather. Then shove the bag sideways as I move in the opposite direction. As it swings back towards me, I aim a sidekick right into its middle.

The chain rattles, the bag careening to a halt.

But I keep moving.

Can't stop.

Leno has the most to gain. It wouldn't be the first time a second son killed the firstborn. But other members of the Family, capos and soldiers and wannabe climbers, have tried to claim the throne in his honor for years, and he's never once embraced them.

Maddox is a little shit, but his pranks, his games have never gone anywhere near this far. I can see him shooting me with a paintball gun, but to shove a blade into my back, only just missing my heart?

My jaw clenches. I hammer my right fist four times into the bag before hitting it with my left.

The scar burns.

The memory the ward triggered becomes a little more in focus, and I can almost recognize that damn soap...

But then it's gone again.

And all I'm left with is the end of my deductions.

Only Talon and Rudy remain, and Rudy abhors violence.

There is a reason I made him a cleaner. So he can come in after everything is all said and done and work with the peacefulness of death. Even when it's dirty. Even when the bodies are butchered and no longer look human like with Jerry, Rudy prefers the silence to the screams.

Not that his world is ever silent.

His innate power is more like a curse and one I wouldn't want even if it gave me magic. Even if it meant I would no longer be an abomination.

My punches start to weaken as I think about Rudy being the traitor. Out of all of my brothers, his betrayal would hurt the most.

I taught him how to ride a bike when Father left. Patched up his skinned knees. Told him all about the Roman Empire and the Mongolian one and the lost city of Atlantis as he fell asleep on my lap, terrified of his dreams, of his magic slipping free to haunt him. I killed the monsters in his closet and under his bed, gained my first three scars because of them. He can conjure the physical manifestations of one's greatest fears, and I faced mine and his every night.

He is only nine years younger than me, but I almost see him as a son. A boy I raised and protected. Who I taught sign language to because Mother was hit by magic while he was still in her womb, so he was born mute.

Pulling on all my grief, I start to funnel it into a strike. But then I catch the whiff of waffles right outside the door.

Closing my eyes briefly, I let my arm drop, my emotions settle. I turn to grab the towel off the bench just as the door opens. My senses all run to her as she steps inside the gym. I can smell the flour and sugar that clings to her hands, can sense the rapid beat of her heart that increases with every step she takes.

And I can feel the pull between us. The same one that pulled me to her room last night, caused me to seek her out rather than wait for her to come to me. To ask her about her dreams. To be bothered that she doesn't have any, hasn't put herself first at all. Even I have dreams. And I can feel the pull to go to her now, to find comfort in her presence despite the pain in my chest.

Rubbing the towel, I clean the sweat off my face. *Our child might die because of me.* To pursue anything between us would be wrong.

"Put it down and leave," I say without turning to look at her.

I can practically feel the stiffening of her spine, the hot glare of her eyes as she tries to kill me with it. I am finding Micha Black does not take well to orders. And I'm finding that just makes me want to give her more.

"Yes, *sir,*" she says, no hint of respect in the mockery of those two words. She draws closer, the hairs on my neck aware of her every movement, and stops at the bench right beside me. After placing the plate down, along with a bottle of syrup and a set of cutlery, she turns to leave but stops halfway round.

Her eyes narrow as she snatches the fork up and offers it to me. "Hold this," she says.

"You're leaving."

"You can't, can you? Because you fucking destroyed your hands."

"It's none of your concern."

"I did *not* spend the last hour making you waffles just for them to go cold because *you can't hold a fork.*" She glares at me, her lips tight. "Now sit."

Surprise flickers across her face when I do.

"Any other orders?" I drawl.

She blinks, a blush spreading across her cheeks. Then she snatches up the plate. After smothering the waffles in syrup, she raises the fork to my lips. "Open," she says briskly, but there's a slight strain to her voice. Holding her gaze as I try to discern what's turning her on, I slowly part my lips.

She pushes the fork inside, her breath hitching. Then she pulls it from my mouth leisurely, the blush on her cheeks darkening under whatever naughty thoughts she's thinking. My cock twitches, but before I can pull her onto my lap, she steps back.

"Why haven't you used a wand?" she blurts. An instant mood killer as I'm reminded why I broke my knuckles to begin with.

My voice flat, I say, "I can't."

Her brow furrows. "But everyone can use a premade."

Those wands created for non-witches to use, those with low dormant magic inside them. My lips tighten. "I never hit my ascension."

"But you're a *witch*."

I know what she means. Unlike humans – as in all beings made in the gods' images rather than the stolen terminology by the "humans" of Earth, witches don't have to wait until they're past their ascension to use a premade wand. Our magic isn't the byproduct of another gift. We don't get a glimmer of it due to our ability to shift like werewolves or phase like vampires – glimmers that come out only during our ascensions. We have the raw deal from birth, even if we can't access it; a premade wand should work in our hands as soon as we're out of the womb. They should work for me.

"It doesn't seem to matter," I say.

She shakes her head. "That doesn't make any sense."

"Take it up with the gods."

She stares at me, thoughts whirling behind her eyes. But I have already asked all the questions she's thinking. Have already spent years researching why I was born without magic. How I could get it so our father would come back. Not just for me but for all my brothers who I robbed of his love. *Is that why one of them wants to kill me?* "The wand is in the cabinet," I say, glancing at the one beside us.

She shakes her head, snapping herself out of whatever thoughts she had. Then she puts the plate down and raises her arms in front of me. Heeding the silent command, I lift mine, and white magic flows from her palms. It's soft, not that strong, but it is enough to heal the fractures and reduce the swelling.

The magic fades, but she keeps her hands on me. Her eyes search mine. The pull between us strengthens. I can feel her heartbeat in the tips of her fingers; it pulses down my arms and into *me*.

My heart rate quickens to match hers.

My eyes dip to her lips.

I can practically feel them beneath mine, and I ache with the need to taste her. To cross that line of intimacy I have no right to cross.

The door to the gym opens, and she jerks away, turning as Khalid enters. Lowering my arms, I rise to my feet.

"Get out," my brother says to her, and she is moving in an instant. No lip. No rise of her hackles. Just a respectful nod before she leaves.

My eyes narrowing, I glare at Khalid. He looks at me, and I am quick to shove down my jealousy, to remove it from my face before he gets any stupid ideas about how she's my girl and I should treat her accordingly. Because to Khalid, a man doesn't make his girl worry, doesn't make her serve him. No, to him, a man *serves her*. Makes her want for nothing. Discovers her dreams and gives his life to make them come true.

My chest tightens at the idea of pulling back her layers, seeing parts of her that even she hasn't seen. Dismissing the foolishness, I focus on my brother.

"It's Lincoln," he says, the words a clear trial leading to an execution.

My gaze sharpens, the last comforting beats of Micha's pulse squashed down by the need to believe this truth. That it wasn't one of our brothers who tried to kill me. That he somehow found evidence in a few hours even though we've been looking for months without a single trail.

"How do you know?"

"His wife got drunk last night and let it slip she wasn't with him."

"He could've been off with a whore."

"She also said he's been meeting with Antonio."

My jaw tics. Lincoln's a shapechanger, able to change the forms of other living things. With a single touch, he could have destroyed Jerry's body, causing his skin to bubble and slip off like we saw last night. "The territory he runs borders Antonio's. They would have reason to talk."

"Perhaps," Khalid says, but I know that tone. He has no doubts.

"Who did she spill this to?"

"Vinny."

Our cousin. Uncle Myers' son. He's practically our eighth brother. His word is reliable. Still, I'll not kill a capo without being utterly certain, not when we're on the verge of a war and need all the soldiers we have. And Lincoln is a damn good fighter.

"I want evidence."

He nods and heads for the door. I watch him go, words burning my tongue, but I swallow them down. A reaper needs to be able to kill anyone, family included, and so he has always kept a bit of distance from us. I will not ask him to broaden that gap.

Stopping at the door, he says, "Don't do anything stupid, Varius."

And then he's gone, leaving me alone with my paranoia, my dark thoughts, and my cold plate of waffles.

TWELVE

HER

Within a week and a half, I'm utterly exhausted in every sense of the word. I'm up at five or six in the morning to make breakfast, depending on what Lord Varius desires that day. Then I help with the cleaning. Since Sau can't use her magic anymore, I end up doing most of the work simply because I'm faster. But to slow down means I'll get a shorter nap, and *gods* do I need my noontime nap before I begin my lessons on how to be a lady in the Shadow household.

I have to have great posture *all the time*. Including when I'm on the toilet. Sau doesn't go in with me, but somehow she still knows and will zap me with her magic. And then Khalid will find out, and he made it really fucking clear on day one that if Sau uses her magic at all because of me, he will hold me responsible.

So I'm constantly on edge, my sixth sense on overdrive, screaming, "Danger, danger, danger!" every second Khalid is in the house. At four or five, we start making dinner. I am not the best cook and live on packet noodles and take away, so to say it's been easy learning is like saying my ass and vagina have gotten used to Varius' dick – a blatant fucking lie.

I'm learning how to do "professional looking" make-up, which *ouch* but fair. I've only ever learned the basics to help Dayne when he wanted to try crossdressing, and he soon out-learned me anyway. I'm learning how to walk more sensually and less like an assassin, how to smile just the right amount of pleasing, how to wear high heels and long dresses that are designed to limit movement. I'm learning how to laugh so it sounds like bells, how to keep my voice level even when I'm pissed. It's a miracle Sau hasn't killed me herself, though, with how badly I'm progressing.

The only thing that I *am* excelling at is learning all the parts of the business – or rather, the bare basics. I won't learn the more in-depth stuff until after we're married in case I don't become part of the Family. Though honestly, I don't see why it matters either way. If our engagement falls through, I'm dead, and any secrets I learn will die with me.

But I've memorized the faces, backstories, innate powers, likes and dislikes, dietary requirements, et cetera of all his capos, and I've met all his brothers but Talon. He's currently 'out' – on business I am not yet trusted enough to know.

At the engagement party, I'll meet all the big players, and I am expected to make them feel both like I'll service them in every way while also remaining untouchable. A desire, a fantasy that will never happen. So of course, I then have to learn how to put a stop to a man's advances without punching him in the nose or setting his dick on fire – two of my current preferred methods.

After dinner, I help clean up, and then I go to Varius' room. A few hours later, I hobble and stumble back to my own, one hand on the wall, my pussy thoroughly wrecked and my legs incapable of supporting me on their own. By that point, it's after midnight, and I'm to be up in a few hours to start the cycle all over again.

"I'm not joking, Dayne," I mutter into my phone at five in the morning on day ten. My eyes are heavily bagged, so I'm dutifully putting on my make-up. Gods forbid, I do this *after* I make seven men their breakfast, but a lady must look the part at all times. Shit, if Varius ever wants me to sleep in his bed, I'm not sure what I'm supposed to do. "I'm actually researching ways to jumpstart and then elongate my period just so I can sleep," I say.

He laughs, and I'm so tired, I'm not even mad.

"Is he seriously lasting hours every night? Because that's impressive."

"Not really. He comes in a few minutes, then does...other stuff until he's ready again. I need to introduce him to naps in between. Or quickies." Yawning, I accidentally jab myself in the eye with whatever this make-up stick thing is called. I pull it away to look at it, and then I curse. It's mascara. I'm putting fucking mascara on my skin.

Dammit.

Dropping the thing on the counter in disgust, I turn on the tap and start scrubbing at my face.

"So has he got it in all the way yet?" Dayne asks.

I snort. "No. Not even close. He'll literally become Vlad the Impaler if he tries."

His laughter rings out and doesn't stop until I manage to remove all the black gunk from under my eyes. I stare at my reflection, trying to decide if how I look is good enough but knowing it isn't. Sighing, I reach for the foundation.

"Our stint in North Korea was better than this," I mutter.

"You mean that time we ended up with a whole country after us and our healthy asses plus my utter whiteness stood out?"

"Mmm." I flick the brush of foundation across my cheeks in small back and forth strokes. Given I'm half Vietnamese, half white, I didn't exactly fit in skin-wise either, but Dayne might as well have been a Christmas tree at an Easter party. He nearly got shot so many times.

"It can't be that bad," he says sympathetically.

"It's worse. At least then I got to kill people. Here, I can't even yell."

"Maybe you can go to the gym?"

"With what time and energy?"

He laughs. "Don't worry, Micha. No guy can keep this up for long. I bet he only makes it a few more days."

"Varius isn't a guy. He's a –" I stop, the word 'god' on my lips. Although it has been centuries since a person has been struck down by lightning or turned into a spider for comparing themselves to the gods, it's just one of those things you don't risk.

Then again, if I really put some enthusiasm into my claims, maybe Zeus will strike him down in a fit of jealousy and I can get some sleep.

"You think I can fake a period?"

"I don't see why not. It's not like he's going to check, but it might make it quite awkward when you hit it again in a week or two."

I wave my brush at the mirror, happy enough with my foundation to call it done. "Eh, that happens to some girls, so it's not outside the realm of truth."

"Will he punish you if he catches you in a lie?"

"I'll just say I'm pregnant. He won't hurt me then."

"Micha," he says flatly, his humor suddenly gone.

I sigh as I start working on my eyes. "I don't think so."

"Just because no one's hurt you so far –"

"I know," I say. I am well aware of the honeymoon phase a lot of bought wives go through. The calm before the storm.

He pauses for a moment, then grumbles, "I don't like not being able to feel you. I keep thinking the worst every time I…"

My chest squeezes. "I'm okay, Dayne. Honest. I'm just tired. But you got an invitation to the engagement party, right?"

"Yes."

The tightness in my chest eases. "Good. Then I'll see you in a couple days. You won't even recognize me."

He doesn't laugh, and my forced smile drops. I always loved who I was, and he knew it.

"I have to go," I say hurriedly, not wanting to dwell on things I can't change. "I'll see you soon."

"Yeah."

Hanging up, I close my eyes briefly. Then I finish putting on the finishing touches to my make-up and thread my nose stud back in. The piercing in my eyes, implanted under the clear surface of the sclera, mocks me with their presence. As dangerous as they are to get for humans, so much so many doctors won't perform the surgery, I need them to see my ethereal flames. The piercings are platinum alloy runes, no more than a few millimeters wide, and they were a bitch for me to create. But glasses are too easily knocked off and are a pain to push up against a scope or binoculars. So Dayne put them in for me when I was twelve, when I was foolishly determined to be the best damn assassin there ever was. So I'd be too valuable for my father to lose, to trade...

A fucking fool.

Turning from the mirror, I head downstairs, my new life shackled around my ankles.

THIRTEEN

HIM

Talon stands as I enter his sleek, modern office, a smile on his face, his green eyes easy. My skin is pulled tight by paranoia, and my nostrils flare slightly as I breathe in his scent, checking for the sour tang of fear, the rich odor of adrenaline or rage. But there's nothing under his deodorant, applied liberally beneath his simple black tank top. Still...the hairs on my neck do not relax. And my fingers twitch with the desire to pull one of the many knives I never go without. I have a gun too, but there's just something more calming about holding a blade.

"Congratulations on the engagement," he says, his smile stretching across the full of his face. There isn't any strain to his lips, no tightness that belies genuineness. I want to just ask him if he wishes to kill me, not tiptoe around the real reason I'm here, but if Talon isn't the traitor...I do not want to destroy the relationship we have.

So I keep my mouth shut and simply nod as he lifts the

phone off its receiver on his large black desk. The piece of furniture is perpendicular to me on this side and a wall-to-wall, floor-to-ceiling window with an amazing view of Miami Beach, Florida, and the crisp, blue-and-green stretch of the Pacific on the other. He presses the button to call his assistant. "Louise? Bring in the good stuff."

"Yes, sir."

Hanging up, he looks at me. "I knew you had it in you to last more than fifty-nine seconds. Won me twelve hundred, that did."

My expression doesn't change, but he laughs anyway as he gestures to the seat in front of his desk. I move towards it, no hesitation in my steps despite the rising of hairs on my back. His preferred way of killing is by blasting a person with a bolt of electricity, and I can sense the charge in the air before he does it. I can move faster than him, grab the gun in my shoulder holster, and fire it into his skull before he can use his magic.

My finger twitches in the phantom pull of a trigger.

Bang.

"Should've gone for the full minute. The odds on that..." Talon whistles as he rounds his desk to stand in front of me, then leans back on it, his arms crossed.

I don't ask him how he got the information on my time. Indulging my brothers only leads to them taking the piss for longer. Instead, I start by developing a baseline to discern his lies, asking a question I already know the answer to. "How many Ricks did we move last month?"

That's the street name for our incubus potions, derived from the shortening of the word "erections" given that is what they create – albeit with ridges and bulges and extra parts like feelers and tongues and hooks and sacs of cum for those obsessed with breeding.

He shakes his head, his buzzed black hair not moving. "Oh, come on," he says in exasperation. "Forget business for a sec. You're *engaged*."

The door to the office opens, and Louise Warner strides in in a well fitted dark-blue suit, her brown eyes sharp, not one strand of hair free from her tight bun. She carries a tray with a mini bottle of helfire on it, a corkscrew, and two glass tumblers. After placing it on the desk beside my brother, she turns to leave. Efficient and quick. The door *clicks* within six seconds of her entry.

Talon grabs the corkscrew and black bottle. A green wax seal covers the top, stamped with the Heldron Family logo – a fiery H. Steam hisses from the beverage as he pulls the cork free, and he pours a generous shot into both tumblers, the liquid as black as tar. That amount will kill a human and will practically floor us, but I take the offered glass with a slight nod.

"To the loss of an old man's virginity." Talon smirks as he lifts his glass. My body buzzing with the expectation of pain and adrenaline, I raise mine to clink with his. And as I move closer, his eyes sharpen. His smile drops. And his shoulders tense as he goes on high alert – but it's nothing suspicious. Just the normal reaction to drinking helfire.

Created in the Underground of Halzaja, the plane of the angels and demons, it's brewed by the family of demons that guard the backdoor of Niflhel. They fight the souls of the escaped, keep the dead from coming back to the world of the living, and party like fucking animals. Each batch of helfire is imbued with the actual flames of the underworld, so it isn't a drink you indulge in for pleasure. It's a beating of chests, a "tradition" in our family to see who's the biggest dumbass, started when Talon stole a bottle when he was nine, wanting to be cool like Father.

"Louise is on standby," he says, referencing the fact that she's a healer. We wouldn't be the first sups to die from drinking this, and for a moment, I wonder if this is a trap, if Louise is in on it. And the glass in my hands feels heavier than if it was solid gold.

But if it is, then I want to get it fucking over with. And being drunk when I kill him might be a blessing.

So I raise the tumbler to my lips, and Talon quickly does the same. His eyes sparkle with this dumbass challenge, but I would be lying if I said I didn't feel that same need to win. Though no one ever wins drinking helfire. Case in point, the few sups who have actually died from it, their souls burned by the flames of Niflhel.

My nostrils sting with the heat of the liquid, like the smoke of a forest fire wafting up to them, clogging them, making my eyes water. My lips start to tingle with phantom pain. My fingers flexing, I take a deep breath, still holding my brother's challenging gaze, and then I chuck it back.

Instantly, my throat and stomach feel pelted by acid rain.

So I only manage to down about a third of it before I'm leaning forward, coughing up my balls. Talon is having a similar fit, but his comes with full on tears as he struggles to suck in air.

"Holy...shit," he wheezes as he pounds on his chest.

My throat is on fire, as is my stomach and lungs and every other inch of my godsdamn body. Sweat gleams on my face and neck, and the pain has me sagging down into the chair. As I sprawl out, familial memories rise, and I start craving some Carolina reapers to eat like a bag of chips. A few years ago, Maddox had the bright idea that if he could "handle" helfire, then the hottest pepper on Earth couldn't be that bad. Turns out, the high concentration of alcohol in the drink naturally dissolves the capsaicin in the chillies that makes them spicy. They have a pretty good flavor when they're not just "hot, hot, and more hot" – something you don't get to experience before first having a drink of helfire.

As I start to sit up, Talon laughs in that broken, crazed way that speaks of pure agony. My lips twitch as exhaustion hits me like I've just run a hundred miles, that rush of bone weary exhilaration, that delicious heaviness of well-worked limbs.

"Fuck," Talon says as he pushes himself further onto his desk, his knees hanging over the edge. "How did Father ever manage to drink this with his dinner?"

"Balls of steel," I say flatly.

"Clearly." Shaking his head, he looks at me. "Soooo tell me about your neeeeew *boooo*. Is she as scary as the stories say?"

I shrug a shoulder, and he rolls his eyes.

"You haven't asked her a single thing about herself, have you?" He shakes his head again. "That's a terrible start to a marriage."

"We're not married."

"But you will be."

"If she conceives."

He stares at me, twirling the remainder of his helfire. "Have you told her?"

"That Khalid might kill our kid? Or that he'll kill me too?"

His smile is flat. "Could do a good news, bad news in that case."

I laugh wryly, imagining just how well that'll go. Hey, bad news is our kid needs to be murdered. Good news, so do I. She'd probably kill me herself. And then Khalid would have to kill her because that'd technically be treason despite me already having a death sentence. Because politics.

"Then again," Talon says, "they might both be good news to her."

My gaze sharpens, demanding he elaborates.

He stares at me. "You don't know Micha specialized in killing kids? Any time a bulletin went out for anyone under fourteen, she took it. Some people say she keeps trophies of them. Teeth, fingers, hair, you know? Others say...she does something else with them." He gives me a pointed *look* that has my fingers tightening on my glass.

"Mother wouldn't have picked her if she did."

His lips tighten ever so slightly, and the hairs on the back of my neck start to rise. There's a hardness in his eyes, an unresolved anger as he raises his tumbler to his lips. He doesn't take a drink though, suddenly remembering perhaps that it isn't a soothing brandy in his hands but a touch of demonic fire. Placing it down on the desk beside him, he settles into silence.

But I need to know what anger he is hiding. If whatever it is is the reason he might've tried to kill me...

Fighting through the fog of the helfire, I study him. There was surprise in his eyes that I didn't know her speciality but no disgust. Dead kids are nothing new in our line of work. We might be at peace with the vampires, the hardships of war no longer forcing us to do the unthinkable, but there are two thousand years of war crimes on all sides. What counts as a child today was either a soldier or a breedmare only a few decades ago – and with Mother, Antonio, and Aleric all being much older than that, their memories are still sharp. Their lines between what is a child and what is an adult is heavily blurred, and that confusion still bleeds into the bellies of the three gangs.

As for the vampires who feast on blood, they have a preference for the younger "animals." Veal instead of beef. Lamb instead mutton. Most things on the American meat market in all practically – their farm animals forced to grow so fast their bones break from the strain, making them unfit to walk. The vampires have followed suit in their morality, seeing them with the same eye as humans do chickens and sheep and cows.

When Talon was but a teenager, he fell in love with a bloodbank – one of the humans passed around Aleric's gang like a bong for everyone to take a puff from. Mother and I both warned him away from her, knowing the outcome of one of their "farm animals" is always a brutal death, but young love is foolish and irresistable.

The day she was eventually bled dry was the last day Talon ever cried. So I am certain his anger isn't directed at Micha. He doesn't care enough about nameless kids. He has seen too much shit, is almost numb.

Which means the anger is personal.

"How many Ricks did we move last month?" I ask again, steering the conversation to something less emotional so I have a baseline to work from. To compare his lies to. His anger.

"Ten percent more than last January, and this month is looking to be even higher."

"Already?" The incubus potions are one of our biggest products, giving those who take it a fancy new dick with various bells and whistles, but we're only in the second week of February.

Talon nods. "I reckon we'll hit quota around Valentine's. I thought of a good slogan – 'ain't cheating if it ain't your dick' for men and 'ain't cheating if it ain't real dick' for women." He looks so fucking chuffed with himself. "I've emailed that out to the other capos today, so should see a rise in sales across the board." A slow smirk spreads across his face. "Want a couple Ricks to take home tonight?"

"No."

"The cum bucket helps with pregnancy." It creates a rigid sac, knot-like, that fills up with extra cum right below the head.

My eyes narrow, but I don't repeat myself. Using any of our products myself is a rule I will not cross. None of my capos are allowed to use anything other than Ricks, and if they do, they're monitored. Addiction leads to distractions, loose fists on their territory, stealing from the top... An ever downward spiral that only ever ends in death. Either by their hand or mine.

Chuckling, Talon holds up his hands. He ducks his head and breaks eye contact, instantly and casually submissive. I focus on the muscles of his face, but his jaw doesn't clench. His nostrils don't flare. His eyes don't harden as he stares at the floor, having tried to duck his head so I can't see his hidden rage. His hands don't twitch with the burn of magic. His feet don't kick in a restless need to jump the distance between us and kill me. There are no signs of him hating me. Nothing to give suspicion to his loyalty.

My eyes narrow slightly.

"You bringing anyone to the party?" I ask, steering him towards more personal topics. Swirling the black liquid in my glass, I relax back in the chair. But my senses sharpen on him, picking up every twitch of his jaw muscles, every released hormone, every sharp inhale and exhale as dark clouds thunder across his eyes.

"No," he says, his lips tight, his emotions written across them in broad strokes. And I know he's thinking about the guest list, how Aleric will be there. Both Bosses have been invited out of respect to the treaty that is technically still in place, but Talon doesn't give a shit about Antonio Garcia. He doesn't even care that he's slaughtering his way through the vampires; in fact, he applauds it, of the belief that we should just sit back and let it happen. Or actually help the wolves get rid of them for good.

"Aleric will be there," I say, goading him, pushing buttons I know are there.

Jackie, his first love, didn't just get drained dry during a party that got a bit out of hand. They waited until Talon took her on their first date – a picnic beneath the stars on the night of a meteor shower. She loved space, dreamed of being an astronaut, and Talon had bought her a promise ring inlaid with a real meteorite. He promised to buy her from Aleric – the only way a bloodbank can be free outside of death and then free her immediately after. He'd applied to colleges on her behalf, knowing she hadn't because she didn't expect herself to still be alive, having sold herself to the Blood Fangs in order to save her brother, to buy him protection when they lived on the streets. He had promised her so many things, and I want to think she died believing them. That for once in her miserable life, she found hope.

But Jackie was too experienced for that.

Talon left her on the beach while he went back to the car to grab something. And when he got back, he found her on death's door, with "Witch Whore" written on her forehead in her own blood. She died in his arms, and her lost dreams, their lost future has haunted him ever since.

His lips tight, Talon barely manages to stop his growl. "I'll behave. Just don't fucking seat us together."

There is pure anger in his words, but it isn't at me. I study him, making sure, and then I finally start to accept his innocence. My chest expands in relief, only to instantly cave back in. Because if he isn't the traitor, then who is?

My skin itches and crawls, feeling too tight across my bones, but I don't shift to relieve the building pressure. I don't give him anything at all to pick up on, don't want him to know I'm looking for a traitor in our own godsdamn family. He might not hate me now, but I do not trust he will side with me if whoever it is forces them all to choose.

"You'll stay away from Mother too. I don't want you two scheming," I say.

And there is that anger again, but there's also a flash of relief. He doesn't want to be around her, and I suddenly realize he hasn't been home for nearly a month. That isn't unusual for Talon; he often works late and sleeps here or at one of our other warehouses, a suite of rooms upstairs for him, but the look in his eyes says that, this time, it's more than that.

I backtrack dates, and my shoulders stiffen, as does my spine. Father's birthday was last month. The anniversary of his death was the one before that. And Talon always was a daddy's boy.

He was devastated the first time our father walked out. His grades dropped. His motivation to do anything died. He barely ate, barely slept. He didn't speak a word for months. Mother pushed him into counseling, and he gradually got better.

But then Father came back, getting up his hopes, only to destroy them again just as fast. This time, it wasn't grief that came. It was rage. When he hit his ascension, electrical fires started popping up all around town. When one of those fires had the body of another kid in it, some runaway girl who had snuck into the abandoned building, I started giving him jobs in the Family business. He needed an outlet, and at eighteen, I had no idea how the fuck to parent him.

It was a good call though – blind fucking luck that I take no credit for. By the time he was sixteen, he was damn near back to being a model citizen. Back in school. Excelling at math and economics. He even came over to Mother's side, finally understanding that she'd kept this family together when he walked out. So whatever beef Talon now has with her, I know it will pass.

My eyes dip to the helfire still in my hands, that train of thought leading to somewhere dangerous. Phantom screams of Father's disgust soon knock round my head. Smashed bottles. Thrown chairs. Cocked guns pointed at his own temple. Then comes the sound of crying. All my brothers other than Khalid and Enoch did it openly. Our mother and Enoch did it behind closed doors. But I heard them all, my senses sharp since both. And now here's the guilt that I tore our parents apart. Tore everyone apart.

Looking up at my brother, I ask, "Do you blame me for Father leaving?"

Talon's mouth drops open as he rears back, his green eyes wide. Silence descends with a heavy fist, but then he shakes his head.

"No. No, of course not." His face twists both in pain and anger. He runs his hand through his hair as he ducks his head. Then he sighs, the alcohol loosening his tongue, and he looks at me, his eyes strained. "I blame *her.* Father had his faults, but to have hated her so much he killed himself?" He shakes his head. "What did she do to him? His birthday was last month, and that's all I can fucking think about."

The glass feeling heavy in my hand, I'm almost tempted to knock it back. But I want my head clear enough to drive home.

Back to Micha so I can work out my growing restlessness between her legs.

But before I go, I have one more question… One more thought that's been bugging me for over a year, pulled out of the shadows of my subconscious by the suspicion in my brother's eyes. Or perhaps by the burning of the helfire.

"You think she deserved the curse?" I ask softly.

His jaw works. The vein at his temple ticks.

Then he says, "Don't you?"

FOURTEEN

HIM

My talk with Talon has left me restless and wanting to fuck Micha until I can't think, but when I get home, she's out. Mother's car is gone from the drive. They're most likely shopping for the engagement party, Micha's clothes not fit for her new station, but this is the first time she hasn't been here when I want her.

Grabbing the bag of goods I purchased on the way home, I step out of the car. When I enter the house, I can hear two of my brothers shouting in the living room, but there's a sense of emptiness to the place I do not like. My skin itches, becoming too tight across my bones. The restlessness builds. Like a fucking addiction only she can soothe.

It's just the fucking alcohol, I tell myself even as I dig out my phone and shoot a text to Mother.

Varius: *Bring her back.*

Shoving the mobile back into my pants pocket, I enter the living room. In the room adjacent, Enoch and Ezriel sit across side by side at the table, their laptops open, a video game flashing on their screens. Irritation, anger, and stress seep from their pores – all markers of an attack. If they're the traitors and I'm alone with them, I'm as good as dead.

But neither of them so much as turn around to look at me. They're screaming at each other way too much to even notice I've come home.

"I told you to buy wards!" Ezriel shouts, clicking madly on his mouse.

"And I told *you* to stop face-checking bushes and to keep an eye on the fucking map. You can see where everyone is, dipshit; you shouldn't be getting ganked."

"That's your job! Oh my gods, you are the *worst* support ever."

"You want to see me be a bad support?"

"Go ahead! I won't notice a fucking difference!"

There's a moment of silence as I head up the stairs to my study, my paranoia dwindling, the hairs on the back of my neck settling. But as soon as I reach the top, Ezriel shouts, "You KSing piece of shit!"

Enoch laughs, but it quickly dies under, "Hey! We agreed no telekinesis! Give me back my mouse, you fuckwipe!"

"You want it? Go ahead, take it back. Oh, you can't, can you, you weak ass telekinetic."

Stepping into my office, I close the door, automatically activating the silence rune Khalid drew on the wall. In an instant, their bickering is cut off and they won't be able to hear a thing I do up here either. Walking over to my desk, I toss the bag of stuff I bought onto the gray fabric couch on the way. It's pushed up against the wall on my right, lined by a filled bookcase and a wooden filing cabinet.

My desk is a large slab of oak that's hundreds of years old. A piece of brown vinyl is inlaid into it at the front – an addition my father added to make it easier to clean when severed heads were delivered to him.

My gaze settles on the pile of paperwork in front of my black leather chair. Rudy has left landscaping blueprints – drawn up drafts for our clientele that have been printed out and then marked with a red pen with notes on either what to change or what to do. Pinpricks dance across my skin as my vision narrows on them. Will I end up on one of those sheets? A carefully coded message about where my body is hidden written in red ink? Because that is what these papers really are – maps to all the corpses we have buried under flower beds and pools and paving stones.

Rolling my shoulders, I force a bit of the tightness out of my skin. Behind my desk is an abstract painting of colorful blocks, and behind that is a high security safe, secured with both human electronics and a hidden spell that will trigger an explosion should anyone other than me or the reaper try to access it. There are fake bomb components inside to fool any human police should we fuck up badly enough to get searched.

Opening the middle drawer of my desk, I pull out a box holding a single needle spelled to stay sterile and sharp. I take it out, having done this a thousand times before, but just as I place the needle against the pad of my forefinger, a sudden thought slams into me. Leno knows where I keep this. He could coat it in a slow acting poison. I could prick myself, put the needle back, and go about my day before randomly collapsing. No one would suspect I was poisoned hours ago or days or weeks. It would be the perfect crime.

Pinpricks dancing across my fingers, I force myself to breathe. Leno doesn't want to be Boss. He's too worried it'll put a target on his dog's back.

And it would. Because the easiest way to destroy Leno is by killing Krypto. The easiest way to blackmail my brother is to kidnap his dog. Krypto isn't just Leno's eyes. There's a bond between them that runs deeper even than the blood we share.

So I force the needle into my skin. My pulse increases at the sight of blood, but there's no turning back now. I either die or I don't. No point fucking worrying about it.

After placing the needle back in the box and in the desk's drawer, I grab the painting off the wall with my other hand. A black metal safe about the size of a microwave sits nestled in the wall. I squeeze out a drop of blood onto the top of the safe's keypad.

The air shimmers like a summer haze, the drop of blood disappears, and I quickly put in the access code. Sucking on my finger to stop the bleeding, I open the door with my left hand and grab the black leather-bound ledger inside.

As I settle into my chair, I pull the landscaping blueprints towards me. The first on the pile has seven notes written on it. The highest one says:

Plant mullein one foot apart.

Mullein is associated with the planet Saturn, which is the sixth body in our solar system. Therefore, the body is hidden under the sixth note. But they aren't counted left to right or top to bottom or even the reverse of that. They're counted in the order of the blood code in *Mortal Kombat.* A is up. B is right. C is down. And double B is left. If you can't go any further, you loop it around the page, so sometimes a B is so far right it's left, and an A is so far up it's down.

Putting the blueprint to one side, I start to make two piles: one with the highest note on it containing anything about the sun (ex: *"No sunflowers. Allergies."*) and the other with everything else (ex: *"Plant mullein one foot apart."*). In the end, I have five for the sun and two referencing planets in one way or another. The addresses in the sun pile get added to the ledger, along with yesterday's date (when the bodies went in), and whose bodies are hidden there – their names swapped out for Disney characters. Then I put the ledger away, rehang the abstract painting, and study the two remaining blueprints.

After committing their information to memory, I shuffle all seven pieces together. Opening the second drawer of the wooden filing cabinet, I stack them inside, then head out. As soon as I open the door, the commotion from downstairs thunders up.

"They're backdooring!" Ezriel shouts as I cross the hall, my nape hairs rising despite his voice coming from the floor below. As a telekinetic, neither of them needs to be up here to kill me.

"Don't stop pushing. We've got this!"

"But –"

Entering my studio, I shut the door. Lock thoughts of them out. It's a small room with various paintings leaning against the three walls to dry. The fourth wall, opposite the door, is filled by a large window and shelves on each side of it, housing supplies and empty canvases. In the middle of the studio is an easel with a half-finished painting on it – abstract, similar to the one in my study.

After turning on the radio to classical rock, I settle on my stool, roll up my sleeves, and begin to paint the information I have memorized. Coded sins fill every line, every shape, every color. The precise movements of my paintbrush reflect back truths only I can decipher.

For this is the true ledger, the sun related notes meaning nothing, the book in my study a fake. Left there to be found by any thieves or police or even a traitorous brother, to make a fool of them when they think they've cracked the code. When someone thinks they've outplayed *me*.

But someone has *outplayed me...*

Someone I love has made me believe that they love me back. When all they want is to see me dead.

Dying.

Broken.

My brush quickens across the canvas. My emotions rage inside of me. Do they hate me because I'm an abomination? Because I made Father leave? Or because of one of the sins painted onto this canvas and the one in my office?

My fingers tighten on the brush. My pulse jumps hard, then starts to gallop. Or do they hate me because of Father's death? Have they found out why he killed himself cursing Mother? That just as I split them apart when I was young, I also triggered that? Caused it in some way or another? Is my lack of magic –

I claw the painting from the easel. Set it aside. Snatch up another, blank this time, and grab a different set of paints. Red meets black meets a sea of other colors, all muted dedications to pain. Silent screams flow out of my brush. Unwanted questions lurk on the edges of the canvas. My chest tightens with every broad flick of my wrist, every movement cut sharp and hard and wild.

"Do you think she deserved it?"

"Don't you?"

My breath becomes shallow, like it doesn't dare exist, terrified of drawing attention to itself.

My head grows dizzy.

My breath nearly nonexistent now.

Is my lack of magic...

The brush wavers from a shaking hand, but I push on, don't stop, no mercy even to myself. I drag that thought kicking and screaming from the dark depths of my mind, from the cobwebbed corners it's stayed in for so long and shove it full force into the light.

Is my lack of magic...

Because Caden isn't my father?

FIFTEEN

HER

When Sau told me we were going shopping this morning I didn't want to leave the house, didn't want to lose another part of my self identity under draping silk and glittering jewels. Now that we're back, though, I don't want to get out of the car.

Because I've been summoned, our trip cut short.

And I hate that.

Hate how he can just demand I come back to spread my legs.

Hate how I can't tell him to go fuck himself.

Hate it even more how much it bothers me that he didn't even text *me*. He texted his *mother*. And now she *knows*. And this whole ride back was super fucking embarrassing.

In the week I've been here, Varius hasn't even looked at me outside of the bedroom. I'm pretty certain he could spot my pussy in a lineup, but I doubt he even knows what color my eyes are. And I hate that.

I hate him.

Because I know *exactly* what color his are. As tired as I have been, as annoyed with him as I am, I still know every fleck of color in that damn intense gaze. And isn't that just pathetic?

So when he storms out of the house, my back is already up, my levels of annoyance skyrocketing with every step the damn neanderthal takes. Sau somehow disappears in the seconds it takes for me to undo my seatbelt and for him to yank my door open and drag me out. He crowds me against the car as he grabs my bicep with one hand and leans into the interior with the other. He grabs a random dress from the backseat, then drags it and me away.

"Get off me," I snap as I wrench my arm free. I stumble a step from the momentum, surprised that actually got him to release me. But then his arm is around my waist and he's hauling me over his shoulder. My ass in the air, my face low, I growl at him. "Put me down!"

When he doesn't, I bare my teeth. Gods, I'm so fucking tempted to bite him. I yelp as his hand lands hard on my ass.

"I told you to be here when I want you."

I glare at him – or rather at the back of his jacket given I can't see his face. "That's the first time I've left the house in over a week. You have a hand. Use it."

He spanks me again, and I jolt. The sting of the blow is rubbed out by the palm of his hand.

"You have a brain. Use it before you speak to me."

My eyes widening at his *audacity*, I lean forward and bite him. Perhaps it's not the best plan I have had, but I'm tired and exhausted, and I have spent ten full fucking days keeping the real me weighed down with cement shoes and chicken wire. I have done nothing *but* think before I did something this past week and a half, and it feels so damn good to break that.

Until I hear his deep-throated growl – a warning of hot, imminent danger.

Swinging me off him, he slams me into the side of the garage, out of view of the house. My breath whooshing out, I'm left momentarily stunned, and then even more so when I'm hauled into the air and he kisses me.

Arousal explodes in my belly, and I wrap my arms and legs around him, momentarily ignoring the fact that I'm angry at him. Because I've never felt the touch of his lips on mine, and I'm craving that connection, that binding of souls that makes it seem like he sees *me* and not just the offspring I can pump out. But the kiss isn't sweet and romantic. It's rough and hard and a desperate, raw demand of pure need.

His tongue pushes into my mouth, and I open for him as I grab his hair. I grind my pussy against his waist as he kisses me. There's no technique, no slow exploration as he learns my mouth as he has every other part of my body. He is just greedy in his claim, lapping up every inch of me, pushing his tongue as far down my throat as it'll go. Like he's desperate to get inside of me one way or another.

Moaning against him, I trail my fingers down his neck, scratching my claim into his skin. His hands bunch in my ass as he rocks me faster against him. I clench and unclench my legs, my body aching with the need for a release.

My tongue pushes against him, and his retreats, letting me into his mouth. It's enough of a shock, that lowering of his guard, that offering up of control, that I break away. I stare at him, and he stares at me. Our breaths collide hot and heavy in the cold air of February.

My chest tight, I rasp, "Do you know what color my eyes are?"

His gaze doesn't waver as it pierces directly into my soul. But he doesn't just say the color he can clearly see. He doesn't even give me that. Instead, he sets me down, then bends low to pick up the dress he dropped. It's a red Ozgur

Masur, a draped shoulder gown worth a few grand, and the dress I'm planning on wearing to the engagement party tomorrow.

"Put it on," he says.

"Not until you answer me."

He towers over me, looking down, his gaze searching mine. My lips tingle as I stare up at him. "Why?" he finally asks. "What does it matter if I know the exact color of your eyes? All you are is a womb, Micha."

But the way he says it makes my breath catch. Like he knows every shade but is refusing to admit it. Like he wants something more than what he dares to ask for, to demand I give him. Like he wants what I do – this undeniable pull between us making him terrified of what will happen once it finally snaps into place, so he pushes me away. So he keeps his guard up. His feelings safe.

Holding his gaze, I undo the button on my pants, then push them off. Next comes my shirt, leaving me practically naked in the cold air. All I'm now wearing are some plain black cotton panties. Goosebumps rise across my arms and belly, and for a moment I think he's going to forego the dress part and just fuck me, but he lifts it higher. A silent demand, and I grab it from him and put it on. The red silk caresses my skin like a lover, the deep V-cut of the frontline plunging low between my breasts and pulling his eyes to them.

Then he looks up, his eyes dark and dangerous, and I suck in a breath of pure adrenaline and need. Electricity arcs through my legs, the urge to run making them itch to move.

Grabbing something out of his jacket pocket, he flicks it open, and I recognize the butterfly knife he put inside me when I first arrived. This time it's the blade that he lines up with my pussy. My heart hammers in my chest as I watch him slowly slice through the expensive fabric of my dress, trailing the knife down to my knees. Then he puts it away, and from that same pocket, he pulls out a toy.

It's bright pink and shaped in a U, one side bulbous, the other a thin tail. Like a curled up sperm, in all honesty. I stare at it, wondering what exactly it does. But I don't have to think for long because he shoves aside my panties and pushes the egg-shaped end inside. The tail curves around my pussy and presses against the front of it. I kegel, but he isn't done, pulling out another item, a thin cord with a bulge in the middle, that causes my eyes to widen and my breaths to come out hard and fast.

Sliding his hand inside my dress, he secures one end of the set of nipple clamps to me. I arch against the wall of the garage, hissing in a breath at the new sensation rocking my body. I barely give my breasts attention when I masturbate, but fuck me, I've been missing out. The utter deliciousness as he pinches the other clamp around me has me kegeling again on a moan.

Ducking his head to my neck, he kisses the base of it before running his tongue up to my ear. "The color of your eyes," he murmurs, "has nothing on the color you go when you're on the verge of coming."

My brain spasms, then short circuits completely when he takes my earlobe in between his teeth.

"Now run, little monster."

Stepping swiftly back, he releases me, but it takes me a moment to find my legs. My heart pounding at the hunger in his dark eyes, I stumble away, heading for the woods surrounding his home.

My pace quickens. My strides lengthen. And soon I am running in an awkward gait. The curved tail, combined with my underwear, though, holds the toy snuggly in place.

As the fresh, crisp air fills my lungs, I start to get into a rhythm. My arms pump. My legs eat up the ground, and my chest expands with the thrill of the chase. My ears strain, alert for every sound behind me. But there is only silence. My skin buzzes with the anticipation of him coming out of nowhere, his arms grabbing me around the waist as he hauls me to the ground.

But it never happens, and after a few seconds of silence, I chance a look behind me. Varius is still standing where I left him. His attention isn't even on me; it's on his phone, and my feet grind to a halt as powerful emotions clash inside of me. Hurt. Annoyance. Fear that he's already bored with me and will toss me aside so my worth becomes even less than it is now.

My fingers crackle with the building of anger. And then I gasp as my knees give out, and I stumble forward.

His head lifts. His eyes find mine. And a slow, wicked smirk curves his lips as the toy inside me vibrates. Varius' thumb moves across the screen of his phone. The vibrations intensify, making my thighs snap together. I pant hard as the cold air wraps its arms around me, making my nerves sensitive to every single brush against them.

The toy stills, and Varius takes a step towards me. He walks slow, purposefully, his stride confident in his capture of me despite the lack of speed. My pulse in my throat, I spin for the woods. Just as I duck between the first set of trees, though, the toy goes off again, and I cry on a small stumble. The vibrations themselves aren't very arousing, the sensation too new to my body. But the feel of being hunted, of being tracked and played with by this powerful man... *fuck me,* is that hot.

My nipples tighten from the arousal coursing through me, deliciously pinched between the clamps. Dried twigs crunch underfoot, and the smell of the still blossoming flowers shifts to the bark of the trees as I head deeper into the woods. I duck beneath a branch, then cry out, my eyes popping wide as I stumble to my knees. The clamps on my nipples are vibrating *hard*, and dear gods, that's working for me way more than the toy in my pussy. I struggle to suck in air as the sensations build on those two sensitive buds, a near painful crescendo that has me curling in half, my right hand reaching between my thighs. Needy. Desperate.

"Run!"

Whimpering, I squeeze my eyes shut. I want to tell him to go to hel, to let me have this, but my words escape me, so I just show him with my actions. My fingers press on my clit. My pussy clenches tight. He doesn't get to just boss me around like some –

I cry out as his body slams into me. His hands find mine as we roll, clamping over my fingers and ripping both my arms away from my body. I struggle beneath his grip, but he's too strong, has entire dominance over me.

My breaths exit on rapid bursts that have the clamps sending spasms through my nipples with each movement. I try to wrap my legs around him, to use him as he so often uses me, but he rolls me onto my back, stretching out on top of me. He sits up and yanks my arms behind me. I toss and turn, my cheeks pressed into the cold, damp earth. "Varius, *please*," I beg, not above begging, never above begging. Too desperate to keep the words in.

"I told you what would happen if you disobeyed me."

My eyes widen as he slaps a fuzzy cuff around my wrist. A thrill shoots through me. I struggle harder, not wanting to give in even though my pussy is begging me to. To stop being such a brat and let him rail me until I forget my own godsdamn name. But I keep fighting him, keep denying him until he clamps my other wrist, binding them both together. I breathe heavily as he sits back, but I can just *feel* that damn smirk on his lips as he looks down on me.

Baring my teeth, one cheek pressed into the earth, I strain the muscles of my shoulders. My wrists burn from the force of the resistance and then... *Snap!* The chain between the cuffs rips apart. I smile smugly, taking a second just to breathe in his surprise.

But he isn't surprised.

He's prepared.

Because the next second, a small chain, its metal slightly warm to the touch, wraps snug around my wrist. My eyes pop open. I jerk my arm up as I twist my head around, my heart slamming inside my chest. "You fucker!"

There's a thin golden chain dangling from my wrist, no thicker than what you'd find on a necklace. But there isn't a single weak link on it; every single part of it hums with power. For nothing, absolutely *nothing* can break a witch's snare other than the release word spoken by the person who put it on.

Grabbing my other wrist, Varius flicks the end of the chain around it. It wraps around me, circling my flesh to morph into a perfect loop. There's no lock, no snap to undo. It's just a solid gold chain binding my arms together.

Moving off me, he rolls me onto my back. I wiggle to get a bit more comfortable with my arms behind me, but before I can, he pulls out his phone, and the clamps on my nipples vibrate. I twist on a cry, my torso lifting, the air pulled out of my lungs like a puppet on a string.

He increases the vibrations until I'm crying, my nipples so sensitive just the soft wind on them hurts – the straps of my dress having fallen down my arms. My thighs press together as I writhe on the forest floor. My eyes squeeze shut, tears flowing down my cheeks. Panting and moaning, I chase that orgasm he's building inside of me.

But then it stops.

The vibrations end, and I am left whimpering in a mess of need.

"Varius..." Opening my eyes, I look at him, begging him to not stop, to keep going, to let me come so I can remember how to breathe.

He straddles my knees and cuts off my underwear with

his knife. Bringing them to his face, he inhales. I pant as I watch the arousal on his face. Then he shoves them inside his jacket pocket and pulls out a rose. My eyes latch onto the purple silicon toy, then trail to the rest of the pockets on his black down jacket, wondering what other delights he's hiding.

He twists the vibrator inside my pussy so the tail isn't in the way, then presses the rose onto my clit. I scream on a jerk as it starts to lick and suck just how I need it to to be able to come.

But just as I'm about to, he pulls it away and raises it to his lips. My eyes on him, I watch as he licks it clean, then slips it back into his pocket.

"Varius, *please*," I beg, spreading my legs in invitation as my chest heaves.

He shuffles down my body until his face is lined up with my pussy. He pulls out the toy inside me and pops it into his mouth as his eyes hold mine. He groans as he sucks, and my thighs quiver with anticipation. My skin flushes over the hot sounds emitting from deep inside his chest.

"You want to come, little monster?" he asks as he stands and starts peeling off his jacket.

I whimper, my eyes never leaving his. "Yes, please. Yes, Varius. *Please*. Please let me come. I need to come."

Hauling me to my feet, he says, "Then run."

SIXTEEN

HIM

The sound of her whimpers alone are going to make me come in my godsdamn pants. The sight of her wobbly legs as she runs away from me is going to bring me to my knees. I want her below me. Under me. Crying out as her pussy smothers my face. I want her hands in my hair, her nails in my back.

I lift my fingers to my neck and trace the ridges she left there. Her claim. *On me.*

The nerves on my back flair where she bit me, and I hope she left another mark. Another claim. Another sign that she wants me like I do her.

With a rumbling growl, I pull out my phone and turn the nipple clamps on. She cries out and stumbles, one shoulder on a tree as her knees knock together. As her legs shake. As her arousal flows down her pussy and beckons me to taste her. To throw her down on the ground and bury my face in the warm embrace of her thighs.

I shouldn't want her like this. Shouldn't *need* her to calm the damn storm raging through me. But there's a *pull* to her, a desperation. It's fucking ridiculous. Looking to a Black, a fucking assassin who specializes in killing kids, for *comfort.* To ease the demons riding my ass about which brother is out to kill me, which man my mother fucked to have me. If that is what even happened or if I really am just a freak of nature.

It is ridiculous, and yet, I can't stop my pursuit. Can't stop this *need* to have her down on her knees and begging. To look at me like she'd never betray me, never do anything to make me deny her the pleasure she craves.

If I can break her. If I can get her entirely focused on her own need to orgasm, then she won't see the comfort I am taking from her, not just in her body but in her presence. The balm I need but will never admit to even wanting.

So I stop the vibrations of the nipple clamps. Give her the ability to keep running, and I walk after her, never letting her get away. But never reaching her either. Just teasing her, building her up, making her so desperate she starts to cry. I can hear her whimpers. I can smell the salt of her tears as she struggles to put one foot in front of the other. Her pores seep with adrenaline and arousal and then she finally falls to her knees, unable to take another step. Unable to move without coming.

She turns her head to look at me, and her fear spikes at my slow approach. Like a destiny she can't outrun, a reaper of Hades' she can't throw off. She wiggles backwards, her hands still tied behind her back. I move to her side and push her with my foot, rolling her over. She stares up at me, her eyes wide.

And there it is.

That look of utter obsession.

The one that'll allow me to lower my own walls without her knowing – at least temporarily.

When her legs fall apart, I don't hesitate to fall between them. Lowering my head to her pussy, I lick her between her lips. Lifting her hips, she welcomes me. Won't hurt me in this moment, too needy for what I can give her. The tension in my shoulders easing, I wrap my arms around her thighs and haul her closer to my lips.

She moans as she rides my face, but I know she can't come from this alone. She needs pressure on the outside of her pussy, a teasing of her clit – two things I deny her as I take my time spreading her cum all inside my mouth and over my chin. As I drown out my thoughts about my family and their sins and just exist in the melody of her cries.

"Varius, *please.*" Her voice is broken. Her body shudders, and I relent, moving my lips up to latch around her clit. She jerks beneath me as I suck on her. I lift my eyes to her face. She gasps as her thighs squeeze my head, and I watch her as she nears her O.

The rich brown color of her eyes, like a pile of curling leaves before winter's embrace, has nothing on the shades of arousal that paint her cheeks and neck when she's about to finish. Has nothing on the precise pitch of her cries, the growing desperation in her song as she begs me to let her come.

My cock painful in my pants, I rock my hips into the cold ground. I groan around her clit at the slight ease of pressure, and she jerks on a scream. But then she falls back down, her cries lowering to where they were before. I still, trying to recall what I just did that made her jolt.

I flick my tongue across her clit. I get a moan but nothing more. I change how I'm sucking on her, the speed and the strength, trying various things. When none of that gets the right response, though, I growl in frustration.

Then there it is. That cry of desire that has her jerking in an uncontrollable spasm.

"*Shiiit!*" she screams as she lifts her hips, riding me hard.

Her pants leave my balls aching. I hum against her clit, then groan again, the pressure in my cock building too much to fight off.

"Shit! Fuck! Variuuuus!" she cries out, and I come at the same time she does, mine triggered by hers, by having given her what she needs. I bury my tongue into her pussy as I groan from deep within my chest. My cock pulses, shooting cum all in my boxers.

Breathing heavily, I kiss her pussy slowly. She trembles beneath me, her legs jerking every so often when she gets overwhelmed by the sensations I'm forcing on her. A small sigh escapes her lips, one of content and utter exhaustion. Lifting my head, I look at her. Her eyes are closed. Her lips have the smallest of tilts, and I realize she's on the verge of sleep.

My chest tightens as I stare at her. Does she really trust me that much? To let her walls down so fully as to leave herself utterly vulnerable? I could do anything to her while she sleeps. I could slit her throat or push my cock in as deep as I want without her awake to stop me.

"Micha," I say sharply, telling her she's being foolish. No one should have that level of trust from her, least of all me. But she's already asleep.

Her chest rises and falls slowly. Her mien is one of pure unconscious bliss. And fucking hel, I've never seen anything more beautiful. More precious.

My chest tight, I crawl up her naked body, then turn her onto her side so I can remove the witch's snare from around her wrists. She sighs as she brings her arms up under her head. She nestles her cheek into the crook of her elbow.

Moving into a crouch, I watch her sleep.

She's so peaceful.

So ignorant in what she's giving me. I am the monster people run from, the beast in the dark that should be killed. And here she is, her guard fully down as she sleeps.

My lips tight, I reach a hand out to wake her, to chastise her for being so stupid. But instead of shaking her, I run my fingers over the soft skin of her shoulder. She's warm, the fire in her veins protecting her from the cold.

Trailing my fingers up her neck to her lips, I trace them slowly. She sighs, and I pull away, my heart beating fast. My lips flatten into a thin line. Fucking hel, I wanted her home so I could work out my frustrations. But she's only giving me more, teasing me with things I can't have.

Standing abruptly, I slip the witch's snare into my pocket and leave.

SEVENTEEN

HER

My muscles are stiff from having slept in the woods, but I've spent the night in worse places. The engagement party is tonight, and with Varius having destroyed the dress I was originally going to wear, I now need to pick another one. I could do that myself – obviously, but last night, something changed between us. I felt it. And now... I'm not quite sure, but maybe... Maybe I can...I don't know...

Fuck. Is this stupid? Should I just pretend like last night never happened? It's not like he's going to be open to being open with me. If I start this, put in effort, attempt to squeeze through the holes in his walls...it's not going to end well. I know it's not going to end well. I might chisel away a little bit, maybe even a good-sized chunk, but as soon as he realizes he has a fault in his defenses, Varius's going to start chucking burning oil over his walls. And every single drop is going to land on me.

"Fuck it," I mutter as I grab a handful of random dresses

off the rack. The worst thing he can do is slam the door in my face. It's not like that'll change our relationship at all. But the best-case scenario is he lets me in – both into his study and into the first of his ninety-nine walls that are erected all around him. Barbed wire and armed guards and mines buried every step of the way.

This arranged marriage could be something then. Maybe. Potentially. Hopefully. And then I wouldn't just be a *womb.* I would be a part of this family. Because although a Shadow doesn't divorce, they do commit murder.

Scooping up the bottom of the dresses with my left arm while still holding the hangers in my right, I make my way over to my door. Then down the hall. Up the stairs. I stop at his office. Taking a deep breath, convincing myself this isn't a dumb idea, I kick it in lieu of knocking.

"Can I come in?" I say.

There is utter silence.

I wait patiently, thinking maybe he is just finishing a page or a report or whatever it is he does in there. But the time ticks into clear "fuck off" territory.

My irritation growing, I kick the door again, still gently though. Like a lady. Wearing combat boots. Aimed to go up his ass.

My skin prickling despite knowing Sau is out right now, meeting Stefaan to go over the final details of the party this evening, I turn to glance over my shoulder just to double check she isn't here to witness my unladylike behavior. At the sight behind me, I jump out of my skin even though outwardly, I don't flinch.

Varius is right fucking there, walking towards me from the direction of the bathroom.

Ah.

I awkwardly hold up the dresses, lifting both of my arms. "I need help picking out a dress since you ruined my first choice."

"Ask my mother."

"She's out."

"Text her."

"I thought it would be nice if we matched."

"I'm wearing black. It'll go with anything."

He goes to move past me, but I not so subtly shift in front of him, blocking his reach for the door. His eyes narrow on me, and although my pulse spikes at the base of my throat, I don't flinch away. Don't give up a single inch of ground. Nor do I kick him for being a fucking neanderthal about this even though I *really* want to.

I smile sweetly. "Well, I'd like your opinion on which one you'd like."

"I'm too busy to watch you try on dresses."

"You only have to give a two second opinion for each one." I quickly glance at the pile. "That's only ten seconds of your time. I can get in and *out* of these on my own."

Ha! Idiot. The shift of his eyes as his gaze roams down my body tells me I have him. I keep my face carefully free of my internal gloating about how easy he is to manipulate. At least when it comes to his dick.

"Fine."

He reaches for the door again. I move to the side with a small smile. He enters first, and I'm right on his tail in case he had the bright idea to slam the door in my face.

I kick the door shut gently behind me as I sweep my eyes around his office. It's a lot cozier than I expected with a well worn sofa pressed up against the right-hand wall and an abstract painting hanging up behind the desk. I stare at it, wondering what he likes about it. Personally, I have always been a paintings of stormy seas and smirking ladies in bold yellow dresses kind of girl.

Crossing the room, he moves behind his desk. He opens his laptop and promptly ignores me, his fingers flying across the keyboard.

Telling myself it's too late to wuss out now, I place the five dresses on the sofa. My cheeks heat as I think about stripping in front of him. Although he's seen me naked multiple times, there's a very big difference between him tearing my clothes off before or after doing the same to his and me taking them off in front of him. While he sits at his desk. Fully clothed.

Shit.

Come on, Micha. You can do this.

Breathing deep, I decide to just go for it and bend down to grab the hem of my simple blue dress – one of the many ones I've been forced to wear this past week. I start to yank it over my head in one quick movement, but just as it passes my knees, he says, "Slower."

My cheeks heat as my head snaps up to look at him, my arms frozen where they are, my body hunched. His eyes are on his computer screen. His fingers are still tapping away. But there's no denying his attention is on *me*.

Fuck.

Goosebumps tickle across my skin, raising the hairs on my arms and neck. Shifting awkwardly on my feet, I release the hem and then straighten. Reaching around me, I slowly undo the zipper, pulling it and a row of shivers down my spine. With the cool air kissing the small of my back, I reach up to slide my left sleeve down my arm. I hold the dress to me as I do the same on my right. The whole time, he doesn't look at me, his eyes still on his screen, and a flash of nerves suddenly hits me. I'm terrible at this. I'm making things worse between us. I've never stripped for someone before. Am I supposed to move more? Supposed to sway my hips –

Varius looks up at me then, his gaze dark and piercing. "Keep going," he murmurs.

Electricity arcing between us, I wet my lips and slowly drag the dress down my body. The soft polyester rubs across my bare nipples, making them hard. I've never bothered with a bra, my chest too small to be worth the effort.

His gaze drops to them, hunger darkening his visage as his fingers finally still on the keyboard. I pause a moment, letting him look his fill before letting the dress fall freely to the floor.

He lingers a second, still focused on my breasts.

Then his eyes lower ever so slowly to the V of my thighs. Feeling a bit bolder, I hook both my thumbs under the sides of the black lace that's all that's covering me. My breathing turns heavy as I tug them off inch by tantalizing inch until I expose my shaved pussy – my attempt at being "fancy" for tonight's party.

A flash of thunder crosses his face, and I swallow hard, my pulse suddenly racing. His eyes lift to mine, and it takes everything I have not to step back, an instinctive urge to increase the distance from the monster in the dark staring back at me.

"You shaved," he growls.

"Um, yeah?" My eyes flick away nervously, not knowing what I've done wrong. "The party is tonight and –"

"Don't do it again."

I blink as I gape at him. "What?"

"Your pussy, little monster, is mine. If you want to do anything to it, you're to ask me first."

"That's barbaric."

"That's my right and one I will not hesitate to enforce."

I snort. "You can fucking try."

He stares at me, a wolfish smile on his lips that tells me in no uncertain terms that he won't just try. He will fucking succeed. And punish me for it too.

"Try on the dresses, Micha," he says softly.

To a young, naive girl, that might sound like he's giving up, bowing out, throwing in the towel and letting me have this one by changing the subject, but I know he isn't. I back up, my senses flaring, screaming, "Danger, danger, danger!" But then I root my feet, a thrill shooting through me, not just over the wicked promise in his eyes but in the way it feels like the world is shifting. My world. Our world. Where perhaps I become more than just a womb and he becomes more than just a neanderthal.

He sought me out yesterday, needed me despite his lack of words and declaration. He used me not just as a thing to breed but a *person* to find connection with. Comfort from. A lifting of his pain.

He might not've voiced anything at all, and I might have no idea what's bothering him, but to a man like Varius – to a paranoid monster who trusts no one and carries his heavy burdens alone... Yesterday speaks volumes. It means I could truly have something here as long as I take my time wooing him and don't fuck it up.

So with that goal in mind, I grab the first dress, a white floor-length number by Tom Ford. The *click-clack* of the keyboard starts up again as I remove it from its hanger. I pull the invisible zipper on the back of it down all the way, then shimmy into it. All of the dresses have already been tailored to fit my size, and it goes on beautifully, fitting to my specific curves.

I never liked shopping for fancy clothes before I went with Sau, but bloody hel, she knows how to pick the right clothes to make you feel beautiful. Strong. Happy to try on another one. And another.

I run my hands down my thighs, smoothing out wrinkles that exist only to gather my strength before looking up at Varius. "What do you think?"

It's plain white of a completely plain design other than a ruched effect flowing off one shoulder. But it's sophisticated and glamorous in its simplicity.

When he looks over at me, I rotate in place so he can see the full thing. He stops me when I have my back to him by saying, "Bend over."

My pulse spiking, I hesitate for a second. The slit up the back already runs up to mid-thigh. If I bend over, there's a good chance he could see everything. My breathing turning shallow, I keep my knees straight as my hands touch the floor.

"Spread your legs."

Ever so slowly, I shuffle them apart. The lips of my pussy open, and heat rushes into my face as I wait for his next order. Not a movement, not a sound comes from him. And then...

"Not that one." His fingers fly across the keyboard once more.

The next two are dismissed by him even quicker. The black Jenny Packham Ingrid cape gown, fully embellished with hundreds of sparkling crystals, and the Roland Mouret black-and-white asymmetric cady maxi dress – although two of my favorites for their feel of grace and power, are simply not "pervy" enough. Meaning there aren't any slits for him to run his hands up. No deep Vs or low necklines for my breasts to accidentally escape from. He doesn't say that, of course, but it's there in his eyes.

Which leaves just two more dresses to try on for him – or rather one more because I've just realized what the last one I grabbed is. It's a mostly sheer piece of red beauty I got for me rather than for him. A dress to hide in the back of my closet but never wear.

So I grab the final choice, a Maria Lucia Hohan crafted out of pure silk with a deep wide V between my breasts and a slit running high up my thigh. It's a certain winner, a very pale dusty pink that glimmers under the light of his office. With a small smile, I run my hand up my thigh, pulling the slit up higher.

He doesn't say anything. The speed of his typing doesn't slow.

"Well?" I push after a couple seconds of silence.

"Show me the red one."

My cheeks flush. "That's not for the party. I didn't mean to grab it."

He doesn't look at me. Doesn't push again, but the air crackles with his demand. Electricity arcs through me until every part of my body feels too sensitive, and I just have to remove the dress from my skin. I can just put the blue one back on, then demand he pick from the –

"Good girl."

My brain short circuits. My pussy spasms.

My arm damningly reaches for the Nensi Dojaka laid out on the sofa. The deep red of the silk sings to me like a siren song – a beauty ready to punish me for listening to it. The draped cut-out maxi dress is a sleeveless piece that is sheer everywhere but in the two small triangles of fabric covering the breasts and in two more pointing inwards at the waist, the tips of those triangular pieces having been sheared off and attached to a cord that criss-crosses over my stomach, a few inches above my belly button. Dangling between them, hanging from that same cord is a sash of fabric that runs all the way to the hem on the floor. There's a lighter area of sheer fabric cut in angular lines over my midriff, but the rest of the dress is just as see-through – including everything from my hips down. *Everything.* The only coverage is from that thin sash that barely covers the V between my thighs.

"See?" I turn and show him that my ass is not covered in the slightest despite the draping of silk over it. Facing him again, I'm hopeful to see agreement on his face.

I do not.

"I'll wear a red shirt," he says as if it's final.

My mouth drops open.

"I can't wear this! You can see everything!" Grabbing the sash, I lift it away from me, proving my point.

His eyes heat as his gaze lingers there. "If anyone looks,

I'll cut out their eyes." His gaze hardens. "And those of their family. And friends."

Lost for words, I just stare at him. His attention returns to his work.

"But…" I finally get out.

"Wear the dress, little monster," he says without looking up. "I'm looking forward to fucking you in it."

EIGHTEEN

HER

"Holy fucking shit!" Dayne exclaims as soon as I step back from the phone I'm FaceTiming him on so he can see the dress in its entirety.

"Right!" I blurt. "It's way too much. I can't wear this. I never should have bought it."

My bestie laughs, and my irritation softens at the way the tension leaves his eyes. When he first came on, he was so stiff, concern for me tightening his shoulders and neck. Now that loosens, leaves a bit, and I know he's checked out every part of my body he can see – which in this dress is practically all of it, and is relieved to see no bruises.

Although I've been convincing him I'm fine, he knows me well enough to know I'd lie about it. Because if he even suspected I was being abused, he'd risk everything to come and get me, and I wouldn't put him in that position.

"Look, I need you to concentrate," I whisper as my eyes flick to the closed door. I'm hiding in my bathroom, building up the courage to go downstairs so Varius and I and his *entire fucking family* can finally drive to the venue for the party. I have about ten minutes until we're supposed to go, and I need this answered in honest truth so I don't chicken out and grab another dress to wear. The gods only know what punishment that would bring.

Taking a deep breath, I hiss, "Let me know if you can see my vagina when I walk." Varius doesn't want me wearing any underwear, but to hel if I'm going to listen to *that* in a room full of some of the most powerful people in the world if my coochie flashes every time I move.

I take a few small steps towards the phone, then turn and shuffle perpendicular to it.

"Don't worry," Dayne laughs. "Walk like that, and I assure you no one is going to look at your *vulva*."

I roll my eyes at his correction of my terminology. Vulva just doesn't sound as fun to say.

"They'll be too busy trying to figure out if you're doing a penguin impression or if you've received a lobotomy."

"Fuck off."

"Walk properly, Micha."

Inhaling sharply, I take a step forward that feels like I'm jumping across the damn moon. His laughter increases, a soft melody given the low volume of the phone. "Not quite regular, but at least it isn't a waddle," he says. "Just walk. Don't think about it."

I pace around the bathroom, my gait still awkward as all hel. "I can't stop thinking about it, Dayne. Look at me. This dress is ridiculous. I kid you not, I just spent an hour on the toilet so I could make sure I wouldn't have to take a shit at the party. I wipe well. I know I wipe well. I check every time, but I'm still worried people will see shit or something stuck to me if I go in this thing."

My face heats in horror at the idea.

He, on the other hand, laughs his ass off.

"Stop laughing at me!"

He does not.

It doesn't even wane.

A slow smile spreads across my lips as I watch him howl. Tears fall down his cheeks, and it takes him a few moments before he calms down enough to wipe them away. "Why'd you even buy that one if you're that worried about it?"

My cheeks heat as I glance away from the eyes that can read me so well. I shrug. "Not for the party. Just to, like, hide in my closet."

"You brought it to play hide and seek with Varius?" he teases.

"No!" I groan. "Maybe. I don't fucking know. It's just... there's this *pull* to him. Like...I want to maybe try to make this work?" A burning heat creeps down my neck. "Is that dumb? I mean it's Varius fucking Shadow. He's a monster." I wave at the phone. "You've heard the stories. He sentences kids to die."

"Does he?"

I stare at him. "Of course he does. Everyone knows it doesn't matter how old you are. You cross him, and you're dead."

He looks at me pointedly, silently communicating that the stories surrounding us are just as bad.

"That's different."

"You don't know it is."

I snort. "Come on, it's *Varius*. The guy practically oozes 'I will kill your entire family and your puppies.'" I snap my fingers as I properly get into my pacing now. "He said if anyone looked at me, he'd cut out their eyes! And the eyes of their family. And friends. That includes babies. The man's A-okay with blinding babies."

He gives me a you're-being-dramatic-again look.

"And he told me himself he'll never love me. Not that I want him to love me – Not that I'm ever going to love him. I couldn't. But like...I don't know. Maybe we can have one of those content marriages? Where it's not fully cold on both sides? Where he doesn't skip the whole divorce thing and murder me instead when he finally gets tired of me?"

He stills. "Are you worried about that?"

"Uh, yeah!" Seeing the sharpness of his eyes, I shake my head. "Well, no. Not at the moment. But it *could* happen. Dayne, I'm just a womb. There's no safety net in that."

"But you think getting him to what, fall in love with you will?"

I don't say anything.

His eyes soften. "Micha...a man like Varius, even if he did fall in love with you...that might honestly be worse. If you did *anything* to make him mistrust you, he'd punish you harder for not just turning against him but hurting him. I wouldn't advise it."

"But..." I swallow down the words even as they slam into me, triggered by his. A truth I can no longer pretend doesn't exist. About how my heart aches for him. How the cold mafia boss sometimes reminds me of the kids we save. The ones with their backs to the world. Their fists up. Their hearts locked away so no one they love can ever hurt them again. How sometimes Varius makes me feel like I'm all that matters. How he makes me feel...whole. Like I was missing this giant fucking piece of myself and that piece was him.

"Yes?" Dayne prompts softly.

I shake my head. Such thoughts are fucking ridiculous. I don't even like him. Not really. "Nothing. You're right. So we all good or should I change?"

He stares at me for a moment longer. Then he accepts my change of subject. "You're all clear. That sash thing or whatever it is hangs right in front of it even as you move. I saw nothing."

"Great." I breathe out in relief. Only to instantly regret it as I realize I now have to wear it. In public. Where my sister and father and two brothers will be attending.

"Breathe, Micha. You look hot. I'll see you later."

He ends the call, and I take another deep breath. After reaching for my phone, balanced on the sink and the wall, I head into my bedroom. The door to the hall opens just as I toss my phone onto the bed, not taking a purse with me tonight.

"I'm ready. I was just coming out," I say as I see Varius enter in my peripheral. I turn towards him with a small smile. Then stop, my eyes dropping to what's in his hand. My heart racing, I try, "We're going to be late."

But I know he didn't bring the black fox tail butt plug for a quickie. He knows I know that, but that doesn't stop the wolfish smile from curling his lips as he shakes his head.

"Bend over."

"I'm not wearing that."

His eyes dip to my hips, then back up to me. Tossing the tail on my bed, he holds up his other hand. It's just a regular black plug in that palm. No tail for anyone to see.

"For listening about not wearing underwear, I'll let you wear this one," he says.

My mouth drops open as my eyes dart to the tail. If that was the punishment for not listening about the underwear, what the hel would've happened if I'd changed my dress?

"Now bend over before we're late."

"It needs lube," I try pathetically.

He pulls out a bottle from his pocket.

I stare at him.

He stares at me, then glances at the tail.

Pivoting fast, I turn towards the bed. Bending in half, I rest my elbows on the soft mattress. He steps in behind me. Drags my dress up slowly until my ass is bare. At the sound of the plastic bottle being squeezed, my breath catches in anticipation.

It's cold, and I jump, but a strong hand on my hip holds me still. I roll my lip in as he stretches me, both my nipples tingling from a jolt of arousal. The base presses against my ass, fully seated, and I spasm around it.

His fingers trail lower, sliding through the lips of my pussy but not going in. Back and forth. Back and forth, he continues to pet me until I get used to the sensation of my ass being filled. A moan starts to build in my throat. Then escapes on a breathy whimper.

Varius presses a finger in, and it feels so godsdamn tight with the plug already filling me from the back. He growls as he pushes deeper into me. Then he withdraws and moves back from the bed, giving me space to stand. I turn around on numb legs, teetering in my four-inch stilettos. Strappy and black, they seem like a terrible decision all of a sudden.

He grabs me around the waist, holding me up until I find my balance. His other hand raised, he licks the finger that was just inside me. My cheeks hot, I step back from him and smooth out my dress. Then we head out of my room, no longer touching.

We enter the living room just as Enoch and Ezriel come down the stairs, wearing white tuxedo jackets with black lapels and pocket liners and black pants. I start to duck behind Varius' bulk, feeling naked, but then I notice one of them has a new haircut.

Whereas his twin's ginger hair is the same as before – cut short on the sides and ruffled at the top where it's a bit longer, he's buzzed most of it off, leaving only a mohawk… and four lines of hair in the shape of the arms and legs of a gecko gripping his head. My mouth falls open as my eyes light up.

"That's fucking metal," I say as I step out from behind Varius to get a better look. He grins at me as he ducks his head.

"Thank you," the other brother says. "I did it myself."

I glance at him. "You did a bitchin' job." I ran a hand over my shaved head. "Maybe I should grow mine out to let you have a go at it."

He inclines his head as his twin straightens. "I would be honored."

I turn to Varius, only to find he's already walked off, his back disappearing down the hall as he heads outside.

"Shall we?" Gecko Head asks as he offers an arm.

I smile at him, my neck burning only slightly as I recall what I'm wearing. But neither of the brothers have looked anywhere but at my face, so I nod and breathe and thread my arm through his.

"This is definitely going to make it easier for me to tell you two apart," I say as we walk. "Which one are you?"

He grins. "Enoch, m'lady."

To my slight disappointment, we don't ride with Enoch and Ezriel. They ride with Rudy, Leno, and his dog Krypto while Varius and I climb into the backseat of another car. Maddox and Khalid are already inside it, the former at the wheel. Maddox places his arm on the passenger seat as he turns around and reverses. His eyes find mine, dip low and then back up again.

"Looking like a babe," Maddox sings, making me blush. "A babe with the power."

My brow furrows. "What power?"

"Power of voodoo."

I grin. "Voodoo?"

"You do."

I laugh as he turns back around and peels off down the drive, having completed his three point turn. "You are way too young to have watched *Labyrinth*."

"No one's too young for that classic." Raising his arm, he

jiggles it, and I notice his shirt is white and loose, similar to the one David Bowie wore in the movie.

Excited, I lean forward between the seats to try to get a better look at his outfit. "Holy shit, you look amazing. All you're missing is the hair."

"Blame Varius. He vetoed the wig."

"Varius!" I tease as I move back in my seat, but he does not engage at all.

"Said he didn't want me to upstage his lovely fiancee."

A warmth spreads through me even though I know he's teasing about Varius having called me lovely. Even though Dayne's advice to keep my walls up around him whispers in my skull. Ignoring my bestie, I glance at Varius. He doesn't look at me, his eyes on his phone, but I knew it wouldn't be easy wooing him. No, it would be like pulling fucking teeth.

"So, Micha," Maddox says, pulling my attention back up front as he starts drumming his hands on the wheel. "I hear you have a sister."

My eyes narrow, my defenses up quick. "She's sixteen," I growl.

He might be the youngest of the Shadow brothers, but he's still an adult and closer to my age than hers.

"Nah, not like that." I relax a little bit but not much. "I'm interested in her demon summoning ability," he continues. "Mind introducing us tonight?"

I study him warily, but he's twenty-two and a Shadow. He's also very desirable considering his innate ability to shapeshift. Stefaan would die if he could get those genes in our family tree. Just think of what an assassin could do with that power.

Sourly, I say, "Oh, I'm sure you'll meet her with no help from me."

He shakes his head. "Lie, Micha. Say you'll introduce me. That way you can call in a favor later."

I blink in surprise, but I'm not dumb enough to hesitate.

"I'll introduce you," I say.

He laughs. "Good gi –" He suddenly jerks in his seat, his body twisting as he yelps. Khalid casually reaches over and grabs the wheel, keeping the car straight. I stare at him, then at Varius, suddenly clocking him moving as he settles back in his seat.

"Um, what just happened?"

"The fucker stabbed me," Maddox grumbles. White light emits from the front, a soft glow to tell me he wasn't cut too deep. Probably just a flesh wound.

"You know better than to tease him," Khalid says as he releases the wheel back into his brother's care.

"Tease..." I start, but then it dawns as Varius' hand lays claim to my thigh.

Maddox almost called me a good girl... A dumb-as-fuck grin spreading across my lips, I grab Varius' hand in mine. He starts to pull away, but I thread our fingers and hold him there. I don't look at him, knowing he will fly away, back inside those walls, if I do. Instead, I turn to stare out the car window, that wide-as-fuck grin still on my lips.

As the Floridian landscape passes outside the window in a blur of lights, Varius' hand slowly relaxes beneath mine.

And yet again, my world shifts...

NINETEEN

HIM

When we park in front of our destination, a gated estate in the Markham Woods Corridor, I pull my hand away from Micha, then dig the jewelry box out of my jacket pocket.

"Here," I say, tossing it to her as Maddox opens my car door. She catches it, and I step out, flexing my fingers down by my side, getting used to the feel of her absence.

"So romantic," Maddox says. "Can't wait to see what you do for Valentine's Day."

Ignoring him, I turn to the car that's pulled up behind us. Rudy's sitting in the driver's seat, a small smile on his face. Given his innate ability to see the darkest fears of those he meets, driving is one of his favorite pastimes. The distances enforced by the road are enough to keep other's nightmares at bay – the only peace he ever gets outside of our house.

He smiles at me, telling me he'll be okay tonight, and I turn from him with a growing knot in my stomach. Because I wasn't thinking about how he'd fare in a crowded room. I was wondering if he was the traitor and how I would deal with him if he was. Even Khalid, with all of his training and skill, would be hard pressed to kill our brother if he wanted to fight back.

But Rudy has a weakness only I know. He's fucking Aleric's second, the underboss of the Blood Fangs. So if I grabbed Vlad first, my little brother would offer up his own life to save him. Because when Rudy loves, he loves in its entirety. Regardless of their faults. Regardless if that love is returned. He's just too damn pure like that.

Fuck. I don't want it to be him.

The car door opens, and all my senses snap to Micha. I don't turn my head to her, but I watch her in my peripheral. My fingers tingle with the phantom feel of her hand on mine, insisting I reach over and touch her somewhere, to find that comfort only she can give.

Pressing my hand to my thigh, I turn for the house.

"Did your mom pick it out?" Micha asks as she steps up beside me, holding out her hand to stare at the diamond ring.

My eyes narrow. "No."

"Oh. Is it a family heirloom then?"

"No."

When she doesn't ask another question, clearly fucking baffled what the other choice could be, my lips tighten and my pace increases.

Before we make it to the line of pillars at the front of the house, both of the double doors open. A woman dressed in a dark-blue gown invites us in. Diamonds and sapphires hang from her neck and ears. Gold bands dangle from her wrists, and more jewels adorn half of her fingers. Stefaan Black clearly wishes to make an impression – dressing his staff in attire fit for a queen.

As soon as my shoes touch down on the black-and-white marble inside, Stefaan and Mother enter from the far side of the room, walking through the archway beneath the double stairs. Micha slips from my side to slightly behind me as my brothers fan out in the great hall. Maddox picks something up off one of the fancy side tables. The whole place screams of pompous fanfare, so if he breaks something, he's paying for it. If he steals it, he better not get fucking caught.

"Varius," Stefaan says in greeting as they stop in front of us.

I incline my head at him. "Stefaan."

"I hope my daughter has been serving you well."

"She's learning."

A muttered, "Says the fucking neanderthal," is said so quietly at my back, I almost miss it even with my enhanced hearing.

My fingers twitch as a warmth spreads from them to my chest. Only to immediately go cold as Stefaan's eyes finally start to shift to his daughter, a darted look of aggression. I move forward, forcing his attention back on me as anger flares deep in my veins. If he wasn't her blood, I'd fucking cut him down for that. No one gets to discipline my fiancee but me.

When we get to the party room – a regal living room decorated with "Congratulations on the engagement" tat strung all about the godsdamn place, I glance at my mother, a silent demand she takes Micha away from us. If Stefaan tries to look at her like that again, I'm liable to kill him.

She steps in smoothly, having been the one to teach us all to talk this way. By using the slightest of expressions that you can't even identify while looking in a mirror.

As Micha comes out from behind me, she steps in close, and her hand brushes against mine. Even though she does not look at me, does not acknowledge me at all, I feel my blood start to cool. I watch her in my peripheral as she follows Mother to a group of women.

The rest of my brothers fan out, mingling with the guests

who are already here. Maddox grabs a glass of champagne from one of the waitresses milling about and pretends not to notice how everyone tries to avoid him. No one wants him to study them enough to be able to shapeshift into them. Spotting Uncle Myers and cousin Vinny in the crowd, he heads towards them, his glass to his lips.

Rudy lingers at the edge of the room, but Talon, who is already here, sees him and makes his way over, two women by his side. I want to intervene before T reaches our brother, knowing Rudy is too polite to decline their company, but I also want to see who he talks to. Who he might be in bed with. Who he's working with if he is the traitor. So I don't go to his rescue, turning the surface of my attention back to Micha's father.

"Look at my fiancee like that again," I say, "and I'll cut out your eyes."

"My apologies. I –"

"Your claim of territory has gone well," I cut in. I do not care to hear his apologies; they mean nothing to me. If he fails, he loses his eyes; simple as that.

He hesitates for a second, then, "Thanks to your support." Humble right off bat. That means he wants something.

Good. I want something too, and I have way more power to negotiate than he does.

"You should deal with the Mad Hatters before they cause trouble," I say casually.

He shakes his head. "They won't. We have reached an agreement given our different businesses."

A waitress moves over to us, and I grab one of the Ricks on her tray. Stefaan's eyes widen as I toss the vial to him. "You could expand."

"The Mattos twins don't sell to non-established Families."

"I assure you, we are well established."

His mouth going slack, he glances down at the vial of blue liquid in his hand. My gaze roams around the crowd as

I give him time to think it through, what a war with the Mad Hatters will mean – going back on his honored word, potentially losing good men. But also gaining the backing of this Family even if I never marry his daughter.

A low growl builds in my throat, but I shake it off before it can sound. If she can't get pregnant, then there's no point keeping her. But that thought, for some unknown reason, only makes me more irritable.

"What would your cut be?" Stefaan Black asks, pulling my attention back to him.

"Fifty grand to set you up with the twins. Then a forty percent cut."

He mulls it over before he counters, "Seventy upfront and thirty percent."

"Thirty-five."

"With the seventy?"

I nod. He could get a better rate elsewhere. He has the men and the reputation for getting things done. Hel, he could probably approach the twins himself in a few years. But his is a new gang, and he wants the prestige and open doors the Shadow name can give him.

After a moment, he gestures over one of the waitresses, all of whom are dressed in black jumpsuits with white Gucci belts. She glides over, her movements too controlled to be anything other than a fighter, and I like that he's doubled the staff as the security. It gives the place a much more sophisticated and laid-back feel than having armed goons mulling around.

When he reaches for a champagne glass, Khalid does the same. My brother offers it to me, having just checked it for poison with his magic – a subtle spell he learned long ago so as to not insult the men I go into business with.

I take it from him and lift it towards Stefaan.

"To new beginnings," he says.

We drink, then I move away, accepting congratulations

from one of my capos while my attention stays on Rudy. He's looking pale beneath his smile, beneath the glass of champagne raised to his lips. There's a glimmer of sweat beneath his red curly hair as he talks to three others, and I can smell the sickly sweetness of his terror. Instinctively, I let a crack open in my defenses and push out one of my greatest fears – line dancing goats.

His head whips to me. A smile lights his face even as my stomach drops and I want to down a whole bottle of helfire to get rid of the image now in my head. Goats are fucking scary on their own with their demonic eyes. If they ever become organized enough to line dance? Ain't no fucking way humanity survives.

But Rudy likes goats for some bizarre reason. The freak.

He tips an imaginary hat to me, and a smile twitches at my lips. He can't be the traitor with the genuineness of his relief, with the thankfulness in his eyes. Staring at him, I feel disgusted with myself that I ever thought he could be.

But that doesn't stop me from moving to the next brother on my list of suspects. One of them stabbed me in the back, wants me dead, and I need to find out who it is before they try to finish the job. Because they will – all of my kin are fucking stubborn like that.

"Varius!" Uncle Myers says as he approaches along with Maddox and cousin Vinny. He clasps one hand on my left shoulder, champagne in his other hand. "Congratulations on the engagement. It's almost been two weeks." He sighs as he releases me and takes a drink. "Ah! How romantic would it be if you find out she's pregnant on Valentine's Day?"

Maddox snorts. "Bro's idea of being romantic is probably throwing a bouquet at her face and calling it done."

Our cousin laughs. "Did you really just chuck the ring at her?"

When I don't give them a response, Maddox deepens his voice to mock mine. "What difference does it make? We're already engaged."

Uncle Myers jumps in, mimicking his voice to be exactly like mine with his magic – more experienced than Maddox. "What's the point of being romantic when she can't say no? I already own her."

"Yeah. Don't even need any foreplay," Vinny adds, and I want to smack the lot of them. But doing anything will just get this trio riled, so my face stays flat, without any emotion whatsoever.

Maddox nods sagely. "I've never heard her scream."

"There's a silence ward in my room," I point out.

"You were in the woods with her all night last night, and there wasn't *one* scream," he counters.

My eyes narrow minutely, but I can't exactly tell him I was watching over her while she slept. Although she was dumb enough to fall asleep without taking any precautions, and by all means, that should've been her problem alone, I couldn't just leave her out there with a traitor somewhere on the premises. But revealing that will do nothing but cause Maddox, with his damn psych degree, to ask a million questions I don't want to answer.

"Khalid, you were there when he fucked her the first time. Did she scream?"

He nods, and my chest puffs out. *Fuckers.*

"Loudly," Khalid affirms, "but it was someone else's name."

Uncle Myers spits his drink everywhere. Vinny laughs his balls off, and my face flattens as Maddox shouts, "She did what?"

A few heads turn towards us, including hers. She looks at me curiously, and the urge to take her in front of everyone so they can hear just how well she screams has me itching to go to her.

"She was playing a joke," I say. I don't want to mention Dayne being there at all. Don't want to reveal he had a tracker on her. Slights like that can't be ignored when you're a Boss with as many targets on your back as I have. Any show of weakness will have traitors crawling out of the woodwork, and Khalid already killed nearly half of our men only a few years ago due to an attempted coup. The capos in this room have been promoted because of their loyalty, but clearly not all of them are that loyal. My eyes fall to Lincoln as he talks with another capo at the far side of the room.

Maddox whistles. "I wonder if her sister is just as good a liar."

Vinny snorts. Uncle Myers full-on laughs.

I turn my head to him and deadpan, "You can find out during your engagement."

"Hey!" He backpedals, holding up both his hands. "That's not funny. I'm too young for that shit. Also, she's sixteen."

"A marriageable age in more than half the states," I say seriously. "More if you can get her pregnant."

His eyes widen in horror, and I smile on the inside. As disgusting as those laws are, I enjoy riling the little shit up.

He backs up further, shaking his head. Then turns and leaves entirely. Someone calls Uncle Myers away, leaving Vinny and I alone.

My cousin punches me lightly in the left shoulder. "How have you been anyway? I haven't seen you in over a year." About a month after I nearly died. "You heal okay?"

"Yeah."

"You ever remember anything about the attack?"

"I've started to."

"Oh yeah? Anything to help you track him down? Or her?"

My skin prickles, the paranoia of his questions irritating me. I stare at him, a promise of pain in my eyes, psyching him out in case he is the traitor. A cousin rather than a brother... I don't know if that's better or worse. Myers is like a fucking father to us. Killing his only son would wreck him.

"Yes," I say, holding his gaze. "And *he* won't be around for long."

His smile drops ever so slightly. There's a flair of fear in the catch of his breath, and my heart stops for the barest of seconds. Lincoln's wife supposedly told Vinny about his sins...meaning Lincoln might be nothing but a patsy, thrown under the bus by a man who is getting worried he needs someone to accuse. To point the finger at before the noose tightens around his own neck.

Keeping my composure, wanting more evidence than just my fucking paranoia, I set my glass down on the tray of a passing waitress, then grab a couple Ricks. I toss them at my cousin. "Enjoy the evening, Vinny," I say deathly calm. "Nights like this...they're to be remembered."

He forces his smile up as he pockets the vials, but his hands shake. His face pales. "In that case, I'm going to go find Alexis."

Refusing to hold my gaze, he hurries off in her direction. I watch him and his girlfriend for a moment, their heads low as they talk, stress emitting from his pores. Will he sneak off and do a runner with her now that he thinks I'm onto him? Or am I just seeing monsters that aren't there?

"Do you know where Vinny was that night?" I ask the reaper.

He steps up beside me, his lips tight, his eyes dark. "At his office in North Carolina."

"Any witnesses?"

"His secretary. Alexis. Jason Terry – his second. He was on call with him for most of the night."

People who know him, who might give their loyalty to him rather than their abomination of a Boss.

"On camera?" I ask.

Khalid nods.

"Get the tape to Talon and see if it's been messed with."

he hesitates. "Have you cleared him?"

My body stills. "Have you not?" Although Khalid seemed certain Lincoln was the traitor in the gym, I shouldn't be surprised he's been looking into our brothers as well. He is a reaper, and he doesn't have the luxury of ignoring what will hurt to deal with.

"I haven't found anything to convict him," he answers tightly.

So no.

Fuck.

Turning my head, I search the crowd for Lincoln. He's standing beside his wife, his back to the wall, one hand in his pocket, his eyes darting everywhere. Tension rolls off his shoulders like an approaching storm despite his attempt to look casual. He looks guilty as all hel.

But now so does Vinny, and I trust him more...

My teeth clench. I'm tired of this fucking puzzle. Turning to Khalid, I keep my voice low. "My memories got triggered when I walked through that ward and it hit me in the back in the same place I got stabbed. If I grab Louise" –a healer almost on par with Mother– "will you stab me?"

His eyes sharpen, curses clearly firing off inside his skull. But he doesn't say no.

Sending chills running down my back, he nods.

TWENTY

HER

"Fucking neanderthal," I mutter as I finally find myself alone. I've barely been able to concentrate on those I've been meeting and having conversations with because I've been distracted by the damn plug up my ass. I'm feeling way too hot with it in there, and every time Varius moves a hand into his pocket, I tense, expecting a vibration. I don't even know if butt plugs can vibrate, but the potential has me on edge.

And with every passing minute, I'm getting more and more irritated that the bastard *hasn't done it.*

Like, is he not thinking about me at all?

You don't even know if it vibrates, Micha.

I look down at the diamond ring, trying to find comfort in its presence, in its security that I matter. But he didn't even pick it out himself. Otherwise, he would have said. He hasn't once looked at me in the hour we've been here, and this damn party is filled with better dressed, better behaved *whores.*

Now you're just being an ass, Micha.

Fuck off, conscious. Whores. Whores. Whores. Whores. Whores.

Blue-haired Double Ds over there, even though she is the wife of one of the capos, would absolutely get down on her knees for him right here, right now. In this crowded room. With her husband watching. As would Blonde Hair Model and Dressed Even Sluttier Than I Am Vixen.

Gods, he's turning me into such a bitch.

Yet another reason why he's an ass. I'm a *nice person.* Like, seriously nice; not like one of those "nice guy" rapists who –

The back of my left hand suddenly burns in heartless mockery, and I'm jolted out of my thoughts. My throat tight, I drop my eyes from the ring to the stag tattoo right below it. A *nice person* wouldn't have hurt that little girl. A *nice person* wouldn't have ever taken the job. Wouldn't have begged her father to turn her into an assassin just so she wouldn't have to marry. A *nice person* would've sacrificed her own life rather than choosing to take the lives of others. I might save a few kids here and there, but there are just as many that I don't.

Kids that don't wake up after I pull the trigger because my aim was off. Those are my failures. My sins.

Clenching my hand into a fist, I drop it.

But just as I start to convince myself that maybe I don't deserve a happily ever after, I hear, "Hey, giiiirl, congrats on your engagement!"

My eyes light up as I spin towards Dayne. He is my happily ever after and the first to tell me the world doesn't care about what you 'deserve,' only what you will make of it. So with my eyes on him, I shake away the dark thoughts that were trying to claw me down.

He wiggles his eyebrows as he approaches, reminding

me I owe him a punch to the face. Just as I start to raise an arm though, I catch Sau's stern gaze as she talks to someone across the room.

Dear fucking gods, it's like she has radar for this shit.

Lowering my arm, I smile at him sweetly. "Step a bit to the right so I can hit you without Sau seeing."

He laughs and steps to the left. The fucker.

I smile innocently at Sau. She raises an eyebrow slightly, a look of amusement on her face, but I'm not foolish enough to think I'm not being told off. My mother was Asian, and I've long learned that smiles mean *nothing*.

Placing my hands demurely in front of me, I look at my bestie. "How has everyone been?" I ask as I incline my head at him, ladylike as Sau taught. Given he's my only friend though, he knows by 'everyone,' I mean the kid I shot in the head a couple weeks ago. Perhaps those dark thoughts, that guilt hasn't quite left me.

"Good." He cocks his head to the side, his smile slipping a bit. "Well, you know."

Yeah...I know. My eyes flick back to Varius as he walks across the room.

Consumed by pain and betrayal, they become terrified of being hurt again, so they survive the only way they know how – by shutting everything and everyone out. Accepting a hand here and there, only to fall even further back behind their walls, thinking they're getting too soft. Too vulnerable to survive.

"They still talking?" I ask softly as I look back at Dayne.

"Single syllables."

Better than some. Worse than others. My heart aches for him, hoping he is stubborn enough to turn out stronger. But only time will tell if that little boy survives what happened to him or suffers through it until he takes his own life.

"And how about you?" Dayne asks. "You planning any vacations soon? Maybe for Valentine's Day?" AKA: do you want to run away with me?

My smile turns soft as I touch his arm. "Nothing yet." *Even if I'm irritated with him right now.*

It probably doesn't even vibrate, Micha!

Yeah, well, a fucking look every now and then don't cost nothing!

Dayne stares at me as I argue with myself, seeing deeper than my words. I glance away just as his eyes widen.

"Micha," he starts, his voice low in warning.

I shake my head. "Don't. Please, Dayne. I need to believe in something or I'm going to go mad just being his *womb.*"

His jaw tightens as he struggles with wanting to tell me something – that I'm being an idiot. That a monster like Varius isn't capable of love. Real love. That all he could ever give me is a twisted concept of it that will leave me broken and bleeding, how I am such a fucking *fool* to even wish for otherwise.

In the end, he nods sharply. "Just stay safe, Micha."

Before I can answer, Maddox barges over, cutting right between us, and it's only then I realize I still have a hand on Dayne. Or *had* before I was so rudely forced to remove it. But where I scowl at Maddox, my bestie laughs.

"Noted," he says, holding up both his hands as he takes an exaggerated step back.

I look at him like he's an idiot, wondering what the fuck just happened, but Maddox laughs and says, "I like you." He looks him up and down as he wraps an arm around my shoulders and pulls me a step back. "So was it you she called as she…you know…" He wiggles his eyebrows as my ears burn. "Pretended to come all over my brother's cock?"

"Maddox!" I hiss, throwing an elbow into him, not giving a damn that it's not very ladylike. Some people just deserve to be hit, and this little shit is definitely one of them.

He gasps as my elbow connects with his solar plexus. His arm leaves me as I twist away, and he leans forward on a groan. "Shit, Micha. Don't go giving me a boner with your moves, or Varius will cut it off."

"You would absolutely deserve it."

"*Haaarsh.*" He lifts his head to look at me. "And here I was doing a good deed by saving your friend from losing his."

"What?"

But my confusion quickly gives way to understanding as I recall what Maddox did as soon as he arrived. He forced Dayne and I apart.

"The fucking neanderthal," I hiss, lowering my voice so no one around us can hear. "Varius can't be jealous of me merely touching someone."

Maddox cocks his head to the side. "Eh, less jealousy and more simply doing what's expected from a Boss. You're his, Micha. So don't go touching other guys unless you want them dead."

My heart rate spikes for my friend. "He's gay," I blurt.

Maddox lifts a brow as he looks him up and down again. His eyes settle back on Dayne's face. "You like redheads?"

"I'm more of a personality kind of guy."

"Ah. Pity. Rudy's personality sucks."

"Rudy is the best one out of the lot of you," I cut in. He's sweet. He brings his plates to the sink and cleans up after himself. Plus, I caught him saving a spider from a cobweb the other day. He spent thirty minutes cleaning its legs with a pair of chopsticks, then set it up in a new corner inside the house.

Maddox snorts. "The boy can't even commit murder."

I start to tell him that doesn't matter, but really? It kind of does in our way of life. Besides, there's just something really hot about a man willing to get his hands bloody.

Especially if he does it while wearing a button-up shirt.

With the sleeves rolled up.

His tie loose.

First few buttons on his shirt undone...

Mmmm.

Fuck. I shift on my feet, growing more and more aware of the plug in my ass. My cheeks growing hot, I glance at Varius again. My heart drops like a stone. He's talking to a gorgeous lady with dark hair pulled into a bun atop her head. He leans in and whispers something in her ear. His hand is on her arm. He's touching her. In public.

She's classy, dressed in black, and my eyes narrow as I wonder if she's a gold digger. Not that I have an issue with them; you can't tell women their worth is only ever on their back and then get mad when that's exactly what they try to do, but she is way too fucking close to my fiance. Way closer than Dayne and I was. I have half a mind to go force them apart. See how he likes it.

A low growl in my throat, I beeline straight for them. Sau breaks off from the people she's talking to, casually gliding in my direction, still staying the epitome of grace as she flits from one group to the next with the perfect smile, but I know she's coming for me. I know she's going to stop me, so I pick up my pace, ignoring people trying to talk to me, and make sure I reach him before she does.

My chest heaving, I stop beside my fiance. "Varius," I say sweetly as I grab his wrist. "Come dance with me."

He glances down at me, not moving, and my heart jumps into my throat as I stare up at him, so painfully aware that this classy-ass bitch is about to witness his rejection of me. But what did I possibly think was going to happen? He's Varius fucking Shadow. Of course he won't want to dance or care about making me look like an insecure fool. *No. No, he cares at least a little. He won't –*

"Leave us, Micha."

My heart tumbles into my stomach, where it gets sloshed around in waves of acid, only to tragically drown.

I drop my arm, feeling sick. But that's soon washed away

by anger. Pivoting, I storm off to the bathroom so I can take out this damn butt plug, wash off his fucking claim. I pass Dayne, and he looks at me sympathetically, but I don't stop. Don't listen to his, "I told you so," even though he's too sweet to actually say it.

Yanking the door to the bathroom open, I step inside and lock it behind me. "Fucking asshole," I mutter as I yank my dress up, bunching it around my waist. If he doesn't want to acknowledge me at all while he touches others, then he sure as hel doesn't get the pleasure of my submission.

Reaching between my legs, I grope for the plug, but just as my fingers grip the base of it, it vibrates.

Bzzzzz.

Shock flows through me as I freeze. The toy stops too.

Bzz. A short pulse rips through me, and my knees knock together as I reach for the sink.

Bzzzzz.

My dress falls back down to the floor as my ass clenches around the toy. My breath escapes as I realize he's thinking about me.

Bzz.

Maybe I interrupted something secretly important? He is a Boss, and although tonight is a time of celebration, all of his capos are here. Shop talk would nearly be impossible for a man like him to avoid.

Bzz. Bzz. Bzzzzz.

I groan into the crook of my arm as my other hand tightens around the sink. Sagging against it, I clench my eyes shut. Or am I just being stupid? Looking into things that aren't real? Letting him lead me on because I want so badly to believe that my life with him won't just be one of misery?

Bzzzzz. Bzzzzz.

Perhaps this is just a gift to appease me while he goes and fucks that lady. It's not like a man of his station has to be monogamous. Perhaps –

Bzz. Bzz. Bzz. Bzz. Bzzzzz.

My eyes snap open as I recognize that sequence. That's morse code for the number four. He's talking to me through the fucking toy. He wouldn't do that if he was with another person, right?

No. He wouldn't. I might not know much about him, but I do know that if he was fucking someone, she would have *all* of his attention. And right now, that attention is on *me.*

My arousal starts to build, heightened by the feel of his presence despite the closed door between us. But perhaps that is what he needs in a crowded room – an illusion of separation. A way to hide his feelings so others can't see. Those might all be allies out there, but his allies have a way of often turning traitor.

Biting my lip, I concentrate on the buzzes of the toy so I can work out what he's trying to tell me.

Bzzzzz. Bzzzzz. M…

Bzz. E…

My eyes snap open.

Cum 4 me.

A low moan in my throat, I slide a hand to my hip and slowly start pulling up my dress.

"Cum for me, little monster. I want to smell your pussy the next time you ask me to dance."

TWENTY-ONE

HIM

One hand in my pocket, the other on the low of her back, I lead Louise towards the stairs. People glance at us, hushed whispers on their lips just waiting to fall when we're no longer around to hear them. Mother moves towards Stefaan, no doubt to soothe any concerns he has about me taking a mistress at my own engagement party. Though I doubt he cares. As long as I introduce him to the twins and marry his daughter, he'd probably lie to her for me about where I've been.

My dislike of him grows, but I shove it down. It's not like I am really any better, leaving her here to deal with the judgment of not being good enough to hold my attention. Or worse, the pity that she can't do anything to stop me from taking as many women as I want. Whenever I want.

My finger taps on my screen hidden inside my pocket, controlling the vibrations of her toy. It's a poor apology for what she'll walk out to, but it's the only one I can give her.

No one can know what we're about to do. If Vinny finds out I still don't know what actually happened that night, he will have the upper hand. He could plant whatever evidence he wanted, frame those closest to me. And if the traitor is one of my brothers instead, they could send a lackey up to interrupt Louise from healing me in time to save me. Khalid will have to nearly kill me to replicate what happened that night; Mother said the blade almost scraped my heart. Even though the lackey would undoubtedly die in the fight with Khalid, all they'd need to do is buy a few minutes for me to bleed out.

So despite the tightness in my chest about hurting Micha, I don't take my hand off Louise as I guide her up the spiral metal stairs. We enter a bedroom on the second floor. The door shuts behind us, and I drop my hand immediately.

Louise and I stay by the door as Khalid heads forward and strips the sheet off the king-sized bed. He tosses the black fabric to Louise, and she bundles it in her arms. The air crackles with dark magic as my brother calls upon his shadows. He wraps them around the base of everything in this room, stripping it bare and taking it all into the Plane of Monsters. Louise presses her back to the door, the pulse at her neck beating erratically. One touch of the shadows, and she can be pulled into a nightmarish world where she will be ripped apart by claws and fangs, where only a Shadow can survive.

When nothing but a cold floor remains, Khalid releases his magic and turns to us. He holds out his hand, and Louise hesitates a moment, her back still to the door, her breathing panicked. Inhaling an attempt at control, she pushes away from me and slowly walks towards my brother.

I pull out my phone and look at the app connecting me to my little monster. I want to stay with her as she comes, as she slides her fingers between her lips and uses her palm to apply the pressure she needs. One of these days, I will get her to orgasm from my dick alone, but for now I need to deal with this.

After setting the app up so the vibration is continuous, I lock the phone, then slip it into my pocket as Louise returns to my side, the sheet now spread out on the floor. Leaving my blood for another witch to collect and use would be suicide. They might not be able to kill me exactly like Khalid does his targets, adding my DNA to a soul doll that looks exactly like me, but there are many dark spells that will kill someone just as quickly. So I start to strip.

Louise turns away from me, her face now to the wall, giving me privacy despite the looks I've seen her give me over the years. It is a reaction I don't understand, and it makes my hairs rise, wondering if an attack is imminent. If she's turning away from a potential explosion.

"In respect to Micha," she says, calming my paranoia. I stare at her for a moment, reading the truth of her words in the calm beat of her heart and the smell of her slight arousal that she's fighting.

My respect for her grows, and I continue to shrug off my suit jacket. I let it hit the floor as I undo the chest holsters holding my guns, one on each side. The knife holsters. My shirt. My shoes. I lay my pants down gently, taking care of the phone inside them. My fingers itch to pull it out and check the app, to draw Micha to me one last time before I put my life on the line.

But I don't.

I will see her soon.

If I can't trust Khalid, I can't trust anyone.

Once I'm completely naked, I stride over to the spread-out sheet Khalid stands beside. My brother, also stripped of his clothing so it stays free of any blood splatter, draws his shadows to him once more, this time forming them in the palm of his hand. They swirl around his arm, restless and ethereal.

"Are you sure?"

When I nod, he reaches into the shadows on his palm, his arm disappearing up to his elbow. When he pulls it free again, he's gripping a combat knife in his hand.

Turning from him, I kneel on the middle of the sheet, my hands resting on my knees as I wait for him to strike.

I breathe in.

I breathe out.

I breathe –

Clenching my teeth to bite back a scream, I arch my back as pure agony ruptures from the blow. He's used a magical tool that increases pain tenfold, that stops one's brain from shutting down the nerves around the wound in an attempt to keep you functioning. There's no adrenaline to cover up the pain, to hide it until I pass out from blood loss. No numb relief.

Gasping, I fall forward, feeling every scrape of the blade as Khalid pulls it free from my body. My skin sticks to it, the edges of the cut tugged at by the metal. In the gaping hole that's left behind, blood rushes in, overwhelming my system as it goes where it's not supposed to be.

My arms instinctively reach forward to stop my descent, but as soon as my hands touch the floor, my strength leaves me, and my arms buckle beneath my weight. My head hits the ground. My vision blurs, and my consciousness is pulled from this world and tossed back into the past.

To that night when I walked home from the warehouse and someone I trusted came up behind me and stabbed me before I could turn.

The smell of familiar soap teases my nose right before the rich tang of blood assaults me. I stumble forward. The lights go out.

I hear a scream.

Feminine. Close. Full of terror.

Did she witness what happened? Did she see my would-be murderer? Was she the reason he ran away before he made sure I was dead?

I get a flash of a face. Dark-blonde hair, nearly brown. Long and straight and matted in blood as it clumps around her face. Sharp nose. Hazel eyes. Sunken cheeks. Is she an addict? Or someone too poor to eat? My gaze lands on her neck. It's been ripped out. Whoever attacked me had to get rid of the witness.

My chest burns. My heart struggles to pump, like there's something wrong with it. Like the blood isn't making it out of the arteries.

I shake my head. Try to clear the fuzz.

No. Mother said the knife missed it...

I must have turned right before he cut me. Thrown off his aim. Otherwise, I wouldn't have been able to make it to the warehouse... Maybe it's a lung that's the issue. Maybe...

More screams, this time men, familiar voices of those I work with. I'm back in the warehouse, stumbling forward, my feet heavy. I couldn't have been stabbed that far away. There were no sirens. No one saw me on the way back and called the police...

I'm back on the street, but I can't pinpoint where I am. I'm too fatigued. Too dizzy from the loss of blood –

No.

No, that's not it.

All the signs...

They are a blur. All the recognizable features too. The blade must have been coated in something to stop me from remembering. Or maybe it was his magic.

Familiar soap.

I know that smell...

I know...

I gasp as I come to, lying on a sheet in a room I don't recognize. Sweat coats my skin, replacing the blood of my memories. A warmth flows through me, spreading across my back.

"Varius," Khalid says, and I latch onto his voice, using him to draw me out of my head.

I look up at him, but I don't tell him anything that I have learned. I trusted Louise to heal me after my brother stabbed me. I don't trust her with any information. I nod, and he stands up, still naked. Turning my head, I look to the door, to where I left my clothes and weapons. My phone.

Dragging a shaky breath into my chest, checking my lungs now work, I push myself to my feet. Louise stands with her face to the wall, her hands behind her back, in view so we know she isn't weaving any spell. *Smart girl.*

Donning my clothes and gear, I open the door and let her out before turning to my brother. He pulls the shadows to him once more, this time depositing the taken furniture back where it belongs. The sheet with my blood, however, gets swallowed into the Plane of Monsters to never be seen again.

As he does all this, I pull out my phone. My fingers hover over the screen as I debate sending what I want to send. It isn't wise to let her get close. It isn't right when I'm hiding so much from her.

But after being on the brink of death...

And recalling the hurt in her eyes when I dismissed her earlier...

My skin tight, I tap out, *Will you dance with me?*

A small smile curls my lips as I slip the mobile back into my pocket. A silence ward snaps into place inside the room, and my smile falls, back to business. "There was a woman killed where I was attacked. Find out everything you can about her."

The reaper nods sharply. There was never any mention of another death. No blood to find. Neither mine or someone else's. Everything in the area was pristine, the killer having cleaned up after himself with magic. But even though there wasn't a body, there might be a missing person's report. Or perhaps her body was found somewhere else at a later date. "She had dark-blonde hair, nearly brown," I say. "Oval face. Mole on the left side of her chin. Malnourished. Caucasian. Hazel eyes."

They flash in front of me, wide and afraid, already taken by death.

"So you didn't see who it was?" the reaper asks.

"No."

"So we're still grabbing Lincoln tonight?"

I nod. "And Vinny."

One of them knows something, and tonight, I will find out what.

TWENTY-TWO

HER

I lean against the sink with the dumbest fucking grin on my face. My legs are shattered. My pussy is soaking wet. I can smell myself all over my fingers even though my hand is nowhere near my face, and I don't know if I should wash them or not, wanting Varius to lick them clean.

He asked me to dance.

My grin widens. My cheeks now hurt, but I can't stop the joy from leaking out of me.

Don't be stupid, Micha. You know he stepped away when he left the toy on vibrate.

But still...

He "chased" after me when I stormed off, and I doubt Varius fucking Shadow chases after anyone.

He left your ass in the woods all night, the smart part of me counters.

He let me sleep. I sigh dreamily. *I didn't even have to make anyone dinner.*

So what you're saying is he let you go hungry.

Rolling my eyes at the pessimistic voice in my head, I turn on the tap. I hesitate before sticking my hand under it, thinking he might punish me for denying him the taste.

He might have to take me upstairs to get his fill then...

Picturing his head between my thighs, I shove my hand under the flow of water with a sly grin. Grabbing the soap, I apply it thickly. He did, after all, still act like a dick to me in public. My eyes narrow. And what the fuck was up with him touching her like they were lovers?

He had his hand on her arm, his lips near her ear. *And I know what those lips can do.*

I growl. The water around my hands starts to steam and boil, my magic bleeding through my skin.

He learned with you, Micha.

The jealousy in my chest eases a bit, knowing that she wasn't a lover before me. I try to think who she is, having been forced to memorize most of the faces here before we arrived tonight. His thirteen capos. The other Bosses he invited, their Families dealing closely with his. The wives and girlfriends of those powerful men.

But her face comes up blank. Perhaps she is someone's secretary. Or a new mistress. Maybe she is a party crasher and he was telling her she better *get outta here* before he killed her.

I smile at that. Then my lips fall as I realize the security in this place is top-notch. I recognized half the waitresses as high members of our Family, esteemed killers who get paid even better than I. Andrea Turner. Jaclyn Hoscheid. Sharee Smith. Fuck, there's no way an assassin of my skill level got in with just one of them on watch, let alone all three of them. If I actually got round to planning who to hire to kill Varius...those badass fatherfuckers would've been in my top five.

So who the hel is she?

Feeling the need to break something, I head for the door. Just as I grab the handle though, I pause and take a breath. As pissed off as I'm getting, I'm still Varius' fiancee. I have a certain image to maintain. If I make an actual scene, he'll be forced to discipline me – and not with a toy. All of his capos are here. Six Bosses and their underbosses. If I make a fool of him, I'll break his trust, and I do not need to know everything about him to know Varius will not give it back easily.

If I'm wrong in this... If there's an innocent explanation for him having touched her...I'll destroy any chance I have at making this marriage real.

So I take a breath.

Calm myself down.

Then leave, looking every inch the calm, cool, collected woman Sau turned me into.

Having not chosen the bathroom closest to the party, I step out into utter silence. This part of the house is empty, but my eyes still flick across the place in surprise. Varius might not make a habit of following his women, but Dayne *always* follows me when I'm upset. Just as I do him.

An uneasy knot starts to form in my stomach as my pace quickens. Did he make a scene for me? Was Varius forced to punish him? My throat tightens, and I push out with my magic, searching for the tattoo I drew on him years ago and have strengthened every year since.

My feet slow as I feel him. His heart rate is normal. He's alive and not being tortured. He's either searching every room of the house (which will take time as this place is massive and he knows I wouldn't have hesitated to step outside), or he's being held up by Sau so he doesn't make a scene.

Breathing out slowly, I recollect myself. On regal strides, I make my way back to the party.

A few heads turn to me as I enter, but the only person

I'm looking for is Varius. When I don't see him, my pulse misses a beat as a sickness fills my stomach. My gaze darts around the room again, and I realize I don't see *her* either.

Sau starts to head towards me, and I know where my fiance is just by the face she's wearing. Wary yet full of pity.

My throat burns, and I turn to engage the closest man beside me in conversation. I don't want to hear what she has to say. That it is Varius' right to fuck whoever he wants to. That this is the real life of a Shadow woman. That I was a *fool* to trick myself into believing he cared just because he pressed a few buttons. Was he with her the entire time the butt plug vibrated continuously inside of me? During that moment he left?

My chest burning, I fight the rising anger. I will be calm about this. I will be cool and sophisticated as I come up with a thousand different ways to hurt him like he's hurt me.

"You're fucking hot in that dress," the man in front of me says.

My creep-o-meter goes off as his eyes roam up and down my body, but I smile at him politely like a lady is supposed to do. "Thank you." If the words come out a bit sarcastic, he doesn't seem to notice.

He leans in, and the alcohol on his breath hits me hard enough I wrinkle my nose even though a lady should never make a man feel like she's judging him. But holy hel, am I judging him. He's clearly fucking drunk, his eyes bloodshot and his speech slurred as he says, "Want to dance?"

"Varius has my first dance," I say with a polite smile even though the urge to just knock him out cold is making my fingers twitch. But a lady doesn't hit important men like Jason Terry – the right-hand man to Varius' cousin Vinny. She doesn't hit any men. She is the epitome of a damsel in fucking distress, showing the world that her husband is so powerful and so feared that no one would dare hurt what's his.

What's his...

I ain't fucking his.

Glancing around the room, I look for Dayne, wanting the comfort of his friendship. But in the middle of my sweep, Jason puts his hand on my waist and pulls me close. I lean back as he leans in.

"Come on," he says. "I'll show you what it's like to be with a real witch. Not some abomination like –"

Swinging my arm up, I slam my fist into his nose.

He stumbles back, his hand going up as blood spurts all over the floor. "You whore!" he shouts, raising his own fist.

I catch Sau moving quickly towards us, already relatively close due to her earlier approach. A *lady* is supposed to take any and all punishment. A *lady* knows her place.

But screw being a lady. The fucker called my fiance an abomination, and I might be pissed at Varius right now, but he's. Still. *Mine.*

My fist still tight, I go to punch him again.

Just as my knuckles are about to connect with his face, a band of fingers wraps around my wrist. They squeeze hard enough to stop my projection, and I wince as the pain flows through my crushed fingers.

My eyes widen as I glance to the side to see who's been foolish enough to stop me. I expected Dayne. Or maybe Maddox. But it's Varius himself who's holding me back.

"He –" I start, but he cuts me off.

"Jason is an esteemed guest of mine," he says, his words a thunderstorm of anger. "Now get down on your knees and beg him for his forgiveness."

I almost tell him to go to hel, but just as I open my mouth, I catch sight of Dayne beside Khalid. His face is pale, and I know the only reason he hasn't already tried to intervene is because he knows doing so will just make this whole situation worse. Varius doesn't just punish those who disrespects him. He punishes their family. Their friends.

I couldn't care if he hurt my father or my two brothers – both of whom are glaring at me. None of them have said a single word to me tonight. But I can't be the reason Dayne dies. And even though my little sister Lou isn't here right now, currently sick in bed, Varius *will* drag her into this.

So despite it going against every part of who I am, I drop to one knee and then the other in front of this entire crowd of people. Angry tears burn my eyes, but I shut them down as I look up at Jason's sneering face. His nose, at least, is still bleeding, and I take some comfort in that.

"Please forgive me, Jason," I say sweetly, the acid of my thoughts not even bleeding out into my tone. "I do not know what came over me. I'm just a stupid woman who asks for your forgiveness."

"You know how I make my wife forgive me? She sucks on my cock until I come all down her throat. And then she begs me to do it again."

My blood stills, then burns hot as the magic in my veins urges me to let it out. I could turn Jason into a pile of ash before Varius can even break the hand he's still holding.

"Then get it out for her to apologize on."

My eyes grow wide as they snap to Varius, but he isn't looking at me. He's looking at the right-hand man to his beloved cousin. A man he's most likely broken bread with, invited into his own home. A man he holds in much higher regards than he does me.

Looking at the cold indifference on my fiance's face, I realize he's actually going to make me do it. In this crowded room, Varius is going to force me to suck this man's cock as an apology for hitting him. For *sticking up for him*.

And I can't do a damn thing but obey. Not if I want my best friend and sister to not get punished alongside me.

My arm shakes with rage as I watch Jason fiddle with his pants. The alcohol in his system is making his movements jerky, uncoordinated, but he finally gets his small prick out.

Or perhaps it's only small compared to Varius'. Not that it matters. I don't want a single inch of it in my mouth. The damn thing smells, like he hasn't washed it in weeks. There is even something crusty on the end of it.

Bile burns the back of my throat, but before I can force myself to do what I have to, two things happen.

1. Jason screams.

2. Blood splatters all over my face.

I jerk back in shock as I turn my head. My eyes close automatically so nothing gets in them. Stumbling onto my ass, I wipe an arm across my face. My eyes open just in time to see Varius kick Jason in the stomach. The shorter man doesn't even flail his arms to stop himself from falling back, his hands too preoccupied with cupping his junk.

His *missing* junk I realize as Varius bends down and picks up a severed penis. He wipes both sides of his knife on the sleeve of his jacket as he walks towards a whimpering Jason. The man is balled up at this point, his hands still cupped low. Screaming and crying, he begs for mercy.

"Please!" he wails. "Don't kill me. Please, please!"

"You want to live?" Varius asks as he stops in front of him.

"Yes!"

"You want my forgiveness for trying to steal from me?"

At the mention of 'steal,' my eyebrows come together. Then they shoot straight up as I realize he must have heard Jason asking me to dance. Trying to steal that first moment from him.

"I'm sorry. I'm so sorry."

"Then get on your knees and beg me."

He sobs on the floor for a few more seconds, no doubt building up the courage to move. I hope he stays there. I hope he insults Varius so much, he kills him where he is. But then Jason begins to move, his cries increasing as he works himself onto his knees. Blood pisses out of his hands.

His face is pale and clammy; he's going into shock.

"Please," he starts to beg, but Varius cuts him off as he offers him the severed dick.

"Beg me like your wife does."

Jason's eyes widen in horror, a mirrored image of mine. But just like I realized there was no other choice when I was down on my knees, so does he. Whimpering, Jason Terry lifts a trembling hand to take his cock from Varius' fingers. Then he opens his mouth, closes his eyes, and –

"Open your eyes like a proper whore," Varius snaps.

Another whimper escapes poor Jason's lips, but he does as he's ordered. Tears and snot and blood run down his face. He cries pathetically as he reaches forward with his lips. But no one intervenes. Not even Vinny, the man who made him his second.

He gags as soon as the head of his cock meets his mouth, and I wonder if it's from the smell, the taste of the crust left there, or from the act itself. Are the tears from the pain or the utter humiliation?

My stomach twists as I watch him jerk his cock in and out of his mouth even though I have no love for him. The sound of his choked sobs makes goosebumps flare across my skin. I've seen a lot of dark shit over the years, have taken part in my fair share of it, and yet, I still want to turn away.

But I don't.

I can't, my eyes frozen on Jason as he bobs up and down his own severed cock.

After what feels like an eternity, Varius finally breaks the silence. "What do you think, Micha?" he says. "Did he do a well enough job to live?"

My mouth drops open as he says my name. I stare at his back, then at the poor excuse for a man on his knees with his own dick in his mouth, sucking it like a champ even as tears run down his face.

A *nice person* would give him mercy, see his punishment

as having been carried out. Perhaps if all he'd done was hit on me and been too bold with his request of an apology, I would be *nice*.

But he called my fiance an abomination.

So holding his tear-stained, hopeful eyes, I say, "No."

Without any hesitation, Varius' knife slashes forward in a quick cut. Jason's throat opens all the way. Falling onto his face, he chokes around his cock and bleeds out.

The party is silent as Varius wipes his blade once more on his jacket sleeve.

Then he looks up at those surrounding us. He seemingly holds each and every one of their gazes. "Does anyone else wish to steal from me?" he asks, his voice cold enough to give me shivers. When no one answers, his gaze lands on me. And I hear what he doesn't say. What he can't in this crowded room full of masked enemies.

You're mine, little monster. And if anyone ever tries to take you from me, I'll kill them.

A shiver shooting down my spine, I smile.

TWENTY-THREE

HIM

The urge to fuck her as she stares up at me is making me hard. She's still down on the ground, her arms behind her, her knees up and spread. The sash of her dress lies on top of her pussy, hiding it from my view, but I can smell the cum lathered all around it. The intensity of it tells me my little monster came like I told her to. A low growl of approval rumbles from my chest, and I slip my hand into my pocket.

She tenses in anticipation, her legs closing together. But just as I go to unlock the screen on my phone, the hairs on my neck rise.

Aleric.

The fucker appears out of thin air, right beside Mother. He's covered in blood from head to foot, his short black hair slicked back and matted, his skin and tux painted red. The only other color on him is the white of his eyes. Vlad, his Underboss, stands beside him, dripping in the same amount of blood.

"Why, hello there," Aleric says as he flashes a megawatt smile.

In an instant, the waitresses all become armed, knives and guns pulled, hands alight with red magic. The trays they hold are poised on fingertips ready to drop them or throw them at the two vampires. We might be at peace, but no one likes to be caught off guard.

"You should have come through the front door," I tell the Boss of the Blood Fangs as I pull my hand free of my pants pocket, leaving the phone locked. Micha rises slowly to her feet behind me, her heart rate calm, her pores pumping with adrenaline.

I shift in front of her as I move to greet our new guests. Khalid trails beside me while the rest of my brothers slip through the crowd to surround Talon, knowing he is liable to do something stupid. As is Mother. I glance at her as we approach, noting the tightness of her posture before looking back at Aleric.

He smiles at me, not a single flair of fear in his eyes at being in a room of forty-odd witches all ready and willing to kill him. "And track blood all over this lovely place?" he drawls. "Bit of an asshole move."

Lifting a hand, I signal everyone to stand down. Despite the weapons being put away and the magic fading from raised hands, the atmosphere of the room still stays frigid and ready to crack.

"Aw, that was so thoughtful of you," Micha says as she comes up beside me. And although she is merely stepping into the role of hostess that Mother is currently incapable of being, I bristle at the kindness she is showing him.

Her smiles are mine.

She hugs my arm. The thunderous irritation in my chest starts to calm as she pushes her body against me. "We shall move the party outside then," she says. "It's about time we turned on some music and danced." Her fingers trail down my arm to my hand, raising a line of goosebumps in their wake.

Aleric's smile widens, his fangs on full display. "I do love dancing." His eyes dart to the floor behind us, to Jason's butchered body. "Though I am a bit peckish," he drawls. "I might fall over if I don't eat."

"You're gorged," the reaper says, and it isn't a lie. No vampire would deliberately linger in the same room as a shapeshifter without being covered head to toe in blood and recently fed. Witches can cast a spell to protect their DNA from being studied by a shapeshifter, although it is a heavy drain on their body and they can't keep it up indefinitely. But when vampires feed on blood, it doesn't just sit in their stomach. It gets pumped around their body, which allows them to get high if they eat high prey and a damn good buzz if they feed on a witch. But it also hides their own DNA, making it a lot harder for a shapeshifter to get a reading on.

Eventually, Uncle Myers will be able to crack it, but it'll take him a couple hours of close observation to do so. Being a lot younger, Maddox isn't quite skilled enough.

Aleric laughs. "There's always room for dessert." His eyes twinkle as he turns to Mother. Bowing in half, he rolls his hand in front of him as he extends his arm and keeps his gaze on her. "I'll take the first dance."

Before she can answer, he vanishes, phasing away and leaving only a dark bloodstain on the floor. Vlad is gone a second later, having followed his Boss outside.

Smiling tightly, regaining a bit of her composure now that he isn't in the room, Mother ushers the guests outside. As the crowd moves around us, two waitresses come over to deal with Jason's body.

"Leave him," I say. "Vinny."

He steps forward, his face pale. His father moves behind him, his lips tight in the absence of his usual smile. Jason was Vinny's second. He vouched for him to be here. His crimes are my cousin's.

"I'm sorry, Varius," he says. "I should've watched how much he had to drink. I didn't –"

"He tried to steal from me, Vinny," I cut in softly.

He swallows, the panic seeping from his pores in a sickly sweet smell. "I'll pay for the damages. New dress. New tux. The cleaning of the house."

"Compensation," Uncle Myers adds.

"Of course. Yeah, yeah, of course. And compensation for the trouble he caused." He swallows again as the last of the other capos and bosses leave so it's just us five. Even the staff has disappeared. Soft music whispers from outside.

I turn my gaze to my uncle. "When Pauline was alive," I say, referencing his wife and Vinny's mother, "what would you have done if another man tried to steal her away?"

He stills, two predators facing off, the reaper he used to be now staring back at me. I don't flinch even as chills run down my spine.

"I would've killed him just like you did Jason."

"Mmm. And was there any compensation you would've accepted?"

"No." His gaze doesn't waver. "But I loved her."

I still, my heart skipping a beat as I am acutely aware of Khalid's presence beside me. If I say no compensation will sate me like I want to, like the truth of it is, then I will be claiming Micha not just as my fiancee but as my girl. And with that claim comes heavy consequences. Khalid will side with her on all arguments. He'll protect her even from me, and if she cannot conceive, I'll have to marry her regardless or suffer my brother's wrath. A girl is not claimed and cast aside. She is for life. And all the lifetimes after.

A smart play on my uncle's part.

My eyes hard, I turn to Vinny. "Wire me a million on top of the damages. But you steal from me again, and your *pal* here" –I nod at the corpse behind me– "will be nothing but a daydream for you to remember."

His head bobbing nervously, Vinny pulls out his phone to transfer me the money now.

"Uncle Myers?"

His eyes glint with the focus of a snake unsure if it should strike. He loves me, but he also loves his only son, the last remnants of his beloved wife. Any other capo would have died for his second's sins.

"Yes, Boss?"

"Don't let Mother kill Aleric. And come get me if Lincoln leaves."

He nods, relaxing fully as I pull Micha towards the stairs.

"Can she really do that?" she asks as we climb them.

I glance at her, though half my attention is on Vinny. If he thinks we're falling for his lies, he'll put his guard down. And so he does, the fear spewing from his pores decreasing. The likelihood of him running while I'm fucking Micha is low enough I can risk it; he'll hang around and see how much more damage to Lincoln's reputation he can do.

Focusing on her, I say, "She's named the Reaper of the Sired for a reason."

"*That's your mom?*" she exclaims, her feet coming to a halt on the second floor, her eyes bugging out of her skull.

"Yes."

"Shit. Fuck. That's so cool. You think she'll give me an autograph?" Her eyes widen even more, having basically just found out who Jack the Ripper was. A sup doesn't get a name for just anything. They have to be powerful and have done something ridiculously insane. There are only seven named sups on Earth. Maybe eight, depending on whether Sebastian the Ancient Destroyer is actually hiding here or not.

"Do you know what happened?" she gushes as we make it to the next floor. "All the stories say she killed a hundred sired vampires on her own. That's it. Nothing else. There's so much mystery around it. Even where it happened or who the vampires were or who did it." She laughs and shakes her head. "But fuck. That's your mom. I have to tell Dayne. He's obsessed with named sups."

Micha starts to turn back for the stairs, her excitement making her forget what we're up here for. My eyes narrow. I grab her arm, swing her around, and duck low. When I straighten, she's on my shoulder. I slap her ass and stride towards the nearest bedroom door.

"Hey!" She pushes off my back as she wiggles to get down.

My other hand dips into my pocket, and I pull out my phone. I glance down, turn the toy on max, and put it away again. She yelps as her legs come together, and she collapses back onto my shoulder. Burying her face into my back, she struggles not to moan. I slide my hand up the smooth silk of her dress, trailing it up her thigh to grab her ass.

Opening a random bedroom door with the other hand, I step inside. Khalid takes up position outside it as I kick the door shut behind me.

Finally alone with my little monster, I take a second just to bask in the warmth of her presence. Where my cousin isn't out to kill me. Or one of my 'loyal' capos. Or a brother if I have everything wrong. Where it's just me and her and no other pressures weighing down on me.

My hand rubs her ass, then lifts off and goes down to her ankle. Slipping under the fabric of her red dress as I stride towards the ensuite, I slide my fingers up her leg.

I feather them between her pussy lips. She's soaking wet from her earlier play. The toy vibrates in the hole above me.

"You came for me, didn't you?"

She nods against my back as she moans.

"How did you do it?"

She makes a little noise, but she doesn't answer. I slap her ass as I enter the bathroom. My eyes go to the mirror above the sink, and I think about fucking her in front of it. My cock hardens as I set her down on the marble counter, her legs hanging over the side.

"Take off your dress, little monster, before I tear it off you."

Not trusting myself to touch it, I step back and start to strip out of my own clothes and gear. Her eyes darken as she watches me, and I go slowly despite wanting to remove everything in seconds.

"Tell me how you made yourself come," I say as I undo the buttons on my shirt one by one.

Her eyes latch onto my fingers. Her lips part.

"I pulled up my dress," she murmurs as she slides the red silk of her skirt up her thigh. The hem of it rises up her shin. "And I bunched it around my waist."

She wiggles as she keeps pulling her dress up. Until her bare ass is on the counter. A low growl emits from me as I think about her making contact with the marble rather than my face.

With the last button on my shirt undone, my fingers buzz with the urge to shirk it off, but I fight it. A flash of defiance narrows her eyes, wanting me to go first, but then she's continuing her story.

"I spread my legs."

Rewarding her, I let my shirt fall off my shoulders. Her breath catches, and she parts her thighs.

"Wider," I growl when her legs still, not quite far enough to open her pussy lips.

She doesn't move. "Take off your pants first."

"Micha," I warn.

"Then go fuck one of your whores."

She starts to hop off the counter. My hands go to my waistband, stilling her.

"I don't have any whores," I say as I flick open the button on my pants.

Her eyes harden with pain that quickly turns into anger. But she doesn't say what's on her mind. I pull down my zipper, then kick off my shoes. Stepping towards her so I can reach her face, I cup her chin. "There's only you, little monster."

She sucks in a breath, and I like that I got it right. That I could ease a bit of her pain like she does mine. My chest tightens, and as I stand here with her cheek in my palm and her looking up at me like she wants to believe me, trust me, allow herself to...love me, I realize I might want her for more than just a womb.

We stare at each other, breathing the same breath.

My cock jerks with needy attention, but all I want...is right here. Just touching her like this.

She reaches a hand up to entwine with mine. My heart skips a beat as I watch her. But just as she's about to make contact, I drop my arm and step away.

My pulse hammers in my skull.

I can't cross this bridge with her. Can't tell her about what will happen if our child is born without magic. She might not even conceive. Then telling her, giving her that pain and stress, would've been for nothing.

So I hold her gaze, ignoring the hurt there, and strip off my pants. I step out of them and toe off my socks. "Now wider," I demand, my gaze dipping to her pussy, away from those eyes that ask me for things I can't give.

Micha hesitates a second, then slowly spreads her legs apart. But as beautiful as her pink pussy is, as hot as it is to watch her lips open for me, the sight can't compete with the look she gave me just seconds ago. Like I could be her entire fucking world if I just let her in.

Suddenly restless, I yank down my boxers. In the same movement I step out of them, I move forward and grab her hips. I yank her to the edge of the counter, to me, and as she sucks in a breath, I push in deep. Or try to. But she's too fucking tight, the toy in her ass blocking me, pushing the walls together, filling up the space so I can't. The vibrations of the toy feed into my tip, and my balls draw tight with the need to sink into her, to feel her clenching around me.

So I rip the plug out and toss it. Then line my cock up with her gaping hole and push in deep. She cries out, her nails digging into my shoulders as her breasts arch into me.

I pull out, then slam back in. Grunting and groaning, I pick up the pace until I'm hammering into her. Until I'm fucking out my frustration as she pants and writhes against the counter and me. Her nails scrape trenches into my back, and I growl at the feel of the pain. Dipping my head, I bite her neck. She cries out again as her legs wrap around me, her ankles locking as she bounces her ass up and down on my cock.

I release her neck and push her back until she's leaning half against the mirror, half on her hands. "Show me how you came for me," I demand as my eyes dip to her pussy.

Shifting her weight, she reaches forward with one hand. She presses her fingers against the outside of her pussy, applying hard pressure as she lifts her hips. I bring a hand up to join her, trailing two fingers back and forth between her lips.

"You want me to finger fuck you while my cock's in your ass?" I ask, overcome with the need to fill every hole of hers at once. To claim her as mine in action if not in words. The tension in my chest claws at me, demanding I don't wait.

But I want to hear her say it. I want her to want me everywhere.

"Yes," she pants as she grabs my wrist with her other hand, leaning back on her elbows, her neck awkwardly bent against the mirror. "Yes, please. Fuck. *Varius.*"

She arches on a cry as I push a finger in. Her eyes close. Her mouth opens. When she sags back down, I shove that finger into her mouth as my other hand goes to her pussy.

Her eyes pop wide as she stares at me, as she tastes her own cum on my finger.

She freezes for half a second, then she's sucking me as she fucks me with wild abandon. My balls grow tight. Her ass slides up and down my cock. And in another few bumps, I'm coming inside her as her tongue swirls around the length of my finger.

Grabbing both her hips, I lift her off the counter and take her inside the walk-in shower. She yanks her dress over her head quickly, just barely managing to get it off and throw it before I turn on the spray, draw the door shut, and press her against the wall. Lifting her up off my cock, I ignore her yelps against the cold as the shower heats up. With her breasts now at my face, I suck on them.

Her fingers dig into my wet hair. Her legs wrap around my torso. As she holds me to her, I start my worship of every inch of her body. All we can ever have is good sex. Great sex. But we can't have anything more. I don't have anything else to give.

So I give her this. Give her every fucking thing I can, sucking and licking and biting her breasts until she's on the verge of coming. Her moans increase. Her breaths hitch. Her body trembles beneath my lips. I wrap my mouth around her nipple. Flick my tongue across it. She screams out as she orgasms, and I shove two fingers inside her as I suck her entire breast, small as it is, into my mouth.

She pulls at my hair as she jerks beneath my attentions. A few strands come loose and the bite of the pain has me biting her, leaving a mark on her skin so everyone knows she's mine.

Jason, the fucker, tried to steal her from me.

I growl with her titty in my mouth.

The fucker is dead though, and I'll kill everyone else who even *thinks* they can have what's mine.

My cock hard and aching in its need to claim her pussy, I

yank her down the wall, pull her directly under the spray of the shower, and bend her over. Her hands rest on the tiles cascading with water. She turns her head to look at me over her shoulder, but I'm not where her eyes went. No longer standing. I'm dropping to my knees behind her. One hand on my dick, I wash it under the spray as the other grabs her thigh, and I bury my face in her ass. The mix of cum and lube touches my tongue, and I growl at the knowledge that she is mine. That she is marked by me. Claimed by me.

Is fucking mine even if I can never vocally admit it.

"You want to dance for me, Micha?" I ask before I rim her asshole with my tongue. She moans as she trembles beneath me. "You want to grind your body on my face?"

She pushes back as I lick around her ass. My nose digs into her flesh. My hand quickens on my cock, now clean and hard and ready to slide into her pussy.

But first, I'm going to eat her out. I've never acquainted my tongue with this part of her body, and I want to take every inch of her and make it mine.

"Then dance for me, little monster," I growl. "Ride my face until you come."

Spreading her cheeks, I lick her fully, then thrust my tongue into her hole. She squeezes around me as one of her hands comes back and fists my hair. She grinds herself against my lips, panting and moaning. I keep my head still, letting her position herself, to find the angle she likes so I can learn what makes my little monster come.

"*Varius, please,*" Micha begs as her legs start to shake. I continue to eat her out slowly, leisurely, knowing it isn't speed that gets her off. It's technique. It's pacing. It's taking her to the edge and leaving her there to quiver.

I run my hands up her legs, going over her calves, her knees, the corded muscles of her thighs. My fiancee's a little warrior, an assassin, and she has a body for fighting. How will it change over the years? The decades she stays by my side? Will she lose the muscle, replacing it with more of a lady's physique, or will she keep training even when she's locked away in our house?

She hasn't been to our gym yet other than that one time she brought me breakfast, and the idea of her losing this, this part of her that makes her her, that shows she once had dreams even if she doesn't now... I don't like that. She put in so much effort to get her body like this. It isn't just the effect of a few hours a week of exercise. It is a constant upkeep, a show of pride. She chose the life of an assassin rather than the life of a bride, and anger fills me over the idea that she will lose something she wants. That being with me will take that from her.

I will not give her back to her father, but I can try to not kill all her dreams.

Spinning her around, I lift her right leg over my shoulder and bury my face in her pussy. Both her hands dig into my hair as she rides me, but she rarely comes from oral alone, so I know all she's doing is building up her own frustration. I let her fuck my face as my tongue fucks her for a few minutes and then I'm pulling her down to my cock as I run my tongue up the full length of her body. Her leg still over my shoulder as she sits on my lap, I push my cock into her pussy.

She groans as I growl. Wrapping one hand around her throat, I haul her mouth to mine. I don't kiss her like I did in the woods. I take my time, learning her lips, her tongue, what makes her turn away, and what makes her desperate for more.

Cupping her breast with my other hand, I kiss her as she rides me. She doesn't slide down all the way on my cock, stopping when I hit her cervix. I pull away from her lips and look down to where she's gripping me. She looks so fucking beautiful with her lips around my cock, glistening from her arousal. But my eyes narrow at the reminder she shaved it without my permission and the punishment I still owe her.

Pressing my palm over her pussy, I let her grind against my hand in the way she likes. "I'm going to tattoo my name here," I say as I lift my gaze to hers.

Her eyes widen. "No, you're not."

"You think you can stop me?"

"It's my body."

"It's mine, Micha." *Whether or not we marry, it's fucking mine.*

Her mouth drops open, and I haul her lips to me before she can speak. The words I didn't utter bang around my skull as I fuck her hard and fast, pumping my cock up into her. She nips me as I hit the back of her cervix. Then she's pushing me back, and I'm letting her, just for this moment. In this singular lowering of walls as I let myself imagine a future we can never have. I let her take control.

Her hands on my chest, she rides me until she comes. Until I'm joining her in orgasm, triggered by the blush of her cheeks, by the honesty of her desire. As she collapses onto my chest, tucking her face into the nook of my neck, I wrap my arms around her and breathe.

Just for this moment…

I hold her close and breathe.

TWENTY-FOUR

HIM

Micha is up in an instant as a body appears right beside us. I bite back a sigh as I look up at Aleric, half expecting to see naked bloody balls dangling above me. There isn't, but I'm too pissed off to feel thankful he kept his damn clothes on before phasing into our shower. Two seconds. I got two seconds with my fucking gi–

"Don't," I order Micha as I sit up. Water is steaming from her hands, and although I can't see her fire, I can sure as hel feel it in the air. "This is just how he likes to meet."

"In showers?" she growls.

"By violating people's personal spaces. Now get out and get dressed."

"Yes. Don't want to start a new war by tempting me into eating you. I have a thing for feisty women."

She lifts her chin. "I'm a fucking lady."

He laughs as he leans against the wall, but his eyes stay perfectly on her face. "So you are."

"Wait in the bedroom, Micha," I say as I stand.

She throws a look at me but doesn't argue as she files out of the shower. Grabbing a towel from a cupboard and her dress off the floor, she leaves the ensuite.

"She's delightful," Aleric drawls as he starts to take off his suit jacket. He drops it on the floor as I leave the cubicle, assuming he wishes to get the blood off him now that he isn't worried about Maddox seeing him. He'll leave after this little chat, and I wonder if Vlad is still downstairs or if he's already gone. Probably the latter; otherwise, Mother, Talon, and Uncle Myers would be wondering where Aleric is.

"What is Antonio doing to your men?" I ask as I grab a towel and wrap it around my waist.

"And you're not in any way delightful," he says, ignoring my question entirely. He sighs as he rips the buttons off his shirt, popping every single one of them. Given the piece is already wrecked from the blood, there's no point showing it any care.

I keep my eyes on his face as he strips. It's a tactic he likes to use. Make people uncomfortable so they turn away and he can strike at their back. He'll just as easily hit from the front, but a predator like him? Can't resist an easy kill.

"You should learn to engage in small talk, Varius. It will make you much more likable." He grins as he starts to lather his hair. His voice rises in pitch as he mocks me. "I'm Varius fucking Shadow. I don't need to be likable when I can just cut off people's dicks and make them choke on it." Lowering his hands, he applauds slowly. "Bravo, by the way. I wish I'd arrived a few seconds sooner to see that." He cocks his head as he goes back to washing his hair. "Then again, I can just reenact it tonight. Mmm. No, not tonight. I'm busy tonight. Got a date with a bottle of lotion in an empty house, you know?"

"Have all your missing capos had their skin fall off?" I

ask, ignoring the shit that comes out of his mouth, which is practically every fucking word.

He waves a hand at me. "My Family's business is mine, just like yours is yours. You don't go around kidnapping my men to get answers, and I don't go around telling you who tried to kill you thirteen months ago. That's how this whole treaty thing works."

"This 'whole treaty' is about to fall apart if Antonio is picking you off this easily."

He laughs from deep in his belly, then gives me a look. "You really trying to play it off that you don't want to know what I know?"

I don't move a single muscle. But it doesn't matter if my poker face is completely flat. He knows I want it. I know he knows. A stranger on the street would guess I'd pay top dollar for good information about that night. "What will it cost me?"

"Leave Cara Jervis alone."

"That's it?"

He shrugs. "I have a soft spot for the girl." He lowers his arms to clean the blood off his hair-free chest. "And she has a soft spot for dangerous men with dogs. She gets stupid brain when Leno's around." He rolls his eyes as his hands dip further south. My eyes stay on his neatly trimmed face as I try to discern what's real and what's just a smokescreen to throw me off.

He's given information too freely. So either he genuinely likes Cara Jervis and will do whatever he can to protect her, or he wants me to think he does so he can use her as bait. She'd be a hel of a lot easier to ambush than Aleric would. If he really liked her and our Families turned on each other, I could grab her to draw him out.

But he singled Leno out as the one to draw her in. Leno is my second and liked by our men much better than I. Does he plan to grab my brother while he attacks me so it forces my Family to choose which one of us to save? It would be a clever way to take us both out. Use more men to attack me first, get me pinned down along with Khalid. Then when Leno tries to sneak in to get Cara Jervis, there's an ambush waiting for him. My backup would be rerouted to Leno...

Except for that to work, Aleric would have to have a full nest, and his capos are being picked off one by one. Even if he's making a dozen more sired every night – something that would utterly drain him, a sired vampire only has the fraction of power a born vampire like Aleric does.

So the alternative is Cara is a complete red herring, and he's only using her as an excuse to finally tell me about who tried to kill me. Which means he wants me to deal with the traitor now, the timing being the important part.

Perhaps because his Family is getting slaughtered, and he needs to make sure my Family isn't being torn apart on the inside so we can stop Antonio for him.

"You finished in that head of yours?" Aleric teases, his hands dipping low to wash his balls and cock.

"If we leave Cara alone, will you tell me what's going on?"

The vampire boss shrugs. "Not much to tell. Antonio's throwing a tantrum because I fucked his mom."

"His mom's dead."

"Yeah...he's especially pissed I dug up her grave."

The Garcia family has always eaten their own kind, but I don't point that out because I really don't want to know what he'll come back with.

"You have no idea what he's doing to them, do you?" I say, fishing.

He snorts. "I know exactly what he's doing, and good on him for making them last so long."

My eyes narrow as I try to work out what he means. Is whatever poison Antonio pumping them with meant to kill them a lot faster than it has been? But why would he want to drag out their deaths in a way that makes them incapable of speech? He can't be interrogating them for information. So is he trying to make it contagious? My stomach twists at the thought of it jumping from vampires to witches. Getting anything out of Aleric, though, isn't going to happen.

"Deal," I say, focusing on what he will give me. "Who was it?"

He turns off the shower. "Not who you think."

My eyes narrow.

He pins me with a look of exaggerated annoyance. "You are terribly boring to play with. Ask me how I know it isn't who you think." When I don't say anything, he sighs. "It'll hurry this whole thing up if you play along."

"How do you know?" I ask flatly.

"Who do you think cleaned up the mess?"

I still, having assumed it was the assassin, but the look in Aleric's eyes... "You?" I ask. "Why?"

He turns off the shower and steps out, water cascading down the valleys of his muscles to splatter on the tiled floor. He walks over to the cupboard, turning his back to me so easily, not afraid I'll kill him while he isn't looking.

"Fortunately for your assassin," Aleric says as he starts to dry himself off, "there was a rogue vampire in the area. We found the leftovers of his lunch and another large bloodstain nearby. We assumed that was also his kill, so we cleaned up." He snorts. "If I'd known it was yours, I would've kept some of it, but alas." He sighs in pure disappointment. Then he smiles as his gaze dips to my neck. "Although, I could –"

"So you caught the rogue," I cut in, "and asked him what happened."

"No." His eyes lose his humor for the first time, a flash of red coloring the gray as his bloodlust bleeds out. "No, that fucker's still out there somewhere. But the woman he bled dry? She was a tourist taking photos on her phone, and in one of them she caught a man I would recognize anywhere.

Granted, it was just his back, but that was all I needed to identify him."

My patience wearing thin, I ask, "Who?"

He smiles at me, taking pleasure in the pain he is about to dole out. "Who else could carry out something like that, fail, and still get away with it? No one but a reaper."

Everything inside me shuts down. Not a muscle twitches. Not a hair rises. I'm numb at the thought of Khalid, at the brother I trust the most, being the traitor. *No. No, he's had so many chances to kill me and never took them. Aleric is just fucking –*

"Well, ex-reaper," he says, cutting into my thoughts and giving me breath that I suck into my crippled lungs. But I don't feel any better. Because that means that the traitor –

"The traitor is your uncle Myers."

TWENTY-FIVE

HER

With my ear pressed to the door, my heart stutters. *His own uncle...* A man who, only a few hours ago, welcomed me into the family and joked about what my life here would be like. I liked him, thought he was funny. Nothing about him made me uneasy. He seemed so genuine in his love for the Shadow brothers. For Varius.

"He's an abomination."

My heart twists as Jason's words come back to me. Does Myers think the same simply because Varius doesn't have any magic? Before I can think of anything more, the hairs on my nape rise. *Danger!*

Instinctively, not thinking at all, I drop to the ground and roll to the left, away from the bedroom windows and the threat that's just entered from them. My pulse is steady as I come back to my feet, but my body is already swaying, the spell the fucker threw at me having grazed the top of my head. I'm dizzy. My vision blurring. My tongue feels heavy.

I lift my hands and throw up a shield around me, pushing the fucker's spell out of my bloodstream, but it's stronger than mine. I've slowed it down but haven't stopped it. My vision starts to narrow. All I can see is blurred shapes with no definition, and I'm starting to feel tired.

Knowing I'm outmatched in my current condition, I yell for Khalid, hoping like hel it isn't him who's attacking me. People always underestimate the effect of yelling in a fight, but this person hasn't. I opened my mouth, but no sound came out. *Fuck.*

The figure, nothing but a blur of red, darts towards the bathroom. I'm out of their way, and the fact that they don't try to kill me when they so easily could makes me realize I'm not the target. I'm the fucking patsy, and all that red I'm seeing in front of me is a dress similar to mine.

Myers.

I drop to one knee as his knock-out spell starts to take me down. The bathroom door starts to open from the other side, making my heart spike for the first time in a fight.

Frantically, I pull on the magic of one of my tattoos, a custom spell I use often, and grab hold of the door. I slam it shut, then throw my fire at the lock and hinges to meld them to the frame. Varius might be the Boss of the Shadow Domain, but he can't help in a fight of magic. He'll only get in my way. He'll be safer inside the ensuite.

The spell on me releases instantly as Myers turns in my direction. My vision comes back full force, and I blink to try to adjust to the overload of sensory information. But his fist hits me before I can, and I fall to the ground.

I twist as I go, landing on my hands and lifting my lower half up to slam my feet into him. He staggers back, the dress he's wearing tripping him up.

It's fucking uncanny fighting yourself, his face looking exactly like mine, but I don't hesitate as I jump to my feet and lift my arms up. I start to weave a ball of fire, but he barrels into me. The fucker has changed tactic, and I need to figure out what his gameplay is. Khalid's absolutely in the dark, the room having been warded in silence. And no one suspects Myers of having disappeared inside to kill Varius. They probably think he's just gone to the bathroom, and will be back in a couple minutes. So there's a timer, at least, a length of time I need to hold out before someone starts to wonder where he is.

Hopefully.

He charges forward, instigating with a jumping kick to my face. I duck, neatly avoiding it but stepping right into the line of his other leg. His foot slams into my solar plexus, knocking the wind out of me. I'm down on my knees, then rolling, trying to breathe as I find my feet again. He doesn't attack me while I'm down though, and that flags something inside my head, something important. But I'm moving too fast to think of it, throwing my hands up to block another kick to my chest.

My forearm aches like hel from the force of his blow, and there's a moment I wonder how he's moving so well in this fucking dress. Then I realize he ripped the seams down the sides while I was down. I want to do the same, but I know he won't give me the chance.

My legs restricted, I do my best to dance out of the way of his attacks. Something rams into the bathroom door from the other side.

If Varius is shouting at me, I can't hear him, the ward of silence around the room still engaged. It's not a hard spell to maintain, so I don't bother trying to think of a way to break it. His magic is obviously stronger than mine. He has nearly a hundred years on me, and he's an ex-reaper on top of that.

Which begs the question of why am I not already dead?

He must still need me as a patsy.

He darts forward, but this time I throw up a blue shield of magic. Knowing he is strong enough to break it, I let it down just as he starts to counter the spell. My other arm shoots forward, and a fireball of purple flames erupts from my palm. It slams into his own shield, just barely erected in time, but the thing about my fire that no one knows is that it feeds on magic. The flames grow higher, consuming his shield as fuel.

He staggers back, surrounded by a wall of fire he can't see but can absolutely fucking feel. The door to the ensuite slams off its hinges, and Varius barrels into the room. He looks at Myers, who still looks like me, but then his gaze shifts to me.

I try to tell him I have the threat contained, but I still can't fucking speak. That niggling red flag starts to wave again. Why would Myers have bothered both warding the room and stopping me from speaking?

Before I can figure it out, the hairs on my nape start to rise as Varius slowly moves towards his uncle. Because his steps aren't right. There's no rage in them. There's no sign that he's moving towards someone who had all his trust and broke it. No...no that look is aimed at me.

Varius. What are you... My eyes widen as I get it now. What's causing his paranoia.

Myers is a hel of a lot stronger than me. A lot faster. A lot smarter. So how the hel did I manage to get the upper hand?

The sly mother fucker played me, and now Varius thinks I'm the imposter.

TWENTY-SIX

HER

Fuck.
My.
Life.
Both of my hands are needed to hold the flames in place around Myers, meaning I can't use them to protect myself. If I let them down, Myers will be at Varius' back. He'll kill him in a second. Then do whatever he's planning on doing to me – probably knocking me out, kidnapping me, then killing me later as the 'hero' who dealt with the traitor.

Looking into Varius' eyes, I don't see the man who held me a second ago. I only see the monster behind the stories I've heard. The boogieman to the boogiemen. The heartless, hollow bastard who will kill friends and allies just as fast as he will his enemies.

If I don't try to protect myself, he'll kill me. Then Myers will kill him, my flames dying with me unless I allow them to have a mind of their own – though if I do that, this whole fucking house will go up in flames. Potentially the whole continent given nothing can put them out but me. I have no idea if they can traverse across the ocean if given enough time.

Fuck.

My.

Life.

Because I get it now, why Myers warded both the room and made me mute. I can't argue my case, can't give up information only the real me would know.

So I do the only thing I can do that will force Myers to reveal himself. Ignoring Varius' sudden charge forward, I push my flames towards his uncle. His eyes too fucking calm, he jumps straight up and uses his magic to latch onto the ceiling like a gecko, transforming his hands and feet.

A knife embeds itself into my hand just as Myers crawls towards a window. I flinch my arm back as I twist out of the way of another blade. Able to dismiss my fire now, I throw up a shield over the windows, blocking both the exits, then concentrate on avoiding the knife slashing through the air, aiming for my throat, my chest, my eyes.

I've lost track of Myers in all this, and his game is up. He doesn't have a reason to hold back anymore, to pretend like he can't kill us in a second. I might've just made things worse by forcing the ex-reaper into a corner, but I didn't have any other choice. I pray to the gods I at least brought us enough time for someone to realize Myers is missing.

But the door doesn't open.

And I've just caught sight of Myers dropping from the ceiling behind Varius, with a knife in his hands.

Thinking fast, I throw a blast of magic into Varius. It knocks him across the room and into the door leading into the hall. The silence ward will stop all sound from escaping, but it won't stop the vibrations. As long as Khalid hasn't left his post outside, he'll see it and –

Pain explodes in my side as Myers closes the distance to me. By having moved Varius, I left myself wide open – an opening he took. I guess he doesn't want me as a patsy anymore.

Staring into eyes that look exactly like mine, I try to push him back, but he rips the knife up, opening me from my hip to my breast, cutting through my ribs like butter. That isn't a regular knife. It's cursed with magic. Lethal.

I stagger back as Varius turns to me and the door bursts open behind him. Khalid takes half a second to study the room, and then he's moving on Myers. Guess it's clear I'm not the stronger witch now that I'm dying.

Stumbling to my knees, I press a hand to my side, only to curse myself like a fucking fool. There's a knife in that hand, pushed all the way through, and in my dumb, shocked state, I've just stabbed myself with it.

Fuck.

I sway, the ground rushing up to greet me.

My.

No one comes to my aid, both the brothers focusing fully on Myers. He's strong. Old and powerful and too fucking experienced to not demand all of their attention if they wish to live.

Life...

I'm bleeding out, my intestines and organs sliding out of me. I want to live too, but I don't know if I can. I can't find the magic to heal myself. Don't have the skill even if I had the energy...

My eyes fluttering close, I look at Varius.

But he never once looks at me.

TWENTY-SEVEN

HIM

For situations exactly like this, I've ranked everyone in my family. Who would I save if forced to choose? These thoughts allow me to bypass all emotional conflict during the moment and act without hesitation.

I would save Rudy over any of the others. As much as logic would dictate he is at the bottom of this list, capable of protecting himself if he must and self-sacrificing, I can't bring myself to leave him even in just my thoughts. So I must save him first so I can then concentrate without any distractions, so that hesitation leaves my body.

Then Maddox. He's the craziest and smartest of us all, but he isn't very strong physically or magically yet. He'd be least likely to survive a fight.

Then Khalid. Though he's reaper and capable of holding his own, he is the only one I truly trust. Life without him would be too hard.

Then Krypto.

Enoch.

Leno.

Ezriel.

Talon.

Vinny.

Myers.

Mother. She would kill me herself if she wasn't at the bottom of my list. Her children always come first.

So I have a list. One I've thought long and hard about so I can act without hesitation when the time comes.

Micha, obviously, isn't on that list.

She *shouldn't* be on that list. I barely know her. Don't even want to know her. I am willing to give her up if she can't conceive. There's a chance she's only temporary, that within a year, her face is one I'll never see again.

And yet...

My concentration keeps breaking with every inhale that is filled with the coppery scent of her blood, with the smell of her stomach ruptured, its acid seeping into the rug she's lying on. I know there is nothing I can do for her. I am not a healer. And even if I was, I can't turn my back on Myers, can't leave my brother alone with him. Khalid might be a reaper, but he's over a century younger than our uncle, and Myers taught him almost everything he knows. In a one-on-one fight, my little brother will die.

And yet... My eyes go to her.

A mistake that I pay for instantly as Myers launches a ball of red magic at my brother. Khalid throws up a blue shield to protect himself. I swing my attention back to our uncle just as his knife jabs in towards my face. I dodge but only barely, getting a cut that nearly takes out my eye. As it is, the blood is blinding.

His blade comes in again. Rapid strikes that I only just manage to avoid. I don't have time to strike back at him, but I don't need to. I just need to buy my brother time.

So when Myers starts to turn, aware that Khalid needs dealing with now that his magic is no longer pinning him down, I slash out at him, leaving my side open. It's a small hole in my defense, minuscule, one most people wouldn't even see. But Myers isn't most people. He twists back to me, and his blade slides into my side.

I drop my own knife to wrap both hands around his wrist as pain buckles my knees. "Why?" I ask as his other hand comes up to blast me with a spell that will undoubtedly kill me.

"You're an abomination," Myers says as he strikes.

He didn't stop to monologue, but that was all the reaper needed. That turn, that slight distraction as Myers focused on the weaker prey. Khalid has shifted into his shadow form behind him, a black mass that connects this world to the Plane of Monsters.

Just as Myers' ball of red magic burns the hairs on the side of my head, I let both my knees buckle. He staggers off balance. I headbutt him in the stomach, then roll over the knife. It opens my side up more, but he expected me to go the other way, so threw his ball of magic in that direction.

He tumbles to the ground and spreads his arms just as Khalid races forward. Our uncle must sense my brother has changed, must know he is coming for him, because feathers shoot out of his skin. His left arm shrinks. His legs come up, merging with his body as his magic starts to change him into a crow. I draw a new knife and stagger towards him as he hits the ground. He claws himself forward in his half-shifted shape, using his arm that's still human, his blade still in his hand. He's not aiming for the open door or even away from me. He's just trying to escape the black mass chasing him.

But he can't.

My brother's shadow form wraps around one of his scaly, twisted legs, and he screams. A mixture of human and crow, the sound chills my spine. But I don't stop, don't hesitate in my strides towards him.

Although not every Shadow is strong enough to hold the portal to the Plane of Monsters open long enough for the monsters to make their way to it, Khalid is. And now they are eating our uncle, sinking their teeth and claws into his flesh, using his body as a handle to pull themselves out of that pitch-black world and into this one. They can't come all the way through, Khalid isn't strong enough, but they can eat whatever is pressed against their cell door.

As our uncle shrieks in agony, I step through the black mass surrounding him without hesitation. I might be an abomination, but I'm still a Shadow by blood. The monsters will not grab me.

Just as I get close enough to skewer him though, Myers slashes his blade at my ankles, forcing me to jump back. Then he swings his arm low and severs his own leg above the knee. He drops his knife, that arm now shrinking back into the shape of a wing. I dart forward, drawing on my secret speed, but before his blade even hits the ground, Myers has transformed fully, not even missing a leg now given his much smaller shape.

He twists out of the way of my blade, his black wings flapping. He darts over my head and out the door. Knowing the fight is over – a shapeshifter shrinking their mass that much is always a last resort, I rush over to Micha.

"Get Louise!" I snap as Khalid shifts back into his human form. Her pulse is weak, the fight having only taken a few seconds, maybe a minute, but it's still there, and I work on shoving her organs and intestines, par her open stomach, back into her body. Then I gently remove the knife I stabbed her with and slide it away. Louise can fix her. *She'll be okay. She has to be.*

When I sense my brother still with us, I turn my head to yell at him even though I know he won't leave my side to save her. He won't even leave to chase down Myers. But his phone is in his hand as he stands guard by the door, and a second later, Louise answers. "Yes?"

"Upstairs. Now. Bring Rudy and Maddox with you."

"No," I snap. "Not Rudy." As much as I'm trying to fight it, I'm terrified Micha will die in my arms. If I can't control my fears by the time Rudy gets here, his magic might make them come true. "Dayne," I say, knowing she'll want him here. "He can help Louise."

Khalid relays the change, then hangs up before dialing a new number. Mother answers this time. "Don't let Vinny leave," he says.

"He's already contained."

"By who?"

"The twins."

"And you didn't use any magic?"

"Just my sixth sense." That won't use up her life-force. "I'm coming up with Louise."

"No," I bark, raising my voice so she can hear me through my brother's phone. "Stay there in case Myers comes for his son." Although a shapeshifter cannot grow mass, only ever able to shrink or stay the same, they can combine their innate ability with a spell that allows them to use mass from somewhere else. If Myers has a stash of meat somewhere – something I would not put past him, then he can regain a bigger form. "Get Stefaan to get everyone else out of here."

He hangs up just as I sense people coming down the hall. I move Micha's sash to cover her as Khalid moves out of the way for Louise, Dayne, and Maddox to enter.

"Micha!" Dayne rushes in, dropping to his knees across from me. I want to tell him to get away from what's mine, but I'm the one who steps back. Louise needs the space. My hands are trembling as I stand, and I press them against my thighs so no one sees. Micha shouldn't matter this much. I barely know her.

My eyes snap up from my little monster's pale face as Louise steps in front of me. White light glows from both her hands as she reaches for my side. I grab both her wrists, my fingers biting. "Her first," I growl. "I'll survive until then."

Shock flickers across her face, but then it's gone, locked under her professional composure. Louise turns and kneels beside the ruptured stomach I left on the ground, thinking the leaking acid would cause more damage. Her white light wraps around the organ, patching it up and cleaning it of any harmful germs. She puts it back in Micha's body, then moves her hands up, still inside the wound, patching the internal damage.

Dayne's hands are over Micha's chest, above her heart. His face is one of concentration, and I tune my senses to her pulse, praying it doesn't stop in the time it takes these two to heal her.

My head grows dizzy, and I sag back against the wall. Khalid's head snaps to me. "Louise," he starts.

"No! Her first."

Micha's heartbeat stops. I feel it. Feel its absence. Feel its weight on my chest as it squeezes out every breath of air in my lungs.

I push up off the wall and stagger forward just as Dayne says, "Get out of her."

Louise pulls her hands away, and a second later, Micha's body jerks like she's just been hit by a defibrillator. I stop, my heart in my throat as I strain to hear the beat of her pulse. He curses and jolts her again with his magic.

Wake up, Micha. That's a fucking order.

But my little monster does like to defy me.

Dayne waits another second, then hits her again, the charge of his magic now strong enough to move her across the floor.

And there. There it is. The soft beat of her heart. I sag back against the wall, then all the way to the floor, my legs giving out for a different reason other than the hole in my side.

"Heal her," Dayne tells Louise, and the white light of her hands flows over the wound in Micha's side.

"She'll need rest," she eventually says as she rocks back on her heels. She takes Micha's bloody hand in hers. "But she'll be okay."

I take a deep breath, my head dizzy, my throat raw with silent screams. My focus latches onto Micha's face, waiting for her eyes to open. Louise moves over to me, blocking my line of sight. My pulse trips at the sound of her raspy voice calling Dayne's name. Always calling his fucking name.

I don't move my head to look at her though, instead lifting my shirt up for Louise. As much as I want to go to her, she wouldn't want me right now. After a tragic event like that, all you ever want are the people you love.

My chest aches at the memory of wanting Uncle Myers alongside the rest of my family the last time I nearly died. He came in so concerned, so convincing in his desire to help Khalid find the bastard and kill him. And all this time...

All this time, he was just staying close so he could find another opening. Because I'm an abomination, a freak.

As soon as Louise's magic heals my physical wounds, I stand. The cuts were clean, so they didn't take her long. I start to head for my brothers, watching Micha with Dayne only in my peripheral vision. Their arms are around each other, neither of them paying attention to me.

"You good to talk to Vinny?" I ask Maddox, knowing Khalid has already filled him in.

He doesn't smile like he normally does when given permission to "talk," but he does nod.

"Then let's —"

"She's the fucking Reaper of the Sired," Micha says, her voice light, and I turn my head to see her smiling.

"What?" Dayne asks, no doubt confused where this came from. But my chest feels lighter from hearing her words, her excitement. She really will be okay.

"Sau. She's the fucking Reaper. Varius told me –"

"What?" Dayne shouts, absolutely fangirling.

Her smile falls as she turns her head away from him, searching the room. As if she's looking for something she's certain she won't find.

Then her eyes land on me.

And the biggest fucking smile lights up her face, pushing back every bit of darkness clawing around inside my mind.

Locking my muscles down before I do something stupid like go to her and 'claim her as my girl' in Khalid's eyes, I nod, then turn. "Let's go," I say sharply to my brothers.

But later, when Micha and I are alone, perhaps…

Perhaps I will finally let myself get to know her.

TWENTY-EIGHT

HIM

Vinny is sitting in a chair at the table, his arms and legs magically restrained in gold binds, a mute spell drawn over his lips, red and glowing, looking like a line of stitches. His face is stoic, though, giving nothing away. His pulse is calm. He doesn't sweat. Doesn't fidget. Uncle Myers trained him well, just like he trained all of us to be able to withstand a "talk."

My eyes flick to Maddox as he splits off from Khalid and I to search through the cabinets. He moves casually, without any tension, without any hesitation, and I know he's locked himself down into that dark place inside of himself. Where people stop being people and just become *things*.

Where the pain of Uncle Myers' betrayal no longer hurts. It's just a fact. He's no longer the man who raised him, the only father Maddox remembers, Caden having left before his final son was born.

"Everyone else out," the reaper signs as we stop on the

other side of the table to Vinny. All of our brothers stand behind him. Mother is off to the side, a mask of calm, ever the collected lady. But beneath that facade, she is trembling with so much fear, an absolute mess of emotions. I've never seen her so afraid, and I wonder what she knows. What she is so worried Vinny might know...

Or perhaps I'm being paranoid, and all she's concerned about is Khalid hunting down an ex-reaper after this.

Although my brother has an ace up his sleeve, able to pull the monsters to him while he's in shadow form, it is severely risky to use. For the more often he does, the more agitated the monsters become, and although an ancient pact with a djinni stops them from eating us...they can still touch us. They can still drag us into the Plane of Monsters, and once there, we're no longer able to use our magic, including our ability to open a portal and escape.

Theoretically, another Shadow could pull him out just like we do the items we keep in our etheric storage, but that requires us to know exactly where our stuff is. The Plane of Monsters is vast, and we'll have no idea where Khalid ends up, and he will have no idea how to make it to one of our storage areas. So Khalid *could* use that technique to kill our uncle, but if he uses it and then is unable to grab hold of Myers, the monsters will grab hold of *him.*

The twins, Rudy, Leno, and Krypto file out instantly, knowing it wasn't their brother that gave the command to leave. It was the reaper. Vinny's reasoning could potentially resonate with them, and that would put a risk to the Family. Khalid will listen and then share only what he deems appropriate.

Talon and Mother, however, linger.

"He's family," Talon says, his voice raw. Vinny is his age, and the two of them have always been close. Always getting into trouble together. When our father left the first time, Vinny was the only one who could get him to eat. When his first crush died in his arms, Vinny was the one who took him on a week-long bender through our nightclubs in Miami. Watching over him. Letting him work through the pain. Alcohol never helps, not really, but whatever Vinny said to him during that time did. These two are as close as brothers, and for a moment, I wonder if Talon *should* be here. If he should be sitting right beside Vinny... If we need to "talk" to him too.

But I can't handle that right now. If he's a traitor, I'll deal with him later. After I've recovered from the loss of Vinny and Uncle Myers.

"I know," I say softly.

Mother grabs Talon's arm. "Come on, son," she says. "If Vinny is innocent, you know they won't hurt him."

Talon doesn't budge, his eyes swimming with tears and hatred and pain. But then he shudders, the pain winning out, the need for a mother's comfort, and he turns to her as she pulls him from the room. As she looks over her shoulder at us, her eyes are supportive, urging me to do what needs to be done.

Yet, there is still so much fear seeping off her, and once again, I wonder just how much she knows. If she's afraid Uncle Myers found out she cheated on his older brother. If I'm not his.

My fingers twitch down by my sides, wanting to ball into fists, to slam into a bag or a wall or an opponent as I work out my frustration, my paranoia. My thoughts that have no evidence.

Instead, I shift my gaze to Vinny as Maddox comes over to join us, a bowl of walnuts and a nutcracker in his hands. He hops up onto the table in front of Vinny, crossing his legs under himself as he faces our cousin. "Do you mind if I eat while we do this? I didn't have anything before the party and I'm low key starving."

Without waiting for an answer, not that Vinny can speak

with the silence ward still active on his lips, Maddox takes out a walnut and places it between the metal jaws. "Did you know there is a thing called a nutcracker fracture?" he asks as he gestures with the tool at Vinny.

"It's when the bone in the middle of your foot breaks because it's been *crushed* by the bones in your heels and toes." He *crushes* the nut between the metal teeth, popping its shell in a splinter of shards. "Can you guess why it was named that?"

Vinny doesn't move, can't speak, but his eyes latch onto the nutcracker as his pulse spikes for a few beats. He forces it to steady, keeping hold of his training.

"Exactly." Maddox nods as if he answered. "Ballerinas are so fucking metal, they have a fracture named after them. Have you ever seen them perform the *Nutcracker*? It's a beautiful dance." He opens the metal teeth and extracts the nut from inside its broken shell. Popping it into his mouth, he chews as he tilts his head to the side. "We should go after this. What they put their bodies through...it's breathtaking." He places another nut inside as he smiles wistfully.

"Watching them, you might even forget what it felt like to have your balls crushed in this."

He snaps the metal teeth together *hard*. The nut splinters. Vinny pales. I have the sudden urge to step back and cup my balls.

"Granted," my little brother says as he pulls out the nut and brings it to his lips, "your eyes might not have grown back by then." He chews, swallows. "Did you know you can dig out your own eye with your fingers? And as it dangles on that bunch of nerves, you can still see." He holds up the nutcracker with a new nut. Then he touches it to Vinny's cheek, right below his eye. A chill races across my skin as I can practically feel the coldness of the metal on my own.

"How high do you think it'll splatter?" he murmurs. Then he snaps the jaws together, and Vinny flinches as bits of shell fly everywhere. Our cousin turns his head away, his pulse spiking, a wild hammer against the base of his neck.

Maddox puts a new nut in. Touches the cold metal to Vinny's other cheek. Slides it up to his eye. Our cousin closes it with a hard swallow.

"Trick question," my brother says. "The optic nerves will hold it in place, you see, so I'll have to crack it while it's still mostly in your socket."

He smiles as he *cracks* the nut. Vinny jerks in his chair as Maddox pulls back to free his next bite of food.

"Thankfully, this nutcracker isn't one of those wooden man ones. That would've been fucking annoying to use." He laughs as his head turns towards the kitchen. "Although, getting him to chomp on your balls would be hilarious." He grins. "I'll have to add one to my Christmas list this year. Seeing all the blood running down his teeth and chin would be hilarious." His grin widens. "Maybe I can meet with a ballet company and run a thriller twist on the *Nutcracker* by them."

He pulls back, looking relaxed. "So what do you think, Vinny? Which part of you shall I start on first?" He nods. "The answer can be, 'None,' if you answer our questions."

Placing the nutcracker down on the table beside him, he reaches forward and rubs off the silence ward on Vinny's lips. "So first question, Cuz. Have you ever been to a ballet before?"

Vinny doesn't move, doesn't speak. He knows answering any question, even one as casual as this, is a gateway to breaking.

Maddox sighs in disappointment. He hops down off the table, then moves behind Vinny's chair. He pulls it back, the wooden feet dragging across the floor. Bending down in front of our cousin, he starts to undo Vinny's belt.

"I am aware you can handle pain," he says as he pulls the strip of leather free. "I'm also aware torturing you like this is pointless." He snaps open Vinny's button, then pulls down his zipper before he reaches for the nutcracker. "However, I want you to know what this feels like. I want every pulse that reaches your left testicle to remind you of the pain."

Placing said ball inside the teeth of the nutcracker, he squeezes it hard.

Snap!

Vinny jerks in the chair as he screams. His head falls back, his arms pulling tight on his binds. He shudders as Maddox straightens, removing his blood-splattered hand. He places the metal tool on the table. The jaws open and a testicle rolls out, the flesh of his torn ball sack sticking to it. Then he walks behind our cousin. Shuffling the chair, he points it towards one beside him. He steps away, pulls that chair out, and turns it to face Vinny.

He doesn't sit in it though. He stays standing as he pulls on his shadows. They swirl around his feet, and chills run down my back as I realize what it is he's doing. I didn't give him the order to take Alexis, Vinny's girlfriend, but Maddox must have grabbed her at some point because he pulls out a metal cage with her in it. She's screaming as she sits in the middle of it, her eyes closed, her knees pinned to her chest, her hands over her ears as she shakes. Saliva coats the bars, and angry hisses come up from below. One side of the cage has been dented in, and her leg on that side sports an ugly gash that cuts to the bone.

Vinny's scream trails off as he drops his head forward, his eyes widening at the sight of his girl.

"Open your eyes, Alexis. Vinny is here to save you," Maddox says as he vanishes his shadows, then pulls open the door of the cage after unlocking it.

She lifts her head slowly as tears continue to run down her cheeks. A few months ago, Talon told me Vinny was thinking of popping the question. They've been together for over three years, been living together for nearly one.

Jerking in his chair, Vinny scrapes it across the floor as he gnashes his teeth, fighting the urge to speak. To break his silence and ability to stay strong.

She calls out his name between sobs as Maddox hauls her into the chair. He ties her down, applying pressure to her wound when she tries to fight him. She collapses back on tear-stained cheeks and broken screams.

He picks up the nutcracker. A bit of blood and flesh is still stuck to it.

Stepping up behind Alexis, he places one hand over her chin, aiming her face at Vinny. Our cousin glares at him, then drops his gaze to his girlfriend, his eyes misting but trying to give her strength despite his silence.

Waving the nutcracker in his other hand, Maddox then trails it across her left cheek. "You focusing on that pain, Vinny?" he asks.

"Please," she begs. "Just let us go."

"That depends on your lover here. Although..." He looks down at her as he lifts her chin up. "You've moved into his house, haven't you? Stayed up waiting for him to come home. Do you know who his uncle is?"

Alexis nods, not smart enough to know she shouldn't answer. Or perhaps she's smart enough to know that she should. Our beef isn't with her if she had no knowledge of it.

"Have you ever heard the two of them talking about killing anyone?"

Her eyes widen as they flick to Vinny. He shakes his head at her, and there is a moment where she struggles to believe in him. Where her love for him shines through.

But then comes that desire to survive. To believe she will be let go if she just answers some questions.

"Yes," she whispers.

"Who?"

She starts to tremble. "I don't know. Some guy who stole

from him a few months ago."

Vinny closes his eyes so briefly, it could've been a blink. But I saw his flicker of relief. He'd talked about killing me with her home and thought for a moment she'd heard.

"Anyone else?" Maddox asks, and she shakes her head.

"A pity," he says as he trails his hand up to her eye. "I was really looking forward to letting you go."

She screams as his fingers dig deep. Her head thrashes around as he curls his grip around her eye. Her legs kick as he raises the nutcracker. "Vinny!" she screams. "Vinny!"

"Focus on the pain, Vinny," Maddox says as he pops her eye out of the socket far enough to get the nutcracker over it. He starts to squeeze. Her screams turn raw, grow higher in pitch. Her hands fist, clawing at the arms of her chair. Blood vessels burst behind her eye, coloring it red. The eye starts to deform, squeezed –

"Stop!" Vinny screams. "Just let her go. Let her go, you piece of shit!"

Maddox drops his hands, and her screams turn into heart wrenching sobs. But there's no relief in them, no belief that the pain won't come back. She's an associate of the Family, and she knows exactly what we are capable of.

"So have you been to a ballet?" Maddox asks our cousin, his words calm. Setting up the groundwork before he gets to the important stuff. Start low, make them comfortable with answering questions that don't matter.

Vinny grits his teeth together, his eyes fastened on his girlfriend. When Maddox starts to raise his hands again, he sharply nods. "Yes."

"Did you like it?"

"It was okay."

"*Okay?*" Maddox asks in disbelief. "They're the epitome of grace and power." He shakes his head, his long dark hair swaying. "But we're all allowed our differences in taste, I suppose. What about you, Alexis?" He trails his fingers down her cheek. "Do you like ballet?"

She cries as she keeps her head tilted back, her eye still popped out of her socket. "I've never been," she sobs.

"No? A shame. I'd say you should get Vinny here to take you, but, really, you should see it with one who appreciates the hel ballerinas go through so you can fully appreciate the gift they give us as spectators." He pauses a second, then grins. "I'm free on Valentine's. Assuming, of course, you're no longer dating my cousin. I'm not a fan of cheating."

The constant reference of them still being alive, of them making it through this gives them a bit of comfort. Makes them believe that they can end this, that they can survive this as long as they just give us what we want.

She trembles as he caresses her cheek, her entire body shaking.

Vinny jerks forward in his chair. "My dad is going to kill every single one of you," he spits, desperately trying to get Maddox's attention off his girl. "None of you deserve to rule this Family. You're a stain to the fucking Davenport name. *Uncle Caden* is the one who built this empire into what it is, who turned it from the backwater trash it was under Sau's father. It should be *me* who is Boss. It should be *our* line that gets passed down! Varius is a fucking joke who can't even use a fucking premade!"

His chest heaves as he spits out his rage, as he demands Maddox's attention, pulling it off Alexis. "You want to know who stabbed you in the back thirteen months ago?" Vinny asks as he turns his head to me. "I did. I thought I stabbed you in the fucking heart though. I would have cut off your fucking head if I'd known I'd missed."

He glares at me, and I stare calmly back, inhaling the sickly smell of his fear. His adrenaline. "Myers stabbed me," I say, my gut trusting Aleric's claims over his. Although both of them have motives to destroy this Family, Vinny would die for his father. Aleric would die for no one but himself.

Vinny sneers, "He wouldn't have missed your heart."

The first tendrils of doubt wrap themselves around me. "Myers was spotted by Aleric, who had the sense to capture it on camera."

Vinny pales, not knowing that was a lie. He tries to come up with a reason for what "Aleric showed me," but it takes him too long, and he knows it.

"He's my father," he says simply.

"And we were your *family*. Talon thinks of you like a brother. He would've fought for you," I say.

He scoffs. "He fucking left, didn't he?" There's a tear in his eye that he angrily blinks back. "None of you deserve to live after what your whore of a mother did to this family."

I still, wondering if he knows. "What did she do?" I ask, my voice flat.

"She killed Caden. He loved her. Tried to give her the world, and *she killed him*."

"He killed himself," Maddox says, the first crack in his mask, in the raw, wavering words that show he can still *feel*.

"Because she drove him to it. All she had to do was love him back, and instead she asked for *space*. He was with her for thirty years while she lay in a fucking coma, feeding her, combing her hair, removing her piss and shit so she would not wake up to tubes. He gave her *everything*, but then she became *woke*." He sneers at me, his eyes hard and so full of a hatred I've never seen, never suspected until tonight.

"She wanted to know if what they had was real, if it wasn't just because her father sold her to him, wrapped her up in a godsdamn bow and told him she was his, so she demanded space. He loved her enough, he left, but when he came back three years later, she still wasn't ready! He was my uncle, the only family my father had left, and she killed him!" He's shaking now, full-on yelling, and I know that he believes what he's saying.

But Father didn't leave because of *her*.

He left because of *me*.

Or is that just my paranoia talking? A coincidence of timing? Are the memories I have false, crafted from the mind of a boy feeling guilty over breaking up his parents – something so many kids feel? Did Father really yell at her about me? About my lack of magic… Or did he actually leave because she asked him to, and Mother never told us because she didn't want to be the bad guy? Is that what she was so afraid of us finding out when she left this room? Not that she cheated on Father when she had me? Just that she's the one who tore this family apart?

My jaw locks. There are too many questions in my head. Too many doubts.

But right now none of that matters. All that matters is Vinny is guilty.

"The Shadow Domain never would have followed you."

He lifts his chin. "We were going to rebuild the Red Demons." The Family my father's father ruled in New York before the human gangs ran them out and they came down to join ours. When Caden married Mother, their men, what few remained of them, came with them, but they all died during the war between the Blood Fangs and Death Hunt.

I stare at my cousin, wondering how I missed all this pent-up rage. Was it always there? The entire time we grew up together? Are all the memories I have of us nothing but lies?

Or did it recently fester?

My gut says it is the latter, that perhaps Myers acted alone when he tried to kill me thirteen months ago. Then his son found out somewhere along the way and demanded to know why.

Or perhaps that's just me being sentimental, not wanting to believe that two people so close to me hate me this much.

At least it's not just me they hate, a dark voice says. *It's all of my brothers too.*

"You're a traitor to this Family, Vinny," the reaper says calmly, having clearly heard all he needs to hear. "For that, the punishment is death."

"Fuck you all." He opens his mouth and sticks out his tongue, but Maddox is on him before he can bite it off. His fingers pinch Vinny's jaw, forcing his teeth apart. He shoves the nutcracker sideways between his lips, then he forces it to stay there with his magic. Vinny is to die, but it will be by our hand.

With our cousin bound, silenced, and helpless once more, Maddox straightens, then steps back.

"Kill him quickly," he says as he walks away, and I know he isn't coming back to this mess. He needs a breather from it all, and I can't blame him. So do I. I want nothing more than to turn on my heels and find Micha, but I can't.

I am the Boss of the Shadow Domain.

And this fucker wanted to kill my entire family.

They might've wanted to rebuild the Red Demons, but they were going to do it with *my* gang, a gang that only follows the rule of a Shadow. Which means for Vinny to be accepted as Boss, he would have to have our magic in his veins...or be the father of someone who does. And with Mother being the only female Shadow...

My fingers burn with the urge to squeeze his fucking neck. He would've killed all her children, then raped her.

Beside me, Khalid draws his shadows into the palm of his hand. His reaper mask is deposited there when the shadows fade. It's a skeletal face that isn't human, made of tar-black metal. Two sets of gold horns curve out of its forehead, and nestled above them is a gold rune that says: *Death claims all.*

He lifts it to his face, walks around the table, and pulls a knife from his shadows. He shoves it sideways into Vinny's throat, then jerks out. As Vinny slumps forward, gurgling on his blood, Khalid wipes both sides of the blade on his tux. Then he turns and heads for the door, off to hunt our uncle alone.

Although he has magic that can kill him from a distance, he will want to question him first. Will want to make sure there are no other secrets that will tear this family apart.

I watch him go, slipping through the archways leading to the front of the house. My chest tightens as I wonder if this is the last time I'll see him. Myers is weak at the moment, having used an excessive amount of magic in our fight. If a witch isn't careful, our magic will turn on us, literally eating away at our organs until it finally kills us. Khalid might have a chance of surviving...

I want to go with him, to follow him and make sure he lives, but this is reaper business, and if I join him, it'll look too much like a hit rather than a serving of justice.

So I glance at Vinny, but there are too many thoughts in my head. Too many questions. Too many doubts. Too much pain.

Turning for the stairs, ignoring Alexis' whimpers, I make my way to Micha.

TWENTY-NINE

HER

Neither my side nor my hand hurts in the slightest, but my head is fucking killing me. As the Shadow brothers leave the room, my eyes turn to the woman who healed me. She looks exhausted as she rubs a hand over her eyes. Like she's about to fall over at any moment.

Exhaling with a silent grumble, I ignore Dayne gushing over Sau being the Reaper of the Sired still, and climb to my feet. My dress immediately starts to fall due to the tear in its side, and I grope at the flaps as I glare at it. Pinning them to me in an awkward embrace, I head over to the dark-haired woman.

"Who are you?" I ask, trying not to sound too much like a jealous bitch. I don't know Varius well enough to trust his claim that I'm the only one he's fucking even though I want to.

She drops her hand as she looks at me, a small smile on her lips. "My name's Louise Warner. I'm Talon's secretary."

"You know Varius well?"

"Not really. He doesn't exactly let people know him, you know?"

My lips twitch. *Don't I fucking know.* "But you left with him earlier."

She nods, a blush running up her throat.

My lips flatten as my eyes narrow.

"It was strictly business, but he and Khalid both got naked."

"Together?" Dayne asks, popping into the conversation like a fucking meerkat popping its head up, and I roll my eyes. Of course *that* is what would grab his attention away from the whole Sau is a named sup thing.

"Well, they were both naked at the same time, but ah –" She clears her throat, that blush streaking across her cheeks. "Not like, *together.*" She makes a little noise. "Not like the twins sometimes do." A choked breath of air escapes her. "I mean, they don't fuck each other either, just the same chick. Or at least, not that I know of. Though they are identical, so one could argue that morally, that'd be okay and is akin to masturbation –" Her eyes widen.

"Not that I think they're the same person. They're very different, obviously. Enoch is so sweet and his twin is less so. Not that I think Ezriel is an ass." The reddening of her cheeks says she thinks *something* about his ass. "Just that there wouldn't be any genetic issues. Though there wouldn't be anyway, obviously, due to them being the same sex, so they can't have kids even if they wanted to – not that I think they want to. Together I mean. But like...you know... Ah..." She trails off, red as a fucking tomato, and my smile spreads across my cheeks.

I like her.

She seems embarrassingly honest and open, and gods is that a breath of fresh air compared to a certain neanderthal.

"Aw!" Dayne says. "She rambles just like you." His smile

has the power of the sun as he turns it on her. "You're cute."

Louise blushes even more as her eyes dart up and down his body. He's well in shape and has that rugged alpha look like he knows how to get down and dirty in the outdoors.

I give her a sympathetic smile. "Sorry, he's gay."

"Ah. Ah, of course he is."

"So what were they both doing naked?" I ask, curious as all hel.

Her spine straightens though, and she lifts her chin. "I can't talk business. Sorry."

"But it was business?"

"That required them both to be naked?" Dayne chimes in.

She nods, and fuck it, I believe her. There's no guilt in her eyes, no sign of gloating from a woman who knows she can steal another's man. Also, there's the whole fact that she's able to string sentences together. Ain't no way she would be able to if she'd had both Varius' and Khalid's dicks inside her. I have seen the bulge in Khalid's pants. He might be bigger than his brother. And gods, do I feel sorry for any woman who catches *that* thing's eye.

"Well, thanks for saving me," I say.

"I couldn't have done it without Dayne. You died for a few seconds there before he brought you back."

I shiver, remembering the pitch black of Purgatory. I felt like I walked that barren plane for days. Screaming into the abyss, unable to tell if I was the right way up or not, no ground beneath my feet, no sky above. Just utter darkness, and the feeling that I was being hunted.

I rub a hand over my shaved head to calm my nerves. "Well, anyone know what we're supposed to do now? Have they just left us here or..."

"Maddox is having a talk with Vinny, which means the house is probably locked down tight." She strolls to the open door, then pokes her head out. "Six 'waitresses' are outside, as is your dad." She asks them, "Is she allowed to leave?"

"If she wants," Stefaan says.

Louise leans back in. "I wouldn't recommend it though. Varius doesn't like having to find things he wants."

"Yeah, well, he shouldn't have just left then, huh?" I head for the door, wanting to give Varius a reason to punish me tonight. The fucking bonehead won't come to me otherwise, and no one should hurt that much alone. He might think himself tough and capable of taking on the world, making it bend the knee to him, but I see him for the boy he is. The one who can't trust anybody so doesn't let anyone in. The one who needs comfort before he breaks but doesn't know how to ask for it.

Entering the hall, I look at Stefaan. "How'd Myers slip away?"

His jaw tics, and I fucking love how much it pisses him off to submit to me. "He went into the bathroom and had a recording of him taking a shit that he played to fool Sharee."

I glance at the assassin standing closest to me, my eyes widening. Despite wanting to hate the guy, I can't help but be impressed. "He saw you?"

"No, but he was smart enough to know someone was watching."

"Fucking paranoia clearly runs in the family," I mutter.

"He snuck out the window, and you know the rest."

I glance back at Stefaan. "Where are Aaron and Teak?" My two brothers.

"I sent them home."

"Why?"

"To guard Lou."

I blink, surprised he'd bother. Even if Myers did plan on going after her to get to me to get to Varius – something utterly pointless given I doubt he'd care if Myers had me, Lou is over eight hours away. Why would he remove two damn good assassins from tonight's detail given how much he was trying to impress Varius? If he actually cared about his kids, I would understand, but as it is, I'm fucking baffled.

My head hurting too much to think about anything, I rub my temples. "I'm going for a walk," I say.

His eyes narrow, but he doesn't glare at me like he would have done just a few hours ago. Nor does he tell me what to do. He simply shrugs off his jacket, hands it to me, and then steps to the side. Dumbly, I put it on to hide the opening in my dress.

More weirded out than I was when I fought Myers with my own face, I walk quickly in front of him. Dayne comes up beside me. "Are you sure this is wise?" he asks in the language we made up together years ago.

"Going for a walk after nearly dying? Louise healed me, so –"

"Pissing Varius off when he's already pissed off."

"Yes. He'll need a reason to visit me that doesn't make him look weak."

He sighs. "What happened to you agreeing that getting him to fall for you was a bad idea? Men like him don't love in sappy poems and mixtapes. And when they hurt, they lash out without thinking. This is a dangerous path, Micha."

"My whole life has been dangerous, Dayne. Besides, I'd rather die still being me than living until I'm three hundred, having been forced to be someone I'm not. This marriage is my cage," I say, referencing his childhood, where he spent over a decade chained inside a dark room and beaten like a dog. Worse than a dog. He understands what it means to die fighting.

"I just want you to be safe," he says softly.

"I know," I murmur as I turn my head to him. "And I will be. I'm getting him to fall for me, not the other way around." I tap my head. "I'm keeping it cool."

He gives me a look that I'm too tired to decipher, then he grabs my arm to stop my forward march. Opening the door we're beside, he shoves me into the room. "We've gone far enough," he says. "You need rest if you're going to tease him tonight."

Grinning, I stride over to the bed as he shuts the door behind us, leaving my father and the other assassins out in the hall. Louise broke off at some point during our walk, perhaps going to find her boss Talon.

"Fuck yeah, I'm exhausted." I flop onto the mattress, right on top of the neatly tucked in duvet. I close my eyes, and two seconds later, I'm out.

"I told you not to make me search for you."

A smile tugs at my lips as I'm pulled from my sleep by a hand on my thigh. Lifting my head up, I'm not surprised to find we are alone. "If I had your phone number," I mumble as I drop my head back onto the pillow, "I could've texted you."

"You had Mother's."

"I'm not running everything past your mother. What if I want to send a topless pic? Or sext you?" I raise a brow as I twist onto my back to look up at him. "You going to reply back through her too?"

His eyes narrow slightly, and I know he knows what I'm doing. He's too fucking paranoid not to. I expect him to brush me off, to hide behind his walls still, but he surprises me by pulling out his phone as he sits down on the bed beside me. His fingers swipe across his screen. Curious as to what he's doing, I sit up and peer at his phone. He's on his messenger app.

Varius: *Show me how ready your pussy is for me.*

He presses send, and my heart hammers as he turns to me. But there isn't any heat in his eyes. There's just sorrow and pain and a need to yell into the void about what his own family has done to him. All hidden behind a solid mask, of course. Only readable to me because I've spent years deciphering such looks from kids. After Dayne and I "rescue" our targets, we keep in touch with them, visiting every so often to make sure their new life is better than their old one. A couple times, they haven't been, and their new parents ended up six feet under.

Swinging my right leg across both of his, I straddle his lap and loop my arms around his neck. I moved slowly, non-threateningly, but even still, he is tense beneath me, ready to fight for his life.

I drop my hands to his chest, pressing my palms flat to him so he can feel every movement of my fingers and know I mean him no harm. His eyes hold mine, and I can see that first wall creak open. I smile at him, a light teasing on my lips. "So I hear you got naked with Khalid."

"Louise talked?" he asked, that wall slamming shut, that curtain coming down as he paints her as yet another traitor. Someone who broke his trust and *talked*.

My pulse jumps, fear for her making me blurt, "No. She said it was business. That's it. She only mentioned you two got naked because I basically accused her of fucking you, but she's actually annoyingly tight-lipped."

There's a moment where Varius doesn't move, doesn't believe me, and my throat closes as I realize just how fine of an edge I'm walking. A single sentence is enough to raise his suspicions, to lose his trust, to turn him from a man seeking comfort into the monster who stalks the dark. If I make one wrong move, say one wrong thing, I could be the one he "has a talk with." Maybe Dayne was right. Maybe trying to get him to like me is a fucking stupid idea. Having the attention of someone as dangerous as him...

But then he relaxes, accepting my answer, and my brain grows heady. There is something addicting about having the trust of a powerful man. *I'll be careful,* I tell myself. *I'll never give him reason to suspect me of anything.*

Deciding teasing him about his brother will just make him think I'm trying to get him jealous to drive a wedge between them, I change tactics. "So I've been thinking," I say, "about my dreams."

My heart pounds inside my skull at the vulnerability I'm opening myself up to. I swallow as I glance away, suddenly feeling like I'm being a fool with foolish dreams.

"What are they?" Varius asks when a moment of silence settles heavily between us. I start, looking back at him.

My cheeks and neck hot, I make a noncommittal noise. But one of us has to break the distance between us, and the gods know it'll never be him. So I take a deep breath, then squeak, "I want to try karaoke."

He stares at me without a word, and I want to kick myself for having such a dumb dream. But I wanted to start small. Manage my expectations. And the idea of going out with friends – having friends to go out with, and then being able to just enjoy all the normal things I missed growing up because of my assassin training...it just seems nice.

"Okay," he finally says.

"Okay?"

"We can go for Valentine's."

My jaw drops. My pulse spikes. *I've changed my mind. This is a terrible idea.* The thought of standing up in front of a crowd and singing sounded like a straight-up nightmare. When I dreamed of it, I never thought it'd actually happen!

He nods, the decision final, and I let out a little squeak before I control myself. *This is a good thing*, I tell myself. It's progress. I can suffer a night of embarrassment for that. Exhaling slowly, I nod back. "Okay then," I finally manage. "It's a date."

"Why did you become an assassin?" The abrupt turn in the conversation throws me off, and my mind blanks for a second. I blink a few times to get it back up and running.

I shrug. "I'm a Black." I'm not ready to trust him enough

to tell him about Lou. About what she means to me. He already has Dayne as collateral. As someone to torture if he ever needs to break me. Dayne, as much as I hate the idea, can handle it. But Lou? She wouldn't last a second under a knife.

"You could've married into a different family." His hands grip my hips, a subconscious movement that locks me to him.

"Would you want to be someone else's toy?"

"No." He pauses, then asks, "Do you like burgers?"

I blink, trying to figure out how we possibly got onto this question. "Um, yeah. I guess."

He nods, but his lips are tight. Like he isn't quite pleased with himself.

Remembering he said he likes them too, my lips twitch. *Is he trying to ask me on another date?* "We could go out to eat after karaoke if you'd like. Just the two of us."

"Mmm," he says noncommittally, but there's an easing to the tightness of his lips. "Why do you specialize in killing kids?"

I tense, then force myself to relax, not giving anything away. If anyone finds out Dayne and I've been scamming our clients, not even the Shadow name will stop me from being blacklisted, and there will be absolutely nothing to protect Dayne.

The thing about charging six figures for a kill, as well, is all of your clients are stupid rich, and the rich get especially bitchy when they get played for fools. Given they clearly have no morals against hiring hitmen, they'll hunt down not just us, but all the kids too. There are more than a hundred of them. It would be impossible for Dayne and I to save them all while we're also on the run.

"Easy kills," I say with an indifferent shrug.

He watches me, his eyes looking past my words, and I struggle to keep my breathing even, my face free of any sign of deceit.

His fingers tighten minutely on my hips. He opens his mouth slightly, hesitates, then says, "If my lack of magic gets passed down..." He stops, his lips pressing together as he looks away. My brow furrows as I try to figure out what he's attempting to say. Whatever it is is clearly weighing on him.

And then it hits me.

The line of ascension follows the Shadow bloodline due to the magic in their veins. If Sau had ever decided to cheat, her firstborn would have been the legitimate heir to the throne. Her husband would have lost all status, only able to rule because of his connection to her. It's why most of the coups in this Family have tried to put Leno on the throne rather than their own children. Their sons would never be recognized as Boss.

"The Boss has to have the shadow magic," he says. "Or at the very least be able to pass it down."

"And if you can't?" I ask, my throat tight.

"Then it is the reaper's duty to kill me and any children like me."

My heart plummets past my stomach and into the soles of my feet. I can't speak, can't move. I don't even want to look at him. How could he have ever asked me to do this? To have a child and fall in love with them, only to watch them die in their teens?

Because he's Varius fucking Shadow. A fucking monster.

I start to shake as I climb off him. But his fingers dip into my hips, refusing to let me go. "Get off me," I snap.

"I don't have a choice."

"Everyone has a choice! You could step down and just let Leno be Boss!"

"That would be a death sentence. I know too much."

"But they're *kids*. Innocent fucking kids and you —" I stop, horrified at what I've just revealed.

"The Family will pay you for them. Your going rate is a hundred thousand, is it not?"

I clamp my mouth shut. I need to put my mask back on, my indifference, but I can't stop the word from crawling out. "*Them*?"

"We don't know if I'm incapable of passing down the shadow magic until our firstborn is in their teens. We don't have thirteen years to waste when we're on the verge of war." His voice is utterly flat, a heartless monotone. "We need the soldiers."

"That's barbaric," I whisper.

"I know." And in those two words, I hear everything. His frustration at what he can't change. His terror about what he will lose. His uncertainty over whether he can really go through with letting his own children die.

"If that happens...run with me," I say. "I have a network. They'll hide us." I swallow, everything inside me wanting to take those words back, keep the secret about the kids Dayne and I've rescued under lock and key. But I need to convince Varius that running is a viable option, or he'll never go for it.

"Khalid..." He stops, but he doesn't need to spell it out.

The reaper will have their DNA.

He'll be able to kill them from any distance.

I shake my head slowly. "You picked me because of my speciality," I say, feeling so fucking sick that my attempt at a good deed has led to *this*.

He doesn't say anything.

"Did you not?" I demand.

"Mother picked you."

"Your mother?" Angry tears burn my throat as I scoff. "Your *fucking mother*? Because of that though, right? She thought I would be fine with it because I take jobs killing kids."

"I think so."

"You think –" I cut myself off as I stare at the monster in front of me because he's unable to hold my gaze. His eyes are open and pointed at me, but there is an absence in them. A devastation. He is as stuck in this life as I am, and my heart aches for the boy who can't escape his chains.

"So Sau is okay with killing her own grandkids?" I ask, my voice raw.

He shakes his head. "She's convinced my magic will pass down." But Varius isn't. I can hear it in the tightness of his words.

"Why?" I ask, and for a moment I'm not sure what I'm asking. Why is she so certain? What does she know? "Why are you telling me now?" *Why tell me at all when I'm just a womb?*

My lungs stop working as I wait for his answer, feeling the pinpoint edge we're balanced on. The silence stretches, grows taut and heavy until it's damn near unbearable. My heart stutters as I realize he doesn't know. The words just came out, his conscience demanding that there're no secrets between us. Cupping his face in my hands, I rasp, "We can stage both our deaths. We can run away together."

The shock in his eyes breaks something inside of me. "Why would you take me with you?" he murmurs.

Because you remind me of the kids I save. Because no one should have to suffer like this. But none of those words come out. None of them seem right because what I really want to say is...I don't want *you* to die. I don't want to lose *you.*

My feelings for him twist in undecipherable knots. That pull between us draws taut, but I can't pinpoint why. I know I don't love him. I don't even know if I really like him. But the flickers of depth I've seen in him, locked away under all his mountains of betrayal and pain and paranoia...they call to me.

We could have something one day.

He could become something so godsdamn important to me. I know that in the depths of my soul.

I start to answer, taking the courage of that first step. "I don't –"

But a knock on the door interrupts me. A quick rap that instantly gives way to the *whoosh* of the wood swinging open. "It's Khalid!" Sau says, breathless and terrified as she runs in. "I can feel him dying."

THIRTY

HIM

If Khalid dies, I could run with Micha.

The thought has me shoving her away and standing. She will never mean more to me than a brother, especially not Khalid. He has saved my life more times than I can count, not just by stopping assassination attempts and killing my enemies, but by being the only one I can trust.

As Micha turns to face the doorway, Talon skids into the room behind Mother.

"Vinny!" he says, his face pale.

I start to tell him it was necessary, that our cousin was planning to kill us all and rape Mother to take the throne, but before I can get a word out, he shouts, "He's gone."

Mother spins on her feet. "What?"

I'm out of the room in a few strides, needing to see for myself. Khalid didn't just slit his throat; he fucking tore it apart, severing half of it with his knife.

But when we get down to the kitchen, his body is gone.

So is Alexis, but she was moved out not long after I went up to find Micha so Louise could heal her. Our beef is not with her.

"*Varius.*" Mother's voice is close to cracking, and I turn to her, my heart hammering in my ribs. Her sixth sense has always been strong, doubly so when it comes to the welfare of her children.

Khalid needs me now. Vinny's mystery will have to wait. Striding through the house, I start to bark orders. "Micha, get Stefaan to comb the house to see if he's still here or if anyone saw anything. Talon, have Leno watch over Alexis, then tell Enoch and Ezriel to gear up. They're coming with me. And get Maddox's ass in here for a location spell."

"No," Mother says. "That'll take too long. Hand me your phone."

I pull it out of my pocket and place it in her hand. She taps my contacts, then Aleric's name. She steps away from us as she raises it to her ear. My eyes narrow, wondering why she is calling him.

All the times Mother has ever spoken of Aleric, it's been with the urge to kill him clear in her tone. We are not the first 'batch' of children she's had. Born as a breedmare, she started young, having seven children in six years. The next batch, she had seven more, and Aleric killed or caused the death of most of them in only a month.

If she's calling him, pleading with the devil himself, then Khalid must be close to dying.

My pulse jumping, I turn to the chair where Vinny was restrained. Micha and Talon have already split, and Stefaan now comes running in from one of the archways.

"Two of my assassins are dead," he says. "They've been ripped to pieces." His eyes drop to the empty chair with the bloodstain on its seat. "Was he a shapeshifter?" he asks.

It would explain how my cousin survived a knife to the throat. He could have rearranged his anatomy, moving his vital parts somewhere else.

I shake my head. "He was a telekinetic. *Is.*" Fuck.

"So how did he survive?"

"Myers knows a lot of dark magic," I say, my lips tight. "He most likely spelled his son before he attacked me. That would explain why he didn't come back for Vinny; he knew he would make it." *Fuck.* He probably rejoined his father immediately. Is Khalid fighting the both of them right now? I turn to Mother and only just catch Aleric's last words.

"...lotion every night."

"If he lives," she hisses, her knuckles white. Then she hangs up. She takes a breath before looking over at me. She pales further before lifting her chin and striding over.

"Get everyone back to the house," she says, then she looks at Stefaan. "The party was wonderful. Thank you for hosting it, and we apologize for the mess. Send us the bill when you have it." Her words are clipped and rushed, but if he's offended, he doesn't show it.

"It was a pleasure hosting," he says with a formal nod. Then he turns to me. "I'll call you when the Mad Hatters are no longer in business."

When I nod, letting him know I'm still keen on our deal, he walks off.

"What about Khalid?" I ask, turning to Mother.

"He'll be there," she says.

My eyes search hers, niggling questions at the back of my mind making me tense. "Why is Aleric doing this for you?"

"Khalid is dying. I need to get home."

"We'll talk on the drive then."

She pales, a tremor shaking her. But then she's back in control, locking down her fear. She starts to stride past me, but she barely takes two steps before Aleric appears, his shirt covered in blood, and I know it is my brother's. His chin is too, and I take a step forward, seeing red. Without even glancing at me, he grabs Mother's wrist and phases away.

My pulse spikes at the idea of him having fed on Khalid. Then spikes again at the thought of my brother dying before I can even make it home. It's over an hour's drive back. *No.*

No, Mother will save him.

She's the strongest healer on this side of the Atlantic, and she'll trade her life for his. And if Aleric did drink from my brother, then it was in order to save him. Mother wouldn't have traded that lightly.

So Khalid will be there. Alive and stable. Then I'll have a fucking long chat with Mother.

Khalid is alive and stable, but fucking hel does he look like shit as he lies in bed, still unconscious. Mother told me he was stabbed sixty-nine times. Both his hands were nearly hacked off. To most witches, the loss of one hand is a death sentence in a fight. We need them to control our magic, and without both, the energy becomes wild and unstable, much more likely to kill us rather than to do what we want. With the loss of both, Khalid would've been forced to rely on his speech as a conduit – a skill most witches do not have due to even trying it once will normally end up with them dead. Or worse – alive, locked in a twisted form of their body that is crippled by constant pain.

Thank the fucking gods Khalid's a stubborn idiot, though, who's practiced speech magic in secret. It's a skill we have kept from everyone – including Uncle Myers and all the brothers now sitting around us, crowded in his bedroom alongside Mother as we wait for him to wake up. Khalid hasn't mastered speech magic, not by a long shot, but it's probably what allowed him to win the fight. Even still, he wouldn't have survived if Aleric hadn't saved him.

If Mother hadn't made whatever deal she had with the Boss of the Blood Fangs. *"...lotion every night."* My eyes flick to her, kneeling beside Khalid's bed, both her hands clasped over one of his. What the hel does that mean?

"I can't believe Uncle Myers did this," Talon whispers in the quiet of Khalid's bedroom. There's no furniture other than the bed; prison cells are more decorated than this. So everyone but Mother is standing; some of us are leaning against the walls, others are pacing.

Talon runs his hand through his hair. "He raised us," he says. His voice catches. *Breaks.* "And Vinny..."

A brother in all but blood.

"He was really willing to kill every single one of us?" He looks over at Maddox, a subtle, subconscious sign that he doesn't trust me to answer truthfully. Doesn't trust that I'm innocent in all this. He needs confirmation from someone else.

Maddox nods. "They want – *wanted* to resurrect the Red Demons."

"Is it 'wanted?'" Rudy signs.

Normally we would all talk with our hands in respect to his presence, but no one seems to have the energy. "How could it not be?" Enoch asks. "Khalid ripped out his throat before he left." He looks at me. "Right?"

I nod.

"Did you just suck him into your shadows, T?" Rudy asks hopefully. It is an honor given only to those who are family. Had Vinny died any other way, he would have been 'buried' like that without question.

"Two assassins were killed," I sign as Talon shakes his head. He wanted to though. I can see it in the pain of his eyes.

"Myers knows how Khalid kills," Leno says as he squats down beside Krypto and scratches him between his large pointy ears, taking comfort in his canine friend. "He could have easily put a spell on Vinny before he went upstairs to kill Varius and frame Micha." He swallows, taking a small break before he pushes on. "As a shapeshifter, he'd know how to rearrange a body so a knife to the throat doesn't kill him."

"A shapeshifter can't change someone else though," Rudy signs.

"But Lincoln can," Leno says. "Krypto saw him talking to the two of them earlier. I didn't think anything of it at the time…" He trails off. His fingers stop moving. His dog turns to him, pushing his head into his hand, and Leno smiles as he starts scratching him again. "He could've helped them."

A dry laugh escapes my lips as I realize just how well they played us. "They framed Lincoln," I sign when heads turn to me. "So even if I'd seen them talking to each other, I wouldn't have expected they were working together. There was no way you could have known." The last part is directed at Leno.

He nods at me, but his guilt still lingers.

"Fuck," Talon says, rubbing his head again.

It's a word that resonates through all of us, and as we fall into silence, waiting for Khalid to wake up, I can't help but wish Micha was up here with us. Beside me. The back of her hand brushing against mine.

But I sent her to her room. Louise said she needed rest, and it is inching towards midnight.

Mother lifts her head to Khalid's face, the first movement she's made since she's knelt by his side, and we all tense, knowing she's sensing his return to consciousness. His eyes open a second later. They flicker around the room, seeing all of us.

"You must be losing your game," Maddox teases, "losing to an old man like Uncle Myers."

"What did he do?" Rudy signs. "Shift into a woman with big tits?"

"Nah, Khalid's too focused for tits." Enoch laughs. "He'd have to shift into a shiny new blade. Oooh, look at the edge on this thing."

"Feel its balance!"

"Come stroke your fingers along my handle. Oh yeah, just like that. Stab."

They rib him for being rubbish, hiding their fear behind jokes and smiles, but I keep quiet as I recognize the look in his eyes. The pain in them that someone he loves is missing from this crowd of people welcoming him back to the world of the living – the woman he started stalking two years ago after she bumped into him on the street. *His girl.* The only one he really wants to see.

"Vinny?" I ask, cutting through the rest of my brothers.

"Dead," he says, the word flat, and I know he is grieving.

He needs to see her, needs her to recover.

So I nod, silently communicating we can talk later, and before my head even rises, he's shifted into his shadow. As exclamations of, "What the fuck," resonate around the room, with one, "You need to rest!" yelled by Mother, Khalid peels off under our feet and races out the door.

I wish to do the same as him. To leave all this darkness behind for one fucking night and take comfort in my girl.

But I have too many questions that need answering.

And she isn't my girl...

"Meeting tomorrow at dinner." I walk out of the room. The others follow behind me, their nerves still drawn tight even as they start joking again about Khalid trying to catch the last hour of some gun and knife show. Out in the hall, they all head downstairs, no one wanting to face their grief alone. Mother stays behind, as do I. She looks at me, and I turn for my study.

Once inside with the silence ward activated, I pivot to her. "Why did Aleric help us?"

She crosses the room to the cabinet where I keep the fine

liquor required for toasts in the closing of deals. She pulls out a bottle of single malt scotch and two glass tumblers.

"I don't want one."

"It's for your father."

I half turn towards the door, expecting to see someone behind me. My pulse pounds in every part of my fucking body until even my skin is vibrating from it.

But there's no one there.

I turn back around to see her lifting both glasses. One she raises to her lips and knocks back. The other she holds out in front of her.

"I'm sorry," she murmurs as she tips it sideways, and the fifty-year-old Highland Park pours out onto the floor, then gets eaten by her shadows. For once, I don't mention her use of magic.

"After Caden cursed me," she says slowly, "I took him into my shadows."

"Why? Out of guilt?"

"Out of love." She smiles softly as she lifts her head, then turns to pour herself another shot. Leaning back on the long cabinet, she meets my eye. "I was gifted to him before I was even a week old. He named me, and from that moment on, my life was his. Everything I learned was to serve him. My parents made me believe it was an honor, that he was a prince and I a princess. I loved him before I even knew what love was."

Her eyes drop to the floor, to where she poured the other drink, but her shadows are no longer there. Her smile turns sad, then falls away completely. "Khalid thinks Caden and I never loved each other, but he's only part right. Neither of us really knew what love was, but we believed we had it with each other. But I was gifted to him. I was a thing he latched onto to survive his own hel. If he didn't marry me, his dad would've killed both of his brothers. So he built me up as this great thing, this toy to cherish." Her eyes mist, and I can feel the pain breaking her apart. It cracks her voice, makes her hands shake. "It wasn't love. It was obsession. Just in a kinder way than –" She breaks off on a hard swallow. After raising her glass to her lips, she drinks half of it. "And I had the mentality of a child for years. Decades even... I wasn't raised to think for myself, to have that adult independence. I fell into a coma on my wedding day, and when I woke up...the years had passed, but my mind was the same as it was then...

"It took me a long time, but I realized that I only *thought* I loved your father. I never chose him. I was given to him, then I latched onto him through trauma."

"So you asked him to give you space."

She closes her eyes. "Yes," she says softly, her voice raw. "I needed to see if it was real or if we were only together because we had to be."

"So you let me believe he'd left because of *me*?" I bite out, unable to stop the words from spewing out of my lips, unable to stop the rage, the pain, the feeling of betrayal from someone I thought would never hurt me. Not Mother. Not the woman who so dearly loves her fucking children.

"I told you it wasn't your fault," she says, tears burning her eyes.

"But you didn't tell me it was because of *you*." The words claw at the back of my throat. "I thought that was just one of the things parents say. 'It's not your fault, Varius.' 'Don't blame yourself, Varius.'" I suck in a breath, trying to keep my calm, my control. But my lungs are being stretched over a fire. Its smoke is filling them, killing me. "Father couldn't even look at me those last few months before he left," I say, drawing up all those moments I've tried not to think about. "You cried yourself to sleep. Why would you do that if you asked him to leave?"

"Because love is complicated. You were his firstborn. He loved you. He didn't want to leave you –"

"But you made him."

"Yes."

I look up at the ceiling, my chest feeling like it's being crushed in. I struggle to breathe, struggle to think. For so long I thought I was the one who broke this family, who was the abomination Father couldn't bear to love. And all this time... All this fucking time it was *her*. And she let me believe...

I close my eyes. Draw in a deep breath and hold it until my lungs ache. Until my desire to scream finally goes away. But now something is niggling at the back of my mind. I run after it, focus on it, drag it kicking and screaming into the light because I can't ignore it anymore.

"Did you fuck someone else?" I ask as I look at her. "Is that how you learned you didn't love him? Am I..." I stop, swallow, then force myself on. "Is he even my father?"

Her eyes widen. "Of course he is! I'd never cheat on him, Varius."

"So why don't I have any magic? You and Father are two of the strongest witches of your generation. There's never been a *single* witch without magic."

"I don't know."

"Yet, you never *once* took me to see anyone about it."

"There's no one to take you to."

"But why didn't you even try? You never reached out to anyone about it. You just accepted that I was a freak."

"Varius –"

"Why didn't you try?" My tone rises, so I bite it back. Wait until I'm back in control, my chest heaving, my hands shaking. "If you really don't know why I don't have magic, then why did you never try to fix me?"

"There's nothing to fix."

"I'm an abomination! My own Family has tried to kill me because of it. Khalid just had to kill Uncle Myers and Vinny because of it! How can you say there's nothing to fix?"

Tears fall down her cheeks. She stares at me in silence for a long moment before she whispers, "Your father almost killed you when you were only a baby."

My heart stops along with my breath.

"It was an accident," she hurriedly adds, then swallows. "He had a nightmare, and he didn't know... He hit you with his magic. I couldn't..." She shakes her head; tears splatter down onto the floor. "You were in so many pieces." She lifts her chin, her eyes pleading with mine. "But there's a spell – dark magic where you can trade one's magic for a second chance at life."

A chill runs down my spine as my hands tremble. "You made me a freak."

"I had to to save your life, Varius. You're my son. I love you, and Caden... He wouldn't have survived knowing he killed you. You were our first after so long..."

I swallow down the lump in my throat. "Did you really ask him to leave?"

She hesitates for a second, her pain so agonizing to see. "No."

All strength leaves my legs, and I don't know how the fuck I stay standing.

"He didn't know what he did to you that night. He was still asleep. I cleaned you up and the room, but when you didn't hit your ascension, I had to tell him. It destroyed him. He couldn't look at you without guilt, and he hated that I kept that from him."

A harsh breath leaves me as my thoughts spin. "That's why I can't even use a fucking premade?" I say.

She nods. "I'm sorry."

"But the magic's still in me..." I say slowly, my paranoia settling back in, trying to pick holes in everything she says, to discern any lies.

Fuck, I fucking want to believe she's lying.

"That's part of the spell. It's a Tantalus situation." Named after the Greek king of Sipylus who's being punished in Hades' Underworld. He is standing in a pool of water he can never drink from while dying of thirst.

My chest hurts, but there is one flickering light in all this pain. "Will my kids..."

"It won't affect them," she says, her voice not wavering for the first time tonight. It's strong, honest, utterly certain.

My shoulders cave in. My lungs open up, and I close my eyes as I just take a moment to breathe. I can have a future with Micha. A family... One I won't have to hide from the reaper. My throat clogging fast, I force out my next question before it closes completely. "Why did you call Aleric?"

"Because he can phase."

"No, why did you call *him*? How did you know he would help?"

She swallows. "He wants something from me."

"*...lotion every night.*" I still have no idea what the fuck that means.

"What?" I demand.

She shakes her head. "That's between me and him."

Perhaps 'lotion' was the end of a word. Or it's a name, a code. He fed on someone. Does he want access to them every night?

"Who did he feed on?"

"I don't know."

"Khalid?" I press, wanting to make sure.

"No." The word is hard, nearly violent. Like if Aleric even thought about it, she'd kill him.

I study her, try to spot the emotions she isn't showing, the subconscious micro expressions that will let me know if whatever deal she made with him is going to destroy her. Despite the pain she's caused me, she did it out of love. To save my life when I was only a baby.

"Did Myers know about this spell?" I ask.

She nods. "He must've used it on Vinny beforehand."

Silence descends between us, but it's lacking the tension from earlier. It's lighter now that secrets have been cleared. Now that guilt and shame have been lifted.

Exhaustion suddenly hits me all at once, and I head for the door. Just as I turn, I notice her raising what's left of her whisky to her lips.

Wanting that same kind of distraction, I glance towards the stairs. My brothers' voices drift up as they drown their sorrows, but I don't have the urge to join them. It's not drink I want; it's my little monster.

Shaking my head, ridding myself of that weakness, I start down the hall towards my bedroom. I open my door so I can fall into bed, only to immediately stop.

Micha's sitting on my bed, freshly showered and naked. Her legs are crossed, and her bag rests on her lap. "I brought a set of clothes so no one will know I stayed the night," she says as she lifts her bag.

"You're not sleeping here," but I don't move out of the way for her to leave. I step inside and close the door behind me. Only so I can activate the silence ward though. So no one can hear us.

"I got some gloves off Sharee." She reaches into her bag and pulls out a pair of metal gloves used to restrain a witch. If we can't move our fingers, the majority of us can't cast spells. "And a gag."

My mouth runs dry. "Why are you doing this? You just learned our kids might die because of me." I don't tell her they won't, not yet. I want to hear her answer. Why she's trusting me, putting herself in such a risky position for the second time, the first being that night in the woods when she fell asleep.

"Because I might be yours, Varius," she says, a hard glint in her eye, "but you're *mine*. Now get over here because I'm fucking exhausted."

A weight lifting off my shoulders, I take a step forward.

THIRTY-ONE

HER

My heart skips a beat as I watch him walk towards me. His guard is still up, his footsteps measured and weighted like he's ready to turn around at any moment. Time slows as I wait to see if he makes it, if he's willing to build this bridge with me. Because I now know that running with him will never be an option even if Khalid is dead. I see the love Varius has for his brothers. The responsibility. He might be the boogieman to the boogiemen and even his own family might see him as such, but I see *him.*

I see the pain. The overwhelming agony over his uncle and cousin's betrayal. The last of his solstice has crumbled. The camp he never expected to get bombed due to it being so far back from the front lines has just been hit. Now he'll strike out even harder to prove it wasn't a crippling blow. His paranoia will increase. His guard will triple, his thick-ass walls becoming thicker.

But even then, I will see the truth he hides – his need to

just be loved. To find someone, anyone, who won't ever hurt him.

My heart in my throat, I try to keep myself together. *It's a dangerous thing to fall in love with a dangerous man...*

Stopping at the foot of the bed, Varius says, "I talked to Mother. My magic will pass down."

A tremble runs through me. "How does she know?"

"She used black magic to bind mine in order to save me as a baby."

My eyes widen. "So does that mean there's a spell to counter it?"

"I don't know, but trying to reverse it or find a loophole might kill me." He speaks in a monotone, without any hope lightening it, and I get his lack of enthusiasm even though I couldn't imagine a life without magic. Hope is the deadliest of things – capable of crushing you completely if you keep chasing it only to constantly be let down.

How many nights did young Varius spend trying to find a cure? How many disappointments did he suffer before he realized the next one would break him?

My heart hurting for him, I say, "Tell me to leave if you want me to."

He places one knee on the bed. "Stay," he orders. "Please."

My throat clogs tight at that simple word. Struck mute, I can only nod. My hands trembling, I lift the gag to tie it around my head.

"Don't." That single word is filled with so much hidden meaning.

I don't have the energy to mistrust you. Not tonight.

If you kill me, at least it'll stop the pain.

Can you do something for me, little monster? Can you pretend you love me just for the night?

My throat tightens even further as I let the gag fall from my fingers. Tossing my bag and gloves on the floor, I watch as he strips off his clothes. Then together, we move beneath the blanket. For a long time, we just lie on our sides, staring at each other.

It's a dangerous thing to fall in love with a dangerous man... The reminder fills every part of my soul. He just had his own cousin tortured. *But Vinny betrayed him,* I counter, *and I would never do that.*

Reaching a hand out to him, I cup his cheek. He stills beneath my touch, his eyes fast on mine. I slide my fingers up into his hair, stroking him, comforting him. And gods, there is something dangerous in that – a heady sensation that fills my head, to be able to offer solstice to a powerful man.

His eyes flutter with every stroke of my fingers through his hair. Lowering more and more, but they refuse to close completely. As much as he wants this, at least for tonight, his paranoia is still rearing its ugly head.

So I start to talk in soft tones, letting my words wash over him. I tell him about the adventures Dayne and I have had over the years. Not just the funny jobs, like the time we got lost and ended up unknowingly asking our target, whose face we didn't know, for directions to his address in some backwater town without internet, but the ones outside of work too. The times we loved and laughed and became like family. Varius already knows Dayne is a weakness of mine; sharing these moments won't make a difference. Not in that regard at least.

But they get him to close his eyes. Then eventually fall asleep.

I stare at him, still stroking his hair, still talking in case stopping causes him to wake back up. He doesn't look at peace. Even now when the world should have stopped, he looks tormented and on edge.

And utterly alone.

Leaning forward slowly, I kiss him on the forehead. It might be dangerous to fall in love with a dangerous man,

but I can't help but take that first step...
Varius fucking Shadow is mine.
And just for tonight, I am his.

THIRTY-TWO

HIM

She's gone when I wake up, and for a sleepy moment, I want to go downstairs and drag her back up to bed. I can smell the waffles cooking in the kitchen, though, and know Mother is most likely with her. Given the lies she has told me all these years, I don't trust her to know how much I want Micha.

So instead I roll onto my stomach in the place where my little monster slept and rub my morning wood against the mattress. I breathe in her lingering scent, getting stiffer with every inhale of raspberries and cream. Rocking my hips, I groan into my pillow. But I don't want to come all over my sheets, don't want to have to wash them and get rid of her scent, so I flip onto my back and push off the covers.

Imagining her pussy sitting on my face, I wrap my hand around myself. A tight grip that I jerk with quick pumps before slowing down as I close my eyes, mimicking that pace she likes when I fuck her. Long slow thrusts that slam in at the end. I groan as I imagine the taste of her pussy as it drips with my cum. And in my mind, I've already tattooed my name on her like I promised. The sight of it makes me feral.

My balls draw tight. My pace quickens, and I shoot a load all over my stomach and down my hand. Breathing heavily, I keep my eyes closed, my mind basking in the eating of her pussy. Just taking a moment longer before I have to push all thoughts of her aside and get to work.

My cock growing hard again as I imagine sweeping my tongue between her lips, I slowly stroke myself, the cum on my cock nowhere near as good as hers.

The kitchen is understandably tense as my brothers and I all sit around the table come dinner. The meeting I called last night weighs heavily on all of us even though it hasn't even started.

As Micha walks towards the table with small bowls of middle eastern food for everyone to share, I barely manage to keep my eyes off her. I need to concentrate, need to keep my thoughts focused, and she is already making that damn hard with her mere presence. Looking at her will have me dragging her up to my room and postponing this meeting so I can bend her pretty little ass over and drop down behind her to eat her out.

A mixture of aromas from the various mezze dishes helps keep down the smell of her pussy from rising in my mind. I focus on the tomato dolmas as she heads back for more bowls, Mother helping her too.

"Vinny and Myers both had their heads cut off," I sign, relaying the information I got from Khalid when he came back this morning, after having spent the night with his girl. His mouth and chin smelled of pussy, was absolutely soaked in it, and even now that smell still lingers as he sits on my right. Jealousy curls in my stomach as I'm reminded that Micha left my bed before I could do the same. Khalid licks his lips, tasting his girl, and I've never wanted to stab him more. *Focus.*

Pulling my focus off him, I look at Talon. "I've collected their bodies" –they're currently lying in the back seat of my car in two black bags– "if you wish to take Vinny into your shadows." Despite his betrayal, my brother still loved him. Perhaps this will give him a bit of closure.

Talon shakes his head slightly as he starts to open his mouth, but I cut in, "Take your time to think about it." I turn to Maddox to give him the same option. Myers was the only father he ever knew.

"No," he says before the first word has even been formed by my hands. "He wanted to kill me. Kill all of us. Fuck that bastard."

"Then I'll –"

"May I take him?" Mother asks after she places an empty plate in front of Leno as Micha does the same in front of me. Her eyes are lowered, but she slowly lifts them to mine. "Your father loved him," she says, her hands shaking. "They deserve to be together."

"He doesn't deserve that honor." Maddox's movements are sharp and abrupt, clearly signing his displeasure.

"I love you boys more than anything. You know that. But Myers is dead now, and he can't do any harm in the Plane of Monsters. Please just let me lay him to rest with Caden. He did this for him." Her hands shake stronger. "Would you not try to honor a dead brother?"

"I wouldn't turn on the rest of my family," Talon signs.

"Even if one fell in love with a vampire?" she asks as she turns to him. "Had a hybrid child?"

"That's different. They're –"

"Abominations?" she asks softly, her hands still.

His body shakes as his eyes fall to his lap. Talon's hatred of all vampires is second only to his hatred of hybrids – an opinion shared by almost everyone across the entire Seven Planes. If a mother knows she's pregnant with one, she'll often dig it out herself regardless of how far along it is. The father will often kill them both even if he's the one who impregnated her. And those that are foolish enough to try to carry to term get hunted down while they're pregnant, and their unborn child is ripped from their bellies to be stoned to death or thrown on a fire.

Hybrids are extremely rare, one in a million chances of being born, made even more so by their premature murders. But this is a thought experiment of Mother's, and though my opinion of someone doesn't change just because society tells me it should, I can feel her pain. Myers was the last memory she had of our father.

Their relationship might have been complicated, and she might claim she never loved him, but at the very least, he mattered to her.

"You can have him." I glance at Talon, but his eyes are still down. "And if T doesn't wish to take Vinny, you can take him too."

The tension around the table doesn't ease, but she nods at me as she heads back to the kitchen to join Micha. The flatbread is almost finished baking, its freshness teasing my senses.

"We still need to know what the Death Hunt is doing to the Blood Fangs," I say, getting to the main reason I called this meeting.

Leno and Krypto, who's seated in a chair separate to the table, both turn to me. "I haven't been able to grab Cara yet. I –"

"She's not to be involved anymore," I cut in. "A term of Aleric's for information about Myers." A pointless endeavor that, given my uncle showed his hand only minutes after the reveal. I wonder if Aleric knew he was about to make his second strike. It would be just like the sly motherfucker to get something from me I didn't really need to give. But I am a man of my word, so Cara is now off limits. Which means we need to figure out another way to discern what's going on. "We're going to grab Cid."

There's a heavy moment of silence.

"You're fucking joking," my youngest brother blurts, then quickly signs it with his hands. Rudy makes a gesture to tell us all to stop signing, wanting us to discuss things quicker. The table explodes into conversation all at once.

"Antonio won't let that stand."

"What's it fucking matter if they kill the bloodsuckers for us?"

"That's a declaration of war."

"Let's fucking do this. I've always hated that guy."

"How?" Khalid asks, and his question stops the racket.

Cid Garcia is a werewolf, and like all werewolves, he has a natural resistance to magic, so taking him won't be easy. But he's also Antonio's youngest son, and he's the only one of his brothers with a family. We will get him to tell us what his father is doing to the Blood Fangs one way or another.

"He likes to visit their brothels."

"*Their* being the keyword," Leno says. "They have wolves guarding every door."

"Our Families are still at peace. Talon can just walk in." I look at him, as do the rest of my brothers; he is the one they won't suspect wanting to save the vampires. "Find a woman called Rei. She's been Cid's whore for a long time."

"He's married," Khalid growls. For that alone, he should die according to my brother's code.

I nod at him. "With three kids." They're all adults, with the youngest being twenty-five. Khalid nods at me, a silent confirmation that he'll have no problem using them to get to their father.

I look back at Talon. "Go in, sprout some shit about the vampires like you always do, and try to make some deals. If the werewolves aren't planning to come after us, then we have no reason to join the fight. We could side with them then, wipe out the Blood Fangs like you want."

He smiles as he leans back in his chair. "Might take me a while to get to Rei." Demanding her immediately will be too suspicious. Cid has enough weight, he might even have her reserved as his own.

"Do it as fast as you can, but your safety is priority. If you can't get to her, we'll find –"

"I'll get to her," he says confidently. Ever since Jackie was drained dry, Talon has visited brothels. He only fucks to relieve himself, never sleeping with a girl more than a few times. He doesn't want it to turn into an emotional ordeal; Jackie was the only person he ever gave his heart to. The working girls are unlikely to fall for him – it's just business, but Talon has a soft spot for girls in trouble. So he visits the brothels to punish himself for failing to save his girlfriend. He forces himself to look at all the other girls he can't save. He uses them, discards them, and hates himself for it. But he can't seem to stop. Can't forgive himself for something that wasn't his fault.

But because of this, he makes his rounds from girl to girl, even getting the madams to fuck him eventually. The ones who are 'off limits' due to the exclusivity demand of a john still end up fucking him too. It just takes a little longer. A greasing of hands, a building of loyalty. If he says he can get to her, then he will.

"Let us know when you have," I say as Micha and Mother come over, carrying freshly cooked flatbread and homemade hummus. They set the plates in the middle for us to share, then take their seats. I reach for one of the breads, calling an end to the meeting. As we all fill our plates with the foods we like the most, my eyes drift to Micha. Valentine's Day is in two days, and although I will be taking her somewhere public, we'll have all the privacy in the backseat of a hired limo.

And the item I ordered this morning will have arrived by then too.

THIRTY-THREE

HER

I've had to take a shot from a moving speedboat before in order to save Dayne's life, but even then, I wasn't more nervous than this. This place is absolutely packed, and I'm wearing a skimpy dress (picked out by Varius and left in my room), as well as the remote control nipple clamp vibrator he first put on me while I was pressed up against the wall of his garage.

A chick is currently at the karaoke bar, belting out "Girls Just Want to Have Fun" by Cydni Lauper, and holy fucking shit is she *killing* it. There are a couple tables near the stage, full of men and women, who are literally clapping.

Not ironically either.

One of them whistles.

Fuck. I've only ever sung in the shower before. What if I'm utterly shit at this? Nervously, I look over at Varius, but he's still talking business with the manager at the bar. This is one of the Shadow Domain clubs, with illegal high-stakes gambling taking place in the back. I stare at him as I nurse my gin and tonic, trying to drown my urge to go over there and pull him back to our table.

On the way over here, he didn't take his focus off me, keeping his head between my legs in the backseat of a limo he hired, but I know he'll always struggle to show affection in public. If I'm going to be the perfect wife for him, I will just have to get comfortable with being ignored.

Turning to Khalid, I glance over his shoulder and pretend he's Dayne rather than someone looking like he wants to kill me and everyone else in this club. "If I'm shit, will you clap for me anyway?"

"If you're shit, will we leave sooner?"

I blink. "Um, probably."

"Then no."

"Ah." I smirk. "Keen to get back to whoever's pussy you keep eating, huh?" My eyes widen as my cheeks heat to the temperature of the sun. Shooting out of my seat, I thank the fucking gods the woman singing just finished. *I did not just say that. To the reaper!*

But the words just slipped out of my mouth, my nerves making my tongue loose. As did the whole pretending he was Dayne thing. I'm never fucking doing *that* again.

Making my way to the stage in a very quick walk that is in no way a run, I take the mic from the lady and keep my gaze far, far away from the table where the reaper is still sitting. I pick a song off the playlist, wish I'd brought my drink up or at least downed the rest of it, and then freeze. The song starts to play from the speakers. The lyrics appear on screen. My fingers turn white around the mic.

People stare at me in expectation.

Sweat builds on my palms.

Who the hel ever thought this would be a good idea? I don't even like people. My idea of a fun weekend is curling up with a book. Or petting a dog. I like animals. Crowds less so.

Being 'normal' is so overrated I suddenly decide. What does it matter if I missed out on things I don't really want to do? But just as I start to take that first step to run off the stage, the clamps on my nipples buzz.

I jerk, nearly dropping the mic in my hand. My eyes fly to Varius. He's still talking to the manager, not even looking at me, but his hand is in his pocket. The clamps buzz again.

Sing for me.

My cheeks hot, I start to mumble into the microphone. I don't really know this song though, so I'm forced to look at the screen. Blocking everything out other than the fact that Varius wants me to sing, I start to get a bit louder. Every time I increase my volume and show a bit more confidence, the nipple clamps buzz in approval.

I'm grinning now, singing for all I'm worth, but the song's nearly over, the music dying. But still, I did it, and I'm so fucking proud of myself. I start to head off stage, only to immediately freeze as someone in the front row shouts, "Do another one! You've got this this time!"

"Ah..."

"Yeah, go for it!"

"Show us what you've got!"

My ears burning from the force of my grin, I take my time to actually go through the playlist and pick a song I know. Excited to see, "Everything Burns" by Ben Moody and Anastasia, I click on it and start to sing.

The crowd hushes in anticipation. Closing my eyes, I suck in a breath, then exhale slowly. The lyrics start, and I sing with everything I have.

Cheers and whistles echo out in front of me, and I try not to grin so I can keep my tones right. I hit all the high notes and the lows, change my voice for the male and female parts. I absolutely love this song, and I sing it with every part of my soul.

When it is over, they ask for another.

And another.

Eventually, I plead for a needed break but promise to be back in a couple minutes. I head off the stage feeling like a damn superstar. Who knew I could sing? I could've been the next Taylor Swift if I hadn't been raised an assassin.

Avoiding the table with Khalid, I head over towards Varius, who's still at the bar. I know he doesn't want me to interrupt whatever conversation he's having, so I stop a few paces away from him and lean on the counter of the bar. I order something fruity, my attention more on Varius than the drink. I glance at him. He doesn't look at me, but the buzz on my clamps make me smile. I take a sip as I walk back to Khalid. I have to use the bathroom, and I can't just leave my drink anywhere, so unfortunately I'm going to have to face him.

You're an assassin, Micha.

A damn good one.

You're scared of no man!

Except for Khalid.

Ha! Yeah. Except him.

He could kill me in his sleep.

Deciding I'll just buy a new drink, I leave my cocktail on a random table, then head for the restroom.

I enter the ladies room, surprised to see it empty. Usually, there's always a line a mile long. Guess no one wanted to miss me singing. Grinning, I step into a stall.

The door of the bathroom opens, and a woman instantly sighs. "Holy fucking shit. That woman can*not* sing."

A second woman groans. "A set of bagpipes played by a goat would've been kinder on my ears."

Woman One laughs. "Nails on a chalkboard."

I try to think about who they're talking about. No one I've heard tonight has been that bad. Perhaps this woman has taken up the mic while I've been in here? In that case, I should linger for a bit. Give her time to finish. I don't want to make her feel bad, comparing herself to my standing ovation when I next take the stage.

"Roll up a bit of napkin and put it in your ears," Woman Three says as they all move into the stalls. "That's what I did."

"Did it help?"

"Not really."

"Fuck. And she's going back on." One of them groans as she pisses. "I want to go home so bad."

"Well, you can't. Rio was clear about what would happen to *anyone* if we disrespect the Boss' fiancee."

"Is that guy really the Boss of the Shadow Domain?"

My eyes widen as I suddenly realize they're talking about me. I'm the shit singer. But they've all been applauding me and asking for more...

A dumb-as-fuck grin spreads across my lips as the rest of the situation dawns.

"Yes, and the other guy with him? He's rumored to have killed a hundred men, one of them with a toothpick. So no leaving, Beth."

She groans. "Death might be better than this."

"Not how he does it. That toothpick kill? He shoved it up the guy's dick and waited for him to get sepsis. But look, it's nearly ten. There's probably only nine hours left max."

My grin hurting my cheeks at this point, I exit the stall and then the bathroom without a sound. I linger in the hall until the trio starts coming out. Pretending like I'm heading in for the first time, I nod at them.

"Oh my gods, you're such a great singer!" one exclaims, probably Woman Three.

"Thank you. I'm about to get back on! Why don't you pick the first three songs for me?"

Her smile freezes, fractures.

I turn to the other two. "And you can pick the next sets!"

I barely manage not to laugh as I leave them horrified. I head in to wash my hands, then step out after I've finished and make my way back to the stage.

After Woman Three picks a song, I say into the mic, "Apologies if this is a bit worse than before." I raise a hand to my neck as the entire club seems to die. Trying my best not to laugh, I add, "My throat's a bit sore, but I'll do my best. Please let me know when I should stop."

And then I kill it.

Properly.

Fucking.

Kill.

It.

A set of goats playing bagpipes with quarters stuck in the pipes while the goats themselves were being tortured would sound so much better than me. And that's on the first song. I get progressively worse, but still they cheer me and ask for another.

Varius eventually makes his way back to the table, where Khalid looks like he *really* wants to kill me. But the rest of the bar is actually starting to genuinely get into it because they're all so fucking drunk at this point – alcohol the only thing having helped them through the last hour.

Grinning like a fucking fool who's loved by a man who can only express it in the most obscure ways, I hop off the stage for the last time. Making my way over to my fiance, I grab his hand. "Let's get out of here."

Khalid is on his feet in a second, and I laugh at how keen he is to leave. Being on duty, he hasn't had a single drink, and I kind of feel bad for him.

"Are you sure?" Varius asks, his eyes soft despite how badly his ears must be ringing. But he genuinely means it. He's willing to sit here while all the goats with bagpipes die just so I can live my dream.

My chest squeezes tight. "Yes," I say softly. "I could really demolish a burger right about now."

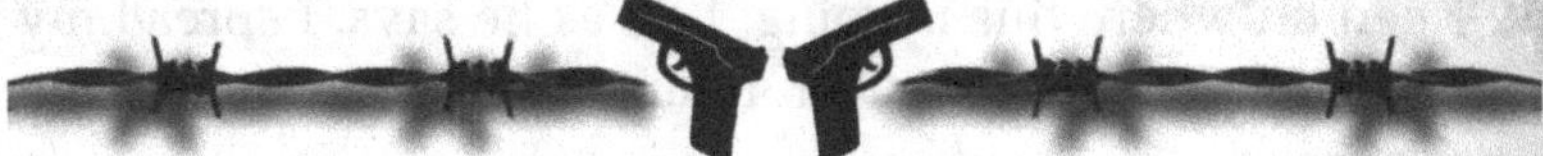

After fucking me senseless in the backseat of the car as Khalid drove us to a restaurant, where he then turned my nipple clamps on and left them for the entire meal, I am dead on my feet. Also horny. But mostly dead. My throat is actually really sore from all the screeching I did – I mean, all the "singing," and my body is crashing from the surge of dopamine I've been getting all evening.

Khalid takes the turn onto the Shadow estate. As soon as the car passes the security ward that keeps all non-witches out, he parks the car and turns off the engine. I start to lean forward to ask him what's up, but he's already gone, having turned into his shadow. I look out the window, but I can't see him in the dark. Still, I know he's heading back off the estate, running to wherever his girl lives.

A smile curls my lips at the idea of the big bad reaper being twisted around the finger of some woman. I bet she's a fucking badass.

"Thank you for telling them all they had to applaud," I say as I turn to Varius.

"I did no such thing," he says, his tone hard. He's been in a mood ever since we left the restaurant, and I wonder if he is upset the date is now over.

"Then thank you for telling Rio –"

"I didn't." Sharp. Clipped.

My eyes narrow slightly. "Thank you for taking me to a place where the boss is a total brown noser?"

He doesn't protest this time, and I smile. Grabbing his hand, I scoot over to him. I lift his arm and loop it around my shoulders as I snuggle into his side. He lets me for a second before removing his arm and stepping forward off his seat. As he turns to grab an item out of one of the cubby holes, he commands, "Lie down and lift up your dress."

Keen on where this is going, I do as he says. I spread my legs, opening my pussy up for him, having not worn any underwear.

But it isn't his dick or his mouth that touches me there. It's an alcoholic wipe. I lift my head in curiosity. My eyes shoot open as all exhaustion leaves me.

"You're not seriously going to –"

The tattoo gun pierces my skin, and I suck in a breath as I clench my fists. I don't look at what he's doing, my head facing the ceiling, but I can feel every line of his name being branded onto my pussy. With every letter that's finished, I start to pant harder and harder, my legs starting to shake as the pain turns me on. His face is so close to me too. I just want him to lean in and lick me as the black bold letters claim my pussy.

"You're soaked," he growls, and I lean up on my elbows to try to discern why he's angry. His jaw is locked. His eyes are boiling pools of fury as he stares at the juncture between my legs.

"Did you get this wet when Dayne tattooed you?" he asks, and my mouth drops open.

"He's gay."

"Did you know that then?"

"Well, no –"

"He's hot." His eyes narrow as he moves the tattoo gun across my skin. I flinch as the bite of the gun feels harder this time.

"He's my best friend."

"People fuck their best friends all the time."

"I've never fucked him."

"Did you think about him while you touched yourself?"

"No! Ew. He's *always* been like a brother to me."

The gun stills as he looks at me, and the look in his eyes causes my pulse to spike. I glance at the door handle closest to me. I could grab it and run, let him work out his jealousy.

"Are you lying to me?" He lifts the gun away from me, and I glance down to see he's done.

Property of Varius Shadow sits in clear bold across my pussy.

My mouth running dry, I answer his question by kicking him in the shoulder. He stumbles back, and I bolt for the door. I'm out before he can grab me, and then I'm fleeing down the drive, the cold air filling my lungs and stinging the bare skin on my sleeveless dress.

I take a chance and veer off the track and into the woods. My heels dig into the dirt, and I trip. I fall to my knees and hurriedly twist to take them off. He's advancing on me, his long strides eating up the ground between us. The door of the limo has been left open, and another car pulls up behind it, honking.

Maddox pops his head out of the window to yell, having clearly just got back from his date with Alexis. He actually did take her to the ballet, and though a part of me wonders how that went, that curiosity quickly vanishes.

Because Varius is nearly on me.

"Don't leave the car there!" Maddox yells in annoyance, but I'm already on my feet, now bare, the heels gone, and running for the trees.

I can hear him chasing me, his footsteps thudding on the winter ground. He's close. *Real* close. I dart left around a tree, a sudden turn that'll hopefully throw him off, but he grabs me around the waist and swings me back around. He cages me against the oak. A glint of metal flashes in the thin space between us as our breaths mix in the cold air.

My skirt is cut open. His hands are on my ass. His cock is already out. Lifting me into the air, he impales me on his eight-inch monstrosity. I cry out as I wrap my legs around him. He pushes in deep, all the way to my cervix, bruising it without mercy. Punishing me for teasing him.

"Answer me, Micha," he growls.

Wrapping my arms around his neck, I lean forward and bite him through his shirt. He groans as he slams me into the tree, fucking me hard and fast. The bark rubs against my skin, the pain of the scratches colliding with the tears of my pussy as it's stretched fast and hard as he brutally owns it.

"Didn't...lie," I pant before crying out. I dig my nails into his neck. "You damn...neanderthal."

"When it comes to you, yeah I fucking am," he growls. "And you better" –he slams into me, hitting the back of my pussy– "fucking" –he pulls out– "remember that." He slams back in, and I scream in both pain and pleasure.

"If you ever *think* about another man, I'll kill him." He picks up speed, his jealousy driving him hard and fast and making me hot. "If you ever flirt with a man, I'll cut off his fucking cock." He grunts as he rails into me. "Even if you never conceive, little monster. Even if we can't marry–"

That last word comes out on a hiss and makes something inside me shiver.

"I'm going to kill anyone who makes you wet."

His cock damn near feels like it is entering my womb, and I close my eyes as the sensation overwhelms me. He tears at the straps of my dress, yanking them down so he can palm my breasts after ripping off the clamps. I cry out from the sharp pain. He kneads me, squeezes me, easing away a bit of the sting.

"And if a waiter so much as slips you his number, his balls will end up on the godsdamn menu."

My eyes snap open as I stare at him. I didn't even notice the waiter being overly friendly at dinner. And he sure as hel didn't slip me a number. "He didn't –"

I cut myself off as he holds a scrunched up napkin to my face. I don't need to unfold it to know there's a number on it. No wonder Varius has been in a fucking mood. "I didn't know," I say, my heart slamming against my ribs just as fast as his cock's pounding into me. *It's dangerous to fall in love with a dangerous man...*

"I know," he growls. He presses the napkin to my pussy, right over the tattoo he's just given me. "Now scream for me, little monster."

Changing his pace, he goes from fast to *hard*, and I'm damn near crying in only a few thrusts. My eyes close. My lips part, and I squeeze my legs tight around him. The sound of a ringing phone, of a call going out rather than coming in, causes me to open my eyes. He has his phone up near my mouth, and a familiar voice answers. The waiter from the restaurant.

"Hello?" he asks hopefully.

My cheeks heat as Varius continues to rearrange my insides. I bite my lip to try to stay quiet, but I can't. Each thrust pulls another cry from me, another whimper, another moan, another scream. And soon I'm forgetting all about our other audience.

Even when the waiter screams in high-pitched agony, and I know someone is cutting off his balls.

My nails digging into Varius' back, I orgasm around his cock. He grunts as he buries himself deep, though still not able to go all the way in, then growls as he comes. I can feel the hot spurt of his seed filling me up, and I close my eyes as I bask in his attention.

He hangs up his phone, then slides it back into his pocket before hauling me up the tree. His lips come down on mine, hot and possessive and demanding that I open for him, that I soothe the temper raging through him.

Parting my lips, I take him into my mouth and kiss him back. He bites my lower lip, and I shudder against him.

"Tell me who you belong to, little monster," he growls against my mouth.

Chucking my feminist card over my shoulder, I kiss him softly and say, "Varius fucking Shadow."

THIRTY-FOUR

HIM

If I'd known that waiter would end up taking his own life, I would've fucking done it for him. He was lucky all I took was his balls. Had he flirted with her openly, though, I would have taken everything right there on the godsdamn table and then fucked her beside him while he lay dying. But he was respectful while he served us. It was only when he thought I wasn't paying him any attention, my eyes on my phone, that he tried to shoot his shot.

Annoyed still three months later, I click off the article about his suicide, then push my chair back in my office. My phone rings, and I answer it after seeing Talon's name flash on the screen.

He's been frequenting the brothels multiple times a week for the past three months, but he still hasn't managed to bag Rei. I'm getting impatient. We need to know what kind of weapon the wolves have, if it's a virus that can transmit to us.

"Yes?" I say as I place the phone to my ear.

"I'm meeting Rei this afternoon. Cid is currently out of town."

"Does it smell like a trap?"

"Nah. She's just really keen to suck my cock."

He's boastful, arrogant, and I wonder if he's being overly confident to hide his real feelings. He's always been a bit cozy with the Death Hunt, bonding over a mutual hatred of bloodsuckers. He's gone there pretending to be sympathetic to their cause, but I wouldn't put it past him to actually fall for their shit hook, line, and sinker.

The hairs on my arms rise as my paranoia digs its claws in. Talon was close to Vinny, and these past few months, he's been becoming more distant as he deals with his grief. If he's siding with them, will he come for me eventually?

Ignoring my suspicions to deal with later, I focus on the importance of the call. "Then fuck her well," I say. We need this to be more than a one time thing so he can work on loosening her tongue. Asking questions the first night he's with her will get him killed.

"Always do." He laughs, still cocky and sure.

"You able to get her DNA yet?" I demand.

"Nope. I'm stripped right after I enter. Then I'm hosed down every time I leave. They're very thorough."

"And she never leaves the property?"

"Nope. All the girls work and sleep here."

Dammit. We need to get her DNA for Khalid. Cid might not break under the threat of his family if he has a regular extra on the side.

"She sneak out?" I ask.

"She might do. And if not, I'll try to convince her."

"We don't have time to build her trust." That could take months or years. The Death Hunt has nearly halved the Blood Fangs' number in only a few months, and they're getting more efficient at it. Seven more vampires have just been reported as not having been seen for the last three days. Aleric is staying tight-lipped about whether they're dead or just out of the state, but I suspect it's the former.

"Figure something out soon," I say, "but don't get caught."

"Aye, aye, captain."

"And come for dinner sometime this week."

He doesn't say anything for a moment, then he sighs. "Yeah. I'll be there."

"I mean it, T. It isn't good to grieve alone."

"Says the man who can't let anyone in."

My fingers tighten on my phone. But he's right. Not even Micha, outside of that one night, has been allowed to see my festering pain. I haven't even shared the real reason Caden walked out with my brothers. They'll look at me with pity, thinking I feel guilty over learning that I really did tear this family apart, and –

They'd be right, I admit in the back of my mind. Our father left because Mother had kept a secret from him, but it was my face he couldn't bear to see. He would've forgiven her, had always forgiven her. He could have lived with what he'd done while trapped in a nightmare if I'd just died.

"Yeah, well, do as I say, not as I do."

He laughs dryly, then hangs up.

Dropping my phone on my desk, my shoulders tight, I lean back in my chair. I focus my thoughts, dragging them away from my guilt.

It'll take my brother a few sessions with Rei to get her to talk about Cid. He's charming and able to learn all kinds of shit from the workers he visits. Plus he knows how to dig out information without seeming to be searching at all, so I doubt he'll be in any danger.

Still, I'll get him some backup for this afternoon. Maddox hasn't given me any reason to doubt his loyalty lately. I can get him to spy on Talon at the same time, make sure he isn't getting too cozy with the wolves.

I hate that I can't even trust my own brothers anymore, but it doesn't stop me from picking up my phone.

Varius: *You're on babysitting duty this afternoon. Trail Talon. Don't let him see you. You know how shy he gets when others see him performing.*

Maddox sends a shit emoji, but I know he'll be there. He won't be able to sneak into the brothel as a client though. Everyone wears full-faced gold masks like off *Spartacus* – a rule that was added after they realized how dangerous my little brother could be with his ability to shift into various sizes thanks to his shadow magic. As Talon doesn't have the identities of any johns to pass back and with the brothels deep inside Death Hunt territory, meaning we can't hang around outside to follow them home, Maddox taking one of their identities is too dangerous.

Even if he copied the exact likeness of one of the johns, pulling off such a deep swap requires intimate knowledge of that person. How they move. How they talk. What secrets they've shared with their ladies. One wrong slip up and they would kill him.

Shifting into an insect isn't much safer for him; he'll be way too easily killed, but tonight warrants that risk. I text back, asking if he needs more meat. If he gets stuck as an ant, Mother will kill me.

Maddox: *Added Alexis to the pot so fine for today but how much am I babysitting?*

Magic can't create mass from nothing. It has to take it from somewhere. If a healer is working with someone who's lost too much blood, like Micha did when our uncle nearly killed her, they have to use up some of their patient's fat or muscle to make more. When they're too far gone, like the reaper was, a blood transfusion is necessary, which is why Aleric brought bags of it with him. For Maddox to shift into an ant, no extra is required, but if he wants to turn back into himself, he will need the entire difference of mass in meat.

It can be animal or human, but he is much happier killing the latter. Animals are far more innocent.

Although Alexis was taller than the average woman, she was slim. She won't even cover one shift on her own.

Varius: *I'll get you more.*

Maddox: *I get the green?*

I tap the side of my phone while I think about giving him the green light to kill as many people as he wants. He has a taste for it. Is a proper little serial killer who's obsessed with the hunt, but I don't like him shitting where we eat.

Maddox: *I'm gonna have to watch T get his dick wet*

Maddox: *Come on, bruh, have mercy*

Maddox: *His cock is so much bigger than mine. Seeing it's gonna make me sleep on the tracks. I need something to look forward to*

I look at my phone dryly. *Dramatic little shit.*

Maddox: *Look*

The urge to throttle him becomes a necessity as he sends a flaccid dick pic through. He's a grower, and given he's dipped it in his sweet tea, it's even smaller than usual.

Maddox: **pleading face emoji**

Maddox: *Even when it's hard it ain't that big*

Varius: *Two weeks of green.*

We need to know what the Death Hunt is planning. If I have to sacrifice a few dozen people to do it, then so be it. The safety of my Family will always come first.

Maddox: *Yeees. If you ever need tickets to the ballet, I've got you covered bruh*

I start to put my phone down, but it beeps again. It's a dick pic, hard, with a frowny face drawn on it in marker. I delete it with a glare.

But just then another one comes through, the frowny face crossed out and replaced with a smiley one.

The fucking little shit.

Deleting the whole chat, I wish I could do the same with

my memory.

But at least we're finally getting somewhere. Once we have a way to grab Cid, we'll interrogate him until we know what the fuck is going on. When we do, though, will we need to make an alliance with the Blood Fangs in order to survive the coming war?

THIRTY-FIVE

HER

Gaining Varius' trust was always going to take a long time. I knew that. But after three and a half months of being his fiancee, I'm starting to get a bit impatient.

"I kid you not, Dayne," I mutter into my phone as I sit in my car, recently gifted to me by Varius. I'm in the parking lot of a grocery store, the backseat filled with stuff I need to take home. No one sits in the passenger seat or trails me as a silent shadow. I'm in Shadow Domain territory, and if I had a bodyguard here, that would be screaming proof that Varius cares, that he won't risk my safety even when there's little chance I'll get hurt. Granted, it also means his enemies are more likely to ignore me as I'm not important enough to kidnap.

"Every time I think we take a step forward," I say, "he shoves me back three times as far. He tattoos my..." My neck heats as I clear my throat. Despite getting absolutely railed nearly every night, I still get a bit flustered when it comes to talking about my sex life.

"Your pussy?" he teases as I managed to choke out the story to him a couple months ago, so he already knows it.

"Mmm. Yeah, that. He gets jealous a waiter gave me his number. Makes me *weak* from railing me so hard, but then he ignores me for the next week. Like, do I mean something to him or not?"

"He's dead, you know."

"Inside?"

"No, the waiter."

"Oh... Really? Did he kill him?" I ask, perking up a little at the thought of Varius' jealousy being that uncontrollable.

"Nah. Suicide."

"Dammit."

"What?"

"Nothing." But I'm pouting. My lips are in a downwards curve, and I'm slumped in my seat.

"He doesn't even trust his family, Micha, and he's known them for a lot longer."

"Yeah." I pinch the top of my nose, then rub it between my fingers. "Yeah, I know. It's just..." *I'm falling in love with him.* It's only polite if the fucking neanderthal falls in love back. "He hasn't even had me test for pregnancy yet," I say so Dayne doesn't call me out for being dumb enough to fall for Varius fucking Shadow. Not that I've actually fallen for him *yet* though.

It's just...he's got his damn name on my pussy, and there are moments where I think he might actually like me, so I can feel myself *starting* to like him. That whole date night was amazing, but we haven't had another one since, and... ugh. Overly frustrated and confused, I ask, "So, like, does he want me for my womb or not then? Because if he did, he'd have me check every day, right? But if he doesn't, then –"

"He's probably just addicted to sex."

My eyes narrow. *Not what I want to hear, bestie.*

"If you're pregnant, he won't have an excuse to fuck you anymore without admitting you *are* more than a womb."

"But if that was the case, he wouldn't be fucking me while I'm on my period, and he does that." My cheeks heat, but my embarrassment can just hold up for a second as I try to figure out if the guy I like likes me back. Dear gods, I sound like a pathetic teen.

"But women can conceive on their periods," Dayne says.

My eyes narrow slightly. "No, we can't."

"Yeah, you actually can. The chance is smaller, but it's not zero."

"You serious?"

"Yeah."

"Fuck. You think he knows that?"

"I don't know."

"He probably does," I grumble beneath my breath. Just like him to annoy me even more.

"What was that?"

"Nothing. So are you saying he *does* like me for more than a womb?" I ask hopefully. "And he's just in denial?"

"I'm saying he could give lessons to Fort Knox. The only one who's ever going to know what he feels is Varius. How is he when it's just you two?"

My whole face burns. "Attentive," I push out.

"Still going for hours at a time?"

"Yeah."

"Then you've still got this. He just needs more time to be sucked in by your charm rather than by your cunt. Maybe start spouting off random, cool facts about yourself while he's fucking you. Like when people are being held hostage, you know? Start with your name..."

I laugh. "Thanks."

I can practically hear his smile. "Keep your head up, girl. He's just another mark, and you always get your mark."

My throat tightens as my eyes flick away. My hand turns

clammy on my phone. "Yeah, just another mark," I lie. "So how's the kid doing?"

"He's talking more. Getting into music. His foster mom says his grades are starting to pick up in school."

"That's good."

"Yeah. Hey, look, I have to go," he says abruptly. "The movie's about to begin." That's our code phrase for 'target's just arrived.'

"Hope it's a good one," I say. *Stay safe.*

"Yeah, trailer looked alright." *Nothing complicated about it.*

He hangs up, and I stare at my phone for a few minutes, a bad feeling growing in my stomach. It's been so long since either one of us has worked alone; what if he needs backup?

Shaking my head, I put the key in the ignition. Dayne knows how to look after himself, and besides, I can check in on him given he still has the tattoo I gave him. If anything happens, I'll know. Reversing out of my parking spot, I head home.

When I get there, I park near the door rather than in the garage where my spot is. As I don't use my car as often as the boys do theirs, I don't get a prime location outside. Most everyone is out at the moment though, only Maddox's car is here, so I'll move it once I unload all the groceries.

Leaning into the backseat, I pick up one of the two fifty-liter backpacks I took to the store and haul it onto my back. I grab the other one and wear it on my front, then waddle towards the house. Maddox comes out just as I reach the side patio. "Hold the door," I say.

"Sorry, can't."

"Little shit."

He grins at me, and despite my glare, my lips twitch. Out of all of Varius' brothers, he's the one I've become the most comfortable with. I like Rudy the best though. He's way too sweet for this world and reminds me of my little sister even though he's a part of this lifestyle and I'm hoping she never is outside of just being blood. But Maddox kind of reminds me of Dayne when he was younger and less mature.

As he passes me, he pivots and raises his arms to push down on my bag. I wobble left, my thigh muscles burning, but he gets me anyway. His added weight literally makes my knees buckle, and I take a knee as he laughs.

"You going to help me up?"

"Nope."

"You ever want a helping of dessert again?"

Sighing loudly, he comes around to stand in front of me, then offers his hands. I grab them, really needing the help with all this weight on, and he hauls me up.

"You not going to say, 'Thank you?'" he asks, pulling a face that says, 'Wow.'

"*Thank you*?"

"You're welcome."

My jaw drops as he laughs and turns for the door of the house. He opens it, then bows, one arm out in a flourish. "Considering you were so polite," he says.

My lips purse, but I bite back my retort. The only way to open the door myself is if I put the bag down, open it, then haul it back up. Squatting with near eighty pounds on my back isn't very appealing.

So I smile brightly and say, "Thank you," like a fucking lady.

"You can thank me by making some brownies tonight. I'm going to be starving by the time I'm back."

I stop in the doorway to look at him. "What are you doing?"

"Watching Talon fuck all night."

He laughs at the burn of my cheeks, then shuts the door behind me as I hurry inside. Despite myself, I can't help but wonder if he was telling the truth or just being crude as a way to tell me to mind my own business. Although Varius is the king of paranoia, his brothers aren't exactly definitions of pronoia.

Slinging the bags off my shoulders, I start putting away all the food. My phone buzzes in my pocket, and I take it out to see an unknown caller.

Probably spam.

I end the call, finish my task.

My phone buzzes with a text.

Hoping it's Varius asking me for a naughty pic while he's out, I grab it and turn on the screen.

My stomach drops at a photo of Dayne.

He isn't being tortured – or at least he wasn't when this picture was taken. I push out with my magic, checking his heart rate. It's normal. He's calm.

The image is of him in some mall, no doubt tailing his target. He's side-on to the camera; he doesn't know he's being hunted. Is his target a fake? A trap? Someone to kill him when they're alone in some corner without a camera?

I tap on the call app and then Dayne's name. I let it ring for a second, knowing it's on vibrate, then hang up when another message comes through.

Unknown: *End the call.*

My pulse settles a bit at that text. Whoever this is doesn't know us that well. Otherwise, they'd know if either Dayne or I hang up before the call hits voicemail, it's a sign that something is wrong. I can't tell him it's him who's the one in danger, but he'll be more alert now. Maybe he'll see the person tailing them and figure it out.

Micha: *What do you want?*

A recording comes through. *"He's just another mark, and you always get your mark,"* Dayne says.

"Yeah, just another mark."

The fucker has tapped my phone. For the first time I'm thankful Varius hasn't trusted me with any secrets. Though this is bad enough. If he hears this, I'm dead.

An image appears. It's a screenshot of a bulletin that's gone out on the dark web.

Shadow Domain ledger. 2 mil.

My eyes dart to the stairs. There's no one home. Is that stellar timing on their part, or are they watching the house?

My attention falls back to my phone as it vibrates.

Unknown: *If you don't want me to send this to Varius, then do what I say.*

Micha: *Go for it. He'll believe me over you.*

My heart is hammering over that blatant lie, but I need to fish for information. Blackmailers don't just ask for one thing. If I give in now, they'll own me. And *no one* gets to own me but Varius.

Unknown: *Get the ledger, Ms. Black. You have 2 weeks if you want Dayne to live.*

A picture of my friend appears again. This time, it's of him sleeping. Not recent but recent fucking enough.

The messages all delete. The number disappears from my phone. I stare at it, wondering if that was tech or magic, and if it was magic, who the hel could have weaved a spell like that?

My lips tight, I look towards the stairs. Does Varius keep the ledger in his room or in his office? Or somewhere else in this large house?

Shit. Am I really going to break his trust like this?

My heart drops as I'm forced to choose between Dayne or Varius.

But this won't kill Varius...

And Dayne is my ride or die.

Knowing I have a bit of time before anyone gets back, I run for the stairs.

THIRTY-SIX

HIM

The fucking vampire has stood me up. I've been waiting for him for twenty minutes behind one of the libraries in St. Augustine – a historical parlay spot blessed by the Peaceful Goddess Eirine. It was here that the treaty was signed. No violence can occur in her lands without invoking the wrath of the goddess herself.

I'm not surprised Aleric hasn't showed, but I'm fucking irritated. I called, he accepted. He said he would be here to talk about a potential alliance as long as I came alone. I've half a mind to let his entire Family get wiped out for this, but I haven't made it this far by reacting without thinking. It might feel good to stick one to the vampire – *real good,* but it'll be a small victory in the war that I know is coming.

Although Stefaan Black has secured his footing up north, having pushed out the Mad Hatters, the increased income isn't going to help us if Antonio has a disease we can't cure.

My teeth grinding together, I head for the car. I try to

appease my frustration by thinking about how Talon has finally taken that first step in grabbing Cid, so we should have more intel soon. But all that leads to is me visualizing Maddox's dick pics, and my irritation grows.

When I make it to my car, a chill races through me as a sudden thought takes root. The Shadow house is now empty – a rare occurrence. Although all thirty acres are protected by a ward that will keep out our enemies, a previous edition of it was broken before by Aleric. Father upgraded the spell afterwards, but it still isn't a hundred percent perfect. Is the vampire there now, working to weaken it enough he can break it when we're all home? Has he not lost as many men as we think? Is this new feud between the two gangs just a ruse for them to attack us together and take us out in one night?

Micha.

My heart stops as I yank open the door and slide into the driver's seat. She only went to the grocery store and left before me. She could be back by now. She could accidentally walk in on Aleric. And he wouldn't hesitate to kill her.

Tearing out of my parking spot, I race for home. I slip a hand in my pocket to grab my phone. I call her, but she does not answer.

Maybe she isn't there. Maybe she's still driving.

But my gut's telling me she's in danger. I speed through the streets with little care for the limit or pedestrians trying to cross the road. I don't slow down until I pull onto our drive. Our ward is still up, and given it accepts me quickly when I pass through it, I know it's still the original thing. New wards hurt like hel until they learn that I'm a witch.

Lifting my foot off the accelerator a fraction, I let myself breathe. The plants filling our acreage are spelled to attack intruders, and not one of them looks stressed.

At the sight of Micha's car in front of me, I frown. I park beside her, then step out and place my hand on the hood of hers. It's cold. She's been here a while. So why didn't she answer my call or call me back?

I dig out my phone just to check, but there are no missed calls. My pulse increases, but I push my paranoia back. She isn't in league with Aleric. She –

Greeted him so warmly at the engagement party...

My stomach tightens as I walk to the front door and slip in without a sound. Making my way through the house, I open my senses, my ears twitching at every sound. There's someone upstairs... I can hear the scuff of things being moved. I take a step in that direction when a muffled noise, almost like a groan, comes from the lower bedrooms.

Thunder crashes around my skull. Red flashes across my vision. A low growl in my throat, I head down the hall in silent steps. If she's fucking someone in my own house, I'm going to kill him and then use his intestines to tie her to the godsdamn bed. She won't be able to speak by the time I'm through with her. Won't know a godsdamn word other than my name.

Stopping outside her bedroom, I take a moment to listen. The door is open a crack, but I don't hear anyone, don't sense her or anyone else either. Grabbing the handle, I push the door open. There's no one inside. I stride in, checking the closet and ensuite. Nothing.

Another noise has me spinning on my feet and heading out. This time I stop outside Mother's bedroom. I know she isn't here. She's meeting Katie Wilks, the regional manager of our legitimate chain of hotels. So is Micha in there with someone? Using Mother's room in some twisted kink?

I shove open the door and catch –

A TV on low that wasn't switched off. It's playing some porno with the lead woman looking too fucking similar to Mother. Shuddering, I stride over and turn it off. As I turn to leave, my gaze catches on a bottle of lotion on the wooden nightstand between the TV and the bed.

"...lotion every night."

My eyes narrow as a sick feeling twists in my stomach. A niggling thought starts to rise, but a noise directly above me cuts in before it can fully form.

If Micha is the only one here, what the fuck is she doing in Maddox's room?

Locking down the rising sense of betrayal, I head out of the room. If she's fucking him... *Shit.* I growl. Her or him, I'm not sure which one of them I'd fucking kill.

I take the stairs four at a time and reach the landing just as she's coming out of my brother's room. She sees me, and her face lights up. Then falters as I march towards her.

"Varius?"

"What were you doing in there?" I demand.

She's standing in the doorway, not yet having closed it, and I peer over her head. No one else is in there. A small movement to the right catches my attention, but I ignore it.

"Maddox was a dick earlier, so I am pranking him, but did you know he has a shapeshifter in there?" Her eyes are wide as she turns her head to look behind her. "He's keeping her in a fish tank. She's like five inches tall!"

"That's Marrabelle."

"Um, okay. Cool. That's cool." She looks back at me. "So he's turned her into what, a pet?"

She doesn't seem worried about being caught out. She isn't trying to block my gaze inside the bedroom. All I can sense off her is genuine surprise and confusion. The knot in my chest eases a little.

"You didn't answer my call," I say, ignoring her inquiries about the tiny woman in Maddox's room. She's a brownie, a species from the plane of Gaera, and she's a total weirdo. Even more so than my brother.

"Your call?" Her brows bunch together. She checks her pocket, then shakes her head. "I must've left my phone on the counter. I took it out while I was putting away the food.

Sorry I missed it. Did you want something?"

"When did you get back?"

"Maybe an hour ago?"

Not long after I left. If Aleric lured me out to come here, would she know? He can't get past the ward, and the house is far from the edge. Unless... Would drinking from a witch, draining them dry, allow him to phase in? "Was there ever a moment you thought someone else was here?"

Micha tenses. Something flashes through her eyes before she looks up at me. "No. Did you see someone when you got back? Recognize them?"

Her questions are too direct. There's no surprise in her voice. No question about how they would've gotten past the ward. Like she already knows someone is here. Is she trying to hide Aleric? Or is it just her assassin training, gathering all the intel she can before she reacts?

My chest squeezes with instant denial that she would turn on me, but I lock it down. I've only known her for four months. I knew Vinny and Uncle Myers for decades, and my judgment of them was still too fucking blind.

"I was supposed to meet Aleric," I say slowly, watching her carefully, "but he never showed."

Her eyes light up as she smiles coyly. "So you thought he was coming to grab me?" She reaches forward and runs her hand down my chest. "So you came racing all the way back even though I'm safe behind the ward?"

My cock jerks as she brushes her fingers over it. My flare of jealousy is still pounding in my chest, demanding I take her rough and hard until she can't remember her own name.

"I guess I should thank you for saving me," she purrs as she ducks past me, perhaps to lead me down the hall to my room. But I grab her arm and push her back.

Her eyes widen. She takes a step back as I advance, my intention clear in my eyes. In my hands as I undo the button of my pants.

"We can't have sex here!"

I pull down my zipper.

"But what about Marrabelle?" she tries.

"Oh, don't mind me," the brownie says with an off-world accent. "I can take care of myself." I am smart enough not to look over. Brownies are utter sex fiends, Marrabelle having mentioned coming from a free-use cult. The reason she's on Earth is because it was her job to invite *everyone* here to an orgy. When she bumped into Maddox, he decided to keep her as a pet.

But Micha is not aware of what a brownie is. She looks behind her at the waterless fish tank. Blushes hard. Her eyes damn near pop out of her skull. Then she whips her head back to me, looking traumatized. "She's fucking the tower," she whispers. "Like, it's actually *in* her."

I dig into my boxers and fish out my cock. Soft moans start up from the tank, and Micha turns bright red. "Can we put a towel over her at least?"

"No. Because she's going to tell Maddox just how much you're mine."

"Maddox?" She swallows as she keeps stumbling back. "He absolutely knows. He's your brother. We would never – *I* would never –"

She sucks in a breath when I grab her by the throat and haul her forward. Leaning down, I take her lips with mine and push my tongue into her mouth. She tries to turn her head, so I tighten my grip until she stills. A strangled noise escapes her. Her hands push against my chest. But as the kiss goes on, her fingers start to curl until she's grabbing my shirt in both hands.

Releasing her throat, I grab her hips and haul her up my body. Dipping my head, I bite her neck.

"This is so wrong," she whispers even as she wraps her legs around my waist and arches her neck on a moan. "He's your *brother*."

"Talk about him again," I growl as I lift my head. "And I'll cut off his fucking cock."

She sucks in a harsh breath as she stares into my eyes. "You have a serious problem, you know that?"

Only when it comes to you.

Grabbing my dick, I rub it against her panties. She arches against me, her lips seeking mine as I tease her with the head of my cock. She's already wet, her pussy used to being fucked daily, waiting and willing at every hour of the day. But I still need to wait until she's stretched. Otherwise, I'll tear her.

"You're going to get yourself off on just my tip," I growl. "And as you're coming, I'm going to fuck you until I'm balls deep."

She whimpers. She's been adjusting to my size over the last few months, but she hasn't made it all the way down yet.

But she nods like a good girl. Trusting me. Giving me what I need as the jealousy in my chest flares hot.

Reaching between us, she slips her panties to the side, then wraps her fingers around my cock. I grab her ass with both hands, keeping her up as my arm muscles bulge. She flexes her thighs as she holds herself up on my hips.

Sagging against my chest, she rubs the tip of my cock back and forth between her pussy lips. My balls tighten, begging me to shove up and into her. To fuck her fast and hard until I get my release. My fingers digging into her ass, I force myself to stay still as she uses me. As all of her focus stays on *me.*

She starts to moan as she humps the tip of my cock. Her other hand dives beneath her dress, and I know it's on her clit, giving herself that outside pressure she needs. Her cum slides down my cock, making me twitch. Her pants become harsher and harsher. She bites my chest through my shirt, and I groan. My fingers dig harder into her. I want to suck her tits into my mouth. Want to lick her pussy as she cries out. But all I do is curl my toes and focus on the feel of her gripping my head. Soon I'm going to sink all the way inside her, but first she needs to come. She needs to relax enough I can push in deep.

"Varius," she whispers as she starts to writhe. Her thighs tighten around me, squeezing me. She grips my cock harder. "Come in me," she moans right before biting me again but in a different spot. "Get me pregnant with your child."

She clenches her pussy around just the head of my cock, and it's so fucking sensitive, I can't breathe. My balls ache. My cock begs me to thrust inside her. But she doesn't get the rest of me until she comes. She doesn't get to tease me without consequence, even if she did so unknowingly.

"You want me to come in you?" I growl.

"Yes. *Please*."

"You want me to fill you until it's dripping all down your legs?"

She whimpers.

"Then tell Marrabelle who you fucking belong to."

"Varius," she rasps, shaking against me. "I'm Varius'!"

"Damn fucking right you are." My hands knead her ass. I haul her down just past my tip, then push her back up. I bounce her up and down at a speed that has both my knees buckling. "Now come for me, little monster. Let her hear you scream."

She whimpers and moans, trembles and shakes. She's desperate for me to fill her and frustrated that I won't. So she moves her hand faster across her clit. She releases my cock to fondle her tits, shoving aside the top of her dress. And then she's screaming, crying out as she arches back. And I'm thrusting up into her as I shoot a hot load so deep into her fucking pussy.

Wrapping my arms around her back, I drag her down as I hold her close. Her thighs fall apart just as she does, and I use her relaxed state to drag her down my cock even more. It's so fucking sensitive, it hurts, but I don't stop pulling her down. Don't stop thrusting up. She's close to taking all of me.

She whimpers, and she winces, but she doesn't deny me. She wiggles her hips, trying to go that final inch. "Shit. Fuck," she moans as she shakes her head, sweat gleaming across her brow.

"You can take me, baby," I growl as my breaths turn hot and ragged. "Be a good girl and sit all the way on my cock."

"I...ahhh..." she rasps.

My hands dig into her skin, forcing her down more.

"That's it, baby," I say, all of my blood, my focus, down in my cock and balls. "Fucking squeeze me."

She kegels, and I jerk.

I fall to my knees but keep my arms around her.

I bury my head into the crook of her neck as I rock back on my ass. "Fuck," I groan, and she kegels again. I twitch hard as I bite her neck, growling around the flesh in my mouth. The tip of my cock is pulsing with a plea for me to stop. To give it a second to recover.

But I don't, too desperate to fill her up again.

Grabbing the front of her dress, I rip it down the middle. Then I tear off her panties, stopping it from rubbing against my cock. I drop a hand between us to cup her pussy, then trail it up to her belly.

"You want my baby, little monster?" I ask as I release her neck to push her back, arching her away. I pinch her nipple with one hand as I grab her hip with the other.

She nods as she places her hands on the floor behind her. She lifts her pussy off me, then rocks it back down. I dig my fingers into her, my thighs shaking as she rides me.

"You want me to fuck you while you're pregnant?"

She whimpers. Pants. Fucking *moans*.

"Then take that last inch, baby. Let me feel you around

every part of me."

Crying out, she slams down at the same time I thrust up. I'm nestled all the way inside her now, and fuck me, I see stars. The brilliance of an exploding sun.

I lean forward and hold her close as I growl in between her boobs. My teeth scrape across her skin as I jerk my hard-as-fuck cock in the tightness of her pussy.

"Good girl," I growl. "Good fucking girl."

I grab her nipple between my teeth, and she cries out. She wraps one hand around the back of my head, her nails digging into my scalp.

"That's it, baby. Mark me." I groan. *Mark me like I'm fucking yours.*

She rakes her fingers deep down my neck, and I hiss in a sharp breath. I can feel her nails all the way down to my cock. Her claim. Her desire. I slide my hand across her belly, imagining it swollen in all the stages. I can feel a little kick, hear a little heartbeat. And the last part of my control falls apart at the idea of holding her as she holds our little boy. Or girl. Fuck, I don't care which as long as they're *ours.*

Groaning, I grab her by the throat and yank her mouth up to my lips. I kiss her desperately, my tongue dancing with hers as I drink in her every moan.

"Fuck. *Varius.* Please." She claws at my shirt, tearing it over my head, then drags ten red lines down my chest. I arch into her fingers, hissing in a breath. "Fill me up, baby. Don't stop until I'm pregnant."

I groan, barely able to beat off my orgasm.

"That's it," she rasps. "That's it. You feel so fucking *good,* Varius. Make me come on your cock. Ahhh!" More lines appear on my back, carved into my flesh as she cries out my name.

Her pussy squeezes me, pulsing tight and fast as she orgasms on my cock. I last only a few more pumps and then I'm emptying myself inside of her. She squeezes out every last drop, sucks my balls dry.

But she's taking more than just my seed.

Panting in my brother's room, with her collapsed against me, her face pressed against my chest, I give her a part of me that is utterly terrifying.

My chest tight, I climb to my feet and carry her out of the room. As soon as we're outside, away from Marrabelle's eyes, I set her down. I start to form words I don't even know how to say. But she isn't looking at me. She isn't giving me her attention, and for the first time in my life, I'm scared shitless.

"Varius…" she starts, but I'm already gone. Her word tickles the back of my ears as I stride away. I need time to think, time to gain a courage I've never needed before.

"Varius," she tries again, but I'm stepping into my office.

My entire body shaking, I close the door behind me.

Firmly.

Without a crack left open.

And then I lock it.

Because fuck me, I think I'm in love with Micha.

THIRTY-SEVEN

HER

Shit, that was close.

I close the door to my bedroom, then immediately fall into bed, my body shaking. I hadn't even realized Varius had come home until I heard him downstairs. Thank fuck, I had thought ahead for once and come up with a reason for being up there if I got caught. It was a prank I'd pulled on Dayne a couple of times – heating his pillow with my magic so both sides would stay warm practically all night.

At the thought of my friend, I squeeze my eyes shut and bite back my urge to scream. I asked Varius to make me pregnant, a knee-jerk idea, hoping that will get him to listen to me if that recording ever gets out. And I *hate* that that request came from something that dirty. A manipulation.

Shuddering, wanting to cry but refusing to, I force my thoughts away from Varius, away from a future that feels so close to falling apart. I need to concentrate on one thing at a time. So I focus on Dayne, on the tattoo I gave him. His heart rate is still calm. Whoever is stalking him hasn't hurt him. *Yet.*

But I only have two weeks to find the ledger, and after his scare today, I just know Varius isn't going to leave me alone in this house for a very long time. All I've managed to search was his bedroom, and it wasn't there. Which means I'm going to have to get creative in how to search his office.

If Varius catches me…

I shudder, knowing what my fate will be.

Unless, perhaps, if I'm pregnant…

But I can't give up. Can't not look.

Not when they're threatening Dayne.

"Fucking idiot," I grumble. The next time I see my bestie, and I *will* be seeing him, I'm punching him for being so obtuse. Who doesn't realize they're being followed? Only a fucking idiot.

Pulling myself together, I get my laptop out of my bag, then stop. I can't trust any electronics I have. I blow out a breath. Which means I need to go old school and write a godsdamn letter because some *idiot* never learned how to scry due to how easy it is to use technology.

"Fucking idiot," I grumble again, this time at myself.

My hands shaking, I try not to think about that last look I saw on Varius. The one that rocked my entire world. The one that changed it in its entirety.

Biting my cheek, I force myself not to cry. The only tears I'll shed because of this blackmailing asshole will be ones of glee when I skin the fucker alive.

THIRTY-EIGHT

HIM

"How did you know?" I ask Khalid as he appears out of his shadow on our porch in the early hours of the morning. It's been a week and a half since Talon started visiting Rei, and with every day that he fails to get info, I've been getting more and more restless. No...that's not true. With every day that passes after I fucking realized I loved Micha, I've been wanting to tear off my skin.

She is a weakness I can't afford, so I've been avoiding her, hiding in my office under the excuse of work.

Like a coward. Refusing to look at my feelings because I'm dreading the two week mark from when I last fucked her. That's the earliest we can find out if she's pregnant with magic. And if she is?

If our enemies kidnapped either of them, they'd fucking have me in the palm of their hand.

How can I be a Boss, how can I protect my brothers, if I could be so easily manipulated?

And Micha...

My chest tightens.

Today, I found something out that makes me so fucking afraid. I haven't been able to sleep at all, so I've been out here for hours, sitting in a chair and watching the flowers bloom. Leno spelled them to open whenever they're looked at. A type of therapy, and fuck, it kind of works.

"About what?" Khalid asks as he steps towards me, the smell of someone's pussy on his breath.

"That your girl was it?"

He looks at me sharply. "You finally claiming her?"

"Just talking, Kali," I say, using the nickname he hates. It is a low blow, but I'm feeling irritable, and besides, it is still vastly better than the one Maddox gave me. Which is Vay Vay. The fucker calls me a vagina.

He settles into the chair beside me. "It just felt right."

"Instant?"

He nods.

I sigh. It wasn't instant with Micha. So maybe I'm not in love with her. Maybe she isn't a weakness.

"Though it took me longer to realize that than it should have."

I glance at him. "What changed?"

He shrugs. "Couldn't fucking resist her."

Couldn't fucking resist her...

Damn, that fucking fits. This last week and a half has been hel to my control. Micha's making me insane. I have never had an issue ignoring any carnal urges before – made it thirty-odd years no problem. But with her...

I'm sleeping in my fucking office just so she can't come to me at night.

And at the same time, I want to burn the entire fucking world down just so no one gets to enjoy her but me.

I fucked her in Maddox's room for gods' sake. Because she felt comfortable enough to prank him. That was it. That was all the fucking trigger I needed.

She's driving me insane.

This can't be right.

"How do you know it isn't a spell?" I ask.

He glances at me like I'm an idiot, but he's the dumb one if he hasn't even at least considered –

"You know it's not," he says.

I glance away, not quite ready to let that hypothesis die. It *could* be true. It would explain so much. She wouldn't be the first woman who tried to seduce me and kill me. She'd just be the first one to succeed.

I frown, not liking the heaviness in my chest. But fuck, my little monster actually could succeed. I would run into a dark alley in the middle of Death Hunt territory if I thought she needed me. Impale myself right onto her fucking knife.

I shift uncomfortably, but I haven't survived this long by ignoring my paranoia.

Then there's the thing I discovered today – the reason I haven't been able to sleep.

"There's a bulletin out on the ledger," I say. "Someone has accepted it." Meaning someone thinks they can actually pull it off. Someone like Micha perhaps… She's the only one who can other than a brother, but if any brother gives it up, they will be damning themselves to a life behind bars given all their sins are listed too.

Khalid glances at me. "The ward's solid." His eyes track across the flowers. "Our second defense is strong, and that's assuming none of us are home, which is rare."

"Wards fail all the time. Aleric broke one just like this a few decades ago." He attacked at dinner with his entire nest. If Mother hadn't realized she could pull monsters out of her shadows, he would have ended our bloodline that night. As it was, many witches died.

"Our magic has come a long way since then."

I incline my head, but I don't verbalize my agreement.

"You should be more worried about Maddox. He killed a WALL member tonight."

"They're nothing but gnats."

The Warriors Against Lycans and Lessers consists only of humans. They might kill a few of us every so often, but they don't have the firepower or the manpower to take us down.

Not like Micha could destroy me... A one woman army.

"They're planning to establish an organized task force," he says, pulling me out of my thoughts. My fears.

"Aleric owns half the police."

"But not all of them."

My eyes narrow. A human task force hunting sups? That would be enough to call the attention of the Special Crimes Unit, and unlike the WALL, the SCU *does* have the means to take us down. They might be mere humans, but they're a division of the Elv've'Nor, which polices the entire Seven Planes. They have a whole bunch of toys that hurt like hel.

"Who relayed the intel?" I ask.

"No one. I've recently taken an interest in politics."

I raise a brow, but he doesn't answer the silent question.

"Get some rest, Vay, Vay," he says as he stands and pats my shoulder. "And stop being an idiot and fucking claim her already. She's good for you."

He leaves me on the front porch, nursing the weight of his words.

She's good for me...

Unless she really is planning on betraying me.

Because I might have been avoiding her for nearly two weeks, but she hasn't exactly been seeking me out either. And I can only wonder why...

My fists clench as ice-cold anger fills my veins.

Don't do it, Micha.

Please just fucking don't.

I'll give you everything if you just make me your world.

THIRTY-NINE

HIM

Talon rocks up a few hours later. I'm still on the fucking porch looking at the damn flowers, hoping Micha doesn't fall for the trap I've left in my office. My gaze lifts to him as he steps out of his car.

"Got him!" he shouts.

I'm on my feet in an instant, my paranoia mixing with my pleasure. "Why didn't you call?"

"Phone's dead. Think I broke the charging port."

I stare at him for a second, then turn to yank open the door of the house. "Everyone in the kitchen!" I yell. They're all light sleepers, but they're not all here.

Maddox hasn't come back yet. He'll need time to regain his strength after shapeshifting back into his normal size, but I know he won't have taken a nap like he normally does. Given he's been an ant on the wall during Talon's sessions with Rei, he'll know it's time to strike against the wolves. He'll be back in an hour tops.

Leno and Krypto are currently out too. They're up north cementing our deal with Stefaan. Enoch and Ezriel are with them, acting as bodyguards.

I stride inside and enter the kitchen just as Khalid and Rudy come in from the direction of the stairs. Talon enters behind me. Mother and Micha are already inside, making us something to eat. Despite everything in me calling to her, I refuse to look at Micha. I'm stronger than my weakness.

I fucking need to be.

"Fill us in, T," I sign as I stop beside the table. I don't sit, my body too restless with finally having a lead a follow. An action to take so we're not just sitting ducks in this fucking war.

"Cid's heading up to North Carolina tonight for three days."

"What for?" Rudy asks.

Talon shakes his head. "Rei doesn't know, but she wants me to take her out."

"She care for him at all?" I sign, wanting to know the chances of this being a trap.

Another headshake. "Hates him. He leaves her covered in bruises. Has broken a few of her bones. He's stabbed her a few times, burned her in others. Shot her once. Opened up her stomach and jerked off with her intestines."

"Fucking hel," Micha says from the kitchen.

We all ignore her, but I catch her attempt at repeating herself in sign language. She's trying to learn for Rudy, and fuck, does that make me hard for her.

Mother corrects a mistake she makes, and I tear my focus away from them.

"He do the same thing to his wife?" I ask. If he does, using his family to break him probably isn't going to work.

Talon shrugs. "No idea. Cid never talks about family with her."

The front door slams open, and Maddox rushes in, out of

breath and a few inches shorter than normal. He clearly did not take the time to measure the amount of meat he needed. He most likely just grabbed one body and called it done.

"I got a fucking wolf," he says, tapping his head.

"Fully or just face?" I demand, adrenaline pumping in my veins. Though either one is a fucking ace up our sleeve.

His grin splits his lips apart. "Face –"

"Lame," Rudy signs, teasing him.

He glares at him before adding, "But he wants to take me out, so I'll get his DNA soon."

"As you?" Rudy asks. "Or some bimbo?"

"Seriously, bruh, if you could experience a girl's orgasm, you wouldn't be knocking me each time I changed to get laid."

"Any other info?" I snap, making it fucking clear that line of conversation is over.

"Full body experience," Maddox mouths as Talon shakes his head.

But that's enough for me to make a plan. "T, you'll get Rei out and get her DNA." His jaw tightens the slightest bit, but he doesn't protest us using her. "Rudy, you're his backup if shit hits the fan."

He nods without hesitation even though we all know what it'll cost him if it comes to that. Weeks of night terrors that have the power to actually kill him. And us. He is a last resort, but fucking hel is he some damn good calvary.

"Khalid, get a team together to grab Cid."

"I can –" Khalid starts, but I shake my head.

"Pick a team. Half a dozen. We need you fully healed for the interrogation. Maddox, you'll stay here."

"I could help with –" He sighs in disappointment when I look at him.

"You're breaking into his house and getting the DNA of his family. You still have enough bodies?"

My brother hums, looking a lot happier. "For a job like

that, I don't know, bruh…"

My eyes narrow, but I don't push. He might need to shift multiple times if things go bad.

"I could use a couple more bodies," he says seriously.

"Go up north and hunt freely." My eyes sharpen. "But do *not* draw the attention of the SCU."

He grins, then mock salutes.

I cock my head towards the door. "Go."

"Before breakfast?" he whines.

"You'll need the time to plan."

Grumbling, he heads for the door. "First, you make it so I can't sleep in my damn room without hearing about your dick, and now, I can't even eat."

"Here," Mother says, and he pivots just in time to catch a lunch box.

"Fuck, yes. Love you, bruh!"

He turns, and an onion sails across the room. It pelts him right in the back of the head, and he yelps as he rubs where it hit him.

"What did I tell you about being disrespectful?" she asks.

"Love you, *ma*," he says grumpily.

"Love you too, you little shit."

He laughs as he walks out the door.

"You did good, T," I say, turning to him.

He ducks his head, then rubs a hand through his black hair. "Rei's had a really shitty life," he says slowly. He looks at the reaper. "If you can break him before you get to her…" He trails off.

Khalid nods. "I'll try."

"Thanks," he says, but he doesn't seem hopeful.

"And Micha," I say, turning to her as she brings a plate of food to the table – scrambled eggs and bacon and toast.

"Yes?" There's no tilt to her tone that demands suspicion, but my gut rolls nevertheless.

"I'm calling Leno back, so I need you to go up north as a

representative. The groundwork has already been laid. Your father knows the terms. You just need to cement what has been established and drink the required toast. Think you can do that?"

Her eyes widen in shock. That isn't the job of a woman in the Shadow Domain. They've always been nothing but breedmares, but I can't stand to look at her right now. Can't stand to have her around. I need to be on top of my game. She's too distracting. And...

The real reason...

I don't want to know if she's a traitor yet.

I want to give myself another few days of bliss. Where there's no way she can get access to the ledger, no way to trigger the trap I've left in my office.

No way for her to hurt me in her betrayal.

A slow smile curls her lips. "Yeah. Yeah, I can do that."

"Good. You and Khalid will leave after breakfast. He'll come back without you."

She nods, then places the plate down in front of my chair. After walking over to me, she leans up and pecks my cheek, and fuck, do I want to grab her and kiss her properly. It's been too long since I've touched her.

But instead I keep my hands at my sides as I take a seat at the table. Until I find out if Micha's yet another traitor, I don't trust myself with her at all.

A one woman army...

FORTY

HIM

I slam my fist into the punching bag, waiting for the call I know is coming. Today is the day we go after Cid. Rei was broken out three nights ago, her DNA taken. She's back in the brothel as we can't risk her not being there. It'd be too suspicious given Talon's been fucking her for the past few weeks.

Maddox has been to the werewolf's house and collected items for Khalid to use in his soul dolls. Hair for the women. Semen-covered tissues for Cid's boy. He's also brought back a few dirty lacy panties, taken from the youngest daughter's room, but they're not to be used in Khalid's soul magic. No, those have been kept by Maddox.

There's a bet going on about whether he's obsessing over her because he *likes* her or because he's planning on her being his next victim. With Maddox, it could be both.

But all I'm interested in is a phone call from Khalid. He went out with the team he picked this morning. They should be bringing Cid in soon.

Impatient, I jab at the bag in quick strokes. Left, left, left, right. Duck. My thoughts turn to Micha unbidden, the main focus of my frustrations. I don't like her not being here. I don't like that she hasn't called. I don't like that I want to, near desperate just to hear her voice.

Ignoring the presence of my phone on the bench, I attack the bag harder. Working my muscles like my thoughts work me.

If Micha goes for the ledger, can I actually hurt her?

My fists hit the bag.

It's just a book. The information in it isn't even true.

She doesn't know the paintings are the real ledgers. If she did, she would've taken a photo of them already and collected the two mil.

It'll be a victimless crime...

But it would still be a betrayal.

And betrayal always means death.

Just not with her...

Fuck. I have it bad.

My phone rings, and for a second I ignore it, striking the bag hard and fast. Needing to let my frustrations out. Then I stop suddenly, remembering Cid. The bag swings back to me, and I step out of its way as I stride over to the bench. For a moment, right as I pick it up, I hope it's Micha calling. But it isn't. Of course it isn't.

This engagement is just a transaction to her, a fate forced upon her. She's at home for the first time in four months. Why would she be thinking about me at all?

Irritated, I snatch up the phone and accept Khalid's call.

"Four died, but we have Cid," he says. "We're bringing him back now."

I force out a breath, force Micha out of my thoughts. "No, I'll get the room ready. Grab his soul, then dump his body inside the city. Fix him to make it look like a heart attack.

We're using the WALL as bait tonight."

They are dumb enough to hunt sups at night but smart enough to know we're the ones who've killed Cid. The idea of a war between us will get them itchy and moving out in full force. I need to see their numbers, and if there are as many as Khalid thinks there are, that big of a group will draw out Antonio.

I have a feeling we're going to be needing to kill him soon. To cut off the head of the snake before it strikes.

"Will do. Back in fifteen."

He hangs up, and my thumb lingers over my contacts.

Hating my lack of control, I press her name.

It rings three times before she answers.

"Hi."

And just like that, my irritation eases.

"We have Cid," I say. "You finished there?"

"Yeah."

Then come home.

"Good." My chest burns as I think about telling her I love her. My fingers tighten on my phone. But I don't blurt them out. I want to make sure they're not coming from a place of manipulation. A way to get her to not betray me. I want her to genuinely want me like I do her.

"When you get back," I say instead, "come see me."

"It's a long drive, Varius. I might not get there until early morning."

I don't care. "I'll see you tomorrow then."

"Sure."

I hang up, then shove the phone in my pants pocket. My irritation is back like it never left. 'Sure' isn't a word you use when you want to see someone.

Looking forward to it.

I can't wait.

Those are fucking things you say when you want to see someone.

Shoving my middle fingers into the black rings I left on the bench, I make my way to the door. I detour first, though, back to the bag and swing an angry fist into it. With my rings of strength on this time, the bag flies across the room, knocked clean off its chain, and ruptures when it hits the wall. As sand pours out onto the gym floor, I yank open the door and storm out.

Rudy is waiting for me, and my footsteps halt at the sight of him.

"You okay?" he signs.

I nod and start to walk past him, but he darts in front of me and puts a hand on my shoulder. His power pushes into me, slamming into my chest with all the power of a bolt of lightning.

Micha flashes in front of my eyes in the arms of another man. And she's happy. Smiling and laughing and looking at him like he's the fucking world.

I swat Rudy's hand away, but I don't tell him to fuck off. If he were any of my other brothers, I would've shoved him, but he isn't. He's a boy I raised, so I breathe out heavily as I look at him.

"You should tell her you love her," he says, and my heart trips over itself.

"It's not that simple, Rudy."

"Why not?"

Because she might be a traitor. This whole time we have been together could have been nothing but an act. I don't know when that bulletin went out about the ledger. Did she take it the first day? Has she been biding her time? Building up my trust? Playing me like a fucking fool while she waits for me to turn my back so she can stab me in it? Just like Vinny and Myers did and so many other Family cousins and uncles?

He reaches out for me, moving slowly, letting me back away if I want to. But I don't. Because I already know what he's going to show me. I already know what I'm afraid of.

His hand touches my chest, causing goosebumps to flair across my skin as I see her for a second time.

She's pregnant and chasing a little boy around the house. He runs to a sofa, then dives behind the back of it where she can't reach. Giggling. Laughing. He crawls away from her as she roars, pretending she's some great beast.

My chest squeezes.

Grows tighter still.

Because then I see me. Smiling. Joining in as we chase our boy around the house. I grab him and lift him in the air before turning him into an airplane to chase Micha.

Rudy drops his hand, and the magic fades. It takes a huge ass part of me with it.

"It's not normal to be afraid of being happy," he says.

"I can't afford to be weak." To have a weakness. To lose my edge when I have thousands of people counting on me to make the right choices for this Family.

He shakes his head. "Love isn't weak, you idiot. Being alone is weak. If you weren't there for me when I was a kid, I would be dead," he signs matter-of-factly. "Needing you wasn't a weakness of mine. It allowed me to grow strong." He smiles at me softly. "You needing her isn't a weakness either."

"That's different."

"That's your fear talking."

I stare at him, then shake my head. "When did you get so fucking wise?"

"When I had to play father to my father."

My jaw drops along with my mask. Just for a second, then I'm pulling it back up so the damn tears don't escape my eyes.

"Well, don't just stand there," he says with a cheeky grin. "You need to get the room ready before Khalid gets here."

Turning, giving me privacy to recollect myself, he heads

for the room of runes. I watch him go, remembering the last scene he showed me. My throat tight, I pull out my phone.

Hesitate.

Then type a quick text to Micha.

Varius: *I don't care about the time. I want to see you when you get back.*

My finger hovers over the send button.

Then the back button.

My shoulder muscles rigid, I shove my phone into my pocket without pressing send. I'll talk to her later when she gets back. Perhaps I can just fucking ask her if she's trying to steal the ledger. As dumb as it would be to give her that chance to play me, we could come back from her *planned* betrayal.

But if she actually goes through with it?

If she actually tries to hurt my brothers by selling info that will damn them?

I'd be so fucking angry, I don't know what I'd do.

Closing my eyes, I take a deep breath.

Upon opening them, I head for the room of runes. I'll deal with her when she gets back. Right now, I need to focus on learning what Cid knows.

A war is coming, and we *have* to be prepared.

FORTY-ONE

HER

The call from Varius has me itching to go home. Or at least talk to Dayne to make sure the Boss of the Shadow Domain is okay. He sounded tense, on edge, and although I left my friend there to watch over him, I have no way of communicating with him while I'm up here. There wasn't a bug on my phone recording my conversations that day, so the blackmailer must have gotten it through magic. Which means I can't use any technology, no burner phone. Can't trust it won't come back to bite me in the ass.

Two weeks ago, after I hung up on Dayne before I got his voicemail, he headed straight to Florida. Having suspected he would come to me, I left the letter I wrote at one of our drop-off zones for him to pick up. I told him to deal with whoever was watching him so I could fuck this blackmailer up.

He told me he had dealt with the guy already, having clocked him the day I signaled him something was wrong.

The man hasn't talked yet. He's tied up and gagged and still with Dayne to keep working on, but he had a burner phone with a single number. So Dayne's been texting updates to it, giving my blackmailer false intel on his whereabouts.

Leaving me free to hunt the idiot who thought he could hunt me.

Unfortunately, they're damn good at hiding their tracks. The only lead we have to go on is that damn phone with a single number. Dayne's been working on trying to trace it, and in the meantime, I have been trying to figure out the blackmailer's identity.

Rolling over in bed, I glare at the ceiling. This is the first time I've slept in in months, it being the afternoon now, and the fucker is ruining it. Once I get my hands on them, I'm going to make them pay for that.

And for threatening Varius' trust in me. My eyes close as my chest aches.

Then I'm on my feet and moving, getting my bag packed and ready to go. Father and I toasted yesterday. The deal's been finalized. I've set up a meeting between him and the Mattos twins. There's nothing else keeping me here, and I have an eight-nine-hour drive ahead of me. More with rests as it's just me driving and the last thing I want to do is die from a crash on the way home.

"You're leaving already?" Stefaan says when I step into his office with my bag on my shoulder and inform him I am going. If I wasn't an official rep of the Shadow Domain, I would've just left, but rudeness in this life can trigger wars.

"Yeah. I have a long drive ahead of me," I say, then pivot to leave. I've done the necessities. He won't get anything more from me.

"Lou will hate that she missed you."

She's spending the weekend camping with a friend in the mountains, but she's scheduled to get back in tonight as she has school tomorrow.

"I'll make it up to her later," I say. As much as I would love to see her and catch up, I need to get back home. I step out into the hall.

"Micha, wait," Stefaan orders, but I don't. I never have to listen to him again.

"It's about the ledger," he says, stopping me in my tracks.

I pivot slowly to face him. If he's the fucking blackmailer, I'll kill him slowly. My fingers flicker with flames he cannot see but is about to fucking feel.

Walking back into his office, I shut the door behind me. "Did you take out the bulletin?" I ask softly.

"Of course not. Our Family does not have the prestige to use the information in it. If we tried to take over any of their operations, we'd be laughed at. Use your head, girl."

I glare at him, but I can't fault his logic. "So what about it?" I ask.

He looks at me, his eyes sharp with the gaze of a man who has survived years of hel. "You must know how it looks that someone has accepted it. No one is capable of pulling that off unless they already have access to the house."

I keep my face flat, giving nothing away. If he finds out I'm being blackmailed, he'll either try the same but with a different requirement or tell Varius, throwing me under the bus so he can use me as a stepping stone.

"Which means Varius must suspect you too."

My knees buckle, but I somehow manage to still stay standing. My mind reels. My pulse spikes in fear that Varius is going to kill me as soon as I get back home.

He's been avoiding me for two weeks. He hasn't fucked me once during that time...

No, I tell myself sharply, pulling myself together. *That was because he scared himself.*

I felt his feelings for me in Maddox's room that day. Saw the look in his eyes when he walked away. He's falling for me, and that simply terrifies him. *That* is the reason he has been avoiding me, and I've been giving him space to work through it. If I rush it, it'll only force him to take those three steps back he so often likes to take.

But he's starting to come around to the idea. I heard his need on the phone. He wants me back home. He misses me.

It isn't death that will await me on my arrival. It is love, and I'm so fucking ready to fall into his arms.

But first I need to deal with this blackmailer. Because I'm starting to suspect it's someone close to him. Someone who knew the house was empty. Maybe even a brother who is planning a coup and wants me as a scapegoat if it all goes to shit.

My heart twists at the thought of it actually being one of them. I like them all, and fucking hel, hasn't Varius suffered enough? First a cousin and uncle... Now a fucking brother...

I almost wish the traitor was me just so he wouldn't have to go through all that pain.

Itching to go, I pin Stefaan with a saccharine smile, and say sweetly, "Don't worry, father. Even if I die, the deal we have made will still go through."

His jaw tics. "I don't give a damn about the deal, Micha. I want to know you're staying safe."

I blink, having not expected that at all. As if he can hear my disbelief despite my inability to find any words, he says, "A man like Varius kills first and regrets never."

My eyes narrow. "He's not like you."

"He's exactly like me."

"He cares about his family."

"And you think I don't?"

"You sold me!"

"I saved you! Do you know how many assassins make it past their thirtieth birthday?"

"You! Aaron –"

"Aaron's dead."

My mouth goes slack, the air rushing out of my lungs.

My brother and I were never close, but – "When?" I croak.

"Two weeks ago. Three days before he turned thirty."

I step back. I want to sit down to process this sudden news, but I don't. "Why didn't you tell me?" I demand. *Why didn't Lou?*

"I didn't think you'd care."

"You didn't think – He was my brother!"

"You two hated each other."

I open my mouth, my emotions boiling and bubbling, but there's no substance in the froth. Just pretty air. He's right. We hated each other. There wasn't one quality I liked about him. But he was still my brother.

"I have to go," I say. I can't stand to be in this damn house anymore.

"Micha," he says softly, and fuck me, I turn back to him.

"What?"

"When your mother died..."

My throat tightens at the mention of her. Stefaan never mentions her. After she died giving birth to Lou, he was never the same. He turned distant. Cruel.

"I know I haven't been the best father."

I barely just bite back my snort.

"But I do care about you." He pauses. "So if you need help with anything..."

"Like if I run?" I ask, a sarcastic bite to my words, but everything in my soul is in that question. I don't want to run. I just want him to be there for me, to be the father he stopped being sixteen years ago.

His piercing eyes hold mine. Honest. No lie. "Then we'll kill Khalid and pretend to search for you."

I stumble back, shocked and reeling. "Just...just protect Lou," I say. "Don't drag her into this fucking life." My throat burning, I open his door and walk out.

My hands are still shaking by the time I make it to my car. I shove the key into the ignition and throw it into drive, but then I hesitate.

I don't have to go back to St. Augustine, Florida. I could run. With the Blacks only pretending to look for me, I could hide from Varius. I'm tempted. I'm so fucking tempted with the blackmailer hanging over me.

Maybe I can run until I figure out who it is. Wait until I have evidence of my innocence before going back to Varius. It'll be safer...

But I can't.

I know in my heart that that would break him.

He'll never trust me again if I abandon him, regardless of the reason. And he is worth risking it all for...

So I press my foot onto the accelerator and speed home. Although the two-week deadline to grab the ledger is no longer hanging over me with Dayne having dealt with his stalker, if Varius is already suspicious of me, I don't have long before his paranoia poisons everything between us.

Will I find the blackmailer in time?

Gather enough evidence for Varius to believe me over him?

Or am I about to lose everything?

About to risk it all for a man who won't risk it back?

Dammit, Micha. You're being a fucking fool.

Maybe.

Maybe...

But he's *mine*, and I will fight to the ends of the earth to save him.

FORTY-TWO

HIM

We're going to lose everything.

Khalid got Cid to talk, and now we know what Antonio is up to. He's trying to make fucking hybrids. Vampire and werewolf – something that should be utterly impossible as a wolf's fluids are poisonous to a vampire.

But that would explain the state we found Jerry in – his skin peeling off, his entire body turning to slush. He was forced to fuck a female wolf, to poison himself over and over until he was no longer able to perform. Then he was discarded like yesterday's trash.

So we're all strapping up, getting ready to hunt Antonio down.

If he actually manages to create the army he wants, he'll grab the archangels' attention, and they will kill us all. The Shadow Domain. The Blood Fangs. The Death Hunt. Every sup in a hundred mile radius just to be sure the information on how to breed them dies with us.

"What the fuck is he thinking?" Talon hisses, electricity crackling in his fingers. The air buzzes with his anger. My phone glitches in and out, and I want to hit the fucker, lash out with my own anger.

I was trying to text Micha, dammit. I think I finally found the right words that time, and now they're all gone. And I wrote a long ass paragraph too. Fighting back the urge to strangle him, I shove my phone into my pocket.

She'll be back soon, I tell myself. Just another few hours. *I'll talk to her then.*

"Aw," Maddox teases Talon as he grabs a few blue vials off the kitchen counter – healing potions made by Mother. "You look like you've just found out your mistress has been two-timing you behind your back. I'd say girlfriend, but it's the Death Hunt. They're not exactly girlfriend material."

Talon glares at him. "Says the asshole jacking off with a werewolf's panties every night. You can at least do it in your fucking room."

"Don't want to see it? Don't come out at night. Or blame Varius. It's his fault I'm out there in the first place." Ducking his head as he swipes another few potions, Maddox mutters, "Marrabelle still won't shut up about your damn show."

A small grin pulls at my lips, so minuscule none of them can see it. I grab a few potions myself, blue for healing and shielding, red for dealing damage. What I'm really waiting on, though, are the cursed tools from Khalid. He's not here yet, still upstairs getting ready, as are our other brothers.

Walking into the kitchen, Rudy clearly catches the last part of the conversation as he signs, "Why don't you give her another show to talk about then? Put on a porno. You can ask Talon for recs. He's into the nasty."

Maddox makes a horrified face as he signs, "I don't want to hear about werewolves shitting in each other's mouths."

Talon punches him in the shoulder, zapping him with electricity as he does so. Maddox yelps. "For the last fucking time, I don't watch that!" he bellows.

"I think thee protests too much." Maddox grins as he dances away from Talon, shaking out his arm.

"Why don't you shrink yourself then?" Enoch asks as he and his twin stroll in. He pumps his hips as he pretends to hold another's waist.

"Because then he would end up killing her because she wouldn't shut up about how bad he was," Ezriel jokes. "And he *likes* her."

Maddox flips him off.

"Works for me if it gets him out of the damn living room," T mutters.

"Just let Krypto in there. He's been dying to eat her." Enoch laughs.

"Absolutely not," Leno says as he and his dog enter. "I taste everything he eats."

"That feels like a you problem. It was a dumb thing to add to your binding. Sharing seeing, touching, and taste?" Enoch shakes his head. "Fucking idiot. You could've been superhuman with having his hearing and smelling instead."

Leno narrows his eyes. "I was young. And I wanted to know what dog food tasted like to him. If he got bored of eating it all the time."

Maddox snickers.

"And you wanted to know what licking your own dick felt like," Rudy signs before Maddox can.

Leno blushes this time, but he doesn't deny it.

Enoch laughs. "So instead of having super powers, now you feed him steak."

He nods in defeat. "Yep. Now I feed him steak."

Krypto woofs as he wags his tail, clearly much happier with this arrangement, and my brothers all laugh.

Mother places another batch of healing potions down in front of us, and the new arrivals grab everything they need. "When you get out there, don't pull any punches," she says.

"We can't let the archangels get wind of this."

We all nod as Khalid comes in. He offers me a sword in its sheath. "It negates all innate healing effects," he says, which means it won't matter if it cuts me. Then he offers me a gun in a holster. "You don't have to shoot to kill. The bullet will dig its way into their heart. Takes up to three minutes if you shoot them in the foot. Don't waste the bullets. They're fucking expensive."

I nod and strap the weapons to me. "Let's go then," I say.

We split into four different cars. Maddox and Khalid in one, their innate powers working well together. The twins get in another, their telekinesis amplified when they're near each other. Talon and Rudy, then Leno and I in the last one as our pace is similar due to Krypto not being able to shift into a shadow either. Streaking out, we head towards the woods north of St. Augustine as the moon starts to climb. It is on the edge of Death Hunt territory and one of the places the WALL loves to hunt. If we're lucky, they get wiped out today too, and their little task force dream is nipped in the ass.

"So Khalid's girl," Leno sings as I drive. "Know anything about her?"

"Nope. You?"

"Nope. But he bought a house three months ago. Nearly dropped a mil on it."

"Near Aleric's street?" It could be useful if he's fucking a vampire too. It would make it easier for me to approach the idea of an alliance with them.

"Don't know. Haven't been able to figure that out yet. I have been checking into all the houses in town that sold around that time at that price, but..." He frowns. "I might need to widen my search as they've all been purchased by other people."

I shake my head at the idea of Leno and Krypto knocking on doors of random houses to see if our brother answers. "If

Khalid catches you snooping, you're dead."

He grins. "Yeah…but what's life without a bit of danger?"

My thoughts turn to Micha, to the scene Rudy showed me where we're chasing our little boy. He has her eyes, her smile.

A life without danger – it's an impossibility for us, but it doesn't look half bad…

"Check for neighbors who are into politics," I say as I turn left onto N. Holmes Boulevard.

Krypto glances at me from the footwell of the passenger seat, nestled between Leno's legs. My brother scratches him on the head. "Oh?"

"He mentioned having a new interest in it," I say, though I feel a bit weird joining Leno in this. Teasing any of my brothers, let alone Khalid, hasn't been something I've done since I was a kid. The responsibilities of Boss widened the distance between us.

It isn't weak to need others. Rudy's words come back to me. *"It's weak to be alone."*

Have I done it wrong all this time? Ruling from up high rather than down below?

"Thanks!" Leno says as he rubs his hands together. "Most politicians are male, so I can check all the women and work backwards. That can't be hard. I can start with the mayor," he jokes.

I shake my head. "I think you can rule her out."

"I don't know. She's fucking hot. I'd risk it to bang that."

Krypto woofs, and Leno stops scratching him to wag his finger in front of his nose. "Bad dog. Bad timing. What have I said about you sounding like you're agreeing to sex stuff?"

My lips curl upwards on the side away from him.

"It's a good thing you're cute," he says as he ruffles his dog's head in both his hands. "Otherwise, I'd have traded you a long time ago."

Krypto woofs again, having no idea what Leno is saying despite his spectacular timing sometimes. He isn't a magical creature himself, just a dog Leno shares a few senses with.

I pull off Interstate Ninety-Five at Sampson, a small town that's mostly made up of eateries, then head east towards the woods. I park on the side of a random dirt track, and we get out. Krypto lifts his nose to the air, but he doesn't growl. At the moment, we are alone. The rest of our brothers are scattered around the woods, waiting to ambush Antonio and his gang.

Kicking off his shoes, Leno leaves them in the car, then walks off the side of the road. Krypto trots beside him, his head scanning left and right, doing as he's been trained.

"Yellow light," Leno says, telling his dog he's free to roam as long as he stays nearby. Krypto takes off like a rocket, his tongue lolling out as he zooms around the woods.

Turning so I'm half focused on my brother and half on my surroundings, I draw my sword. One of these days, I'm going to convince Khalid I'm ready to play with his urumi – a whip sword I have been obsessed with trying since I saw him use it a few years ago.

But to be fair, I'm still shit with a regular whip. Giving me one with blades on the end probably isn't the best call.

Magic hums from Leno as he digs his toes into the dirt and closes his eyes. The plants around him shift, feeding off him like the rays of the sun. Tamping his power down, he focuses it, and the plants near us settle again.

He's searching the woods, traveling along the roots of the trees, through the mycorrhizal network that they use to talk to each other, to feed young saplings that can't quite get enough sunlight. It's a community beneath the earth, right below our feet that most people never know about. But Leno joins it like a long-lost relative finally coming home.

"The WALL is here. Two teams of four, plus a van." He shakes his head, his eyes still closed. "I can't see how many are inside it."

Probably four, but assumptions can lead to death. Unlike the werewolves and vampires, we don't need our hearts to be ripped out or our heads to be cut off to die. Wounds that will kill Earth humans if left untreated will kill us too.

"The wolves?" I ask.

"None yet."

Not surprising, but they'll come. With both us and the WALL here tonight, they won't be able to resist, especially if Antonio is hopped up on the idea of making hybrids. We just killed his youngest son. Khalid also killed Cid's wife, eldest daughter, and only son in order to get him to talk. He burned the first two alive with his magic, having dropped the soul dolls he created of them into a ball of fire. And as he did it, he opened up a channel between his victims and their dolls, allowing us to hear them and them to hear us.

Antonio was fucking Elana, Cid's wife, at the time she burst into flames, and Rudy informed us he'd been fucking Abril, Cid's daughter, for some time too. Whether he was joking about that or not, I don't know. But it doesn't matter. What we've done is a declaration of war.

Antonio will come tonight.

And we'll kill him before he can take everything from us, before he brings in the wrath of the seven archangels. Or just one of the winged bastards. Any one of them is capable of wiping out an entire city on their own. They're used to dealing with the gods. We are nothing but ants to them.

"Either of the WALL teams close to us?" I ask, thinking we can increase the chance of drawing the wolves to us if we're all in a 'nice little bow,' grouped together for them to slaughter.

"One's less than a mile –" His eyes snap open, and he yells, "They're here. Krypto, red light!"

His dog comes streaking through the trees as Leno relays the werewolves' location to our brothers, using the trees and plants around them to communicate in signals we flushed out beforehand.

There're a dozen wolves, and they're slaughtering their way through one of the WALL teams. Talon and Rudy are closest to them, but the others are on the south side.

"What the fuck?" he suddenly mutters.

"What?" I keep my eyes peeled on our surroundings, my grip on my sword strong but not knuckle-white.

"Khalid is streaking towards the van. Shadow form."

"He say why beforehand?"

"No."

"Where's Maddox?"

"With him."

"Shit." I can't call them while they're in their shadows.

"Any wolves near us?" I ask.

"Nope."

I pull out my phone and call Enoch with one hand. "Find Maddox and Khalid. Something's wrong."

"Where are they?"

I relay the information Leno gives me about where the van is – our brothers' destination rather than their current location, which is changing fast.

Hanging up, I slip my phone back into my pocket. There is no point in Leno and I trying to join the fight. We can't move fast enough to reach them before they've moved. The best thing we can do is Leno keeps an eye on them, giving us all intel, and I protect him if any wolves decide to come out this way.

Walking over to him, I pull out nine shield potions, then place them on the ground. Three potions on three sides of him, lined up in a row trailing away from Leno and spaced out a few feet apart. The closest one to my brother is about three feet away. I take up position beside him, my sword ready.

"Talon and Rudy have engaged the wolves, but most are

splitting off. Fuck."

My body buzzes with the need to move. I want to be out there, helping them fight, but Leno is vulnerable while he's like this. Krypto can't kill a werewolf. He's just a dog, and my brother can't concentrate on multiple surroundings at once. He's bouncing back and forth between our brothers, trying to keep an eye on everyone.

We tried comms at one point, but if anyone enters the Plane of Monsters, they become unusable even when they are back on Earth.

Krypto growls, and I dart my gaze to him as I inhale. His nose is a lot better than mine, so all I smell is the forest. But I can see the direction he's facing. The fact both his ears are down means it's a werewolf. Leno taught him to growl with his ears up if it's a vampire. If it's anything else, he wags his tail.

Slinking forward, his ears still low, Krypto steps on the potion furthest away from Leno in the set of three in front of him. He's wearing shoes to protect him from the glass, and he's been trained to hop back quick. A shimmering blue shield goes up, twelve feet by twelve feet. Nothing alive can get past it, and Krypto has been trained well not to touch it. He quickly runs around the other two sides, cracking open the furthest potions, surrounding Leno in a triangle.

Staying inside the shields too, he paws the ground three times. Three wolves.

"Antonio?" I ask as I pull out my gun with my free hand.

Leno takes half a second to connect to the plants around us, searching for the wolves his dog can smell. "No."

"Then keep connected. I have this."

A second later, a streak of red aims for me just as a dark-gray one rushes Leno from the other side. The wolf slows in front of the shield, then darts around it to join the red wolf I'm already engaged with. I slash my sword across the chest of Red, then spin and shoot Dark-Gray. Red howls as she jumps back. Dark-Gray stumbles to a knee, then gets back up. A white wolf tries attacking the shield – too young to know it'll hurt like hel to touch. They howl. Red turns her head, and I lop half of it off with a slice of my sword. I line up my other hand with its chest, and fire the gun. As Red falls to the ground, the bullet having torn through her heart, I swing my gun to Dark-Gray.

The first swipe of her claws I catch on my sword, and the metal bites into her nails. She growls. My arm muscles bulge under the strength of her power, but the rings I'm wearing let me match her. I fire my gun into her chest before she can think to lean forward and bite my head off.

She barely flinches as the bullet enters her. I kick at her knee. She goes down, then rolls away before coming back, her teeth snapping for my neck as she lunges. I step to the side at the last second, and she flies past me and into the shield. She yelps as it burns her. She scrambles away as the white wolf rushes me.

A shot rings out. Dark-Gray howls, and then she turns to flee. Having no qualms shooting an opponent in the back, I line up the shot and take it.

Then I remember she would've died anyway due to the magic of the gun.

"Fuck," I mutter. Khalid is going to be pissed I wasted so many shots on one wolf.

"What?" Leno asks, not connected to this area visually or magically, relying only on the updates I give him.

"Nothing. How is everyone?"

"Talon is hurt."

My pulse spikes. "Badly?"

"Rudy is bringing him to us."

Shit. So yes.

"What about Khalid?"

"He's at the van fighting the wolves."

"Are the others with him?"

"Just Maddox."

"Antonio?"

He doesn't say anything for a second, and it takes all I have not to ask again. He will say when he can, when he can decipher what the plants are telling him as they taste the nutrients in the ground, sense the disturbances in the air.

Although plants can 'hear' and 'sniff' their surroundings, their senses are not like ours. They don't have a brain as we know it. Don't have noses or ears, but they can detect the chemicals and pheromones in the air. Sometimes Leno does not understand what they mean immediately.

"He's running," he says. "No one else seems to be hurt badly. Talon's almost here."

The shields around him start to flicker out, and he opens his eyes, pulling himself out of the world beneath our feet. He opens his bag as he walks east, and I can smell blood.

There's a lot of it.

"Shit," Leno mutters as Rudy comes out of the trees on the other side of the road. He's carrying Talon, using magic to keep all the pieces of our brother together. He's been torn apart, his arms and legs nearly severed, flesh hanging free, bone poking out. His torso hasn't been spared either, his chest caved in on one side, his ribs cut out of him on the other. I hurry forward, locking my fears down as I reach them, able to sense how close Rudy is to losing it.

"Leno!" I snap as the wounds on Talon open up further, the claw marks digging deeper into his body. I can see his lungs. The beating of his heart as I take him from Rudy's arms. "Control your fucking fear."

"I can't heal that," he whispers.

"You don't need to. We'll get him to Mother. Just stop fucking thinking about him dying or get out of here!"

Shaking, Rudy turns and flees back into the trees.

"Head home!" I shout after him, but what I really want to

do is follow him. We don't know if Antonio has left the area or if he's waiting to pick off anyone who's alone, but Rudy is the most capable of protecting himself. The magic that hit Mother while he was in her womb might have taken away his ability to speak, but it also gave him an influx of power.

Telling myself Rudy will be fine, I focus on getting Talon into the car. Leno opens the door to the backseat, then digs in his bag as I settle our brother inside. He pours a healing potion down Talon's throat, but there are too many wounds. It doesn't do anything. Not really. It closes one of the two or three dozen wounds across his body, but it isn't enough to stabilize him. So he pours more down his throat, sitting with him in the back as I climb into the front seat and speed off.

My hand tight on the wheel, I push my fear down.

Come on, T. Just survive the few minutes it takes to get home.

FORTY-THREE

HIM

"Holy shit, how is he?" Enoch asks as he and Ezriel enter the kitchen. Talon's lying on the counter, the knots of the wood beneath him twisting and moving, the air humming with power as Mother works over him.

Leno sits with his legs out on the floor, Krypto on his lap. "I couldn't do anything to stabilize him," he says.

"We got him home," I say. "That's all that matters."

"He could die because of me."

Because of him and Rudy. Because his fear became real, making the wounds even worse than they were.

"Because of *Antonio*," I say. "No one did this but him."

"The fucker is a lot stronger than he's supposed to be," Enoch says as he shakes his head. "We couldn't even get a hold of him." Given they 'get a hold of things' by grabbing their atoms, using scries to control objects further than they can see, that is a big fucking deal.

"Shit," Leno says.

"Where are the others?" I ask, unable to focus on coming up with a plan to take down Antonio until I know the rest of my family is okay.

"Rudy's outside. He didn't want to come in in case..." He trails off.

"And Maddox and Khalid?"

Ezriel shrugs. "Haven't seen them."

"Or heard from them."

I dig out my phone as Mother sucks in a breath, but she doesn't look up from Talon, doesn't break her concentration as she bathes him in a white light, using up her life force to save him.

As I scroll to Maddox's name in my contacts, I can't help myself from glancing down at 'Micha.' For a second, I'm torn between who to call, wanting the comfort only she can give me.

But she'll be back later.

I call our brother, and he answers almost immediately, which tells me that he's most likely out of danger. I let out a heavy breath.

"Where are you?" I ask as I put the phone on speaker.

"Almost at the car."

"And Khalid?"

"Fucking left me, the asshole."

"Why?" That isn't like Khalid at all, and the hairs on my neck rise. If I can't trust the reaper...

"He bonded with a fucking WALL member! He's started a full on fucking blood bond."

"*What?*"

"*The fuck?* Enoch and Ezriel add together.

Krypto woofs, and Leno shakes his head.

A blood bond is a binding of souls, not just in this life but in all the lifetimes after. It's permanent, and I have never heard of one being broken after it's been forged. You can break it before it's complete but only in death. The blood bond requires blood in one way or another. Either you can share the burden with your claimed mate. Or one of you can pay it in full. For Khalid to start one with a fucking WALL member, a woman who hates his guts and is terrified of us? This could literally kill him.

"A fucking blood bond. With a WALL member," Maddox says, driving the insanity home, "and now he's going to get her or something."

"And you let him?"

"*He left me!*"

"Fucking follow him, Maddox, and make sure he doesn't do anything else that's fucking stupid."

Dear fucking gods, can the world not just pause for one fucking second?

"Ugh!" He mutters a whole string of curses. "Someone come get my car. I ain't leaving it out here all night."

"Rudy will get it."

"Fucking stupid fucking brother. *Ugh.*" He hangs up, but I know he'll follow Khalid.

Utter silence hangs in the kitchen.

Then.

"What –" Enoch says.

"The fuck," Ezriel finishes.

Leno laughs. "Of course *Khalid* would start a blood bond rather than just ask her to marry him. He's fucking intense. Dear fucking gods."

"What do you think his price will be?" Enoch asks as he shakes his head.

I still at the thought of my brother having to pay a price that will break him. A blood bond is a giant fuck you to the gods given they've already gifted each one of us a lifemate to find. So to enact it, you have to pay dearly, which is why most blood bond couples don't last more than a year before they start to hate each other. For the only price it'll accept as payment is an act that will destroy the couple.

Khalid could be a shell of his own self within a year.

But it also means he'll never be alone...

"Well, Khalid's jealous as all hel," Ezriel starts. "So either someone else is going to have to fuck her –"

"Not it."

"Me neither."

I shake my head, thinking of Micha. I don't want anyone else but her.

"Dammit," Ezriel says as he realizes he's the last one left. He turns his head to Mother. "Save T will you so I'm not the one Khalid kills?"

"He can't kill those he uses for the blood bond," Mother says as she keeps her eyes on Talon. "It'll void it."

"In that case, I'm in," Leno says with a grin. "I hear he's into the mayor."

"Mayor Davis? Isn't she like fifty?" Enoch says.

"Yeah, but have you seen her ass?" Leno whistles. "She's got the body of a goddess."

"Who is she?" Ezriel asks curiously.

"Hold on, I'll google her."

"Later," I snap. "Tell me about Antonio."

Sighing, Leno puts away his phone. Krypto settles back down beside him.

"The fucker is fast. Like *bullet* fast," Ez says.

Leno's eyes widen. "That's impossible."

"Tell it to him because physics sure as hel didn't."

"And Rudy said Talon was only out of sight for about thirty seconds."

"He did *all* that in thirty seconds?" Leno asks. Krypto's head swings over to the counter. Then he shuffles closer to my brother. Leno's fingers dig into his dog's fur.

"It could have been less," Ezriel says softly. "Rudy says he doesn't know when Antonio attacked him. Talon wanted to spread out a bit so he didn't accidentally hit Rudy with any electricity. They checked in every fifteen seconds. When T didn't, Rudy went looking for him."

"Shit. So he what, ate Cid and the rest of them before he came out tonight?" Leno asks.

When the Garcia family consumes their dead, they gain their power. It started off as a ritual to just keep the souls of their deceased with them, but somewhere along the way, it grew into something more. Something powerful.

"He couldn't have," Mother says as she comes over, her face pale, her hands shaking. She looks like she's just aged twenty years for our kind, though to a human, she still looks young, younger than me.

My eyes narrow. "You better not have used more than it took to stabilize him."

"He's my son."

"You're our best healer. What happens if someone else needs you, but you're dead?"

Her lips purse, but she doesn't say anything.

"Is he okay?" Leno asks, his voice raw. Despite knowing she wouldn't have come over here if he wasn't, he needs to hear her answer.

A part of me does too.

She nods. "You okay with taking over from here, Leno?"

He climbs to his feet. "Yeah. Yeah, of course."

As he heads for the counter, Krypto trotting after him, I take out my phone to text Rudy the news, knowing his guilt is killing him.

Rudy: *I'm glad. Thanks for letting me know.*

As I put my phone away, Mother says, "Antonio couldn't have eaten Cid or the others Khalid killed yet. He needs time to purge that magic from their bodies."

"Then how is he that strong?" Ezriel wonders.

"Maybe he grew his pack over the years, and he has just started culling them off?" Enoch suggests.

It's possible, but it doesn't feel right.

Nothing about this damn thing feels right.

Exhaustion hitting me full force, I rub a hand over my face. "Well, whatever he's done," I say, searching for the fine silver lining, "he hasn't shared it with the rest of his pack yet, so we need to kill them all before he does." Otherwise, he won't even need any hybrids. If he can get the rest of his pack on his level? He'll be able to kill us all himself.

"Maddox ain't going to be happy if that includes Zita."

"Then he can start a blood bond with her," Enoch jokes, "and apologize to her in the next life."

His twin laughs, but my heart skips a beat.

A blood bond is forever.

Regardless of how much you hurt each other in a past life.

Regardless of how much you might hate each other after paying the price of the bond.

It cannot be broken.

I could have Micha without betraying my brothers.

Even if she steals the ledger...

Even if she betrays us in this life...

We could start over in the next.

My pulse pounding in my ears, I pull out my phone.

Varius: *Come to my room when you're back. I don't care about the time.*

Pressing send, I head up and wait for my little monster to come home.

As I drive back home, all I can think about is my list of suspects – the people who would've known the house was empty when they texted me:

Khalid. But he has dedicated his entire life to protecting Varius. He can kill him at any moment. He has no reason to be blackmailing me.

Ezriel and Enoch don't need me to find the ledger. They are telekinetic. They could search the whole house from the comfort of their beds. They might need me to get it, but if that was the case, they'd just tell me where it was.

Leno doesn't want to be Boss. He isn't keen to have that weight on his shoulders. In all of the coups that have been attempted to overthrow Varius, Leno hasn't once sided with them.

Rudy. He loves his brother. But he also hates this life, the violence it brings.

Maddox is a little shit, and anyone who wants Marrabelle

as a pet is all sorts of messed up. It could be a mere game to screw with me. Cruel but...how far would he go for a laugh?

And then there's Talon. Does he want the ledger because he wishes to take over? He's fourth in line though. He'd have to kill Leno and Khalid as well as Varius.

And why now? Why blackmail me after four months?

My fingers drum on the leather of my steering wheel as the car eats up the miles. My rhythm falters as a sudden thought comes to me.

Or is it Sau?

A mother no one would suspect? She loves her kids, and yet...there's something about what she did to Varius that is not sitting right with me.

I'm an assassin. My profession comes with a lot of people trying to find ways to cheat death, to have a backup plan in case they make a mistake. But not once have I ever heard of a black magic spell that would do what she claims she did.

And how fast would she have needed to work it if Varius had been in as many pieces as she'd claimed? She's a good healer, but not even necromancers can revive a jigsaw...

"Fucking *dammit*," I growl. We need to figure out who's behind the number Dayne keeps texting his fake updates to.

If we can figure that out, then I can plant the evidence in their room, make them the prey in their own fucking game.

Or maybe I'll just kill them so Varius never needs to know about their betrayal. Never needs to know one of his own brothers – or mother wanted to ruin him.

But not kill him.

And that sudden thought makes me pause.

Maybe...maybe this isn't about the ledger at all. Or even about hurting Varius. Maybe this is about separating the two of us...

My fingers drum faster on the wheel.

I didn't get the text until we started to be happy.

The ledger is hidden and locked down tight somewhere. I

will most likely get caught trying to get it.

But who in his family hates *me* that much?

My chest hurts as I think about any one of them wishing me pain. I like all of them. Have started to see them all as family... Better family than my own.

"Better me than him though," I murmur as I swallow down my pain. *Better me than him.*

The wheels of the car turn.

I get closer and closer to home with each rotation.

But it's suddenly starting to not feel like home...

I pull up onto the garage of the Shadow house. I turn off the car and just sit here for a moment. The hairs on my neck rise as I think about someone coming out to kill me.

Do they want that though? Or do they just want Varius not to trust me? To wedge something between us so we can never have happiness?

But why would that matter to his brothers? Does one have a crush on me?

Or does Sau wish she didn't pick me after all? Does she think I'm not good enough for her firstborn?

Anger building at the audacity of this fucking family, I grab my bag and step out of my car.

They can try their fucking best, but no one is going to split Varius and I apart. I've worked too fucking hard to get us to where we are.

And I love him.

Despite how annoying he can be sometimes, I love my fucking neanderthal.

My heart pounding, I hurry to the front door. I check my phone, hoping there is a message from Varius to tell me he wants to see me because I need to see him.

Varius: *Come to my room when you're back. I don't care about the time.*

My heart is in my throat now, and when I step into the Shadow house, I don't even care that I might be entering my damnation. Because my salvation is also in here, and he is upstairs waiting for me.

Ignoring the commotion in the kitchen, I take the stairs two at a time to the second floor.

I love him.

I love the fucking neanderthal.

I don't knock when I get to his room.

I just push the door open and then close it behind me.

He sits up in bed. The blanket drops away from his naked chest.

I start to tell him someone is blackmailing me, that I'm trying to find them so he believes my innocence, but he says something that strikes me dumb.

"I want to blood bond with you."

My mouth drops open, and I fall back against the door.

"Do you?" he asks softly, hesitantly.

"I'm being blackmailed into stealing the ledger," I blurt.

He blinks and then he does something else that knocks my brain out of my skull.

He laughs.

And says, "Thank the fucking gods."

FORTY-FIVE

HER

I stare at him, certain I'm dreaming.

Perhaps I crashed the car, wrapped it around a tree in my exhaustion, and now I'm in the final moments of my life, my brain trying to comfort me by showing me what I want to see.

But this didn't happen the last time I nearly died.

My heart flips, the rising hope making me giddy. Slowly, I start walking towards him as he continues to laugh.

He throws the covers off himself and stands. He's on me in a few long strides. I'm in his arms, still entirely fucking dumbfounded, and he swings back towards the bed. He lays me down and stretches above me, leaning on his elbows so his face is right over mine.

"What happened while I was gone?" I whisper, knowing something bad must have triggered this sudden change.

"Too much," he says honestly and then he's kissing me slowly. Lovingly. Tenderly.

He takes my heart right out of my mouth and swallows it, making it his. Making everything about me his.

Pulling away, he murmurs, "So do you, Micha Eurelia Black, wish to blood bond with me?"

I tremble beneath him, wondering if it's wise. I love him, but we've only just started this relationship. A blood bond isn't just for life. It's for all the lives.

"What happens if I can't get pregnant?" I ask. "You need heirs."

"We'll adopt. Or I'll name Leno's kids as my heirs."

"But don't you want kids?"

"I want you, Micha. I don't care about anything else."

"Well, what about your lifemate? What if you find her after?"

"Then you can do the same thing to her that I will do to yours." A darkness flashes in his eyes.

A bubble of laughter rises in my throat. "Let me guess, kill them?" I say.

He nods sharply. A definite answer with no wiggle room for negotiation.

"What about the blackmailer? Don't you want to know what they were using against me?"

"I'm assuming it's Dayne."

I blink.

"But you don't have to worry about him," he says. "I've been watching him for months. I have one of my best men on him at all times. I know how much he means to you."

My mouth drops open. "*You're* the one who was having him followed?" *So did the real blackmailer, what...steal the images from his camera?*

His eyes narrow. "Who *was*?"

"But the number he texts you on isn't your number!"

"I have various phones for various people," he says.

My jaw drops, and I wrench it back up again. "Dayne got the drop on him weeks ago," I say. "He's currently torturing him. Fucking hel, I'm glad he hasn't killed him yet." My eyes snap wide. "Oh my gods, I need to call him before he does."

I start to sit up, but he shoves me back down. "But your man –"

"If he cockblocks me right now, I'll kill him myself," he growls.

My jaw has damn well broken its hinges with how much it's falling open. "Varius –"

"I thought you were going to steal the ledger because you wanted to, Micha," he says softly. "And even then I wasn't sure if I could punish you for it." He leans down to kiss my neck, causing shivers across my skin. "Blood bond with me," he murmurs. His teeth latch onto the lobe of my ear.

I swallow hard.

This is too big of a decision to make without thinking it all the way through.

Varius is paranoid as hel.

Although he might believe my innocence in this matter, what happens when it's a brother that accuses me?

Or his mother?

"I don't –"

He licks the base of my neck and then bites it, his teeth cutting deep. And I know he's drawing blood. He's taking that first step the bonding requires: mixing our blood.

Connecting us.

If we share enough, I'll start to be able to feel him, and he'll start to be able to feel me.

He'll know the truth of my innocence.

I'll know his true feelings about me even when he can't express them in public.

Trembling, I fist my hand in his hair and pull his lips off me so I can look into his eyes.

His piercing dark eyes whose colors I know better than my own.

"Okay," I say. "I'll blood bond with you. I... I love you,

Varius."

He freezes, his mask coming down instinctively. But I know he isn't rejecting me. He just likes processing things behind his walls. I cup his cheek and kiss him. A light touch that I feel all the way down to my toes.

His lips part. His tongue dives inside my mouth as he pushes me into the mattress, covering me with his body. His hands slide between us, tugging up my dress. I spread my thighs, and he falls between them.

"I can't wait, Micha," he groans as he grabs his cock and pushes it in. My pussy stretches with a slight burn, tearing as he forces entry. "I'm sorry, little monster," he growls. "I can't..."

He pushes in deeper, and I wince, but I don't stop him. Can't stop him. I need this just as much as he does. "Don't... ahhh...stop," I say.

He stops, his muscles straining. His cock is only half-way in. He growls, pushes in even more. "I can't..." he says, his voice raw and twisted.

And I realize how he took my words. "*Don't* stop," I say as I grab his ass.

Groaning, he shoves in all the way in one solid thrust. He fucks me hard and fast, with no technique. He's feral, like an animal, like a man without control. He's tearing me apart, unable to take his time, and fuck me, that utter need to use me, to own me is making me wet.

The pain starts to recede.

I can feel my orgasm building.

Wrapping my legs around him, I hold on.

I hold on to the man I love.

"*Fuuuuck*," he growls as he thrusts in deep. He collapses on top of me, his entire body shaking. His cum shoots inside me, and I hold him close as he fills me. Rocking his hips, he uses my pussy to get himself hard again.

My nails dig into his back. He hisses in a breath, and I

scratch him harder, drawing a line of blood.

"That's it, baby," he rasps. "Make me yours. Mark me so everyone fucking knows it."

"You mean it?" I ask, a challenge in my voice as I lift my hips to match his rhythm. He slows a bit as he ducks his head to look at me. I crane my neck up to meet his gaze, our difference in height not allowing our faces to line up while he's in me.

"Do whatever you want to do," he says as he rolls me on top of him. "I'm yours."

Staring down at him, I hesitate for a moment, my cheeks heating. Then I blurt, "I want to tattoo your dick."

He blinks.

I shake my head. "Sorry, no, that's not what I meant."

I place both hands on his chest and look down at him in utter wickedness. "I'm *going* to tattoo your dick," I correct. "But first I'm going to get myself off on your cock. And you can't come" –I lift myself off him– "because I need you hard to tat it." I slam myself down.

His lips part.

I roll my hips, rubbing my pussy against his pelvis. My nails digging into his chest, I make sure I draw blood. He arches his back as he groans, and I swipe my finger through the red liquid seeping out on his chest. Lifting it to my neck, I rub it into the open bite mark he gave me.

My eyes close. I ride him as I open my magic up like the ritual requires. His blood bonds with my power, shooting through me like a bolt of lightning. I gasp, feeling him, everywhere, and he leans up to bite my breast. His growl vibrates against my skin as he sinks his teeth into me. He draws blood. Collects it on his thumb and spreads it across the lines on his chest.

"Ride me hard, baby," he growls. "Ride me until you're coming all over my cock. That's it. That's it, baby. You look so fucking sexy. You feel so fucking *good.*"

Threading my hands in his hair as I arch into his mouth as he sucks on my breasts, I come all over his cock just like he asked.

Like a fucking good girl.

Panting heavily, I collapse against him. I take a moment to bask in the after tremors of my orgasm. Then I kiss his shoulder and ask, "Where's your tattoo gun?"

"In the closet," he says without hesitation.

My lips part.

"Well, are you going to get it? Because if not –" He grabs my hips and thrusts up into me, making me cry out. "Then I'm going to come inside you." He pulls out, then shoves back in. I hover above him as he pounds into me. I scream his name, begging him to go harder, but instead, he rolls us and tosses me off the bed.

I hit the ground and bounce.

"Get the gun, little monster. I want your mark on me."

My pussy spasming, I crawl to his closet. He groans, and I know his eyes are on my ass. Using the door to pull myself up, I take a deep breath, then search his closet for the gun. I get the stuff I need, then walk back to him.

He's lying on his back, the covers off him, his glorious dick pointing straight up. Lying beside him, I clean the area and then start to tattoo:

Property of Micha

"Shadow," Varius growls after I finish the A in my name. "Write fucking Shadow."

My mouth running dry, I do.

EPILOGUE

HIM

Whatever happens with Antonio, whatever happens in this upcoming war, I know as I hold my little monster in my arms, that in the end, everything will be okay.

Because she is here.

And she is mine.

And I am fucking hers.

EPILOGUE II

HER

"Varius, don't do this. Please. I didn't do this. Just listen to me." I tug against the binds on my hands, the straps holding my individual fingers down. He's made it so I can't use my magic. I'm drowning in my panic, my lungs filling with it until it's too hard to breathe. "Varius, please."

He places a long screw on the back of my hand, and my heart jumps into my throat. He holds a hammer in his other fist.

"Don't. Varius. Varius, please, look at me. I love you. I –"

The hammer comes down and slams the screw all the way through my flesh.

I scream, my voice cracking, pain radiating up my arm and across my vocal chords. The hammer resonates across the screw again, pure agony shooting through my body as the metal digs deeper into my flesh, the ridges causing even more damage, making the hole ragged and torn instead of clean.

I look up at him on a cry, and for the first time, he isn't wearing a mask. His face is twisted in equal parts agony and rage, and I know he cares for me. He cares for me, and his heart is breaking thinking I betrayed him. This is killing him, killing us.

But I know he will not stop.

It's because he cares that he's punishing me so severely. He's punishing himself for daring to believe in me. To trust me. Dayne's warning comes back to me, how getting him to love me will be worse.

"I swear, Varius... I didn't let the werewolves in," I try again, my voice, my hand shaking.

His eyes mist. His arm holding the hammer trembles. His chest rises and falls rapidly. His Adam's apple bobs with a wail he'll never release. His words raw and cracked, he says, "You attacked mother. You were here when the werewolves came, knowing we were all out. And you can't..." He breaks off, his face twisting with so much agony before he controls it, flattens it. "You can't be *that*."

He places the claw of the hammer around the screw. His lips tremble. My gut twists in anticipation of the pain.

"Varius! *Please*! I'm telling the truth! I'm –" I scream as he rips the screw free, tearing out chunks of flesh, spraying blood high up between us.

I arch against my binds, screaming as my toes curl, the pain rocking through me in an overwhelming wave. "I did not let them in," I cry, my head hanging, tears flowing down my cheeks. "I did not let them in."

My hand's throbbing too hard for me to feel the touch of metal against my skin again, but I feel it when it goes through another part of my palm. I feel it embed into the arm of the chair. I feel him rip it back out. Slam it back in again somewhere else.

"Tell me where Khalid is," Varius says, his voice tight with his own pain.

"He was with you. He wasn–" I break off on a whimper when he moves the screw to my other hand. I jerk against my binds, but it's a futile, pathetic attempt. I can't escape. I can't stop him. "I'm not the traitor," I say, my throat clogged with snot and pain. "I'm not the traitor. I told you about the blackmail."

"To gain my trust," he spits. "Admit to something small to hide something big. It's a classic trick."

"No –" I shake my head. "No, that's not –"

The hammer comes down.

My back arches off the chair as I spasm in agony. My cries are shrill and cracked, ripping my throat raw. "Just feel the bond," I beg. "Just feel it. I love you. Varius, *please.*"

His hands shake as he holds the screw against my skin. Its sharp end scratches me as his arm vibrates, but I am happy for that pain if it means he'll believe me.

His eyes close. He swallows hard on a shudder.

Hope flares in my chest, but when he looks at me again, it plummets into the acid of my stomach.

"I feel *nothing*," he says. "Now where is Khalid?"

"Varius –" My face twists under the strain of pain and panic. "How can you not feel anything? I love you. We're bonded. I –" I scream. I jerk. I thrash inside my binds as he slams the screw over and over into my hand.

"Where is Khalid?"

"Tell me where Khalid is."

"*Where is Khalid, Micha?*"

"I don't know. I swear I don't… But, Varius, stop, please. I'm p–"

My arms jerking against my binds, I scream.

And this time, I cannot stop.

WANT TO KNOW WHAT THE FUCK HAPPENED?

Read *Broken Souls*.

He suspected me.
He tortured me without evidence.
And now he demands my forgiveness.

WANT TO KNOW HOW KHALID FUCKS?

Read *Cursed to be Mine.*

I've stalked her for two years.
I've made myself a key to her house.
And now it's time to make her mine.

WANT TO KNOW WHAT ALERIC WANTS FROM SAU?

Read *Madness Behind the Mask.*

I am a breedmare.
I have no worth outside my womb.
But when it comes to my children, I'll burn this fucking world.

AUTHOR'S NOTE

Hello everyone!

I hope you enjoyed *Tethered Souls.* This wasn't even supposed to be a book. I started writing *Broken Souls* because after *Cursed to be Mine*, it was supposed to be *Broken Souls* like I fucking said it was going to be when I wrote *Cursed to be Mine.* If you have the earlier editions, you will see that in the back of the fucking book.

But no. Micha wanted me to start four months before.

Thus, there's an entirely new book in the *Book of Shadows* series. I didn't even know I was writing this book until 80k into it and I realized there was no fucking way I was going to even get to the *first scene* of *Broken Souls* (which is now Epilogue II).

So fuck Micha.

Fuck all my plans.

I hate writing.

But gods, do I love this book. And I hope you did to.

Many cheers,

RESEARCH NOTES

That dick tattoo scene is entirely artistic license. You don't need to have your dick hard to get it tattooed. In fact, there's a tattoo artist called Moon who will give $1000 in cash to anyone who can actually stay hard the entire time she does it. She has offered this to hundreds, if not thousands of clients, and not one of them has managed.

Varius, however, is just built different.

SPOT ANY ERRORS?

Please let me know by emailing me at:
authormirandagrant@gmail.com

WANT TO IMPACT THE REST OF THE SERIES?

Drop me a review! Tell me what you loved and want more of or what you hated and want less of.

WANT TO LEARN ALL ABOUT WIPS AND NEW RELEASES?